An *LA Times* Bestseller
One of *People Magazine*'s "Summer's Best Books"

"SUMMER'S HOTTEST NEW BEACH READ,
a juicy tome inspired by real-life Hollywood stories and scandals."
—*E! Online*

"A DISHY SUMMER READ ABOUT HOLLYWOOD'S UNDERBELLY,
featuring twists on real celebrity scandals that weren't fit
for print in their original state."
—*ET Online*

"What a SEXY, FUN READ! It pulls back the curtain, for an
inside look at the Hollywood that's behind the glitz and glamour."
—Kristin Cavallari, television star, designer,
and author of *Balancing in Heels*

"This book is as outrageous as any true life
tabloid scandal—A MUST READ!"
—Jenny McCarthy, talk show host, actress, and
New York Times–bestselling author of *Belly Laughs*

"[A] RACY, rollicking novel by two industry insiders."
—*In Touch Weekly*

"A DISHY NEW BOOK."
—*Page Six*

"Sprinkled throughout this rags-to-riches wish-fulfillment
story are REAL SCANDALS that busy publicists
and managers managed to hush up and hide."
—*Publishers Weekly*

"This novel doesn't just push the envelope but SHREDS it."
—*School Library Journal*

blind item

KEVIN DICKSON
& JACK KETSOYAN

{Imprint}
MAKE YOUR MARK

NEW YORK

[Imprint]
MAKE YOUR MARK

A part of Macmillan Publishing Group, LLC
175 Fifth Avenue, New York, NY 10010

Library of Congress Control Number: 2016040185

ISBN 978-1-250-12225-4 (hardcover) / ISBN 978-1-250-12224-7 (ebook) /
ISBN 978-1-250-15885-7 (paperback)`

Our books may be purchased in bulk for promotional, educational, or business
use. Please contact your local bookseller or the Macmillan Corporate and
Premium Sales Department at (800) 221-7945 ext. 5442 or by e-mail at
MacmillanSpecialMarkets@macmillan.com.

Imprint logo designed by Amanda Spielman

First Hardcover Edition, 2017

3   5   7   9   10   8   6   4   2

First Paperback Edition, 2018

1   3   5   7   9   10   8   6   4   2

blinditembook.com

The secrets of this book
Must never be broken
Lest a lawyer's skills
Be expensively awoken.
If thou dost meet the authors
With liquor you may try
To wrest the real identities
To cajole, seduce, or pry.
The secrets of this book
Will be withheld till we die.
In these pages truth is spoken
In person we will lie.

For Vonnie and Silva,
our moms and best friends.

CHAPTER 1

NICOLA MADE A FAST RIGHT off Sunset Boulevard up into the Hollywood Hills. Her trusty GPS device on the dash said the destination wasn't too far ahead. She looked in the mirror and ran a finger through her light brown curls. She slowly blinked her smoky eyelids and pursed her lips.

"Good enough," she said out loud, knowing that she'd be wading through a sea of cookie-cutter Hollywood hopefuls at the party. Rounding a blind corner, she nearly rear-ended a matte-black Lamborghini that stopped suddenly in front of her.

"Shit!" She exhaled as her car jerked to a halt just a few feet from the sports car. That would have been expensive. The Lamborghini was the last car in the line for valet parking in front of an ivy-covered wall that must be the party address.

Ahead of her were blacked-out SUVs, luxury sports cars, and a tanklike pink Bentley. Knowing what her turquoise 1995 Toyota Tercel must look like at the tail end of such a row of car porn, Nicola was gripped by an urge to just keep driving.

Her plans to escape were foiled when a black Range Rover pulled up behind her, blocking her in. Her eyes widened as she saw Seamus O'Riordan at the wheel, the film star she'd swooned over on her last movie date with her mom, before she left Dayton almost a year ago.

As she watched in her rearview mirror, she saw him leaning back in his seat. He was talking on the phone, loose black ringlets hanging down almost to his left eye. Her mom was going to totally flip out when she got this week's star-spotting report.

Nicola was surprised when his eyes made contact with hers in the mirror and he gave her a half smile. She jolted in shock, but then his hand moved toward the steering wheel and he blasted the horn. Looking ahead, she realized the line had moved. *Crap*, she had just kept a movie star waiting.

She pulled up to the ivy-covered wall, feeling flush with embarrassment, and a valet walked up to her window, a look of consternation on his face.

"Hey, sure you should be here?" he asked brusquely, eyeballing her old car.

Nicola glanced into the rearview mirror. The movie star was still staring at her. She panicked.

"Uh, yeah, I am, but I'm just gonna go, I'm gonna leave," she sputtered, shifting the Tercel into drive and pressing down on the gas as hard as she could. It didn't do too much, and the Tercel slowly veered away from the valet area to begin creeping up the hill.

I'm just going home, she thought. *Straight home*. That was ridiculous, and mortifying. Her car had just been rejected by the valet.

She crept higher into the Hollywood Hills, the engine of her car keening at the steep incline and occasionally throwing in a loud knocking noise just for good measure. She couldn't find anywhere to turn around on the narrow street lined with cars parked all along the road. Valets ran past her downhill in the gathering LA dusk.

She slowed down. A parking space was coming up on the right. Her boss, Gaynor, had made it clear that Nicola had to tackle this party on her own. Hollywood parties were the bread and butter of Huerta Hernandez, the PR agency where she worked. And like bread and butter, in a very short time, Nicola had come to find them bland, greasy, and very white. But Gaynor had done her friend Billy a solid by offering Nicola a job when she moved to LA. She didn't feel like she could blow it off.

Nicola sighed and slipped into the parking spot. Getting out of the car, she inhaled LA's signature sunset scent: smog and jasmine. She tugged at the embellished hem of her black silk, borrowed-from-a-stylist Alaïa dress. It was surprisingly unwrinkled. Running her fingers along the sheer pleats, she glanced cautiously down the treacherous hill she had just driven up. At home she wouldn't have thought twice about running down the middle of this road. But she didn't wear borrowed two-thousand-dollar Louboutins to parties back home. Nicola checked the red duct tape she had carefully affixed to the bottom of the soles so they could be returned to the stylist undamaged, and whispered "Let's go to work" to her reflection in the window of the Tercel. She began a precarious walk down the hill toward the rolling bass and laughter that were floating up the canyon, sounding like any other night at the office.

The valet who'd rejected her car saw Nicola walking up and ran over.

"Where did you go?" he asked innocently.

"You rejected my car," Nicola said breathlessly. "I went and parked it myself."

"I didn't reject your car, lady," laughed the valet. "I just don't understand why Seamus didn't drive you in his own car."

"What?" said Nicola, stopping dead.

The valet smirked. "He was pretty pissed you took off the way you did. Anyway, head on in and enjoy yourself."

Mystified, she passed the gate and approached the door.

Guest lists always terrified Nicola, even though she'd been making them almost daily since she started at Huerta Hernandez. Gaynor had theatrically instructed her that making the perfect guest list was a lost art, much like dating, taking quaaludes, and mixing the perfect Negroni.

The science of a good celebrity party went beyond normal physics, with an equation so complex that it was like $E = mc^2$ with celebrity and notoriety replacing energy and mass. You needed an exact mix of celebrities, designers, bloggers, and attractive flotsam, while making sure that all the right agencies were feted. Reality stars were a last resort, and you had to reinforce your list against the worst party foul—the desperate past-their-prime crasher.

Being on the list meant you were *supposed* to be there—that you were essential to the mix. Nicola always dreaded the moment where she gave her own name, and she was still surprised when it was there. This time was no different. When the standard-issue disgruntled intern actually found her name on her first attempt—a rarity—she grunted and handed Nicola a pink elastic wristband without making eye contact. Nicola let out a short, relieved sigh.

Ushered through a huge wooden door bedecked with gaudy brass medieval doorknobs, Nicola stepped through a living room and out into the backyard of a house she'd seen many times on TV and in magazines.

She was immediately submerged in a sea of fairy lights, lasers, and clouds of pink smoke that smelled like perfume and weed. En masse, the crowd around her turned to see if she was a celebrity, and turned away as soon as it realized she wasn't.

Seamus was nowhere to be seen. The celebrities around her were just a slew of lower-tier teen TV actors. Nicola wondered why A-list Seamus was there at all. If she had confirmed him for a party, Gaynor would have redlined all these CW waiters-who-got-lucky immediately.

Drink. Now, her mind commanded.

A bar made entirely of mirrors and ice, all wet and sharp, was nestled against the ivy-covered wall. Lasers refracted through ice vodka shooters, and a girl who looked fourteen at most, in torn jeans and a bra top, was resting her chin at the bottom while the bartender poured an endless shot down the ice, into the girl's mouth.

Nicola accepted a whiskey soda from a bartender who in any other city would have been a local news anchor and pushed back through the crowd into the house. The music was an endless remix of the latest hit track sung by tonight's birthday girl, former child star Amber Bank.

She paused at a long table beside the living room door. It was covered in gaudy gift-wrapped boxes of all sizes. Tiffany boxes were thrown atop larger boxes that clearly contained shoes. Every agent in town must have raided their gift closet, repurposing things they'd been sent by other agencies over the past few months. There were also lots of small, exquisitely wrapped boxes scattered among the haul.

"Looks like Amber's getting a lot of jewelry," said Nicola, mostly to herself. But she heard a low chuckle behind her. She spun around to find herself face-to-face with Seamus O'Riordan.

"Why'd you say that, m'dear?" asked Seamus in a Scottish burr, with his eyebrow cocked quizzically. *He thinks I'm an idiot*, thought Nicola.

"All these small boxes? They've got to be jewelry or makeup."

Seamus burst out laughing. He put one hand on his leg as he doubled over in hysterics. As soon as he could breathe again, he grabbed one of the gifts on the table, a small box wrapped in silver-and-pink paper with an ornate bright pink bow. He held it up to Nicola's face. He shook it.

"Doesn't rattle."

He held it closer to her nose. "Smell it," he commanded, still smiling.

"Wait—this is pot?" Nicola exclaimed as she inhaled a wave of pungent reefer.

"Yeah, the pot shops here in California make Amber one of the easiest people to buy for."

Nicola suddenly understood why Gaynor had asked, at her job interview, if she knew if it was cheaper to buy pot from a store or a dealer.

"You wanna know a secret?" He smirked. "Probably twenty people here actually know Amber. The rest were sent here by her agent to make her feel popular. She's not even here yet. She'll take one look at this crowd and have a fit and go upstairs and get high. After she checks out the gift table, of course."

"Oh, SHIT," said Nicola, wincing. "I was supposed to bring a gift?"

"Well, madam prefers it. She likes getting spoiled. Hey—do you have a pen in your purse?"

Nicola fished out a pen. Seamus started lifting up presents, feeling them like a kid at Christmas, trying to guess what was inside. After inspecting a bunch of them, he selected one that was wrapped in a solid pale-pink brocade paper. He ripped the card off the ribbon and, using Nicola's pen, scrawled across the entire top of the gift *Dearest Amber! Happy birthday! Sorry we forgot your card in the car. Lots of love, Seamus and*— He looked over at her. "Nicola," she told him. He finished writing her name, looked around quickly, and put the gift back on the table, and then moved some larger presents on top of it.

"Quick, let's go," he said with a cheeky grin. He put his hand out for Nicola's and she put her hand in his.

But their getaway was short-lived, because they turned around and ran right into the birthday girl herself.

"Baby doll," Amber cooed at the Scot. "Did you get me a gift? That is so thoughtful. I love it."

"Sure," said Seamus. "You don't even know what it is yet."

"That's not important," Amber moaned in a messed-up cartoony sex voice. She was wearing a hot-pink chiffon baby doll dress and strappy baby-blue heeled sandals. She was not wearing a bra, and as she leaned forward, Nicola saw the former child star's nipples. Again. They were a regular feature in tabloid OOPS fashion stories, and for some reason, they reliably upset her.

"What's important is the thought. I can't wait to open it."

"Well, you're welcome," said Seamus. "Good seeing you; I'll let you get on with your party."

"What do you mean?" snapped Amber, grabbing his arm. "You're coming with me." She started dragging him, but he resisted and took her arm off his.

"Amber, this is my friend Nicola," he said. Amber stared Nicola down, and raised her chin slightly. Her top lip curled into a sneer.

"Hi, bitch," she drawled.

"Hey, Amber, nice to meet you." Nicola extended her hand. Amber didn't take it but she plowed on. "I work with Gaynor Huerta at Huerta Hernandez; she sends her love and says sorry she couldn't make it. And I believe you know my best friend, Billy Kaye, he . . ."

"Please stop talking at me," Amber slurred, grabbing Seamus by the wrist and attempting to drag him away again, like a spoiled child who wanted to show her daddy something.

"Hey, wait," he protested. "I'm here with Nic, I can't just leave her."

Amber turned and grabbed a mousy woman with a huge cold sore on her lip and a plaster cast on her right arm, and pushed her at Nicola.

"Hey, Courtney, this is my friend whatshername, you guys should totally hang out."

Amber turned back to Seamus. "Look! She's not alone. They're totally hanging out. I just need to talk to you for five minutes."

Seamus leaned in and gave Nicola a light peck. His lips were warm and dry, and his stubble felt electric against her soft skin. "I'll just be five minutes, I promise. Don't leave, please—we still need to properly chat."

And then he was gone.

Nicola felt like she had stuck her finger in a light socket. *Seamus O'Riordan just kissed me on the lips!* Her face burned. Her pulse was racing.

She tried to focus on the crumpled mess in front of her named Courtney. Stringy brown hair, skinny jeans that swam on her, and yellow off-the-shoulder sweater that hung too far off her shoulders so that Nicola could see the ribs between her boobs. When Courtney clumsily pushed some of the hair out of her face, Nicola's stomach dropped in recognition. This was Courtney Hauser, former teen star who was currently more legendary for her drug intake than her work.

"You carrying?" Courtney asked in a voice that almost sounded like a cough.

"I'm sorry, I don't know what you mean," lied Nicola, wrinkling her nose again at a sudden bad smell.

"I'm sorry, how rude of me. We just met. Let's start over." Courtney extended her hand, clad in the filthy cast. As the hand drew nearer, Nicola realized the cast smelled worse than it looked, and she pulled back.

"So you carrying or not?" growled Courtney, with her stinking broken arm still outstretched.

Nicola wished she knew *any*body else at the party so she could pretend to go talk to them.

CHAPTER 2

KARA HISSED AS HER ACRYLIC nail poked a hole in the tip of her black latex-free glove. Again. She sat back and felt her shoulders bunched up around her neck. She forced them down to their natural position and took a deep breath. She blinked hard to refocus her eyes and looked around the living room, decorated in busted Target dorm-room furniture. She was alone.

The laminate table in front of her was splashed with bright green fluid. On top of it sat rows of tiny white bottles that Kara had filled with water and a touch of said green fluid, which came from quart bottles marked ALL-WEATHER ANTIFREEZE. This Saturday, after being watered down with LA's finest tap water, they would be sold to pie-eyed ravers at the Palms Up festival outside Vegas as the best liquid ecstasy that their money could buy.

"Ryk?" she called out over the burbling sound of faceless EDM that had been her soundtrack for the last eight hours. "RYK?"

Ryk's egg-shaped head popped around the corner, his thick glasses magnifying his already-wide pale blue eyes. "What is it, gorgeous?"

Oh great, he's high, Kara realized, immediately toning down her voice.

"Hey, baby," she purred. "How many of these do you need to have filled?"

"How much do you have left?"

Kara lugged a full quart up from the floor and set it on the table.

She glanced at the pile of empty quart bottles on the floor and counted.

"I have one full one left, and I've emptied nine."

"How long does it take you to empty a bottle?" Ryk ambled into the room, barefoot, in skinny jeans and a tattered Electric Daisy T-shirt.

"How the hell do I know?" Kara snapped, noticing a tiny spot of antifreeze on her white suede boot. *Shit.* She'd been so careful.

"Figure it out, princess." Ryk waved his hand at her dismissively. "Because that's how much longer you're working today."

Kara glanced at the neatly packed boxes, each one containing fifty small plastic bottles, now filled with the neon-green fluid. At fifty cents for every bottle she filled, she figured she had earned $500 so far since starting at ten a.m.

"I've filled one thousand bottles, and I need to get out of here soon."

"You asked for this job, gorgeous," Ryk said, opening his laptop and changing the playlist. "I need as much as possible. We get twenty dollars for every one of those bottles, so if you are too tired to make the last two hundred, you're cheating me out of four thousand bucks. So how about you hustle?"

Kara inhaled and exhaled deeply. She bent and picked up a bag from Party City and tipped a pile of small bottles made to contain children's bubble solution onto the table. She counted out fifty into a pile and began to methodically unscrew the caps. She lined the bottles up in five rows of ten, and put the caps into a small box to her left. She popped the foil seal on the antifreeze and filled a large glass beaker.

As she was about to begin pouring the liquid into the little bottles, Ryk came around behind her and put his hands on her bare shoulders. Her skin shuddered with revulsion as he began to give her a limp, useless shoulder rub.

"Man, you're so tense," he murmured in her ear.

"You're gonna make me spill this shit."

"You could make me spill something else," Ryk said, lifting the strap of her black tank and sliding it off her shoulder.

Kara wanted to punch him. In the seven months that she had known him, he'd gone from being Richard Rollins, IT nerd and weekend pot dealer, to EDM DJ wannabe and festival drug dealer Ryk Rollin. He was, unfortunately, a good source of income for her. Whenever he needed weed trimmed or drugs packaged, his unrequited lust for Kara would transform into a relatively good wage just when she needed cash. And now he had a reality TV crew interested in his life—which could mean bigger things for both of them.

Ryk kissed her neck. Kara tensed and forced herself to breathe.

"Hey, baby," she laughed icily. "I have to get this finished tonight. It's your four thousand bucks, remember?"

The back rub resumed.

"You could take a break," he wheedled.

"I could." Kara reached back, still refusing to turn around, and grasped his wrists firmly. "But then I'd never get this finished. Why don't you roll us a joint and play me what you're working on for your set on Saturday?"

She could practically hear the smile spread across Ryk's face behind hers. His hands vanished from her shoulders and he moved back to the laptop at the other end of the table. He pulled a small pill container from his jeans pocket and tapped a nugget of weed onto the table. Kara shifted her attention back to the beaker of antifreeze as Ryk began to roll a joint.

"So what's the latest on the TV crew coming on Saturday?" she asked with fake nonchalance.

"Well." Ryk paused. "I'm not sure they're coming anymore."

Kara stood upright.

"I thought it was locked."

"It was always kinda sorta."

"That's not what you said yesterday. Or last week."

"Yeah, there's been a problem with the lawyers. They're worried about showing the drug stuff, and without it there's no story."

Kara rolled her eyes and tried to control her anger. It had been over a month since Ryk had told her that he had signed on with a production company who wanted to base a show around Ryk's burgeoning DJ career. Kara was supposed to be his stylist and possible rap protégé on the show. She'd signed all the releases. She'd met with the producers and had even agreed to possibly becoming a dramatic love interest if the series was picked up. Filming was due to begin on their drive out to the desert this Saturday—THIS SATURDAY—for Palms Up.

"Ryk," she said in a tone that made him look up instantly, fear in his eyes. "Is there something you're not sharing with the class?"

He nervously fussed with the joint and looked anywhere but at Kara. He hit the space bar on his laptop, killing the music. Silence filled the room.

"Richard! What's going on?"

"Yeah, so I had a call today," he began. "The producers aren't sure they can do the show they want. They wanted to show the true story of how a rave works, and obviously that includes the dealing shit."

Kara felt her anger burning in her chest and fought to keep it at a manageable level.

"So you knew all along that you'd be a DJ *and* drug dealer on the show?" she asked slowly.

"Yeah," he said, shaking his head as if he had said no.

"And nobody bothered to tell me that I was being cast as the clichéd black girl love interest of a drug dealer?"

"You *are* my love interest," Ryk said feebly. "It's not casting."

Kara gripped the Pyrex beaker of antifreeze in her fist, fighting the urge to tip it into the laptop keyboard.

"I did it for us," Ryk continued. "The producers are one hundred percent sure that this show will be so controversial and so real and so edgy that it'll make us both famous."

Kara looked at her gloved hands, spattered again with toxic chemicals. She really needed to rub her forehead.

"Ryk. Nobody is going to make a celebrity out of a black girl dealing drugs at a rave. And as far as I know, this show would make excellent evidence at trial. Why the fuck did you not tell me?"

"They told me not to."

"Who's 'they'? The fucking voices in your head?"

"No, the producers, baby. They made me promise to not tell you."

Kara set the beaker down. She thought back to all the paperwork that she had signed. It had been all releases, no contract. She hadn't agreed to any payment deal or actual appearance on camera.

"Are there cameras in this apartment?"

"No, they're being installed tomorrow."

Well, that was something at least. Her mind raced.

"Are you mad at me, baby?" Ryk walked toward her, arms open, a lit joint between his fingers.

"A little," Kara lied. "Does this mean the show isn't happening?"

"No, not at all," Ryk said brightly. "They're just gonna re-configure and have some meetings and then it'll be all systems go."

You really are an idiot. Kara kept the thought to herself as she felt his arms wrap around her waist. He pressed the joint to her lips. She did a cigar inhale, filling her mouth with the smoke, then blowing it out her nose. She took Ryk's wrist and guided the joint back to his mouth.

"You finish it off, baby," she whispered. "I wanna get these last bottles filled. Go sit on the couch and relax."

"You're not mad?" he said in a baby voice.

"Naw," she lied. "Stupid show. They'll come around."

He released her waist and tapped the space bar on the laptop. The generic dubstep filled the air again.

"This shit is still gonna own the dance floor this weekend." Ryk took a long, slow draw on the joint.

"Yes, baby, it's definitely shit."

"Huh?"

"Sit, baby, and get your chill on."

Ryk fell onto the ugly sofa bed and wrapped himself in a comforter that looked as if it had been stolen from a Motel 6. It probably had. Kara resumed silently pouring the liquid into the little bottles as the room filled with stinky smoke. Kara hated weed. The acrid taste in her mouth was only adding to her worsening mood.

"You're so beautiful, baby," Ryk slurred, and his head dropped back onto the sofa. Kara knew that within two minutes she'd hear snoring.

"Shhhhhhhhhhh," she whispered.

Half an hour later, DJ Ryk Rollin was completely asleep on the couch and she had filled all 1,200 bottles. Tomorrow, she was due back to apply little stickers that would read either EASY LAY or GEORGIA HOME BOY (Ryk hadn't yet decided whether to be direct or ironic), but Kara had already decided that tonight was her last night as the future fake love interest of this particular drug-dealer-slash-DJ.

She pulled off her gloves and stood, stretching her arms lithely above her head. She went to the bathroom and dabbed at the green stain on her white suede platforms. It had faded to almost white anyway. She sniffed in approval. *Thanks for behaving, chemicals.*

She looked in the mirror. Her Afro was wrestling with a simple headband and had pushed it almost down to her forehead. She pulled five elastic bands from her Fendi purse and deftly twisted the entire 'fro into five equal puffs that framed her face perfectly. With robotic efficiency she applied mascara and liquid eyeliner, then matted her cheeks and dabbed her lips with a thick coat of deep violet gloss. She switched out her platforms for her favorite pair of purple-suede Prada open-toed stilettos. As she buckled them at her ankles, she considered leaving the platforms at Ryk's. She hated lugging stuff around. One glance at Ryk, unconscious with a roll of hairy, pasty fat hanging out of the bottom of his shirt, convinced her that it would be better to lug the boots home with her. She didn't want to come back to this place.

She took her phone from the purse. She had no missed calls and no texts. That was weird. She texted her roommate.

Nico! You OK?

Then she opened her contacts and chose Billy Baby. The call went straight to voice mail. Her brow furrowed lightly as she tapped out another text.

Baby boy! Where you at? Mama feels like doing a red carpet drive-by at Bootsy's. HMU if you feel like scammin on someone else's bottle service.

Kara walked back into the living room and scanned the room for Ryk's jacket. It was lying on the floor beside his sleeping body. She carefully lifted it up and pulled his wallet out of the inside pocket and was pleased to see that it contained a thick fold of hundred-dollar bills. She helped herself to six and put the wallet back, dropping the jacket on the floor. She flipped the bird at Ryk as she let herself out the front door and, juggling her purse, phone, and platforms, carefully descended the two flights of steps down to Cherokee, summoning an Uber on the way.

⁕ ⁕ ⁕

Ten minutes later, she instructed the driver to wait on Doheny until she returned.

"Hey, this ain't a cab," he complained. "I don't get any more money for waiting for your ass."

"I'll tip you three bucks a minute, honey, I promise."

She stepped out into the warm night air and looked herself up and down. She took a full-length flash selfie and consulted it. The violet of the Prada stilettos set off her black button-up suede shorts and a sheer black tank. She fished a pair of elaborate gold waterfall earrings from her purse and slid them into her ears.

"Girl, you're better than ready," she said huskily.

She peered around the corner onto Sunset. The line at Bootsy's was long, sluggish, and suburban. She checked her phone one last time—nothing—and waited till she saw that tonight's doorman was conquerable. It was Shawn. Perfect.

Dropping her phone into her purse, she snapped to attention and strode around the corner onto Sunset. She walked past the end of the line, and then along the line. People jeered her. She ignored them. She walked directly to Shawn and kissed him on the cheek. She saw a paparazzo emerge from an illegally parked car.

"Block him, baby," she whispered, and Shawn held a huge hand between the guy's camera and Kara's face. A barrage of flashes washed over her as the door opened and she went inside.

She waited just past the entrance as the white flashes faded from her retinas. It was busy tonight. All the booths were occupied and the tiny dance floor was moving solidly as one unit. Kara surveyed the crowd.

"Dang." She whistled. "This place is full of tall white girls with blond hair."

Methodically, she moved through the crowd, pausing on the periphery of each booth to see who was inside. The first few were filled with boring trust-fund Hollywood kids and their friends. Pop tragedy SaraBeth Shields and her manager, both of them on their phones and texting madly, occupied the booth by the DJ setup. Neither of them looked up as Kara filmed a short Snapchat, captioned it #VIPLIFE, and posted it before moving on.

After not even five minutes inside, Kara went back to the front door. She opened it slightly and Shawn appeared.

"Yes, Miss Jones?" he asked playfully.

"I gotta jet," she whispered. "It's loser lodge in there tonight."

"I hear ya, but it is still early."

"Not for me." She smiled. "I need to be asleep. Set a sister up?"

"Yes, mama." Shawn winked, waving his hand at the paparazzo, who obediently got out of his car.

Kara strode out of the club onto Sunset and the portly photographer struggled to keep up with her, shooting her from the front and the side. As she got back into her Uber, she turned and pulled a card from her wallet. On the front, the card read KARA JONES. ACTRESS. STYLIST. CHOREOGRAPHER. Beneath that, her phone number, e-mail, Facebook, Instagram, Snapchat, and even her KIK. She took a pen from her purse and scribbled on the back: "Outfit tonight: vintage from stylist's own collection." She handed it to the photographer.

"You think you can place any of these shots with the weeklies?" she asked, her voice sounding a bit desperate.

"Depends," the photographer said with a wince. "Who the hell are you? What's your story?"

"Like the card says, I'm Kara Jones. I got a show coming out on A&E, I just broke up with . . ." She paused, thinking of which lies would sell best. "Oooh, I better not say his name. I have a clothing line out soon from QVC and I'm up for a lead role on a Showtime drama."

The photographer didn't look impressed.

"Listen, Kara Jones, I'll trade you. I'll pitch your photos to the weeklies if you start telling me what goes on behind those doors. You tip me off, I'll get you printed. Promise. My name is Gino."

"Thanks, babe." She smiled and shook his hand. He clicked off some final frames. "Call me."

"Are we headed to the home address now, miss?" the Uber driver asked.

"Yeah," sighed Kara, slumping back into her seat. "Actually, no. Change of plans. Take me to Pavilions market. Mama needs doughnuts."

CHAPTER 3

AFTER LOSING COURTNEY, NICOLA HAD walked into the kitchen, where a staff of women were prepping food, cleaning dishes, and attempting to corral a menagerie of small dogs trying to escape from a child's playpen in the corner.

The kitchen was normally where she hung out during parties, but this one was way too busy. *Fuck.* Nicola suddenly really needed to nervous pee. She looked around and saw, miraculously, what appeared to be a bathroom door with no line. She walked over and gingerly turned the handle.

It rotated easily and the door swung open, revealing one of her childhood idols, a sitcom actor from the nineties, her first crush. His arm was tied off and he was injecting heroin into a vein in his arm. He released the tourniquet from around his arm, looked up into her eyes, and asked dreamily, "Don't you people ever fucking knock?"

Nicola slammed the door closed and stood there, a little bit shocked, but a little bit more appalled.

The bathroom door opened again and the nineties star stood there, holding the door open for Nicola as he wobbled on his feet.

"Be my guest," he slurred before stumbling off.

It was going to be a long night.

Needing another drink, she wandered back out toward the bar. Amber's hit, "Hot Connection," was still playing in an apparently endless loop. As Nicola neared the laser-lit ice, a woman with a Louise Brooks bob and black leather minidress gently grabbed her arm.

"Hey, you wanna sign Amber's card?" she drawled, purring like a cat and shoving a Sharpie into Nicola's hand.

"Uh, sure, where's the card?"

The woman nodded at a five-foot-tall, extremely retouched photo of the former child star. Per usual, Amber was playing against her once innocent image, straddling a huge bottle of champagne with a cork popping suggestively between her legs, creating a champagne money shot. Nicola raised one eyebrow as she looked at the monstrosity. People had scribbled birthday greetings all over the board-mounted photo.

She handed the Sharpie back to the woman.

"It's okay; I don't really know her," Nicola said with a smile. "She's not going to want to see my name on there."

"Gurl," sighed the woman, refusing to take back the marker, "just write. She's not going to recognize *any* of those names, but it's gonna make her feel real fuckin' popular. Now write your damn name."

Nicola sought out the smallest space she could find, tucked in between champagne bottle and caramel-smooth thigh, and wrote "Happy birthday to the most beautiful girl in Hollywood, love Gaynor and Nicola, HHPR xoxo."

The pen woman was still rolling her eyes at Nicola's inscription as the pen was forced back into her hand.

"Your eyes will get stuck like that," Nicola snapped, startling the pen woman. Feeling satisfied that her mother's threats still worked on others, she headed to the bar.

She had the feeling that everyone was looking at her. Looking around, she saw it was true. Confused, she spun around to see if something was behind her, and bumped her boobs into Seamus.

"So you found me again," he said with a laugh, brushing off his untucked blue chambray shirt.

"I . . . uh . . . yeah, here I am," Nicola said as coolly as she could.

"Let's try this again. I'm Seamus," he said, wriggling the hand that he had been holding in front of her. "Please properly shake my hand." His Scottish brogue made all of his words sound cushioned. In soft, sexy velvet cushions.

"Oh, yes." Nicola snapped back to reality and took his hand, pumping it up and down like a Realtor. "I'm Nicola."

"Well, it's lovely to meet you at last. It feels like it took a lot longer than it should have. I see you need a new drink. Would you be so kind as to wait here while I get some for us?"

Seamus turned to the bar, and Nicola cursed herself for being unable to resist checking out his butt—the one that routinely made the best ass lists—and sighed. It truly was an ass of beauty.

Pushing his way through the crowd, Seamus was completely oblivious to the stares of everyone he passed, and all the surreptitious cell phone photos. He moved like a shark, not noticing the remoras around him.

"Cheers," he said when he returned, clinking his drink against hers.

"Cheers to you, too," smiled Nicola.

"Hey," Seamus asked with a smirk. "So now maybe you'll tell me why you really decided to do the slow-motion valet getaway back there."

Nicola blushed and quickly considered just running for it. Again.

"All right. Yes. Okay. You got me. I panicked. The valet rejected my car."

Seamus gave her a wry half smile.

"It happens, you know."

"Does it now?" He laughed. "Happen to you often?"

"Hey, look, yeah, it hasn't happened *before*, but let's face it, in a 1995 Tercel, it's gonna happen sooner or later in this town. I'm hyperaware of the situation." She stopped. She hated that she could hear herself rambling.

"Listen," Seamus said, leaning in closer. "I ain't busting your sweet ride. It's what caught my eye. Every asshole at this party and every other fuckin' party in town is pulling up in their look-how-rich-I-am car, even though most of them are sleeping on floors to afford their car lease. I wanted to see who the hot girl was who had the balls to turn up in whatever fucking car she wanted."

Nicola tried to swallow, but her throat had dried up. She took a much bigger swig of her drink than she'd anticipated, and choked, coughing loudly.

Seamus's hand was suddenly patting her on the back.

"It's okay, Seamus," Nicola said between coughs. "I got this."

As the coughing subsided, Seamus's hand stayed on her back, moving softly and slowly up and down. It was very warm. In a good way.

"I just saved your life."

Oh great, thought Nicola. *This is where he moves in*. She tensed up.

But he just kept making conversation. "So tell me about the story where the prettiest girl at a party arrives in a vintage beater, has some crazy fight-or-flight instincts, and then tries to dissuade the nicest guy here from talking to her."

"There's not much to tell, really," said Nicola with a smile, releasing her shoulders. "I'm from Dayton, Ohio. I'm a publicist at Huerta Hernandez PR. I bought that Tercel in the parking lot of a Ralphs for two hundred and fifty dollars and it runs like a champ. I feel like a bit of a cotton head driving it but for now, it's perfect."

"A cotton head?" Seamus raised one eyebrow, suddenly conjuring the movie poster for his last big budget sci-fi superhero epic.

"Huh? Oh, nothing. Ignore me. You can take the girl out of Dayton . . ."

"Exactly. Well, then promise to ignore me after a few more drinks and I start to talk like I left Glasgow yesterday."

"It's a deal," laughed Nicola, noticing that Seamus's hand was still gently caressing the small of her back, not venturing too low or high. She couldn't help it. She relaxed a little toward him, and he pulled her a little closer.

"I don't think that's your whole story," Seamus whispered into her ear.

"Well, of course it's not," Nicola said abruptly.

Seamus felt her tensing. His hand rested at the base of her spine, and she felt the warmth of his palm calming her.

"I didn't mean to pry," he said gently.

"It's fine," she said, making it clear that it wasn't fine. "Look, I got out of a bad situation in Dayton. I've sworn off men for a year. No dates, no nothing. So just know that." Nicola looked him in the eye to make sure he knew that she meant it.

"Otherwise, my whole story is that my mom works as a manager at a Motel 6. My brother's just out of rehab. I abandoned them and ran to LA. I need to make it work here so I don't feel like a total ass-hole for running. I send them money, but I need to do more." She paused, her eyes searching his. "Aren't you sorry you asked?"

Seamus shook his head.

"Not at all, Nicola. Not at all."

His hand resumed stroking her lower back.

"Well, it feels weird telling you. And it also feels weird because I feel like I don't need to ask you your story." She already knew a lot about Seamus. His last three girlfriends had gone straight to the tabloids as soon as he broke up with them. She knew he was fiercely private, apparently loyal, but not generous enough for your average Hollywood star-notching trophy wife wannabe.

"Yeah, I get that a lot," Seamus said, resignation heavy in his voice. "And let me say, you *do* need to ask. The truth doesn't sell. And vindictive ex-girlfriends don't tell the truth."

Nicola raised an eyebrow, unsure how to respond.

"Like you said, it's fine," he continued, "as in, 'fine' means it sucks. And if I complain, I'm a rich titled twat. The real story is,

I'm just a fucking bloke who got lucky, and I'd just like to meet a girl who values laughing over Louis Vuitton."

Nicola stared into his eyes. This had definitely taken a turn for the weird.

Seamus took his hand from Nicola's back and clinked his glass against hers, breaking the moment. He let the silence stand between them until it almost blocked out the endless thump of Amber's music.

"I only have one more question for you," he said earnestly, breaking the silence.

Nicola nodded.

"How much time is left on your man-free year?"

"Six months," she lied.

"The clock starts now." He smiled and gave her a wink. Then he saw someone across the yard and waved. "Look, love, I'm really sorry but I have to go chat someone up for a minute. I'll be right back, yeah?"

"Sure." She shrugged, surprised that she was sad to see him leave again. He lifted her hand and kissed it with a flourish. "My lady, I will see you again soon." And then he was sucked into the crowd.

Nicola tried to find somewhere to stand. Amber's endless remix was still playing. She spied an aging rocker woman with a taste for plastic surgery deep in conversation with a celebrity blogger; a troupe of dwarfs all hitting on models while a female dwarf dressed as Britney Spears did shots with the drummer of a nineties metal band.

"This is a nightmare," she muttered to herself. It was ridiculous that this could be someone's job. She had handled PR for the local CBS affiliate in Dayton. Which meant sending DVDs to the local paper and hoping they'd get a write-up for a Sunday movie or a *Survivor* finale. Now her job was to show up at bizarre parties, make sure that someone knew the agency sent a gift, and mingle a little bit. Thinking it over, she determined her job was probably done here and she could leave. This sounded like a great idea.

But as she tossed her cup in the trash and headed through the living room, the heavy wooden doors to the outside world opened and two policemen entered. They went up to the DJ booth and the music stopped. The sudden roar of conversation dried up quickly as one of the cops took the DJ's microphone.

"We are looking for the owner of a 1995 Toyota Tercel. If you are the owner of a 1995 Toyota Tercel parked up the hill, please identify yourself. You're parked in a driveway and we will have to tow your car if you don't move it right now. Can the owner of a 1995 Toyota Tercel please raise their hand?"

It seemed like every single person at that party was waiting to see who owned such a piece of shit.

"It's blue," said the cop.

"Kind of a turquoise," said the other one.

She took a deep breath and walked over to the cops. The music resumed, and Amber's Auto-Tuned voice was singing "I want a hot hot hot connection / I'm looking for your big resurrection" as the cops walked out front with her.

"Don't worry, this time we ain't gonna ticket you, but we need you to get that car out of Jenna Jameson's driveway right now. She's having a fit."

As they marched up the hill to her car, she could still hear Amber singing, "I don't want a missed connection / I want your hot direction."

A strange chill had fallen over the canyon. She fumbled in her purse for her keys, avoiding small talk with the cops. As they drew nearer to her car, Nicola slipped on a pebble and felt the tape tear off her loaned Louboutins. She felt sick as the pebble gouged into the gorgeous red soles.

"Great." Nicola slumped against the Tercel, which was barely six inches into the porn star's twenty-foot-wide driveway.

"You're not having a good night, are you?" asked the cop.

"No, just a typical Hollywood one."

CHAPTER 4

THE COP AT THE OTHER end of the hallway finally fell asleep in his chair. Billy got up and walked gingerly past four hospital room doors to get a closer look. Yep. The regular rise and fall of the cop's chest, coupled with the adorable baby-kitten snores that were starting to huff out of his nose, confirmed that he was in dreamland.

Too bad. He was cute.

Nobody had been in or out of the room that was currently housing the unconscious body of movie star Ethan Carpenter for at least twenty minutes. Billy wasn't sure if this was a good or a bad sign. He went to the door to Carpenter's room and pushed the handle, expecting it to be locked. To his surprise, the door clicked open and he entered the room.

He flinched at the sight of Ethan, shirtless with sheets covering him below the waist. A tube was taped inside his mouth, and wires were taped to his temples and chest. A drip tube fed into his arm. Under the fluorescent hospital lights, the heartthrob looked ashen and closer to forty than the teenagers he regularly played on-screen. Billy surveyed the wall of small screens that pulsed and beeped as they monitored Ethan's vitals.

"At least you're not dead," Billy whispered as he took his phone from his pocket and clicked off several photos of Ethan lying in his bed. He moved around and took more shots from every angle, finally leaning over the bed and taking close-ups of Ethan's face.

This is just insurance, he reasoned. *This is just in case.*

Billy knew there was a shitstorm on the horizon. Never mind that Ethan had been the one to bring him to Vegas, and that Ethan was the one who had flipped out and eaten every upper and downer he could find. In the celebrity hierarchy, Billy knew that as soon as Ethan's team arrived, he'd become the scapegoat. He needed some ammunition to defend himself and these photos were it.

Billy also knew that no matter how well armed you were, it was still better to avoid the fight if you could, and he started to strategize his escape.

The security goons who had rushed Ethan to the hospital had dragged Billy into the wing alongside Ethan's unconscious body, and they'd been very explicit in their directions. Do not leave. Do not get photographed. Or else. And it was the "or else" that was pissing Billy off. He needed to get back to LA. He had shit to do.

Sliding silently out of Ethan's room, he surveyed the hall. The cop appeared to be dozing still, and there was no other movement. He could detect a flurry of activity through the tiny glass windows in the hall doors. Apparently the Vegas press had gotten wind of the story. Billy looked at his phone. No service. He hadn't had any service since that morning. What the fuck was he supposed to do without service?

He started to sweat. He looked up and down the hallway again. He'd tried to call the elevator twice but the button wouldn't even light up to say that an elevator had been called. And then he had an idea.

He went back into Ethan's room. He went to the bedside table and opened the drawer. He found a notepad and a pen inside. He quickly scribbled a note to Ethan's publicist, the grande dame of Hollywood publicists, Crystal Connors.

Hey Crystal,
Sorry I missed you. If you want to discuss today's events, please

contact my publicist, Gaynor Huerta, at Huerta Hernandez
PR. I believe you know the number.

Smooches—Billy XOXOXOX

He placed the notepad on top of the table and took a hospital gown from the cupboard. All of his own clothes were still back at Ethan's apartment in LA, but he figured they were goners now—and besides, he'd scored the nice free shit he was currently wearing from Ethan's Fred Segal delivery. He unlaced the Alexander McQueen high-tops, undid the J Brand jeans and dropped them, then pulled the Phillip Lim T-shirt over his head. He looked at the pile of clothing on the floor, easily one thousand dollars' worth of clothes that basically amounted to something to wear to a baseball game. At least it made the trip worthwhile.

He dragged the hospital gown over his arms and did the awkward reach-around to tie it all up. He rolled the wheelchair from beside Ethan's bed, stashed his shoes and clothes on the seat, and then wheeled the chair to the hallway, where there was a phone on the wall. He sat on top of his shoes and clothes and spread the gown over them, then picked up the phone and dialed zero.

"Operator."

"Hi," he whispered with an edge of panic. "I'm a patient and I must have pushed the wrong button in the elevator and now I'm on level five and it won't let me out."

"Let me transfer you to security," the woman said.

Five minutes later, the elevator door opened, revealing a harried intern nurse.

"How the hell did you get out there?" he asked, darting behind Billy's chair and pushing him into the waiting elevator. Out of the corner of his eye, Billy saw the cop begin to stir. As the doors slid closed, Billy heard the cop start to yell, so he started to talk loudly.

"I don't know, man, I don't know how I got here. I was just taking myself to the bathroom and then I wanted to go out for a smoke and then I was totally locked in and it was like a zombie apocalypse."

The nurse was nonplussed. The doors closed.

"Which floor?"

"Ground," said Billy, hoping that was the floor that led to the street.

"Do you need me to push you anywhere?"

"No, I'm good."

When the doors opened onto a bustling hallway, the nurse didn't move. Billy rolled himself out into the hallway and guessed that he wanted to go in the opposite direction of everyone else. After twenty yards, a bathroom appeared on the right, with a wheelchair symbol on the door. It was vacant. After several attempts, Billy was able to maneuver himself and his wheelchair through the doorway, and he locked the door behind him. Dressing quickly, he looked at his phone. He had one bar. He opened his Uber app. It wouldn't load.

Why does technology always hate me, he wondered. *Seriously.* Technology did always hate him. From dating apps to laptops, nothing ever did what it was supposed to do for him. He hadn't had cell service for almost twelve hours. Nicola probably thought he was dead. They hadn't been out of touch for twelve hours since they could afford unlimited data.

He quickly put his clothes back on and thought for a second. Billy knew he needed to walk out of the hospital quickly and with purpose. He didn't want to burst out of the door and walk straight into the security hulks that had dragged him here, or even worse, into Ethan's power publicist, Crystal. Neither of those encounters would have a good outcome.

Billy unlocked the bathroom door and kicked it open, immediately scanning the walls and ceilings for exit signs while simultaneously watching for any sign of trouble. Doctors and nurses swarmed the hall, and a huge line of regular, worried folks lined up at the information counter. He rushed toward them and grinned widely as he saw the large glass doors to the outside at the end of the hall. As he drew near, the doors pulled open and the stark figure of Crystal Connors swept in, dressed in her signature tightly fitted man's Armani charcoal suit and even tighter facelift, with her straw-blond hair pulled back into a sharp ponytail that looked like a dagger. Billy was relieved that her enormous pitch-black sunglasses were still on, despite it being close to midnight. He darted behind a column and waited, unable to breathe, until he saw her pass on the other side. He counted out loud to twenty and then headed for the doors. As he heard them swoosh closed behind him, he darted into the smelly, sultry Vegas night, and his phone started buzzing madly with messages as he finally got his service back.

Dodging a driveway full of ambulances and cars, Billy made his way across the street to an outdoor plaza lined with towering palm trees. When he was sure he was a safe distance from the hospital and Crystal, he pulled his phone out. And there was Nicola. But only fifteen texts. He'd expected more. Maybe she was busy. And Kara had done a drive-by at Bootsy's. The most recent text was from Nicola's mom, the woman who'd taken him in at age fourteen after his parents found him messing around with the neighbor boy. He decided to respond to her first. As usual, she answered on the first ring.

"Billy!"

"Hey, Mom Two." Billy felt his shoulders relax as she started talking.

"Listen, I have a feeling that something's up with the two of you, and nobody will answer my calls."

"How many times have I told you?" Billy said, smiling. "If something goes wrong, you'll be the second person I call. Listen, I'm in Vegas, and Nico is working late. How about we give you a group FaceTime in a couple days?"

"Okay, baby boy, text me and I'll make sure Biscuit is here, too. We miss you guys."

"Aww, Mom Two, why you gotta be so perfect. Gotta go. Love you to the moon."

"You too, baby boy. Be careful now. Bye."

He hung up and stared at his phone for a second, still smiling. He needed to get as far away from here as he could, so he tapped on the Uber app again, then thought better of it and dialed Nic.

She answered on the second ring.

"Girrrrl," he squealed excitedly. Before Nicola could say anything, he kept right on going. "You won't believe where I've been."

"Vegas," she snapped. "You told me. And I'm driving on Santa Monica and I don't want a ticket so I gotta go."

"Put me on speaker." Billy smiled as he heard the muffled fumbling as Nico did what he asked.

"Well, for once *I* have a story for *you*," Nicola's tinny voice said in his ear.

"Doubt it," Billy said absently. "Remember that movie we saw last week? Remember how I told you that I was sure that that one kid was gay, that thirty-year-old hot piece of ass masquerading as a teenage zombie?"

Nicola didn't bother answering, so Billy just waited the customary beat.

"Well, we're lovers now."

"Of course you are."

"Well, not lovers." Billy sidestepped her passive aggression deftly, wondering why she was being so cold tonight. "But he's a beautiful disaster. So of course, I spent tonight trapped in the intensive care ward of a Vegas hospital. . . ."

"What?!"

"Well, yeah, things have gotten a bit out of hand. I'm fine, I'm fine, but damn, his separation anxiety mixed with uppers and downers and oh my, here we are."

"Oh great, you're lovers with a drug addict. That's not even funny."

"That was the fastest service you've ever seen in an emergency room."

"And you're okay?"

"Der. Of course I am. I can handle my shit, lady."

"So what are you doing now?"

"I'm on the lam—the place is surrounded by reporters and photographers. They were trying to break into our wing of the hospital. Security hated us. The cop fell asleep and I made a break for it. It's all very exciting."

"You're insane."

"Okay, well, you don't sound too excited to hear from me and I do need to call my Uber."

"Nuh-uh," Nicola barked. "I have a story. It's better than your story!"

"Can it wait till morning? I'll call you from the road. I'll be back in the afternoon, traffic gods willing."

"You're so not going to hang up without hearing my story."

"If it's that good, I'd rather hear it in person," he laughed. "Love you, mean it. And call your mom."

He disconnected the call and summoned his ride. He flicked through the photos of Ethan on his hospital bed and texted the best one to Nicola. Then he scrolled through his contacts until he found the number of a hotel publicist who'd been trying to bed him for a year. He messaged him that he was in town working on a last-minute travel story and had missed his flight and needed a room. Within ten minutes, he had a confirmation number for a free suite at the Wynn. The day wasn't a complete loss.

CHAPTER 5

SQUINTING INTO THE DARK OF her West Hollywood street, Nicola prayed for a gap between the parked cars. There was nothing at all on her block.

"Crap."

This was her nightly ritual. The hunt for a street parking spot big enough to squeeze her car into. She cursed at the NO CRUISING NO TURNS AFTER 10 P.M. sign at the next two intersections that forced her to continue to Melrose. They'd warned her about the traffic before she moved to LA, but nobody had warned her about West Hollywood parking.

Her two-bedroom apartment came with only one parking spot, and her roommate, Kara, had claimed squatter's rights on it when Nicola moved in. Their shady landlord illegally rented the other one to some lawyer who had an office up on Santa Monica. She routinely spent at least twenty minutes searching for a place to park her blue beast.

She found a spot on Melrose that needed to be cleared before nine a.m. the next morning. Killing the engine, she sat for a minute, thinking back on the party. She might as well have been wearing a Dayton Flyers jersey and Ugg boots. It was a good thing she'd never aspired to Hollywood stardom.

The Tercel door creaked loudly as she swung it open to get out and then closed it. At the corner of Melrose and Harper, she skirted a drunken guy sitting in the doorway of a boutique and ignored his garbled request for a blow job.

"Cunt," he sneered as she walked past him.

She bridled, considered going back and slamming her heavy purse into his head, took a deep breath, and turned onto her leafy, dark street. In Ohio, that was a bad word. In LA she heard it more often than she heard "thanks."

It still freaked her out, how rapidly the nightlife of Sunset Boulevard, just two blocks north, dissipated into a silent wasteland. At night the streets were always empty, the residents always hidden inside their homes.

Nicola crossed the street, still one long block from her apartment, and stifled a scream as a figure emerged from the darkness right in front of her, as if materializing from behind the bushes. She reached into her purse and wrapped her fingers around the small rock she carried for occasions just like this, and wished it were a baseball bat.

Nicola squinted to see better in the dark, and softened as she realized it was only Jean, her favorite unstable homeless person. The wizened old lady walked her street all day and night selling crayon portraits to pay for her drinking habit.

"Oh, uh, Jean, hi . . . you scared me," she said.

Jean stood in front of her silently, and slowly pulled from behind her back another one of her artworks. It was too dark to make out what it was, but they were usually Jesus, some hummingbirds, flowers, or Michael Jackson.

"That's lovely." Nicola smiled. "It's your best one yet."

Jean stood there, a vague figure dappled in shadows from the streetlight through the trees. She appeared to have done her hair into a high curly beehive, and she was wearing an old floral dress with a moth-eaten cream sweater and what appeared to be a baby's rattle pinned to her chest.

"You want it or not, sister?" she croaked.

"I'd love it," Nicola said. "How much for this one?"

"Ten bucks," Jean slurred. "Thish one wash a lot of work."

"But all the other ones are five bucks." Nicola smiled, used to this exchange.

"Not thish one, it's a new person." Jean wobbled on her chunky heels.

"You've done Michael Jackson before."

"THIS ISN'T MICHAEL JACKSON," Jean snapped, quickly flicking the paper behind her back again.

"Oh, it's not? I'm so sorry, it's dark. Let me see it properly."

Jean slowly drew the gaudy artwork out again and this time presented it grandly in a shaft of streetlight. It was a generic smiling white man's face with dark hair.

"It's Prince," she said proudly. "He and Michael are together in heaven."

"I was just about to guess that it was Prince," lied Nicola. "Of course it's worth ten bucks."

She reached into her purse and pulled out the money.

"Now don't you go back to the Gold Coast and spend all this at once," she said as she exchanged her bill for the portrait. "Maybe you should go get a sandwich or something."

"What's it fucking matter," spat Jean, snatching the money and stuffing it into a pocket on her cardigan. "I'm sick of those fags and I'm sick of you telling me what to do."

"Well, okay, then," said Nicola. "You just take care of yourself and I'll see you next time. Thanks for the beautiful painting."

"It's crayon," said Jean, not moving.

"Yes, it is, sorry," said Nicola, gingerly stepping around the old lady, who was immobile in the middle of the sidewalk, as if she had run out of batteries.

"Good night," said Nicola, waving, as she began walking up the street. "Take care."

She got about fifty yards farther along the street when she heard Jean yell at her, "Old people aren't retarded, you bitch."

"I was waiting for that," she said into the night air, hurrying the rest of the distance to her building.

She paused at the mailboxes in front of a large, faded apricot stucco two-story apartment complex emblazoned with the words OCEAN PALMS in rusty metal script. The words probably looked jaunty in 1973, but these days they were just rusty and depressing.

The mailbox was empty, which meant Kara had at least been home at some time today.

A raccoon scampered down the pathway ahead of her. What else would this infernal day send her way, she wondered. Reaching the second-to-last first floor apartment, she slid her key into the lock, and heard scrambling noises from inside, and the sound of something glass clashing together. *What fucking now?*

"WAIT! Just a sec," bellowed Kara.

Nicola's shoulders dropped. She just wanted to get inside.

After thirty seconds, Kara told her it was okay to come in. As the door opened, Nicola saw a blanket on the awful champagne-colored carpet, along with some rubber straps and a laptop. Kara came striding out of her bedroom, wearing a bra and yanking up a pair of tight olive yoga pants.

"Sorry," she said breathlessly. "I thought you'd be out later than this."

"Er, okay, but what the hell were you doing?"

"Oh, nothing," Kara said, bending down and grabbing the rubber straps.

"Okaaaay." Nicola pushed past her toward her bedroom.

"Fine, I'll tell you, but you can't tell anyone," said Kara, sliding by her and blocking her way.

"Look, it's late and I'm tired. I just want to go to bed," said Nicola, frustration creeping into her voice.

"Oh my God, did you buy another one of those fucking paintings from that crazy old lady?" Kara pointed to the paper in Nicola's hand.

"Obviously. Now can I please get to my room?"

"How many of those fucking things do you need?" laughed Kara. "Come on, you have like fifty of them. Are you working on her first gallery show?"

"Maybe," sneered Nicola. "Maybe one day she'll drink herself to death and they'll be worth a fortune."

"Okay, okay, sorry," said Kara. "Go put your masterpiece away and come back out here and I'll tell you about the incredibly sexy nude Pilates session I just had with Jimmy J."

"The rapper?" Nicola was suddenly interested. She skipped into her room and pitched the Prince portrait on top of her wardrobe.

Her Pottery Barn bedspread, all bold oranges and yellows, failed to brighten her room's generic LA apartment blandness. The ugly gray vertical slat blinds swayed in the breeze she had created. She plunked herself onto the bed and slipped off the Louboutins. Looking at the sole, she grimaced. It was worse than she thought. The tape had torn clear through in several spaces, and there were deep scratches in the bloodred soles.

"Fuck," she hissed. It would take her two paychecks to pay for these, if she didn't buy food or gasoline in those same weeks, and they let her buy them at cost.

"You break it. You bought it," her boss always said.

Nicola had originally started with HHPR as a three-month temporary intern, making so little that after food, rent, and gas, she'd been living on $100 a month. One day she'd walked into the office just as a man was throwing Gaynor against the wall. Nicola had run up and slammed her work laptop against the back of his head, sending him to the floor. As he scrambled to his feet, demanding that Gaynor fire "this crazy bitch," Nicola had held up her laptop again, snarling, "I don't fucking care who you are, asshole. You raise your fist to a woman again, and you'll need another shitty facelift."

Gaynor had given her a promotion and a raise the next day, and moved her from the intern pool to a desk outside her office.

Nicola slipped off her dress and changed into sweats and an old

T-shirt printed with a group of penguins wearing sunglasses and the slogan TOO COOL FOR SCHOOL. She pulled her hair back into a short curly ponytail and returned to the living room, where Kara was still busy tidying up the evidence of her online lust session.

In their early roommate days, morning person Nicola had rarely seen night-owl Kara, but over the months, as their friendship grew, Nic would force herself to stay up on the rare nights they were both home. Billy had told Kara that Nic was consciously making the effort, and that Nic loved a late-night cocktail. Ever since, it became a ritual that Kara would fix drinks while they caught up.

"I can't have a hangover tomorrow," Nicola called from her bedroom.

"All these limitations," Kara yelled back. "Fine, I'll just make the one pitcher of greyhounds."

Nic settled onto the couch and Kara dramatically stepped out from the kitchen with a frosted-glass pitcher of pale yellow booze and two glasses filled with ice balanced on a silver tray. She placed it on the coffee table that they'd hauled in from someone's move-out trash, and handed one to Nic. She started talking before she'd even sat down.

"So I was dead beat on my feet and needed a treat," she laughed. "Pavilions doughnuts, to be exact. And boom, there's Jimmy J shopping for pastry." She paused and sipped. "He didn't want my number, just my Snapchat. My inner ten-year-old was dying. But my outer twenty-six-year-old wasn't too into it, so I left.

"Ten minutes after I got home, he private messaged me asking how I felt about nude Pilates with a rap legend. I should have asked him if he could hook me up with one, but instead I was bored, amused, and the next thing you know, I'm all, bicycle! Crisscross! Corkscrew! And that fool is rapping about wanting to see my butthole."

Nicola laughed so loud she spat greyhound all over Kara, who demurely flicked the droplets away with a perfectly filed nail.

"I'll take that as a compliment," she grinned.

Nicola was used to Kara's life being dramatic. She was a short and gorgeous black girl whose trademark was her huge Afro. She usually wore it in cute black puffs at either side of her head, but on occasion would go "full natural" and let it reach its maximum width. She'd been "the hot girl" in several famous rap videos in the mid-aughts, and had parlayed that into a career as a stylist. She'd "dressed hos" on reality shows like *Teen Superstar* and *Married to My Baby Daddy* on MTV. Billy had set Nicola up as her roommate before the two even met, and it suited Kara since she was still dreaming of her big break, and Nicola had offered free publicist services.

"So Jimmy J still thinks it's 1999 and that he's the biggest star in the world," Kara said, stretching one of her legs out behind her. "He's mainly into himself and his rapping, but he does like my flexibility."

"Am I the only person who thinks this is all a bit ridiculous?" laughed Nicola.

"No," smiled Kara. "Nude Pilates is definitely ridiculous. He liked it tonight via Skype, but he says 'IRL is coming soon.'"

"You must be ecstatic," Nicola deadpanned. "Or really desperate."

"It's hard to keep a straight face and do the positions, and you should hear the weird sexy talk the guy comes up with."

"Thanks, I'll pass," said Nicola, pushing herself up from the couch. "Okay, good night."

"Wait—didn't you go to some big party tonight?"

"Yeah . . ."

"How was it?"

Nicola turned and faced Kara, knowing that to tell her any more would be a mistake. She did it anyway.

"It was kind of fun," she began. "I met Seamus O'Riordan, and you know, we had fun, strangely."

"The fuck you did," Kara gasped.

"I did."

"Okay, so let me guess. He came and talked to you, and then you got all awkward and blew it, right?"

"You got it," sighed Nicola, walking to her room and pulling her door closed behind her.

After brushing her teeth in her tiny bathroom, she got into bed. Just as she was drifting off, Kara tapped on her door.

"Two things," she whispered.

"What?" groaned Nicola.

"One: Did you get his number? And two: Is he into black girls?"

Nicola dragged the other pillow over her head.

"Good NIGHT."

"Is that another painting of Michael Jackson?"

"No, it is clearly Prince," Nicola barked. "And it's CRAYON."

CHAPTER 6

THE ONLY PARKING SPOT NICOLA could count on in West Hollywood was in the open-air garage beneath the nondescript concrete-box building on Third that housed, among other things, the headquarters of Huerta Hernandez PR. It was still early. The summer heat hadn't set in, and the sky was still discernably blue, having not yet surrendered to the smog.

She was glad she had moved up quickly out of the ranks of Gaynor's intern army—who were mainly young Colombian women she recruited at her church who were not interested in PR—but despite her promotion to assistant, Nicola was still saddled with the job of bringing her boss coffee each morning. She walked out to Beverly Boulevard and headed to Starbucks, to procure the enormous five-shot espresso skim latte that would turn Gaynor into a chattering lunatic for a half hour. At least.

Armed with the latte, and a drip coffee and pastry for herself, she returned to the building and buzzed for the ridiculous elevator. Only in LA would you find an elevator and a perpetually locked fire escape in a three-story building. Arriving at her floor and juggling two coffees and her purse and laptop, she stupidly hoped that the front door to the office would be unlocked.

Gaynor's shiny Mercedes had been in the spot next to hers, so she was probably inside. None of the other girls ever bothered to arrive before eleven a.m. She rattled the doorknob. Of course, the door was locked.

Carefully bending in half, Nicola deposited the coffees, purse, and laptop on the floor and fished out her keys in the darkness. All the blinds were drawn, and rows of empty desks flanked the hallway that went past the conference room and ended at Gaynor's door. Small lightbulbs illuminated the word HUERTA on said door, and provided the only light in the office.

Perhaps Gaynor had taken a taxi to an appointment or just left her car there overnight. Maybe Nicola would have two hours to herself to do a little detective work and see if there was any fallout from Billy's Vegas misadventure, or any photos online of Seamus talking to her at the party. She hoped that neither had happened.

Holding the door open with her foot, she picked up her belongings and transferred them to the small table in the reception area, which was strewn with carefully placed magazine covers featuring some of Gaynor's clients.

Gaynor was one of Hollywood's most feared publicists, and she represented some of the world's biggest actors, all of whom she had started working with at the beginning of their careers, and had defended like a wolf ever since. "My clients don't do scandals" was her favorite catchphrase. Of course, in reality, it was all they did.

Nicola picked up her coffee and the little pastry in its brown bag and began walking toward her desk at the other end of the room. Her dreams of some quiet time were destroyed by a sudden, gravelly bark, which her brain took a second to translate as "COFFEE!"

Nicola jumped, hot splashes of coffee scalding her hand via the tiny hole in the plastic lid.

"Fuck!" she exclaimed, putting her cup on her desk and going back for Gaynor's. Opening Gaynor's door slowly, she saw a massive shock of black hair on the desk, like a wig dropped from a great height. The wig started to rise, and Nicola realized it was Gaynor herself. She had been sleeping at her desk, her unruly mane of overly processed, blue-black dyed hair working as a blackout curtain as she slept.

"*Buenos días*, Nicolita," groaned the wig as it rose from the table.

"You sound like shit," said Nicola.

"COFFEE!" the wig barked.

Nicola set the rocket fuel on her boss's desk. Gaynor was now upright, though her hair was still over her face. In one dramatic move, she used her right forearm to snake under the hair and drag the whole mess to approximately where it belonged, on the back of her head. Her eyes were still closed, and her eye makeup had slipped about a half inch from where it began its night.

With her eyes closed, she reached for the Starbucks. Nicola moved it closer to her hand, and Gaynor grabbed it, holding it to her nose and inhaling its fragrance deeply.

"Careful." Nicola smiled. "The beverage you're about to enjoy may be hot."

"Whatever," muttered Gaynor, taking a sip. Her eyes popped open, huge and bloodshot, as the coffee scalded her tongue. She made a raspy moan. "This is good."

"You slept here?" Nicola asked.

Gaynor stared at her and pointed a finger at Nicola's desk through her door.

"What is that?" she said, still creaking.

Nicola turned and followed the direction of the immaculate red talon.

"Oh, I got a coffee, too," she said.

"No, in the bag, what is it? *¿Qué es eso?*"

"Oh, I got a pastry. I was hungry," she explained.

"Give it to me," Gaynor demanded.

Nicola sighed and went and got her pastry. She handed the bag containing her breakfast to Gaynor, who held it between two fingers as if it were a bag of dog shit. She dropped it into the wastebasket by her desk.

"I can't teach you if you refuse to learn," she hissed. "Look at this, look at this thing you buy, all the sugar, nothing but sugar. It will kill you, but worse, it will make you fat, and you will be like the rest of America."

"Well, thanks for that, Gaynor," sniffed Nicola. "I haven't eaten a damn thing in twenty-four hours, so I think I'm still way under my calorie count for the day. And now I just wasted three bucks."

"Oh, calm down, I'll give you an Adderall," said Gaynor, digging into the huge floppy Birkin purse on the edge of her desk.

"I'm okay, thanks. I'll get a kale salad for lunch, if you promise not to throw that into the trash, too."

"If you listen to me, you'll be able to dress like a woman, not like something from the"—Gaynor paused and physically shuddered—"grunge era."

Nicola pulled at her cute cotton black-and-orange plaid shirtdress.

"This is Zara," she protested.

"Why must you make this so hard? That thing needs a belt, rhinestones, shoulder pads, and tights before it can even be considered peasant chic. Please never again remind me of the nineties. Now get out of here. The damn phones have been ringing like a cocaine hotline on Oscar week."

Back at her desk, the red message light on the phone was indeed blinking. Not a good sign for 9:15 a.m. Nicola picked up her handset and dialed in to the company voice mail.

The robot lady voice inside the phone told her there were seventeen unheard messages. This meant something was up.

She pressed one to access the first message.

"Gaynor, this is Crystal. It's urgent. Call me." Click. Nicola noted the time stamp: last night at 11:54—and started a list of callbacks for her boss. She skipped to the next message.

"Gaynor, you fucking bitch, I told you to call me. I've called your cell, I've called your fucking house, and now this, your answering service isn't even fucking answering. Call me now or I'm gonna stuff a burrito so far up your ass you'll burp like a fucking wetback. Call me."

Because Gaynor insisted that her staff use paper notes for all phone messages, Nicola wrote "CALL CRYSTAL. URGENT" on a slip of paper and took it into Gaynor's office. Gaynor looked at the note, and her eyes widened slightly. Due to her Botox habit, this could have meant boredom or complete terror.

"What does that old *puta* want?" she rasped. "She left me a million messages last night. I don't jump when she snaps her claws."

"I don't know, but she says she tried to call you on all your devices. She sounds pissed. I think she left a few more messages, at least."

Gaynor mumbled something under her breath in Spanish, then added, "Try and figure out what she's upset about before I call her. *Por favor*."

Crystal was Gaynor's former mentor, lover, and current nemesis. Their rivalry was legendary. There had even been a thinly veiled Lifetime movie about them that only the gays had loved.

Returning to her desk, Nicola started playing the rest of the messages. They were all Crystal. Each message was more florid than the one before it, the threats increasingly outlandish and more racist. It wasn't until the twelfth or thirteenth message that Nicola froze.

"Gaynor, who the fuck is this Billy Kaye and why is he saying he is your client? The little twink has me in a world of pain and if you don't call me back five minutes ago . . ."

The handset dropped to her desk, and Nicola never got to hear which traditional item of Mexican descent was going to be forcibly inserted in one of Gaynor's orifices. *Fucking Billy*, she seethed, *goddamn fucking Billy*. Why the hell was he telling Crystal that Gaynor was his publicist? Why the fuck was Billy even talking to Crystal? Where the hell did they meet last night?

"Oh no," she gasped out loud, realization setting in. "Oh no."

Pushing away from her desk, Nicola walked timidly toward Gaynor's door.

"Hey, uh, Gaynor, can I ask you a question?"

Gaynor turned to her, silenced by the tone of her voice.

"*Mija*, what's wrong?" she gasped. "Did you see a ghost?"

"Well, I dunno. But tell me this—does Crystal represent Ethan Carpenter?"

"Darling, how did you miss her? She just signed him a month ago; she's been his shadow at every event; you would think he has a thing for Egyptian mummies instead of the boulevard rent boys. He's her first big new client in years. Why does this scare you? What did that *puta vieja* say?"

Nicola swallowed loudly and began. Even after a year, armed with the knowledge that Gaynor's bark was worse than her bite, it was hard to tell her bad news. Her agency was her life, and any threat to it turned Gaynor from disco-crazed caricature into a snarling pit bull in seconds.

"Billy called me last night from some emergency room in Vegas. He'd been with Ethan all weekend and I guess Ethan OD'd or something and went to the emergency room. Paparazzi followed them, and they were trapped inside, waiting for Crystal to arrive. Billy barely managed to escape."

"Oh, *dios mío*," screamed Gaynor, bursting into laughter. "*Abuelita's* gonna have a manic Monday!"

"Well, hold on, because this is the part you won't like," Nicola continued. "Billy told Crystal that you're his publicist!"

Gaynor's laughing ratcheted up a notch, going from monkey squall to hyena cackle. Billy was outrageous and tenacious, and Gaynor had loved him from the start, even if he had first called her to blackmail one of her clients. She'd offered him access to her clients in exchange for him not selling their scandals to the tabloids. He'd even brought Nicola to her, and for that, Gaynor was grateful.

"This friend of yours, this pretty boy, has a set of *cojones*. I love it.

I love it. Fine, for today, I am his publicist. You call him and tell him to tell her that his publicist said we have no comment on the matter. Then tell him to get the fuck away from Crystal, Ethan, and Las Vegas. Tell him to drive to my office, because I want to hear this whole story, I want to hear every single detail. But please remind him, I'm a publicist, not a pimp, and until he's auditioning for something other than Malibu houseboy, never to drop my name again. But for today, I love him and I love this."

Well, that went better than expected, thought Nicola. She called Billy and got voice mail. She began repeating Gaynor's instructions for him, and Gaynor appeared at her side, goading her to deliver the final piece, about her not being his pimp. When she was done, Gaynor applauded her.

"*Brava, mija*. Keep me posted," she said, closing her door. Nicola heard a thud as Gaynor's head hit her desk, probably a little harder than she anticipated. This was the most hungover she'd ever seen her.

✳ ✳ ✳

Billy texted her an hour later, saying that he'd finally rented a car and would be back in LA around five, and that he'd come directly to the office. Nicola went to inform Gaynor. Stepping into her office, she was shocked to see that her boss was now dressed in a completely different outfit, a skintight low-cut red dress with matching heels; her hair was swept into a thick chignon that sat perfectly against the back of her neck, and her makeup was flawless. Her hangover had vanished along with last night's clothes.

"Did you even leave your office?" asked Nicola, shaking her head.

Gaynor pulled at her dress, ignoring her.

"Billy texted me. He's just leaving Vegas now; he'll be here in the office around five."

"Perfect, *mija*, perfect. That gives us time."

"Time for what?"

"A little makeover for you. For us both. I have a little job for you tonight, and I think you will enjoy it. I need you to escort Paul Stroud to a premiere, so I booked us a little salon time for this afternoon. Is that okay? Can Mama pamper you?"

"Well, sure, I guess," said Nicola, suddenly shy. She looked at her feet. She knew that Gaynor represented her teenage crush Paul Stroud, but he'd never been into the office. She felt a blush starting near her ears and prayed that Gaynor wouldn't notice it. She changed the subject. "Aren't you going to call Crystal back?"

"In time. Maybe I will call her while they are waxing my pussy, so the pain will be less. On my pussy, I mean."

"Wait—we're going waxing together? How well do you think this date is going to go?"

"You're funny," scowled Gaynor, not amused. "I don't care how the date goes; I care how beautiful you look in the tabloids next week. So, we go get a little waxing, we get some hair and makeup and nails, and we swing by a showroom to dress you sexy but not too sexy. Then we have a little meeting with your *loco* homo and you and I get in the limo and pick up Paul. Don't worry." She paused. "I won't make you stay through the whole movie. We can sneak out."

"Oh, okay," smiled Nicola, relieved that Gaynor's *we* seemed to indicate that she'd be chaperoning them all night. Paul Stroud had been her absolute obsession when she was eighteen, when he starred on that CW show about time-traveling superheroes. She hadn't seen too many of his action movies, but hell, she was going to be his red carpet date. She wanted to tell her mother. "This should be fun. When are we leaving?"

"Right now, *mi amor*. Please, don't get your keys, I will drive. Also, I'm going to ask them to move your parking space; it doesn't look good to have that thing you drive, that burro wagon, next to my AMG."

Nicola rolled her eyes and followed Gaynor toward the door.

"Gaynor, who reps Seamus O'Riordan?"

Gaynor visibly huffed as she turned.

"Now what?"

"Nothing. I was just wondering who his publicist was."

"Well, it's Crystal; what the fuck does she want now?"

Of fucking course it is, thought Nicola.

"Oh, no reason, I just met him at Amber's party last night, and he kind of hit on me."

"Finally, a superstar tries to fuck you!" Gaynor crowed, pointing to the office door, expecting Nicola to lock it behind them. "Welcome to LA, big deal. Now let's go get your *culo* into shape."

CHAPTER 7

THE GIRL IN HER BEDROOM mirror did not look like Nicola. That girl was wearing a full-length Gianni Versace couture sheath in deep purple silk, with a strap of emerald across the chest. Her arms were bare, but her neckline sat modestly just below her collarbones. That girl's chestnut hair was upswept, with just one tangle of curls falling beside her right eye. That girl, Nicola had to admit, was beautiful. It just wasn't her.

She had hoped for something a tiny bit sexier, a bit more cleavage, but Gaynor had been firm about it.

"It's your first time out, we can't risk a nipple, and also, Paul has a good imagination; let him use it," she had admonished several hours earlier, as they pawed through the racks of potential dresses with one of her army of stylists.

She turned and made sure that the unforgivingly tight dress did not show any evidence of her thong. She slipped into another pair of loaned Louboutins—silver slingbacks that she had triple taped the soles of—and took a deep breath.

"Better luck this time . . . ," she told herself in the mirror. She took a full-length selfie in the mirror and sent it in a group chat to Billy and Kara.

Her phone dinged. It was Gaynor. She was waiting out front. Grabbing an impossibly tiny purse that the stylist assured her retailed for over six thousand dollars, Nicola put her driver's license, some folded twenties, and her apartment key inside, filling it to capacity. She pulled the door closed behind her and headed right along the walkway out to the street. An old Russian man on a balcony just up from hers whistled.

An SUV like an armored tank, with midnight-blackened windows, sat at the curb, blocking half the street. A window buzzed down and Gaynor's head appeared. She lowered her oversize sunglasses and gave Nicola's apartment building a slow up-and-down gaze.

"So, this is where you . . . *live*?" she asked, barely able to hide her disgust.

"Is it the address I gave you?" Nicola retorted.

"*Mija*, I don't remember, and don't make me bother the poor driver right now; he's busy protecting this car from thieves. Please get in."

Nicola walked around the car and got in, sliding onto the seat and trying to smooth her dress out beneath her.

"Why did you make me get satin?" she asked as she buckled her seat belt. She looked at Gaynor, clad in her usual publicist's armor of black pants and jacket with a red shirt. She had a coke spoon on a chain around her neck, and a solid gold band held her hair back.

"Psh," sniffed Gaynor. "It photographs perfectly and nobody's going to be looking at your ass. Drive, Darell," she commanded. "Next stop, Paul's house, the Mulholland address. *Gracias!*"

The hulking SUV headed up into the Hollywood Hills, the switches and curves of Laurel Canyon making Nicola vaguely carsick. She stopped checking her e-mail and put her phone into her purse, only to find that it now wouldn't close.

"Don't stretch that purse," cautioned Gaynor. "That's a couple months of your salary, even at cost."

Nicola shot her a look, and for once, it seemed to register to Gaynor that she may have hurt someone's feelings.

"I'm sorry, that was, uh, insensitive. But please, be careful; I am responsible for getting all of these things back to the stylist. Speaking of which, did you bring back the shoes from last night?"

"Oh, I totally forgot," Nicola lied. She hadn't had any spare time to call around to find if anyone could repair the soles that she had scratched as she fled Amber's party. "I'll bring them in tomorrow."

Gaynor waved her hand dismissively and lit a cigarette.

"That's fine, that's fine."

Before Gaynor could ask anything else, Nicola defensively changed the subject.

"How did the meeting with Billy go?"

"It was hardly a meeting, *mija*. He told me the full story, and now I am armed with enough ammunition to make that old *coño* sweat through her Botox. I will meet with her tomorrow. You're lucky to have a friend like Billy. He's . . ." She paused and looked out the window. "He's something you don't find anymore."

Nicola went to reply, but Gaynor waved her off and theatrically resumed answering e-mail on her phone. Nicola turned and looked out the window as the SUV climbed higher and higher.

✳ ✳ ✳

When they finally crested Laurel Canyon and headed west on Mulholland, Gaynor broke her silence.

"Paul is a very nice man," she began.

"That sounds like a warning, not a recommendation."

"No, he is," said Gaynor. "But he was very, very famous when he was very young. He got spoiled, and he crashed and burned, but now he is back on track, and I just want you to look as happy as you can walking into the premiere. The only time you are to speak is if someone asks who you are wearing. You are to give a one-word answer. No thank-yous, not a single other word. And then that big smile of yours, and then moving on to the next person on the press line. I will be right behind you."

"I get it," said Nicola, suddenly worrying about what sort of man her teenage crush might actually be. Gaynor's words hinted at danger of some kind.

The SUV turned sharply around a corner, and the road fell away outside Nicola's window as they drove along a sheer cliff. She gasped, and her heart was still pounding as they stopped outside a very modest mid-century house with a vintage sports car out front. This was Paul's place? She'd expected more.

Gaynor texted Paul, and he appeared at the door almost immediately.

The late afternoon sun hit him right in the face and drenched him in golden light, and Nicola was suddenly eighteen again. He looked older, but he also looked better, almost impossibly handsome. His brown hair had been lightened with gold streaks that caught the sunlight, and his tanned face showed the barest signs of crow's feet. He hadn't shaved, and his stubble made his blue-gray eyes pop. His charcoal Tom Ford suit was immaculate. He walked to the car and opened the door, smiling when he saw Nicola.

"Well, hi," he said affably. "I'm Paul." He extended his hand.

"I'm Nicola," she said. "It's a pleasure to meet you."

"Oh, please—no more formalities. From you, anyway," he laughed, getting into the car and sitting opposite the women. "Now you," he said sternly, pointing at Gaynor, "you're late."

Gaynor hadn't even stopped checking her e-mail. She slowly looked up, and a smile wreathed her lips. It was like watching a wolf spy a duckling.

"Señor Stroud, it's lovely to see you, too," she purred, leaning in his general direction and giving the air a double kiss. "I'm never late. Your arrival will be perfectly timed. We will be there in time for you to do only five minutes of interviews, and we will go into the movie for ten minutes, and then I have a table booked for you two at the Little Door. It will all be perfect."

Whaaaaaaaaa? screamed Nicola's brain as she froze her smile in place and turned to glare at Gaynor.

"Surprise." Gaynor smiled icily back at her.

They could hear the screaming of the crowd from a block away as security guards and CHP officers directed the SUV into the line of other limousines and SUVs waiting to deposit their celebrity contents at the foot of the red carpet.

Klieg lights swept the sky, even though the sun was still doing a great job on its own, and electronic billboards along Hollywood Boulevard showed scenes from the movie. Nicola had read it was a clunky sci-fi yarn that had something to do with time travel, spies, robots, and the end of the world. At least it wasn't zombies.

In the posters, Paul's handsome face was half hidden under a mask of circuitry, and his torn shirt revealed a chiseled chest and abs. He was holding a gun that was equal parts candelabra and laser teeth-bleaching kit. Nicola was grateful they were only going to watch five minutes of it.

At the drop-off point, Paul and Gaynor simultaneously started fussing with their wardrobe, and Nicola followed suit. The security guards opened the door on her side, and Nicola realized she was going to have to be the first person to get out. Her insides clenched a little.

She felt Paul's hand on her shoulder.

"Relax; this will either be fun or over before you know it," he said gently, then added, "Is it okay if I hold your hand while we walk?"

Nicola and Gaynor answered at the same time, except Gaynor said no and Nicola said yes.

"That settles it," laughed Paul, pushing past Nicola and exiting the SUV. He stepped out, and immediately the screaming of the crowd went from unpleasant to jet engine. He turned, smiling, and extended his hand. Nicola took it, and very carefully stepped down from the car onto the swirling maelstrom of the red carpet.

Their trip to the doors of the Chinese Theatre seemed endless. Gaynor had said it would be five minutes, but it felt like an hour. First they stopped in front of the screaming mass of photographers. Gaynor expertly, silently placed them side by side. She gently kicked one of Nicola's feet slightly forward and turned her right hip. She leaned in and whispered to Nicola, "Eyes and teeth, big smile, and work them left to right. Just copy Paul."

Paul never let go of her hand. He wasn't crushing it, and it felt reassuring. She saw him maintain a completely unchanging smile as he moved his head, and only his head, from left to right so that all the photographers got their coverage, and she followed suit.

Gaynor appeared at her side.

"Time for some solos," she said brusquely, pulling their hands apart and leading Nicola out of the range of the photographers.

When the photos were all done, Gaynor reunited them.

"Okay, boss, what's the plan?" asked Paul, very businesslike.

"Two electronic only. We have to do *ET*, the stupid movie's Paramount, and then let's do something flirty with the gay guy from MTV. Two minutes each. And don't even make eye contact with the print press or you'll just feel sorry for them and stop."

"Well, they have been standing in the hot sun for about an hour waiting to talk to me," said Paul.

"I don't care if they just won a gold medal in the Special Olympics," hissed Gaynor. "No eye contact, no stopping!"

Nicola tried to be a complete wax figure during the two interviews with the fawning reporters from *ET* and MTV. She smiled along with Paul's answers, nodding occasionally, constantly aware that Gaynor was hovering just out of camera range and monitoring her every move. Sweat started to run down her back, and she felt her composure slip. She prayed it wasn't darkening her dress. She finally understood why people Botoxed their sweat glands.

During both interviews, Paul dodged questions about her identity, deftly changing the subject while keeping his hand on the small of her back. Nicola just smiled and channeled her teenage self as she gazed at him with a reasonable facsimile of love.

As soon as Gaynor abruptly ended the final TV interview, Paul muttered "Thanks" to the interviewer and turned away, guiding Nicola through the final stretch of red carpet. To their right, an army of pleading print journalists and chubby bloggers waved recorders and notepads in their direction.

Remembering Gaynor's words, Nicola fixed her eyes on the door of the theater and walked toward it. She couldn't see what Paul was doing, but she assumed he was waving at the fans piled against the security fence to their left. Their screams sounded both higher and louder than was humanly possible. Occasionally, they grew so sharp that she winced involuntarily.

At the doors, a guy in an expensively bland suit stepped forward and shook Paul's hand, ignoring Nicola completely.

"Thanks for coming, Paul," he said with an arched nuance that indicated that he hadn't expected to see him there.

"Sure, man, no problem," said Paul, taking his hand back and stepping around the guy in one fluid motion. As soon as the doors closed behind them, the noise from outside subsided.

"Well done," barked Gaynor, materializing next to them out of nowhere and startling Nicola. "Who wants popcorn?" she asked, before laughing outlandishly and saying, "Popcorn . . . ha ha ha, that's a good one. Let's go to our seats."

Paul stopped short. "How long do we have to stay, Gaynor?" he whispered. "And which exit do we take to get to the car?"

She pulled him close. "Ten minutes. Exit here, and I will walk you out the side door through the office. The car will be waiting on Orange. I'm going to stay for the screening; the driver will take you to dinner. He's yours for the night."

"Roger. Over. Thanks," whispered Paul.

※　※　※

"I insist on dessert," Paul said, taking Nicola's hand in his. She focused on not flinching, despite this being the twelfth time it had happened since they sat down.

"Okay, if you insist," she said.

He waved the waiter over with his free hand and instructed him to bring them the restaurant's "best dessert." The waiter gave Nicola a strange look and vanished to the kitchen.

"I want to thank you for a surprisingly good evening," Paul began. "I don't usually get to end my premieres like this."

"What do you normally do, then?"

Paul sat and considered the question for a while, like a kid who didn't know the answer to a pop quiz.

"I dunno. I guess I was just being nice."

They sat in silence. A photographer had ambushed them on the way into the restaurant, and Paul had seemed pleased about it but Nicola had been shaken. After they'd been taken to a private table in a back corner of the restaurant, Paul had begun his "insistence" on ordering for them both. It hadn't been cute then, and it was less so now.

However, he'd also been relentlessly charming, regaling her with behind-the-scenes stories from the TV show she had loved, and stories from his movie career. It wasn't until just after they finished their entrées that Nicola noticed that he hadn't asked anything about her.

As they waited in silence for their dessert, Paul excused himself to the bathroom. For the fourth time tonight. As soon as he was out of sight, Nic tore her phone out of her purse. She had texts from Billy and Kara but nothing from Gaynor.

Is he cute? Kara asked. She replied with a *Y* and the whatever emoji.

You keeping your pants on? From Billy. She gave him the same response. As she hit send, a text arrived from Gaynor.

I hear the date is going well. Paul would like you to go home with him. Is this OK y/n?

Nicola took a deep breath. She suddenly realized that Paul had been going to the bathroom to text Gaynor. She couldn't decide if that was better or worse than her original suspicion that he'd been doing coke, which she loathed. Since he hadn't been noticeably animated after his bathroom trips, she'd figured it wasn't coke. She thought for a second, and decided she owed it to her eighteen-year-old self to give him a chance. This was the first action that she'd even been offered since arriving in LA. She downed the rest of her pinot noir and texted back.

Y

Gaynor responded so quickly, she must have had her response typed already.

Good. The driver will wait and bring you home whenever you're ready. Text me when you leave.

Nicola spotted Paul weaving his way back toward her through the other tables full of diners, each one staring and whispering as he passed. When he got to their table, he pressed his hands together and smiled at her.

"Nicola, I want to thank you for today," he said earnestly.

He's an actor, her brain warned. "Don't be silly," she said. "It's been fun."

"It has." He beamed. "So, I don't want to sound too forward, but could I invite you back to my place for a drink? The view is really beautiful. It'll kill any thoughts you have about going back to Dayton. I need to make you fall in love with LA."

"Oh," Nicola said, pretending to be surprised, her eyes widening. Paul's composure slipped slightly, and she knew he was wondering if Gaynor had clued her in or not. "Yes," she said quietly, and his smile returned, with even higher wattage. "That would be very nice."

✳ ✳ ✳

Back at his small mid-century in the hills, Paul tipped the driver a $100 bill from his pants pocket and helped Nicola down the short but very steep driveway to his house, which hid behind a screen of bougainvillea. Once they were inside, he kicked off his shoes and told her that she was welcome to do the same. She gingerly removed the Louboutins from her feet, and when Paul adjourned to the kitchen to make their drinks, she quickly inspected the taped soles. So far so good.

Paul returned with two martini glasses and a shaker and nodded toward a door at the end of a short hallway.

"Could you unlock that, please?" he asked, looking down at his hands to show. "I don't have any spare hands."

Nicola stepped toward a white door with an opaque glass center and turned the lock. As she pushed the door open, she gasped aloud. Below them, all of Los Angeles spread out, a million points of orange, white, and red lights shrouded in tiny circles of mist. She could see cars driving on the boulevards, and the avenues extending off so far to the south that they vanished into a sparkly blur before they reached their end. She could see billboards and buildings, and was shocked to see the Griffith Park observatory perched up above her like a weird White House, presiding over a town of sparkling glitter.

"That did it, right?" laughed Paul, placing the glasses on a long, low table. He shook the martini shaker theatrically above his head, his sleeves rolled up, his muscles flexing. It was cheesy as hell, and Nicola hated herself for swooning a little.

"This is ridiculous," she said. "The view is stupid nuts."

Paul laughed.

"Did you just kick Dayton to the curb?" he smirked, pouring their martinis. She looked off ruefully. She wasn't about to admit that Dayton had kicked *her* to the curb. Her boyfriend's secret meth habit had sucked her dry and almost destroyed her family. Her mom and little brother were the only things that Dayton had to offer her anymore—and to her shame, they weren't enough.

Before she could answer, he clicked his fingers and darted back inside, returning with two spears of olives in one hand. He placed one in each drink and passed hers over. He scooped up his own drink and led her to the edge of the balcony.

"I never get tired of this," he began. "It doesn't matter if it's rainy, or smoggy, or just so damn hot all you can see is the heat rising, I can look at this view for hours."

"It is incredible," she said softly. She knew Paul was working her with a well-worn routine. He probably did this with every girl he brought home. And Nicola didn't give a shit.

This was not a gross place to be, and if she was going to have sex with anyone, a former teen idol who knew how to make a damn good martini was not exactly a misstep.

She accurately predicted that his hand would slide around her back and pull her to him about five seconds before he did it. His lips were wet and salty from the martini, and he tasted delicious.

Each kiss was generically more urgent, slowly increasing the intensity. Everything was by the numbers. She told herself to stop being such a bitch, and relaxed into him. He placed his drink on the ledge of the railing, and wrapped both arms around her. He was surprisingly strong, even if his arms were considerably smaller than those of the usual guys she'd hooked up with in Dayton. In line with the first-date script he was following, his hands quickly dropped to cup her butt. She almost chuckled, and tried to focus on kissing him back. She felt him pull back for a breath, and almost mouthed the words along with him.

"Wow," he said. "You're amazing; you're so beautiful."

She grabbed the front of his shirt and pulled him back into the kiss. He leaned against the railing, knocking his glass off the edge. It was obliterated against something hard, many feet below them. As they kissed, she opened her eyes and stared at LA spread out beneath them.

Paul broke the kiss after several minutes and took her hand, leading her inside. She had felt his erection against her, and had expected him to start something on the balcony. Paul saw the look of confusion on her face as they closed the door.

"Night-vision cameras, long-distance lenses," he explained. "I can't do anything out there. I can't smoke pot, I can't lie out in the nude, and I sure as hell can't have sex out there, unless I want to see it on the cover of the *Enquirer* next week."

"What if we just got photographed?"

"We got snapped earlier already," he said simply. "A kiss doesn't matter."

Paul opened the door to his bedroom and turned on the light, revealing a huge white room with a California king bed in the center, facing a floor-to-ceiling glass window. Framed street art adorned the walls, and some mounted animal bones sat atop a chestnut cabinet. The room, like Paul, was designer bland, like a minimalist expensive hotel. Paul drew the curtains and stepped toward her. *This is where he unzips my dress*, Nicola thought, turning around to help. But he left her hanging and she heard him undressing behind her.

Nicola reached around and couldn't quite get a grip on the zipper on her dress. "Could you help me with this, please?" she asked.

With a grunt, he dragged the zipper down roughly. Nicola's dress fell to the floor, and she fought an urge to ask for a hanger. Instead, she kicked it toward the wall. When she turned back, Paul was naked, sitting on the edge of the bed, stroking his erection and staring at her.

He reached over and dimmed the lights a tiny bit. He was so handsome it made the whole event surreal. Nicola played along, removing her bra with no hesitation and then stepping out of her thong, aiming to look as carefree as Paul, even if she was starting to feel like a hooker.

She walked slowly toward the bed, and Paul's hand gained momentum as it slid up and down his dick. She reached down and touched herself, and he moaned loudly. She stepped in between his open legs and stood over him, expecting to feel his touch at any second. Instead, he continued to lie back, putting one hand behind his head and using the other to point his dick at her.

"You know what would feel great?" he said huskily. "Your lips, on this, right now . . . please . . ."

Nicola knelt down, her knees jarring on the hardwood floor, and playfully flicked the end of it with her tongue. She started playing around, teasing him.

"No, all of it," he said coldly. "All of it."

Nicola pulled her head back to consider it, and thought, *Well, there's not too much of it.* She parted her lips and went down until she felt Paul's manicured pubes hit her nose. She pulled back a little and waited for him to move with her. Several seconds passed and Paul did not move, so she began to move her head up and down. Paul stayed completely motionless.

Nicola prided herself on her blow-job skills. Back home, she'd been able to get most of her boyfriends and one-night stands off within five minutes, and her last boyfriend, Tony, had called her La Reina de la Chupa before things went so horribly wrong. So when Paul still didn't move, she busted out all of her tricks. Nothing. After a while she wondered if he'd fallen asleep.

She paused, sliding her hand up his stomach. "What's wrong?" he asked dreamily.

"Nothing," she lied. "Do you like it like this?"

"Yes," he said curtly. "Don't stop."

Nicola began moving her whole head back and forth. She worked away for ten minutes, her knees starting to scream in pain from the cold floor. Muscles in her neck started to spasm as she determinedly soldiered on. Her eyes started watering. *Great, there goes my mascara,* she thought.

Out of nowhere, Paul's leg started to shudder. She doubled her efforts, and soon, she knew enough to get out of the way. She switched quickly to hand only, pointing him away from her. He thrashed around as his orgasm shook through him and he gave a series of short grunts.

"Stop, stop, I can't take anymore." He gently brushed her away and pulled up his legs.

Nicola relaxed back onto her haunches, the hard floor hurting her ankles. She put a hand on the floor to steady herself, and was horrified as a long, loud fart escaped from Paul's ass, a foot from her face. "Oh God," she exclaimed, springing to her feet, away from Paul and his ass.

"Oh, don't worry," he said, absently mopping at himself with his T-shirt. "It happens every time I come. But it never smells. It's just a thing," he said, avoiding eye contact.

"Yeah, yeah," mumbled Nicola, still horrified. "I . . . um . . . So, uh, every time, huh?"

"What?" Paul looked at her like he'd forgotten she was there. He rose to his feet and walked into his bathroom. He clicked on the light and looked at himself in the mirror. Nicola stood there, uncertain of whether she could handle flatulent fucking. Her teenage idol was gently lifting his genitals and making sure he'd wiped up all of his mess.

"That was great, thanks," he said without looking up. She was being dismissed. She was okay with that.

"Sure," Nicola said. "Hey, listen, I have an early start tomorrow, so I'm just gonna head out."

"Oh, okay," Paul said without missing a beat. Nicola dragged on her panties and bra. She shook out her dress and stepped into it, and failed twice to get it zipped up. She briefly considered asking Paul to help her, but decided she could make it home without sacrificing her dignity any further.

In the bathroom, Paul began peeing into the toilet, door still ajar.

"Thanks for a fun night," she said as emotionlessly as she could, turning and walking out.

"I'll call you," he yelled when she was halfway down the hallway.

She slid her feet into her shoes and stepped out into the chilly summer night. She normally loved the cooldown of an LA evening, but tonight the cold went right to her heart. The SUV was still parked out front, and a wave of shame swept over her as she walked toward it. Darell would know what she'd done. *Grow up*, she snapped at herself.

Darell got out and walked around to open her door.

"Good evening, Miss Wallace," he said with a smile and an understanding tilt of the head. "Time to go home at last?" They both knew that it had been nothing more than a long workday, for both of them.

"Yes, thank you, Darell. Home at last."

As the car began its steady descent through the precipitous streets, she texted Gaynor.

Heading home. All went well. See you tomorrow.

Gaynor texted back instantly.

Nico! Happy for you. Was Paul happy too?

Y she sent back.

Gaynor's next text startled Nicola: **So he farted then?**

Nicola burst out laughing. She sent Gaynor YYY

Within seconds she had a response.

Sleep in. I'll see you at noon. Also, *mi amor,* **keep the shoes. Both pairs.**

CHAPTER 8

THE PEDICURIST PUSHED TOO HARD with her little instrument of cuticle torture and Nicola flinched, waking up from a hazy half doze.

"Sorry, lady," the pedicurist snorted, anything but.

Blinking, Nicola looked up at the screen on the TV. Celine Dion
was still performing her Vegas show, but judging by her defiantly
dramatic arm gestures, the concert and the DVD it was on were
drawing to a merciful close.

Every time Nicola came in to get her nails done, this same concert was playing on the three TVs suspended at various angles
around the salon. They must watch this concert all day, every day,
she realized. The manicurists were in Dion's thrall, and would
occasionally glance up at the screen with open adoration on their
faces.

Last night she'd passed out almost as soon as her head hit the pillow, but Nicola's sleep had been one long stream of ridiculously
transparent dreams that any armchair Freud would have rated "too
easy." In one, her eight-year-old self went on a date with Mr. Hooper
from *Sesame Street*, and in another she and John Oliver had sex atop
a checkout at a Target, in front of a horrified clerk. As she dozed in
the salon massage chair, she revisited the weird moment.

It's probably a good idea if I stop hooking up with my TV crushes, she
thought, chuckling, as the pedicurist resumed the vigorous filing of
her toes. On the TV screen, Dion and her heart full of faux emotion

were taking the string of bows that signaled the end of her show. One of the manicurists reached for the remote to start the entire thing over.

"Hey, excuse me," Nicola called out, stopping her in mid button push.

"Yes, lady?" The manicurist paused, annoyed.

"Can we watch something else, please?" Nicola asked pleadingly. The manicurists all stopped work and stared at the blasphemer.

"What you wanna watch, lady?"

"I dunno, maybe just the TV?" Nicola continued, her voice getting softer as she lost her nerve. "It's just, I mean, that DVD is on every time I come in here. Aren't you guys, you know, sick of it?"

The women looked at Nicola as if she'd said the stupidest thing ever. However, the TV switched over to *Entertainment Tonight*. She learned that Courtney Hauser had gotten another DUI. Shocker. Or maybe it was a repeat.

She zoned out again. She had decided to send one of the pairs of Louboutins to her mom. They wore the same size, and her mother had never owned a pair of shoes that had cost more than fifty bucks. Nicola had already boxed up the champagne ones from two nights before. She'd ship them from the office later. Her mother worked as a manager at the local Motel 6, but the shoes would make her happy. A nail file jabbed into another cuticle and broke Nicola's reverie.

Five manicurists and her pedicurist were glancing from the TV to Nicola, shaking their heads.

Confused, she looked at the screen, where the rapid-fire staccato of vapid banter from the hosts was converted to badly spelled closed captioning, that wondered if yet another starlet had "gone too far" and whether "rehab was only answer." Nothing new.

Nicola slipped back into her thoughts, and this time it was Paul who took over. There was nothing significant about her first LA hookup, even though on paper she should have been dying to gossip about it—but she hadn't told anyone, not even Kara or Billy. It had been a kooky date, a wind tunnel of noise and chatter, and later, just a wind tunnel. Any gossip value had been deadened by a fart.

Actually, she thought, *I do want to tell this story to Billy and Kara, but it has to be in person.* She pulled out her phone and sent a group text to the two of them.

GOSSIP PARTY OUR HOUSE TONIGHT!!!!

Kara responded first.

GURL BRANG IT. I ALREADY GOT YOU BEAT.

Her phone dinged with Billy's response while she read Kara's text.

HONEY MAKE IT RAIN. SEE YOU AT 9.

Nicola smiled, thinking about finally getting his full Vegas story. Billy was oddly gifted with being in the wrong place at the right time, and it had supported him well since he landed in LA.

He'd once unveiled a shocking scandal that had made him nearly twenty thousand dollars. He'd walked into a bedroom at a party, interrupting one of the world's most beloved leading men squeezed into the clothing of his supermodel wife. The guy's leading-man days ended four days later, in an *Enquirer* cover that announced in this relationship, the wife wore the pants—and he wore the dresses.

Lately, however, he'd been getting too close and having to navigate the fine art of screwing over celebrities without getting caught. He'd almost been caught in several publicist-set traps, but the near misses had taught him well.

Nicola had started to text her friends back when the pedicurist jerked her big toe sideways, splashing her foot down into the warm water.

"Lady," she exclaimed. "LADY!"

"Ouch," snapped Nicola, yanking her foot out of the warm water. "That hurt. What the hell . . . ?"

"Lady," the woman repeated, jabbing her nail file toward the TV. "Lady, you on TV. Don't pretend you don't see it this time."

Nicola looked up at the TV and gasped. A title card across the entire screen read, "Who is Paul Stroud's mystery woman?" above a split screen that showed two photos of Paul with his arms around Nicola from last night—one on the red carpet, and one outside the Little Door. Her heart sank as every woman in the salon turned to look at her. She swallowed hard.

"Hey, do you guys want to put Celine Dion back on?"

✳ ✳ ✳

She could already hear Gaynor bellowing in Spanish before she opened the office door, though she couldn't tell if it was at a person or a phone. She made a mental note to buy a set of Berlitz Spanish CDs for her car and pushed the door open.

Gaynor was on her phone, in the lobby, dressed in a plunging ivory dress with roses creeping up from the hem and bloodred heels. Her face was aglow with fury. She turned to Nicola, and smiled. She took two steps toward her and planted a small peck in the air beside Nicola's cheek, then covered the mouthpiece of her phone and hissed, "My *puta* nanny wants a fucking day off," as if it were the most horrifying news she'd ever received.

Nicola whistled to indicate that she agreed with the gravity of the situation. She went over to her desk. The red light on her phone was blinking, and the screen told her she had 148 voice messages to clear. Usually she didn't get that many calls all day. Taking a morning off was not a good thing. She grabbed her pen and notepad, sat down, and prepared to start wading through them.

She felt Gaynor's hands grip her shoulders from behind.

"Good afternoon, mystery girl," Gaynor purred.

"Oh God, what now?"

"Nico, you're the talk of the town," Gaynor crowed. "I'm so proud of you! You did it like a pro. Nobody knows who you are, but now everybody wants to know."

"Oh yeah, I just saw *Entertainment Tonight*." Nicola winced.

"Fuck *Entertainment Tonight*—you are everywhere, you are in the

Reporter, you are in *Billboard*, you are on every tabloid's website. The designer called already; the dress is yours to keep and they want to sign you to wear them for the rest of the season. Paul's agents are trying to set you two up on another date, maybe tonight. . . ."

"I'm busy tonight, Gaynor."

"*Ay ya, mija,* no, tonight is too soon, I agree."

"I don't want to see him again, Gaynor."

"So sensitive. I'll buy you a gas mask!"

Both of them burst into laughter. The four other girls all looked up from their computers, jealous and confused.

"Delete all your messages," Gaynor said, hoisting herself onto the edge of Nicola's desk. She began to outline her vision for Nicola's involvement in the promotion for Paul's movie. She envisioned several more dates, with the paparazzi tipped off to each one at the last minute, right through opening weekend. A steady mystery girlfriend would help keep Paul's profile afloat for the two weeks that the movie would be in theaters.

"I'm not sleeping with him, Gaynor."

"Yes, of course, Nico. You are a smart one. You should see the women who go back for seconds. You're here for the rest of the day, no?"

"Sure, where else would I be?" said Nicola, shrugging. Gaynor smiled mysteriously.

"*Bueno, bueno,*" she muttered, tottering toward her office.

Nicola deleted all the messages in three keystrokes, feeling slightly bad about it, then forwarded her phone to the new intern with instructions to only transfer calls from Gaynor or Billy. The intern, a ravishing teenage Colombian girl named Ingrid, could not mask her contempt.

"Why should I?" she pouted.

"Because Gaynor said so."

"What will you give me if I do?"

"The option to come back tomorrow."

Half an hour later, Ingrid appeared again.

"There's a woman on the phone and she won't take no for an answer. She says I have to put her through to you or she's gonna stick a jalapeño up my twat."

Oh God, it's Crystal.

Nicola took a deep breath.

"Put her through."

"Well, hello, Miss Popularity," sneered Crystal as soon as Nicola picked up her phone. "I'm sure you're having a great day."

"Okay, well, if that's what this call is about, I really have to get on with said day."

"Hold on, honey, don't be so snippy, I need to get your cell number."

"Oh, *do* you?"

"Despite the fact that you're already all over the tabloids with that ghastly TV actor, I need your cell for another gentleman."

"You have my work number," retorted Nicola.

"You do not want to fuck with me," seethed Crystal.

"You're right, I don't." Nicola was angry now. "Is there anything else?"

"Okay, listen." Crystal softened. "One of my clients wants your number; he says he met you at some stupid whore's party. That's bad enough! Then I see you plastered all over town with a . . . *TV actor.* I see the game you're playing, girly, but you have to pick between A-list and the dead zone. Just a bit of friendly advice: If you want to get your claws into a leading man, don't fuck with anyone who's ever made it into syndication, and for fuck's sake, don't even wink at a reality star."

"You should teach at the Learning Annex," snarked Nicola. "Not that it's any of your business, but Seamus approached me, and Paul was a work assignment."

"Hmmmm. You're tough. I like that, even if you do work for that burro fucker." Crystal sounded defeated. "Now listen: give me your number, I'll give it to Seamus, and you can take it from there. But honey, for the love of all that's holy, if you date Seamus, steer clear of anyone who ever got a People's Choice Award, just for the duration."

"Got it, guru," said Nicola, before reciting her cell number. And she gave her the real one, because it didn't pay to screw over Crystal Connors.

✳ ✳ ✳

A short while later, the door burst open and Gaynor waltzed back in, accompanied by her twelve-year-old twins, Sylvester and Patrick, two deceptively adorable boys with jet-black hair and mischievous eyes. They did not look like Gaynor, and the identity of their father was a well-kept secret. Nicola groaned. Last time they'd visited the office they'd started a fire in a trash can.

"What the fuck are we doing here, Mom?" demanded Sylvester.

"Sylbesterrr!" howled Gaynor. "I told you already, you're gonna stay here with Nicola this afternoon."

"What?" snapped Nicola, her head whipping around.

"Don't worry, Nico," laughed Gaynor. "The boys won't make a sound; they just drove yet another nanny away, so they have to be punished. By sitting here in silence . . ." She paused, glaring from one boy to the other. "In absolute silence, you hear me?"

Both boys nodded, and stared at their feet.

"Where are you going?" Nicola demanded. "And why me? Why can't Ingrid handle them?"

Ingrid shot her a death glare. Gaynor looked Ingrid up and down, and shook her head.

"I have to go to the nanny agency and get a new woman for them to torture, and then I have to go and see some clients."

"You don't *have* any appointments," whined Nicola. "And I'm not sure I'm up to nannying today."

"*Dios mío*, I stopped and bought them new iPads on the way here, so they'll be busy."

She reached into her Vuitton and pulled out two boxed iPads, handing one to each boy. They took them without a word and retreated to the office couch, tearing into the packaging and leaving the boxes and papers strewn on the floor. In unison, they plugged their iPads into the wall and began setting them up like miniature IT techs.

"See?" chided Gaynor. "You won't even know my little treasures are here. What time do you need to leave tonight?"

Nicola hesitated. Gaynor was reliably an hour late for everything, and she didn't want to fall into that trap again.

"Seven," she replied.

"Then seven it is, *mija*. I will see you then, if not earlier. They both have their Amexes if they get hungry or if they need anything. They must not buy jewelry, bicycles, or anything over one thousand dollars." Both boys looked at each other, then at Nicola, then smiled. "But apart from that, all of you have fun, and I'll be back by seven."

✳ ✳ ✳

An hour later, Sylvester appeared at Nicola's desk. Even at twelve, the boys had distinct and completely opposite styles. Sylvester shared his mother's taste for fashion, flair, and drama, while Patrick preferred to act and dress like a Beverly Hills frat boy. Both of them were going to be nightmares in five years.

"Can I call you Nicola?" Sylvester asked.

"Sure, I guess." She nodded.

"Okay, Nicola. I'm hungry, and I'd like us all to go get some lunch."

"Okay," she said. "What do you boys like?"

"Well, it's tricky," began Sylvester. "Patrick likes the Polo Lounge but I like sushi."

Nicola had been thinking more along the lines of a cupcake or In-N-Out.

"Yes?" She smiled.

"Well, because *I* asked, that means I get to pick, and I pick sushi."

"All right, then," laughed Nicola. "Let me figure out where to go."

"Oh, I just booked it in Mom's name. We have a table at Kazu in twenty minutes, and Kazu will prepare the secret menu for us. We have a private room so that those fucking PETA assholes don't get their panties in a bunch over the whole live lobster thing."

Nicola was speechless. It was as if Gaynor was suddenly speaking out of this twelve-year-old's mouth.

"Fuck you, Sylvester, you're such a jerkwad," spat Patrick.

Sylvester ignored his brother. He turned to Nicola.

"You're going to need dark glasses and a hat. I don't want to get papped next to you today."

Patrick sulked all through lunch, while Sylvester spoke fluent Japanese to Kazu himself as he sliced meat off the back of a very alive lobster. Nicola had had to glance away each time he did it, catching Patrick's eye at one point. He shook his head and mouthed, "Can we go, please?" Shortly thereafter Nicola announced that they had to get back to the office, and Sylvester paid for lunch with his black Amex.

※ ※ ※

The seven p.m. deadline came and went, the boys locked in a war to see who could buy the most apps in the shortest time. Nicola texted Billy and Kara and warned them that she would either be late, or be bringing some kids home with her, which elicited streams of texted profanity from both friends.

At 7:45, she got a text from Gaynor saying she'd be there within fifteen minutes. "Fucking typical," Nicola whispered to herself. "Your mom's on her way," she said, louder.

Sylvester ignored her, deep inside some video game. Patrick stared Nicola right in the face and said, "Hey, can I hang out with you tonight?"

"Uh, no, Patrick, I have plans. Maybe next time."

Patrick's face fell. Nicola started walking around the office, switching off lights and prepping to leave. She heard the door open and turned to see Gaynor swan into the room in an electric-blue metallic floor-length coat that was unbuttoned enough to reveal thigh-high matching boots and a lot of thigh. She really did have great legs.

"My darlings," she deadpanned. "All three of my darlings. Mama is back."

All three of her darlings ignored her.

Gaynor coughed loudly, looking from the twins to Nicola and back again.

"Oh, hi," Nicola said, continuing to turn off the lights around the office. "So glad you didn't have time for a complete makeover while you were so busy interviewing nannies."

"Fuck nannies," Gaynor groaned. "Fuck them and their *estúpidas* agencies. They can blacklist me all they want. For the amount I pay them, they should be able to cope with two innocent angels. But I will show them. I will pay Ingrid to nanny them. She sucks at answering phones."

"So that makes her a good nanny?"

"No, it makes me not give a fuck and she can quit after two weeks. By then the agency will miss the money."

Sylvester set his iPad down and made eye contact with his brother, grinning slyly. They did a slow-motion fist bump, and Nicola almost felt sorry for Ingrid.

"Hey, Mom," Patrick said. "I ordered a pugwawa from a breeder in Idaho today."

"That's hilarious, *mi vida*." Gaynor bent and pinched his cheek. "You know that dogs are disgusting and are for commoners."

Patrick dropped his gaze. Sylvester stepped in.

"I've been e-mailing with designers, Mama," he crowed. "I think I can have a line of high fashion for tween boys ready for the fall collections."

"That's more like it," Gaynor cooed. She turned and faced Nicola. "So, I see that you have the gift? They behave for you?"

"I suppose," Nicola began.

"I asked if I could take her to dinner tonight, and she said no," Patrick yelled.

"She's too old for you, *mijo*," Gaynor whispered, still rubbing his cheek.

"Well, that's it for me, then," Nicola sniffed, returning to her desk. "You're so welcome. It was a pleasure to babysit for you, Mrs. Huerta. Now I need to get home and do my science homework."

Gaynor kissed the tip of her middle finger and then flipped Nicola the bird.

Nicola shut down her computer and pulled her car keys out of her purse. Her phone rang, the vibration startling her. She didn't recognize the 310 number on the screen, but something told her to answer it.

"Hello?" she said.

"Nicola," said a familiar brogue. "Hi, it's me, Seamus."

CHAPTER 9

THE TV IN THE APARTMENT next door was blasting a muffled Russian news-cast through the wall as Kara let Billy in the door.

"Holy shit," he whistled, planting a kiss on Kara's cheek. "I thought you talked to the KGB about keeping it down." He walked to the table and set a cake box down.

"It's worse in Nicola's room," sighed Kara. "They just put a second TV in their bedroom and it's so loud."

"Fuck that," said Billy with a laugh. He strode over to the common wall that the TV was blasting through and pounded his fist. He waited a second, and the sound did not decrease. He banged again.

"Billy, they're old, don't . . . ," said Kara.

Billy shot her a mischievous grin and went onto the tiny patio and called out to the neighbors. Kara heard the neighbors' door open, then the gruff voice of an old woman grunting something at Billy.

"Nice to see you too, Irinka," Billy cooed. "Listen, we're trying to have dinner and all we can hear is your TV, so unless you want us to play music even louder than your TV, please turn your shit down, could you? *Spasibo!*"

As Billy came back inside, his victorious smile crumbled as Irinka snarled, "*Gryazny gomoseksualist Amerikanyets.*" He paused a beat, about to turn back, when the TV volume dropped. He smiled.

"Thanks, Pussy Riot."

"Where's Nicola?" he asked, peering into her darkened bedroom.

"She's running late, but she's on her way," said Kara, heading to the kitchen and picking up a lime.

"What did Gaynor do now?"

"The usual, I guess," Kara replied absently, slicing the lime and making the two of them very strong drinks with vodka and a splash of soda. "Nicola's pissed."

"Weird," said Billy, taking his drink. "I saw Gaynor today, at the Montage. She came in through a service door and snuck into the kitchen."

"Did she see you?"

"I don't think so."

"Wait—what were YOU doing at the Montage?"

"I'd love to tell you," smiled Billy, "but aren't we saving our stories for a gossip beatdown later?"

"You're such a fuckin' tease," laughed Kara, clinking her glass against his and heading toward the couch.

"I put out," sniffed Billy. "If I tease, I please."

Kara rolled her eyes just as they heard Nicola's key slide into the lock.

A flurry of dry-cleaning bags, shopping bags, and a purse preceded Nicola into the apartment. She stumbled over to the couch that Kara and Billy were sitting on and dumped her armloads onto them.

"Fuck this shit," she barked.

"Hey, hey, crankypants," laughed Billy, pushing the crap onto the floor. "What gives?"

Before Nicola could make a sound, Billy and Kara chimed in.

"Fucking Gaynor!" they both yelled.

Nicola closed her eyes and nodded, taking a deep breath.

By the time she'd opened her eyes, Kara had rushed into the kitchen, and in ten seconds she was returning with a drink.

"Is there any soda in this?" Nicola rasped, eyeing her drink suspiciously after one sip.

"There's water," Kara responded.

"Wait—are we out of soda?"

"No, I mean there'll be water in it if you let the ice melt," Kara laughed.

"No chance of that, then," said Nicola, shooting the vodka and lime in one brisk move. "Thank you, m'dear. I needed that."

Billy started puttering about in the kitchen.

"What the hell are you doing? Making dinner?" she asked.

"Dinner after six is a Dayton thing," he hollered. "How many times do I have to tell you this?"

Nicola's brow furrowed when Billy emerged from the kitchen carrying a cake with one candle burning brightly on top.

"What the actual fuck is going on?" Kara looked from Nicola to Billy and back again.

"Happy LA anniversary, Cola!" Billy beamed, holding the cake in front of Nicola's face. She closed her eyes, made a wish, and blew out the candle.

She remembered her first day in LA, crying on Billy's couch. The end of her time in Dayton had been a nightmarish blur. She had discovered that her boyfriend, Antony, had been dealing meth, and worse, that he had gotten her little brother, Robert, hooked. All it had taken was one distraught phone call to Billy, who had flown home immediately, reported Tony to the cops, and gotten Robert into a community rehab. As they sat in silence with her mom at the kitchen table on that steamy July night, watching fireflies blinking through the window screen, Billy had declared that she would be returning to Los Angeles with him. She'd looked at her mom in panic, but clearly she'd already been told, and given her blessing.

"I'm gonna miss you, peanut," she'd said. "But he's right. It's time."

She shook her head to make sure she didn't cry at the memory. She stuck a finger in the cake frosting and scooped a bit into her mouth.

"The best Ralphs has to offer," Billy said with a bow.

"Are we gonna get this party started or what?" Kara asked, thrusting the Settlers of Catan box onto the coffee table.

"Settlers of Catan?" whined Billy. "We can't successfully gossip and play that. It's too complicated."

"We've done it before," huffed Kara, removing the lid and dealing out the cards. "And you just cheat at Simpsons Monopoly."

"So, while mistress is setting up that game, how do we figure out who's going to go first?" wheedled Billy. "I have so many questions already, and you know, I just bedded a closeted superstar and helped him through an overdose, and we haven't talked since."

"Billy's going first, apparently," sighed Kara, rolling her eyes as she carefully arranged playing pieces on the coffee table.

"Okay," said Nicola conspiratorially, moving to the edge of the couch and leaning in. "And I have a great idea. The winner is the person whose news actually derails the game. All in?"

"All in," Kara and Billy chorused.

While Kara dealt the cards, Billy cut the cake and placed a slice next to each stack. As Nicola made her first play, Billy stood and began his story.

"I was minding my own business down on Santa Monica last week," he began. "And I went into that weird card shop, and I saw this guy who kinda looked like Ethan Carpenter, if the world's cutest muscles-and-dimples action star had been on a crack bender and sleeping in a ditch for a week. We made eye contact and I was thinking, damn, if this homeless dude could just clean up his act, he could probably get a show on the CW or at least TNT.

"Sooooo, it was clear that he was cruising me, but a) I'd already hooked up that day and b) come on, even I have standards. And then he said hi. I said hi back, and moved along, keeping my eyes on the greeting cards. And then it got annoying. Wherever I stood, he was right beside me. I walked out of the card shop and went along to that movie memorabilia store and he followed me right in. Then his phone rang, and he looked at it before answering and I saw that it was Crystal Connors calling, and I was like, holy shit, it IS Ethan Carpenter, but damn, he's been living rough.

"He talked to her for about ten seconds. I couldn't tell what they were talking about; he kept his other hand over his mouth while he talked. When he hung up, he looked at me and said, 'So do you wanna get out of here or not?' I said sure and the next thing you know, I'm in a fucking Cayenne with the darkest windows in the world, speeding to an apartment building in Westwood. Underground parking, private elevator, the whole deal."

"I love how you moved from homeless-phobia to 'hey, let's fuck' in less than thirty seconds," Nicola laughed. Billy ignored her.

"I still don't know if it was actually his place or not. We got inside and he took me into this room; it was weird, it's like in the middle of the condo, no windows. Not sure what it's supposed to be in the real world. But he had it set up as a bedroom, and he wanted to get right down to business.

"He was jibber-jabbering the whole time and I knew he was high, but I just couldn't do anything with him looking like he belonged at a freeway off-ramp, so I convinced him to have a shower, and girls, it was amazing; as soon as the dirt washed off, his star started to sparkle. By the time we got out of the shower, he looked exactly like his movie poster.

"He told me his name was Joe. I said, don't be that guy, I know who you are. He was shocked. He didn't understand why I was so evasive at the card store if I knew who he was. His attitude was kind of shitty all along but I figured, here I am, why not help myself to the biggest movie hunk in the world? So we messed around for the rest of the day and night, and even though I never saw him do drugs, I could tell that he was always a bit peppier after a visit to the bathroom. He never offered me anything, but I could tell. And everyone knows it's rule number one with celebrities—never let anyone see you do drugs. But, you know, he could have offered. . . ."

"Don't even joke about that shit, Billy," Nicola said tersely. "And it's your turn!"

Billy quickly played his cards, picked up his extras, and continued right where he left off.

"That very next morning, I was trying to get some sleep, my phone was blowing up, and I was starting to make my exit strategy when he comes bounding into the room with a package from Fred Segal. He hands it to me and, ladies, it's all this clothing that he had delivered for me. It was insane. This shit was nice, and the price tags were still on. He told me to go shower and change, and he'd have the jet ready in two hours so that we could go to Vegas."

"Wait," exclaimed Kara, "did he ask you to go to Vegas with him?"

"Nope," laughed Billy. "He hadn't mentioned it before. But it was so ridiculous, I just decided to play along. I got ready and put on these absolutely gorgeous clothes and we went to the parking garage and got into another dark limo and sped off to Van Nuys Airport. We landed at some private airport in Vegas, I have no clue where, and he took us to a gated community and we set up in this huge, kind of empty mansion. He wanted to blow me and cuddle all the time. He wasn't particularly good at either. . . ."

"Good to know," laughed Nicola.

"Anyways, that's what we did, though it became more and more about the cuddling and less about the sex stuff. He started talking about how hard his life was and how his advisors were telling him to be straight for a couple years and how he hated them and he hated pretty much everything. It went from being *Lifestyles of the Rich and Famous* to a very special episode of *20/20* really quickly."

"So of course you got bored," said Kara. "And it's your turn again."

Billy played his hand so quickly that both Nicola and Kara locked eyes and laughed.

"Yes, it was boring, and also, I was in Las Vegas, so I started asking when we were going home. Wrong question! He started to cry, because apparently he wanted us to hide out for a week or so. I told him I needed to get back to LA, to get back to work. He offered me money, and you know what, I just couldn't take it. I can joke about being a hooker, but when faced with the reality, I just couldn't do it."

"And that drove him back to drugs?" asked Nicola.

"Yeah, he seemed to have been sober the whole time we were there, but after I said I wanted to come home, he vanished for a while into the bathroom and he came back out and he was fuckin' wired, he was bouncing off the walls and he wanted to fuck, he wanted to talk, he wanted to do everything all at once."

"Meth!" said the girls at once.

"Jinx!" Kara said rapidly.

"Fuck your jinx," laughed Nicola. "I'll make you a drink, though."

"Deal," said Kara, playing her hand.

"Yes, meth," said Billy, rolling his eyes. "I knew I was fucked at that point, so I started trying to look at flights and rental cars on my phone. He saw what I was doing and hit the roof. It was decidedly unpretty. I was a prisoner. The place was totally locked inside and out. I tried to talk to him and he was crying and yelling and he went back into the bathroom, and that was it. I guess he tried to calm down by taking downers, but he took too many so he did a bit more meth, and boom, unconscious superstar on bathroom floor."

Billy paused to see if that had derailed the game.

"Fuuuuuuuuck," said Kara, setting a tray of drinks down. "And it's your turn again."

"Really?" said Billy. "This story isn't good enough to derail the game?"

"We've kind of heard it already, dear," said Nicola. "Not that it's not exciting, but we already know the ending."

"Well, that's where we are now. I grabbed his phone, and used his finger to unlock it, and I called that bitch Crystal. She hardly batted her lizard eyes. She was so matter-of-fact that it was clear this is pretty much a weekly occurrence, but she was not happy that we were in Las Vegas. She has a team here in LA but nothing in Vegas. She had me throw cold water on him and sit on top of him and force-feed him pills from a bottle in the cabinet. Benzos, I guess. Anyways, by the time I got that happening, there was a knock at the door and these two HUGE guys barged past me with a stretcher; they got him up and strapped and wheeled out in fucking seconds. I didn't know what I was supposed to do, but one of the goons fucking grabbed me by the shirt and dragged me into the van with them. Then you know the rest. Locked in a private corridor of a hospital while the world's press waits outside. They brought in some slutty girl to pretend she was with him—I overheard that her payment will be a pilot for AMC—and I waited for Crystal. She got so insane on the phone that I actually escaped just before she arrived. I booked into a fucking suite at the Wynn and got as drunk as I could and the next day I rented a car and drove my hangover home."

"That's awesome," laughed Nicola, "and it's your turn again."

"Wait—neither of you have any questions?"

The girls pretended to be surveying the vintage popcorn-textured ceiling for a few seconds before they both shook their heads.

"My turn," announced Kara. "I'm engaged!"

"Nice try," said Billy, playing his hand. "Game's still going."

"But I am," protested Kara, pulling an enormous diamond ring out of her pocket.

"What the actual fuck?" bellowed Nicola, grabbing the heavy ring from Kara's fingers.

"Jimmy J wants to marry me!"

"But you haven't even met!" sputtered Nicola.

"Yeah, we have. He came over here last night, and he only just left to avoid awkward situations with you two. He left about twenty minutes before you got here, Billy."

"Okay," laughed Nicola. "So he was here when I got home last night? Whoa. Back it up."

"Hey, whose turn is it?" said Billy with false seriousness. "I was at the center of a drug scandal, and nobody halted. Damned if I'm going to lose to the latest post-Kardashian assault on the sanctity of marriage."

"It's mine," said Kara, pausing and dramatically playing her hand.

"So, after we met at Pavilions, we did the whole sexy Skyping thing for a few nights and he was just going crazy, just so blue-balled to get at me. I figured it would be funny, so I let him come over last night. And it was about the funniest thing ever."

"Hang on," said Nicola, playing her cards. "Okay, go!"

"There's actually not too much to it. We fucked. A lot. He's way better at fucking than he is at rapping."

"It would be impossible to be worse," said Billy, moving his game piece. "I had such a crush on him when he was a boy-bander. I can't stand him as a TV host, though."

"Way too smarmy," sniffed Nicola.

"I wanted to come into your room in the middle of the night and tell you but damn, he's a light sleeper," said Kara. "He had me doing nude Pilates for like an hour while he walked around, touching his junk and whispering this kind of sexy stuff. At first I thought I'd burst out laughing, but he was so into it, it was contagious. So finally we got down to business and it was all that and that was kind of nice. So then we were done, the first time, and I expected him to jet; you won't believe this, but he's a cuddler!"

"Shut UP," yelled Billy. "The bad boy of the 213 Crew is a softie? What about all the 'caps he's busted in the popo' and how he's 'never shed a tear'?"

"You know his songs better than I do," smiled Kara. "So, the thing is, he's as controlling when it comes to cuddling as he is with his online sex sessions. He had us cuddle facing each other, and he was talking into my face the whole time, about our connection and about how comfortable and safe I made him feel. After about ten minutes, he wanted to spoon. I turned around but no . . . mother-fucker needs to be the little spoon. . . ."

Nicola guffawed loudly. Billy nearly spilled his drink, and suddenly remembered to play his hand.

"Shit, I thought I had it." Kara rolled her eyes. "Anyway, I spooned him for a long time, and he was talking about how he's an insomniac and how he never feels as relaxed as he was feeling right now, so we did that for a while and he fell asleep in my arms. It was total coyote. My arm fell asleep. So I lay there listening to him snore like a baby, bored out of my skull and wishing I could roll over. Eventually he woke up and he turned to face me and yep, there were tears in his eyes."

"If he wanted to talk feelings, I'm going to puke," said Nicola, playing her hand.

"Grab a bucket, then," continued Kara. "He said that he'd never been able to fall asleep with anyone else ever, and that he and I had a connection that was older than us, deeper than us. That same old celebrity blah blah that you see on TV all the time. I was like, this is fascinating, can you get off my fucking arm? Long story short, after about an hour of him talking and me pretending to listen, he said I was the one that he'd been looking for his whole life. . . ."

"And he fucking proposed?" whistled Billy.

"Kinda sorta. He presented it almost like a business arrangement. He said that he was about to break ground on a four-million-dollar house in Bel Air. He wants us to make the beautiful children that will play in the yard, which is when I should have kicked him out. He said we'd be the most beautiful couple on any red carpet. He started telling me how rich I'd be; I'd have everything I've ever wanted. I was so tired by this point, I actually started to get confused. It was just surreal. And then he dropped the bomb: Would I marry him? I was the one he wanted to make babies with, I was the one who would hold him while he slept every night, he would treat me like a queen and we'd be hip-hop royalty. I was so fucking tongue-tied, I was completely in shock. I just met the guy! Then he added the kicker—as much as he values marriage and the church, he can never be monogamous, and that would be a condition of our marriage. I was like, get the fuck out of here!"

Nicola was shaking her head as she played her hand.

"But you said yes? You have the ring, so you must have."

"Not exactly. He told me to sleep on it. And then he never let me sleep. He kept wanting to have sex. If I fell asleep, I'd wake up with him going down on me. He just never left. Then today a messenger came here with a package for him, and it was the ring. He tossed it to me like it was a bag of peanuts. He told me to wear it while I considered the offer. I practically had to push Jimmy out the door with a broom. He wanted to meet my friends!"

"Am I a bridesmaid?" asked Nicola.

"Am I?" smiled Billy.

Kara raised one eyebrow and played her turn in Settlers of Catan. "That would require me to say yes first."

"Can I sell this story?" asked Billy.

"No," said Kara sternly. "I've seen this shit bite you in the ass too many times to get involved in your stupid shenanigans."

"It could make you some loot," wheedled Billy.

"Like how much?"

"Five thousand? Ten if you went on record."

"I don't know. . . ."

"Listen," interjected Nicola. "As a future publicist, I think this is a bad idea."

"But what if it helped bring me more business?"

"Being viewed as some whore selling out a rapper won't help you ascend as a celebrity stylist, believe me," said Nicola. "And it's your turn."

"You have a point," smiled Kara. "And fuck me, I thought I'd stopped the game."

"Close, but no cigar," said Billy from the kitchen, where he was making more drinks.

When he returned, Nicola stood up.

"Anyways, it's my turn to win," she announced. "I banged my first star last night!"

"Like actual banged?" Kara held her drink up.

"Well, I would've . . . ," Nicola whined.

"Who was it?" asked Kara, disappointed.

"Paul Stroud," sighed Nicola. "You really did spend the day in bed, didn't you?"

"Oh dear, that don't sound good," laughed Kara.

"Yeah, we got photographed together, so all of today, I've been 'the mystery girl'—I'm hoping that there's a fresh celebrity scandal tonight so that my phone stops ringing tomorrow."

"So, you guys got naked?" asked Billy.

"Yeah, but come on, let me tell my story."

"Babycakes, I saw your story on TV all day. And online. And every single one of my friends who's met you called me to get the dish."

"Dish about what?" asked Nicola, perplexed.

"Der," laughed Billy, shoving Nicola back against the couch. "About whether he really farts when he comes."

"What?" yelled Kara. "That's stupid and gross."

Nicola looked down at the coffee table and played her hand. She didn't say a word.

"Oh. My. Gawd!" screeched Billy. "Oh mah fookin' gawd. He farted. Tell me he farted."

"Yes, that's exactly how my night ended," sighed Nicola. "I can't believe it's a thing."

"It's an urban legend that's on its way to being the new gerbil in the ass," said Billy. "But you confirming it is HUGE. It's the same as capturing Bigfoot. I can't wait to tell—"

"Nobody," barked Nicola. "That's who you can tell. Nobody. You know the rules of this. If it's between us, I can say it's off-limits, and this is definitely off-limits. Gaynor would have a shit fit *and* a meltdown. You'll just have to bask in your own private knowledge that our teenage TV crush is a come-farter. And for the record, it was both shocking and gross."

"So you're not seeing each other again, then," laughed Billy.

"Gaynor *wants* me to see him again," groaned Nicola. "But I don't think I physically can. He's a jerk. As soon as he'd blown from both sides, he kicked me out. It was just cold. He expected a blow job as part of the service, and I mean, fuck, he never even played with my tits. He just lay back and took it."

"He's a starfish, too?" whistled Kara. "Dayum. He's got it all going for him. He's lucky that nostalgia is the best pussy-wetter around or he'd never get any action."

Nicola hugged Kara. "I love you, foul-mouthed bitch," she whispered.

"Hey, lezzers, if someone doesn't play their hand, it means we're handing the game to Nicola and her ass-blast from the past."

Kara disengaged herself from Nicola and took her turn. "You're having a shitty week, my dear," she said as she moved her piece. "First you botch things with Seamus O'Riordan and then your childhood crush farts in your face. Well, look at it this way: the rest of your week has to get better, right?"

"Oh, that reminds me," said Nicola dramatically. "I have a date with Seamus on Saturday."

Kara and Billy tossed their cards down on the table.

"YOU WIN!" they both yelled.

CHAPTER 10

AN AMBLING CROWD OF SELF-ABSORBED jaywalkers risked death as Gaynor guided her Mercedes carefully along the congestion of Robertson Boulevard, the midday sun blinding her. When her phone rang, the dash display told her it was Billy. She hit the talk button on her steering wheel, and Billy's voice replaced the constant beat of seventies disco that was the soundtrack to her life.

"Morning, publicist," he chirped.

"Morning, charity case." She half-smiled.

"Oooh, someone's cranky."

"No, *pendejo*, I'm not cranky, I want to commit a murder. I'm trying to drive down Robertson and these fucking heiress *coños* are wandering the streets like the fucking cows of India. I want to hear their tiny bones break under my wheels."

"And you haven't even met with Crystal yet, right?"

"*Sí*, and if I'm late, I'll never hear the end of it. *Abuela* likes to pretend-eat early, so I have to get there fast."

"Okay—I just wanted to check that you don't want me to be there."

"Didn't Nicola tell you I never change my mind? Billy, this is one for the big guns. You didn't do anything wrong, and Crystal wants to destroy you. I will not only save your life, but I will help your stupid career. And in the process I will school that *vieja basura* in a few things. If you came, you'd just get covered in blood spatter. I will call you after this, okay?"

Gaynor pulled her vintage Mercedes into the valet line outside The Ivy. The festering sea of agents, managers, and publicists was Crystal's favorite place on earth.

The valet opened her door. Gaynor smiled when she saw that he was a spectacularly handsome young Mexican guy, with the full lips she had never been able to resist. His dark beard accentuated his bright chocolate eyes. She was wearing the neon-blue metallic vintage Courrèges ensemble she had road-tested yesterday on Nicola. He winked at her as he took her keys. She showed him some thigh.

"*Gracias, guapito*," she purred.

"*De nada, bella*," he smiled back.

Gaynor paused for a moment, staring him down. He stared back and bit his pillowy bottom lip with his teeth. He handed her the valet stub.

"Make sure *you* bring me my car when I leave," she said, only breaking eye contact when the car behind them began honking its horn madly. Gaynor was not startled to see Crystal's plastic-surgery-disaster face at the wheel of her hulking black Bentley.

"Enjoy your lunch, beautiful," the valet said, sliding into her driver seat and pulling away from the curb.

"Gaynor!" brayed Crystal from her car window. "Please stop eye-fucking the help so I can park this beast."

Gaynor flipped her a perfectly manicured bird, pulled the neon-blue fur of her collar tighter around her neck, and walked slowly and defiantly to the sidewalk, where she waited patiently. As the valet opened Crystal's door, she smoothly stepped from the car and began walking away, leaving the valet waving her receipt behind her.

Crystal was known for her stark fashion, and today was no exception. She loped along the sidewalk in her trademark black tailored man's suit and low patent heels. Her hair was pulled back severely into a single ponytail that hung down like a short, motionless stick. Her only jewelry was a blinding single diamond at her lapel.

It wasn't like this when we met, mused Gaynor, watching her approach.

Thirty-five years ago, they'd been two junior agency publicists meeting on the dance floor at a Malibu summer beach party. Gaynor's first marriage had just ended, and she was alone in LA for the first time in her life. Crystal had been dressed in hippie chic, reeking of patchouli. She still had her original face. She had spun Gaynor around to the Bee Gees. They'd gone home together, but Gaynor had never been much of a bisexual when push came to shove. She'd broken Crystal's heart, and hell hath no fury like a shattered Crystal.

They walked toward each other like prizefighters entering a ring. Instead of punches, they traded absent air kisses, and Crystal strode up the steps to the patio of The Ivy. She bypassed the maître d' and walked directly to the corner table known in town as the Cone of Silence due to the waterfall beside it that prevented eavesdropping from other tables.

In a fluid move, Crystal slid into the chair that faced the street, whipped the napkin from the table, folded it across her lap, and produced coal-black sunglasses from her purse. She pushed them onto her expressionless face, and stared as Gaynor took the seat opposite her.

"I'm sorry," Crystal said immediately. "Was that gauche of me? To assume that you want to fuck the valet? I just realized, it could have been one of your sons. But then I realized that the kid is working, something your kids don't do."

"I know you're scattered, dear, but my sons are twelve," replied Gaynor, not skipping a beat. She and Crystal had these lunches four or five times a year, and they were always a bloodbath.

"Ah, I see. Too young even for you," Crystal said absently, snapping her fingers at the nearest waiter and nodding. He immediately disappeared inside the restaurant.

"So, how are things?" began Gaynor with an icy saccharine edge. "Let's see, you have one client who's closeted and on meth, and the rest are all getting ready to die."

"Funny," said Crystal as the waiter reappeared with an enormous martini loaded with spears of olives. She snatched it from him without looking and took a sip. "My clients are booking a lot of things right now; we are very busy."

"The only thing your clients are booking is hospice care," retorted Gaynor. "Although I understand why you keep them around. It must be nice to be charging someone six thousand a month to do absolutely nothing."

"Ten, darling, at least, but yes, it's quite nice. How's your stable of high-powered fuckups coming along?"

"They've fucked up very nicely this year, *wela*," beamed Gaynor. "I'm sure you remember awards season. I ran six strong campaigns, including three best acting potentials. You remember when your clients got awards for movies instead of lifetime achievements, right?"

"My lovely Matthew Dalton will get best supporting, my dear. I will make sure of that."

"Eh," grunted Gaynor with a dismissive wave of her hand. "That's a pity fuck. He's in that movie for six minutes. I guess he did a good job of acting like he didn't have dementia."

"Well, we'll see," smiled Crystal icily. "I keep meaning to ask you, that new kid you're repping, the blond from the show on the CW, does he really have his black Amex on file at that abortion clinic in Beverly Hills?"

"He's a helper, what can I say?" snorted Gaynor. "If the bitches are too stupid to insist on a rubber, then at least they're not spending six months' rent cleaning up after it. And you can't criticize, *reina*. Every boutique in town has your Amex on file for when Miss DaVerne goes on a shoplifting spree after a few Percocets."

"We all have to get our thrills somehow," said Crystal brightly, removing a spear of olives from her crowded martini and sliding it between her lips.

The waiter reappeared at the table. He ignored Crystal, and asked if Gaynor would be eating. Crystal never ate in public, and the martini was her signature dish.

"I'm starving, handsome," enthused Gaynor. "Bring me the fried chicken, but instead of mashed potatoes, can I get that kale avocado salad? And the bread basket. *Gracias.*"

Crystal arched an eyebrow.

"You order like a tourist," she snarled.

"Don't hate my metabolism," said Gaynor.

"It's not your metabolism I hate," rasped Crystal, chewing on her olives. "It's money-hungry little scabs like the whore you're representing."

"You need to be more specific."

"The tabloid queen," whispered Crystal dramatically. "I know you're just doing this to twist the knife in me. Why does a tabloid reporter need a publicist?"

"Because he is a friend, and because he doesn't deserve to be destroyed for giving your client exactly what he wanted."

Crystal pushed back from the table. "I need to use the bathroom before this discussion," she announced, striding dramatically down the hallway to the back of the restaurant. Gaynor had watched this ritual for years, and still couldn't help but lean out to watch as their waiter furtively handed Crystal a sandwich wrapped in brown paper as she strode past him. She would eat it in the bathroom stall, and return ready for war.

Gaynor checked her phone, and then used a small makeup mirror to survey who else was eating on the patio. It was decidedly low-wattage today. Probably the clouds, she reasoned. Nobody went out in LA when it was gray. She spied a smattering of black-suited agents and managers, gaudily dressed Beverly Hills wives with their matching face surgeries, and in the far corner of the patio, a female reality TV star being feted by the president of a youth network.

Gaynor felt sad. Even ten years ago, she would have been surrounded by Oscar winners and authors, songwriters and singers and artists. *This town has died,* she mused. *There is no art anymore; there is no passion. There is reality TV and everyone's a whore with a hard bottom line.*

Her phone vibrated as a text came in from John Smith, one of the many pseudonyms in any good publicist's phone.

Montage. 2 p.m. Room 111. The costume is on bed.

Gaynor involuntarily grimaced, and her eyes rolled. This client was the worst part of her job. "Forgive me, Mother Mary," she whispered, crossing herself.

Out of the corner of her eye, she saw Crystal emerge from the ladies' room, dabbing at the corner of her mouth. Gaynor hurriedly dismissed the text.

Crystal glided back into her seat. *She's turning into Andy Warhol*, Gaynor chuckled to herself. She'd been so pretty when they met. Now she was just like the rest of Hollywood, fucked up and hard. Crystal threw her entire martini back like a shot. She set the glass down and started nibbling on a skewer of olives like it was a corncob.

"Shall we start?" asked Gaynor as her food arrived.

Crystal ran her tongue across her teeth to dislodge any olive scraps, and began to speak, very slowly and definitely.

"Why the fuck do you hate me?"

Gaynor picked up a fried chicken leg and took a bite.

"*Ay dios mío*," she moaned. "This *pollo frito*, it's the best in town. You should really try it. They soak it in buttermilk for like a day. It's a shame you don't eat."

Crystal did not bat an eyelid. Gaynor wasn't sure if she actually could anymore.

"Gaynor, you have someone conveniently at my client's side when he has a drug freak-out, and then I learn that your new assistant is *some*how captivating Seamus. This is a new low, even for you."

"You have always been a little paranoid, my old friend," muttered Gaynor, tugging at a piece of golden chicken skin.

"It's called being careful, Gaynor, my love," Crystal purred slowly. "You should try it sometime. I mean, especially considering that half the town is talking about what's going on between you and Max Zetta."

"Rumors are never bad press," smiled Gaynor. "I've been able to transition Max away from last year's unfortunate incident. The scripts are pouring in."

"Incidents. Plural," countered Crystal. "And nobody is forgetting. The scripts are jokes. Try telling the studios that Max wants a role. Nobody is going to hire him. Regardless of how much you control that side of his life, he's a drunk, and drunks get sloppy. He's a lit fuse. It's just a matter of time."

"I have a two o'clock, so let's do this. What exactly shall we do about the Ethan Carpenter and Billy thing?"

"It's easy. I need to know how much to pay him to make this story not happen."

"It's not happening," said Gaynor. "Where do you get your information these days? *In Touch*?"

"Please, they haven't been right in years," sniffed Crystal. "It's just a natural progression. That little whore basically entrapped my client. He made this happen."

"Before you look even stupider, here's what happened. Your client basically kidnapped mine, and was keeping him prisoner in a Las Vegas drug den. You think you have the upper hand? *Ay*, you're a stupid *coño*. You never learn. Here's what is happening. Nothing. Billy is a decent guy. He has a very strange code of ethics about what he sells to the tabloids. He says he just feels sorry for Ethan; he doesn't want to hurt him. The story goes nowhere."

Crystal set the skewer of decimated olives on the table and stared directly into Gaynor's eyes.

"And you trust him?" she said warily.

Gaynor laughed coldly. "I don't trust anybody, but I believe that the story is contained and you can return to making people believe that their closeted gay superhero meth addict is actually clean. And straight."

"That's the easy part, my brown bunny. You know I've been doing that for years."

"I've always said your office should be in a closet," cooed Gaynor. "You know, just so your clients feel at home."

"That joke's older than your fashion sense," said Crystal. "I'm serious here." She leaned in even closer to the fountain. "You and I both know how much money is riding on this staying completely off the record."

"*Abuela*, do you want to give Billy money? Is that what you're saying?"

"Don't be transparent," hissed Crystal, leaning her head so close to the fountain that Gaynor could see water droplets landing in the thick bed of foundation on her cheek.

"Turn your hearing aid up," Gaynor said coldly. "He does not want money. He is not selling the story. There is no other way to say it. Now quit carrying on about it and start trying to get Ethan into you-know-who's rehab."

"I tried," said Crystal, dropping her guard. "His team won't let him vanish for two months. He has two movies lined up and they can't wait."

"You know where this is headed, right?" said Gaynor softly, with a touch of sympathy.

Crystal closed her eyes and nodded.

"We both do," she said sadly. She paused and took a deep breath.

"So, your assistant. You broke her in with Paul Stroud. I assume they slept together."

"Just a blow job."

"Oh no." Crystal rolled her eyes. "She got a face full."

"She's a trouper; I gave her some Louboutins."

"How long did it take you to turn this one into a prostitute, then?"

"She's been with me six months," laughed Gaynor. "Don't get all high and mighty with me. You've done a lot worse, for a lot less."

"I was remarking on the speed, not the action."

"What do you want to know, Crystal?"

"I'm just surprised that after she connected with Seamus, you still threw her away on a TV actor. I can't possibly let them be photographed together now."

"I believe it's outside your control," said Gaynor, stabbing at a piece of chicken and waving it in front of Crystal tantalizingly.

"Don't underestimate me," said Crystal, steely again. "I've had my guy run three background checks and do a little digging. Nothing so far, but that cornhusker better not have any skeletons in her closet."

"Everybody has skeletons," admonished Gaynor. "But I don't think hers are anything that we need to worry about. You know they're going out on Saturday?"

"Of course I know. My clients keep me very well informed."

"Wait—so you knew that the father of Candy Swenson's baby was actually her happily married TV father?"

"Put your face close to the waterfall, you fucking careless cunt!" seethed Crystal. "And yes, I knew they were fucking. Of course I knew. I even made sure I left condoms in both of their trailers. The idiots didn't use them, of course. Nobody wants to use them anymore. And I told her that as soon as his wife started to suspect, he would drop her like an NBC sitcom, but nobody believes their publicist. You know this."

"Cool story," sniffed Gaynor. "Nicola's not expecting anything. She's a very good girl. You should be paying her! She barely drinks. She hates drugs. As soon as she gives up her pussy, he'll move on."

"We can only hope," rasped Crystal, sticking the skewer of olives back into her mouth to finally finish them off. She clicked her fingers at their waiter, and he nodded.

"Your car will be brought around immediately, Ms. Connors." He actually bowed slightly. Crystal almost smiled.

"It's on me," she drawled, standing and picking up her oversize purse. "Let's go."

"*Gracias*, you're so generous," smiled Gaynor. "But I haven't finished eating."

She stood and air kissed the air about two feet from Crystal's face.

"I mean it," whispered Crystal. "Keep your assistant on a short leash. And if he can really keep his mouth shut, you can tell the little faggot that Ethan wants to see him again."

"Of course he does," said Gaynor, sitting back down to the rest of her fried chicken.

✳ ✳ ✳

An hour later, Gaynor pulled her car into the valet line at the Montage. She looked at the yellow envelope on the passenger seat. The valet at The Ivy had left it there when he brought her car around. She knew what the envelope contained without even opening it: a set of depressing head shots and a clip reel of unwatchable appearances on Mexican TV. Still, the kid was damn hot, and he could probably get cast on something pretty easily. *And nobody fucks like an eager actor*, she smiled to herself.

She had been single since the twins' father had gone back to Colombia five years earlier. She didn't really have a thing for younger men, apart from the fact that they wouldn't want to get serious with a single mother twice their age. It was freeing, like the first hit of poppers when your quaalude was coming on.

Entering the Montage, she did a quick sweep. Nothing alarming. She considered using the freight elevator, but a glance at her watch told her that it was 1:59 p.m. already. Max didn't like to be kept waiting. She buzzed for an elevator right in the view of everyone, and seconds later was boarding. She turned as the doors closed, but not quickly enough to see Billy watching her from behind a huge floral arrangement on a table by the front desk.

She paused at Room 111. The door was slightly ajar. She pushed it and walked in. The bathroom door was closed, and water was running. She laid her purse on the couch and scowled at the costume on the bed.

A ratty old linen robe and a set of black lingerie were laid out with a fetishist's meticulous touch. The rough beige fabric was covered in wrinkles and stains in the dim light through the drawn curtains.

Gaynor rolled her eyes. She took a deep breath and put her hands on her hips. She hated this.

Sighing, she turned and started changing into the lingerie. She carefully hung her clothes in the closet, and paused for a minute. *I'm too fucking old for this shit*, she thought. She had been toying with the idea of letting Max go as a client, but every time she brought it up, he increased her fee to the point where he'd already paid for both her kids' college several times over.

As she smoothed the robe over her flat stomach, she realized that for the first time, she really, *really* didn't want to do this anymore. She took a deep breath, looked at herself in the mirror above the work desk, and barked, "My son, Mother is waiting."

CHAPTER 11

THE EARLY MORNING MIST CLOAKED West LA as Nicola gazed out the window of the black Lexus that was speeding her toward the marina—and Seamus. The windows were tinted so dark that it still looked like night outside. Even the windshield was darker than was legal.

"You all right back there, love?" asked the driver, an affable, sandy-blond Australian with deep laugh lines around his eyes. His accent was so thick, Nicola had not caught his name, despite asking him to repeat it four times.

"Yessir," she replied.

As they peeled off the 10 and crested the on-ramp to the dreaded 405, Nicola rolled down her window and peered north through the fog to the Getty, sitting imperiously above all of LA with a gargoyle's cold stare.

"Such a snob," she admonished the museum, the brisk air blasting her face.

"Who's a bloody snob? Me?" laughed the Aussie.

"No, no, I was talking to the Getty," smiled Nicola. "You know, the way it sits up there on that hill, judging all of Los Angeles. 'Oh, hey, I'm all marble and shit and I'm full of art and you're all just full of yourselves,' you know?"

The Aussie laughed. "So you haven't been up there yet?"

"No, why?"

"Oh, no reason in particular, but if yer askin' me, the building tends to overshadow the art, and the views definitely overshadow it, and that's a bloody shame, mate," the driver said seriously. "The permanent collection is astonishing, and their rotating exhibits are pretty much always spot-on. Do yourself a favor and get up there. Do it by yourself the first time, and just get ready to lose your whole day."

"Really?"

"Yeah; one day, I was waiting for Seamus to do a photo shoot in Westwood, so I just decided to wait up there. I lost myself in the Flemish impressionists and my phone reception wasn't good, and the next bloody thing ya know, it's three hours later and Seamus had been calling and the bastard had to take a fuckin'—sorry, miss, I mean, he had to take a bloody cab."

"Oh no," laughed Nicola. "The horror. Was he pissed?"

"What? No, he was sober. Oh, wait, do you mean was he angry?"

"Yeah, was he mad he had to get the cab?"

"No, he thought it was awesome. I went and got him and took him to a pub and got him drunk."

"Seamus can just go to regular pubs?"

"No, of course not. You're about to see just how hard it is for him to do anything in this town, but we have a network of pubs that are dark, and we pay the owners well so that no staff call the tabloids or develop itchy camera-phone fingers. Over in Highland Park mostly."

"I don't even know where that is," said Nicola.

"It's cool over there. It's where I live; it's east of Hollywood."

"I thought Aussies had to live near the beach," joked Nicola.

"I wouldn't spit on an LA beach," said the driver with sudden seriousness. "I drive to Malibu or down to San Diego if I wanna surf. And I can do that just as easily from Highland Park, and I don't have to deal with the wankers in Venice."

"Ah, okay. Thanks for clearing that up," smiled Nicola, catching the Aussie's green eyes in the rearview mirror. He smiled back, then pulled his phone out of his pocket and checked a text.

"Good news!" he exclaimed. "Seamus is successfully aboard the yacht, and there aren't any fucking pap—shit, sorry, I really have to stop swearing—no paparazzi about."

"That's great fucking news," said Nicola. "And please, swear all you want."

"Fuckin' A," laughed the Aussie as he took the on-ramp to the 91 way too fast, sending them hurtling along a freeway that suddenly seemed to be passing through a swamp.

Where the hell am I? wondered Nicola, pulling her sweater around her as the landscape changed and the mist grew thicker. She wasn't nervous at all, even though she'd been restless all night.

She group texted Billy and Kara.

Headed to mystery date with you know who. Will text upon my safe return.

She leaned back against the seat and wondered about the day ahead. Seamus had been very present for the past couple of days, texting her instructions to follow to make today work. She had not been permitted to tell anyone anything about where they were going. They had to board the yacht and sail by seven a.m., and they would only return after dark fell. She'd had to approve their menu for the day, and send her measurements to a stylist. Seamus insisted that all she had to bring were the clothes she chose to wear from her apartment to the yacht. She hadn't entirely listened. She wasn't sure how she felt about someone else picking out her clothes. She also couldn't help wondering if she would get to keep them at the end of the day or if she had to clean them and send them back?

The freeway ended and the SUV wove its way through rows of flat, faded apartment blocks that reminded Nicola of an awful spring break in Myrtle Beach. The marina appeared on their left; hundreds of megayachts bobbed serenely on the impossibly flat water.

The Aussie drove to the far end of a parking lot where a security gate opened automatically, and he pulled to a stop beside a long jetty that led out to the largest yachts Nicola had ever seen, row upon row of them, swaying gently in the morning tide.

"Okay, this is as far as I can go," he said. "If the paps see me, it's over. So here's what you're gonna do . . ."

The Aussie gave her a set of directions, but his accent was so incomprehensible that all she got was that she had to find space 813, which sounded like "oyt thur doyn."

She gathered up her purse, pulled her poncho around her, and opened the door.

"Sunglasses, love," cautioned the Aussie. "Put your sunnies on."

Nicola pulled her sunglasses out of her purse and put them on.

"Better?" she asked.

"Much," smiled the big Aussie. "See yas tonight."

Walking along the dock, she smelled the sea and fish, and saw signs of life as people emerged onto the decks of their yachts, holding coffee cups and waving hello.

She found the 800 block and followed it. As she drew near to 813, she saw her destination, a chunky multilevel thing that looked like a miniature cruise ship, towering over the yachts around it. As she gawked, an older man in a captain's jacket came out and greeted her.

"Ms. Wallace." He smiled, extending his hand. "I'm Captain Hartman. Welcome aboard the *Spicy Tuna*. Please come this way."

A precarious freestanding stairway went up from the dock to the boarding level of the yacht. As she looked at the stairs with trepidation, Seamus appeared on the deck, barefoot in blue shorts and a threadbare gray hoodie. Nicola's breath caught in her throat. Apparently Seamus O'Riordan's just-woke-up look was almost the same as his *GQ* cover look.

"Mornin', Nicola," he said with a smile. "You look beautiful. Would you like a little help getting up here?"

Captain Hartman took her bag, and Seamus extended his hand. Nicola made it up three steps, then grabbed Seamus's hand. He effortlessly pulled her up the remaining steps and across the perilous gap between the stairs and the yacht.

They stood awkwardly facing each other, neither certain whether to kiss or hug. Seamus started to move forward, then stopped. He awkwardly opened his arms wide to indicate the yacht and said, "Welcome aboard!" Then he leaned in and kissed her chastely on the cheek.

"Thank you," smiled Nicola, dismayed to feel a blush heat her cheeks.

"Okay, Mr. O'Riordan," cautioned the captain. "Let's get you back inside until we're out on the open sea. Don't want to risk getting snapped."

"Yep, got it," smiled Seamus, taking Nicola's hand and leading her inside the yacht's dining room. "Thanks, Cap'n."

Entering the large dining room, Nicola noticed all the photos framed on the walls, of various rock stars and actors aboard the yacht. *If only this boat could talk*, she thought, *but it can't and that's why I'm here.*

After sailing up the coast for a while, the captain moored the yacht a safe distance from the Malibu coastline, in a forest of golden kelp. A gentle swell lifted the huge boat every now and then, before it morphed into tall waves that crashed onto El Matador and La Piedra beaches. They were finally allowed outside to eat lunch on the top deck. It was a deceptively simple affair of lobster rolls on the freshest pretzel bread Nicola had ever tasted, a salad of fresh dandelion leaves, flower petals, and a lemon juice spray, and frosty steins of Seamus's favorite beer from Scotland, an exquisite malty ale that was aged in old whisky barrels.

"What the hell is this beer?" Nicola licked the foam from her top lip.

"Why?" Seamus laughed. "Do you need to hashtag it on Instagram?"

"No, I want to buy a crate of it for my fridge. And I don't have an Instagram."

"No?" Seamus gave her an odd half smile.

"Nah. No social media. It's a time suck and a bummer. So, can you tell me the name of the beer so I can hashtag-remember-it-for-later?"

"I'll have some sent to you."

"No, I'd rather buy it myself, if that's okay with you."

"Well, you *can't* buy it. They make it specially for me."

"In Scotland?"

"Yes, in Scotland."

"And then you freight it to Malibu?"

"Specifically, no. Technically, I freight it to Los Angeles. Or the Port of Long Beach, if you really want to split that hair."

Nicola laughed, then stopped suddenly as she was reminded of how surreal the situation was. She was sitting on a private yacht with an incredibly rich and famous person, and even a seemingly innocuous question like the name of a beer became a window into an alternate reality. A long silence spun out between them, until the slapping of the ocean on the hull became unbearable.

"What happened?" Seamus asked.

"It's stupid," Nicola began. "I kind of keep tripping over your fame. Like I forget about it, and then boom, there it is in the middle of the road like a speed bump."

"You forget what I do for a job?"

"Well, I remember that you make movies for a job. But so far, you're a guy I met at a party who has asked me out on this somewhat over-the-top first date. You could also be a doctor, a lawyer, or a mob boss. It's not like I haven't seen your movies, but right now, that doesn't even feel like the same person."

"It's not the same person," Seamus said earnestly. "You're a publicist. Are you the same as you are at work?"

"I'm a publicist's assistant, and I'm pretty much the same wherever I am."

"Good to know. So when will you be a publicist?"

"Apparently either when Gaynor decides I'm a publicist or when I sign my own client. Whichever happens first."

"And you like the publicity business?"

"I'll get back to you on that one. So far it's okay. I'll be honest, I needed a job when I got here and I got a lucky break. I didn't choose it, it chose me. So now we'll see. It feels weird that I might have found my career. Back home, I couldn't land on anything that I could see myself doing for a long time. This feels different."

"You're an odd one," laughed Seamus, reaching his hand across the small table and brushing his knuckles across the back of Nicola's hand.

"Really?" She laughed. "Is that a compliment in Scotland?"

"No, it's a compliment with me." Seamus grinned. "I can't figure out if it's just because you're so new to LA, but you don't have any of that diva bullshit. The demanding entitlement. I don't think you're gonna grow into it, either."

"Oh, that." Nicola scoffed. "No. I see it. I see it a lot. It just blows my mind. It's awful, these women acting like they're training to be the world's worst trophy wife, or the hot bitch in a rap video. I don't get it. If you ever see me acting like that, please just wash my mouth out. With a shotgun."

"I think you're going to dodge that bullet," laughed Seamus, "literally and figuratively."

"When I left Ohio"—Nicola flipped her hand over, and Seamus began tracing the lines in her palm with his fingertip, never breaking eye contact—"my friends all begged me not to let LA change me. After a year, I know that LA doesn't *change* you, but it can give you ample space to fulfill your potential to be a massive bitch. That's not me.

"My single mom raised me and my little brother by cleaning a Motel 6. She still works there, but now she's in the office. We were poor. That's good training for never being a bitch. When life is hard enough, you realize that being kind is the best asset a person can have."

"Excuse me, you two," said the captain's mate, appearing at their side. "May I clear the table?"

Seamus nodded, standing. He looked at Nicola as she passed her plate to the mate. She was so normal that by Hollywood standards, she appeared strange. He gave her a deep, warm smile. She smiled back. They walked over to the railing, looking out at the coastline. They held hands for a while in silence, until Seamus dropped Nicola's hand and gently reached his arm around her back, resting it on her hip.

"Wanna go swimming?" she asked.

"Sure," he said hesitantly. "Don't we have to wait a bit? We just ate."

"That's an old wives' tale." Nicola ruffled his hair. "Come on, let's do this." She pulled her plain T-shirt up over her head, revealing the black-and-nude patterned Beach Bunny bikini she had grabbed from a stylist's lounge yesterday. She hadn't been sure if it was just right or too much. Judging from Seamus's expression when she reopened her eyes, it was the former.

"Take a picture, tourist," she laughed.

"Your skin is beautiful," he said huskily. "No fake tan!"

"God, no," Nicola retorted. "That shit is banned in France. I'm not microwaving myself. It's not like I tan anyway; most summers I just get a few new freckles, but they don't even survive the winter."

"I see," said Seamus, raising his hand to her shoulder, tracing a few freckles with his finger. "Another pleasant surprise."

"Okay, stop, Casanova; let's get in the water."

"Okay, lady boss." Seamus pulled his hoodie over his head and dropped it onto his chair. He took her hand and began to lead her belowdecks.

"Where do you think you're going?"

"There's a ladder on the back of the ship, it's down two levels."

Nicola put her hands on her hips. "Why can't we just jump from up here?"

Seamus's eyes widened. "No, don't be daft, come on."

"Do not tell me that Mr. Action Hero is scared of heights."

"I'm not scared. It'll hurt."

"No, it won't. I used to dive higher than this at the quarry back in Dayton. It's awesome. Do it once, and you'll wanna do it all day."

"The studio will kill me if I break anything. . . ."

"Don't blame them, you big chicken." Nicola put a palm gently on his cheek. "I'll make a deal with you. I will hold your hand as we jump."

"That's the deal? That's all I get?"

"No, the deal is, if you promise to not back out, I'll kiss you before we jump."

"You drive a hard bargain, Nico." Seamus's whole face lit up. "You bet I'll fookin' do it."

Sunlight pierced the sea so far below them, firing the kelp into a riot of golds and greens. Nicola peered over the edge of the yacht. They'd need to jump out to clear the lower deck.

"You ready, scaredy-cat?"

"I'll take that kiss now, daredevil." He gently pulled her to him, brushing his lips against hers. They were surprisingly soft, and ringed with rough stubble.

Over and over he gently grazed his lips across hers. His warm Scotch-and-beer breath filled her nose, and his hands traced lightly up and down her spine.

Oh fuck it, she thought, and pulled him to her, kissing him as hard as she could.

He wrapped his thick arms tighter around her, groaning a little. The trail of black fur from his chest down his stomach tickled her. He pressed a thigh between her legs and all of her skin came alive. He released a guttural growl so low it vibrated her throat.

Nicola grabbed a handful of curly black hair and pulled his head back, breaking their kiss.

"We had a deal," she rasped, their eyes locked.

"We did," he whispered, pushing his erection against her. "But we didn't say we had to jump in right away. . . ."

"A deal's a deal."

Seamus stepped back. Nicola eyed the bulge in his swim shorts. He followed her gaze.

"Not sorry 'bout it," he laughed.

"Don't be." Nicola took his hand. "The cold ocean will take care of it before I get a chance to."

They stood with their toes on the edge of the deck, the glittering sea roiling thirty feet below them. "I'm gonna count to three," she said firmly. "We have to jump up and out, just to clear the lower deck. I'm going to be holding your hand. If you chicken out, you'll pull me back and I'll Homer Simpson my way down the side of this boat. Just so we're clear."

"Are we gonna do this or fookin' talk about it all day?" Seamus grinned widely.

They stepped back from the edge, and Nicola counted down, "One! Two! Three!"

Seamus did not hesitate. In unison, they leapt up and out into space. Salty air blasted them and ocean and sky rushed up in a kaleidoscope of blues and golds and greens. The deafening roar of their splash was replaced by the sudden shock of cold water as they plunged below the surface.

Nicola never let go of Seamus's hand. His weight pulled her deep. She held tight and scissor-kicked her way toward the surface, pulling him up with her. He was laughing as soon as his head popped out of the water.

"That was fookin' awesome!" He shook his head and showered her in droplets from his curls. He kissed her again. She wrapped her arms around his shoulders and he kept them afloat, his arms sweeping broad strokes in the water. After several minutes, Nicola began to shiver.

"Too cold for you?" Seamus whispered. "I thought you were tough."

"I never said that." Nicola kicked him in the leg. "It's just chilly in the water."

"This is warmer than the ocean ever gets in Scotland." Seamus held her against him and sidestroked to the ladder at the back of the yacht. He helped her up onto the landing and wrapped her in a thick white towel. Her shivering stopped almost at once. She tilted her head back and let the sun do its work.

"Wait there a sec, love." Seamus disappeared inside. Nicola heard a grinding sound as the captain raised anchor, and the engine's hum grew louder. The yacht slowly began to edge toward the shore.

Seamus returned carrying a blue vintage longboard. He set it across the landing, turned, and returned with a second one.

"We're going ashore," he grinned. "I have something to show you."

Before she knew what was happening, he had tugged a surf top over her head, and they had gone back in the water to climb atop the two surfboards. Pounding shore dumpers filled the air between them and the beach with explosions of salt water and spray. Over the din, Seamus yelled at her to wait till "this set of waves" ended and then she was to "paddle like hell" to the shore, so that's what Nicola did.

Over her shoulder, she saw a new batch of waves taking shape out by the *Spicy Tuna*. She paddled with as much hell as she could, and felt the board slide onto the wet sand.

"So now what?" Nicola surveyed the beach. It was only a couple of hundred yards wide, bounded at the back and each end by jagged, almost vertical stone cliffs. A house teetered precariously on the cliff to the north. Its Tuscan stone and tile gleamed incongruously against the rough-hewn California coastline.

"First, gimme your rash guard," Seamus said, pulling off his tight black nylon shirt and then taking hers. He bundled the shirts tightly together and pitched them away from the water. They landed with a spray of sand, startling a seagull the size of a small turkey.

He moved behind Nicola and placed one hand on her stomach. She leaned her head back onto his chest. They silently faced out toward the horizon, their eyes closed. They did not see a man come out onto the balcony of the Tuscan stone house, or the pair of binoculars in his hand. They didn't see him raise the binoculars to his face, or how he pulled his cell phone out of his shorts pocket to dial a number. The man ducked furtively back inside.

After kissing Nicola's neck for a little while, Seamus whispered, "Let's put the boards up here by the cliff."

Seamus thrust his board end-first into the sand and then did the same thing with Nicola's. He took her hand and began walking south, their feet sinking in the fine, wet sand along the ocean's edge.

She could see the Ferris wheel on the Santa Monica pier in the distance. Two men were windsurfing a ways down the coast, and Seamus and Nicola both whistled as one of them caught big air off a wave, sailing airborne, aloft on sunbeams.

They stopped at the end of the beach. The cliffs wrapped around and curved into the ocean, rough boulders splashing in the waves. There was no way she could swim around that.

"Where to now?" she asked quietly.

"Follow me, m'dear." Seamus smiled a curious grin and dropped to his knees. She gasped as he crawled into a small crack in the rocks that Nic had thought was just a shadow. She furrowed her brow. Great. The mouth of a cave, just yards from rushing water. What could possibly go wrong? She watched until only his pale white feet were still visible, then slowly dropped down and followed.

"Watch your head," he cautioned.

The small tunnel opened gradually to a wider space, flooded with light, not water. The sand was soft and wet beneath her hands, and she looked up just in time to stop before she crashed her face into Seamus's famous, muscly ass.

"Well, the view's great," she joked.

Seamus laughed. "It's gonna get better."

In a few feet, he stood upright ahead of her. She crawled faster toward him and gasped as she entered a sea cave. Her eyes wide, she took in the high ceiling of jagged rock, the improbably perfect sand beach at the rear of the cave, and the clear pool of seawater that led out to the ocean, lit by blinding sunlight.

"Seamus!" she exclaimed. "This is amazing." She turned in circles, taking it all in.

"Aye, lassie." He beamed. "It is, it is."

Seamus stepped into the pool and washed the sand off his arms and legs. He pulled Nicola in and gently rinsed her sand away. With his arms around her waist, he guided them to the shallow water near the sand. They fell slowly into it, and without a word, kissed again.

Seamus ran his fingers along the edge of her bikini beneath the warm water, his fingers running lightly down her inner thigh. He began to trace the line where her bikini and her thigh met. Nicola wondered if he was going to pull her bottoms off, and whether she should let him, but he didn't. He just kept lightly touching her leg, kissing her and pressing his other hand into the sandy floor beneath them, keeping her afloat.

The kiss lasted forever, or half an hour. Nicola finally tried to drag Seamus up onto the small cave beach, out of the water.

"Cannae do, lassie," he said. "The water is our protection."

She looked confused.

"From photographers," he explained, crestfallen. "If someone's got a long lens on us, it can't capture anything that goes on beneath the surface of the water."

She looked around the cave.

"Dude, the coast is clear."

A small harrumph sounded in Seamus's throat.

"Of all the coasts where we can do this, this particular one is never clear."

He went to resume the kiss, and got her cheek.

"What?"

"I just . . . ," she began, pushing him away from her. "I mean, I get it, this is beautiful, but I just keep forgetting . . . You know all the tricks, even the tricks of this *cave*. It's all so calculated. This must be the place you bring every girl. It's been so like clockwork and I feel like I'm being played." She paused, and sighed a little. "Let's paddle back to the boat. I'm sorry, Seamus, I just don't like being the latest one on the production line."

Seamus slowly pulled her through the water until she was resting in the shallows. He lay alongside her, propping himself on an elbow.

"Nicola, do you really think most LA women would paddle a surfboard through a Malibu shore break and climb into a tunnel with me?"

"Yes, if it meant making a best-dressed list and getting a seat next to you at the Oscars." She took his hand with a wan smile. "Even if not, I'd still like to slow it down."

"Of course," he said gently. "I'll be honest; you're certainly not the first girl I've brought in here. You're the fifth. But you *are* the first one who didn't complain the whole time."

Silence fell between them, the slap of the waves echoing around the cave.

"Nico, I brought you here because it's beautiful, and I thought you'd like it."

"My dad used to call me Nico," she said quietly.

"Did he then?" Seamus stared into her eyes. "It suits you. So listen, yes, I've been lonely, and yes, it's really hard for me to meet women, so I've used this cave before. I'm sure you had some old favorites in Dayton."

"The bleachers behind the racetrack don't count."

"What can I do to make you more comfortable?"

She relaxed against him. "I don't know," she said softly. "We should maybe head back to the yacht. . . ."

"Well, I'd like to see you again," he said, "very much."

"I'd like that, too," she said. "But next time, can we do something lower key? I'm not looking to be impressed. I just want to go on a regular date. Is there anywhere you can do that?"

"Oh yeah," he said. "Bluey can sort anything out."

"I'm sure he can," she laughed, turning her face up to Seamus's. She kissed him on the lips. "I couldn't figure out what he was saying his name was in the car."

"It's Bluey. His real name is Donald, so you can see why he prefers Bluey. And if you want a lower-key date with a real human being, he is a magician who can make that sort of thing happen for me."

"If that's not too much trouble," she whispered. "Sorry if I sound crazy."

"*Au contraire*," he replied. "This proved to me that you're not."

They started to kiss again, and Nicola noticed that Seamus kept his hands respectfully on her lower back, not pushing it. The heat was gone, but the kisses were still slow and delicious. Either he was empathic or he was a genius at playing women. She was trying to decide which when the yacht emitted three loud, short bursts on its horn.

"FUCK," spat Seamus, grabbing her shoulders. "FUCK!"

"What the hell?" asked Nicola, alarmed.

"The fookin' paps have found us." Seamus looked left and right in the cave. He peered out to the yacht, and saw the mate rapidly lowering a speedboat from the side booms. It dropped onto the ocean with a splash. The mate dove into the ocean beside it, then climbed in. He turned the engine and sped toward the cave.

"Into the water, swim," Seamus said firmly, guiding Nicola out of the tunnel, over the rocks, and into deeper ocean. On the speedboat, the mate was pointing to the beach to their left. At the mouth of the cave, Seamus held his hand up, cautioning Nicola to not swim any farther. Within twenty seconds, the speedboat was almost to them. She heard male voices back in the cave behind them. "Don't look back," Seamus whispered as the mate slowed the boat and drifted up to them. He tossed a rope and Seamus grasped it, while pulling Nicola close to him.

"Wait," the mate said. He gunned the engine softly and pulled the boat around Seamus and Nicola, blocking the two photographers who were standing on the sand where they'd been kissing just a minute before.

The mate grabbed Nicola by the wrists, effortlessly lifting her up and out of the water. He quickly draped a towel over her head. She felt like a Halloween ghost. She felt the speedboat tilt as Seamus climbed aboard. He lay down on the floor of the boat, and the mate threw a towel over him like he was dead.

With a noisy roar and a belch of gasoline, the speedboat hurtled back to the yacht, riding up the face of approaching waves and slamming down to the ocean on the flip side.

The captain was waiting for them. Holding up a sheet, he blocked the photographer's shots as they stepped onto the landing of the yacht. He ushered them inside. The mate hitched the speedboat to the back of the yacht and rushed to the wheelhouse. The engine roared to life and the yacht headed directly out to sea.

Seamus and Nicola took refuge in the cabin she'd changed in earlier. Seamus sat on the bed, his teeth clenched. He took Nicola's hand.

"My God, my God, I'm so sorry," he repeated, over and over.

"It's not your fault, it's okay," she said.

"I just lost one of my trusted spots," he spat ruefully. "I'll let you shower and get your clothes on," he said sadly. "We're going to have to stay belowdecks until we get back to the marina."

"Okay," said Nicola. "Don't feel bad; it's totally fine."

"No," said Seamus, with surprising anger in his voice. "No, it's fookin' not."

※ ※ ※

Things got weirder as they approached the marina. A female mannequin in a long dress, a hoodie, and a short red wig was loaded into the passenger seat of the speedboat. The mate donned a red Scotland hoodie, jeans, and sunglasses, got in beside "her," and took off south along the coast, past the entrance to the marina. A speedboat that had been waiting just behind the seawall raced in hot pursuit.

Seamus and Nicola had hidden out in one of the bedrooms for the sail home. Seamus had been sullen and silent at first. He'd called Bluey, informing him they'd had a "code red" and asking for special help getting off the boat.

When he hung up the phone, he turned to Nicola. She thought he was about to cry.

"Nico. I'm sorry. This is about to get silly." His voice caught in his chest as he took her hand and led her from the bedroom.

She had noticed the four huge shipping cartons on the deck when she boarded. Seamus pulled on the side of one of the containers and a small door opened. He gestured inside and Nicola burst out laughing. This was their escape hatch! The interior of the cube of four cardboard boxes was outfitted with two seats, upholstered in leather, facing each other.

"I'm so sorry, but please get inside."

She obeyed.

It was almost pitch-dark inside the crate when Seamus closed the door. She could barely make him out even though she could feel his breath on her face.

"This is weird," she said.

"I know, and I'm sorry," he said despondently.

"Stop saying sorry. What happens next?"

"Well, they'll lower us to the dock, onto an electric cart," he explained. "Then we will be loaded into the back of a truck."

"Driven by Bluey?"

"Yep. Then he'll take us to an underground parking garage, and we'll transition to another car, and we should be safe." Seamus's voice was tight with anger. "I'm just so sorry; this hasn't happened before. The captain said that he thinks we got sold out by the bastard who's renting the house on the beach. He could even be a paparazzo himself. It just sucks so bad; I've lost another place I can be anonymous."

"It's all kind of James Bond to me, so it's not like it's killing our date."

"Thanks," he smiled. "But it did kill our date. Our first fucking date. That fucking dude on the beach better watch his fucking back!"

Nicola noticed that Seamus was saying *fucking*, not *fooking*. He was seething. He had also called it a first date. She put her hand up to his cheek to quiet him down.

"Seamus, I've had a really sweet day."

"As have I, love, as have I," he said softly. "But a first date shouldn't be like this."

"No, you're right, but everything up to the photographers was something I'll remember forever, so you're off to a good start."

"Can I see you again?" he asked, nakedly pleading, as if she'd say no.

"I'd like that," she said, squeezing his arm.

"Thanks, love. This time, you can choose what we do. You tell me, and I'll have Bluey work out the details."

"You know that's not normally how a second date works, right?"

They sat silently in the darkness for a while, her hand on his arm. They felt the yacht jerk as it tied off at the dock, and a short while later, the crate swayed as it was lifted from the deck. She leaned forward in the near dark and kissed Seamus on his soft lips.

"Wanna know what my favorite part of today was?"

"Sure."

"The look on your face just before we jumped off the boat," she said. "You looked like a big kid. You looked scared as hell. Like a real person and not an action hero."

"You make me comfortable," he said, reaching out and taking her hand. "I don't get that a lot."

They fell silent as the crate swayed in the air until, with a mild thud, it was placed onto the waiting cart. They began the rickety journey to the truck.

CHAPTER 12

LATE THE NEXT MORNING, KARA peered into Nicola's darkened bedroom, to make sure that her increasingly elusive roommate was out. "What you doin', Mrs. J?" chimed a voice from behind her. Kara put one hand to her head, trying to wave away the hangover that loomed in her skull like a queasy storm.

J was lying naked on her bed. "C'mere, baby, c'mere," he started rapping at her, over and over. Kara was exhausted by his trademark five-word raps. She pressed her knuckles into her temple.

"I'm just seeing if my roommate is home," she said wanly.

"Nope." J laughed. "She bounced. Won't be home till later tonight."

"How the fuck do you know?" Kara said, her voice a mix of irritation and bewilderment.

J rolled across her bed and grabbed her phone from the nightstand. He held it up to Kara so she could see the texts on the screen.

She snatched her phone from his hand.

"Mrs. J is pissus J," he rapped. She rolled her eyes and went into the bathroom. As she sat on the toilet, the door handle started to turn. She shot her hand up and pulled the lock.

"Aw, baby baby, come on," J pleaded, repeating it three times. Kara wished she kept a fucking knife in the bathroom.

"Can you just wait?" she barked.

"You liked it last night," J whispered to the door.

What the hell is he talking about? Kara wondered through her hazy brain. She remembered eating and drinking in bed, and fooling around. A couple of times. They'd smoked a huge spliff and passed out around five a.m.

Washing her hands, she caught a glimpse of herself in the mirror. "Rough."

She took a scarf from the towel rack and tied it around her hairline. She deftly yanked it tighter and tighter until it had pulled her unruly morning hair into a high puff. She picked some sleep crust out of her eyes and quickly dabbed her lips with gloss. She didn't want to walk naked out of the bathroom, but a towel would look stupid and she didn't have any clothes in there.

She unlocked the door, and the handle turned immediately. J pushed his way in. She put her hands on his chest and pushed him backward out of the room.

"Heeey, what's all the resistance?" J whined, confused.

"I need to get ready. I'm working today; my ride will be here in an hour," she explained, frustrated because he knew she had to work.

She pushed J up against a wall in the bedroom, to get him out of the way so she could grab last night's T-shirt from the floor and pull on a pair of yoga pants.

"That's right, yoga lady, that's right," J kept up.

"For fuck's sake, do you have an off switch?" Kara snapped, leaving the bedroom and hurrying toward the kitchen, aspirin, and coffee.

"You're not a morning person, that's okay, that's okay," he said, clicking his fingers to create an offbeat accompaniment.

"J, you gotta go, I have to prep for work," she said, exasperated.

"Okay, I'll call my driver." She hated how perky he was. "As soon as you tell me when I can see you again."

"I dunno," Kara began coolly. "Sometime this week?"

"Well, I'm in Vegas tonight and tomorrow. And then I have appearances in Chicago, Orlando, and New Jersey for Tuesday till Friday. I'm back Saturday."

"New Jersey is a state," Kara said.

"Yep," he guffawed. "A state that's payin' me seventy-five thousand bucks to plug my laptop into their sound system and play my gym workout mix for two hours."

She rolled her eyes. "I guess I'll see you Saturday, then." She threw four aspirins in her mouth, washing them down with a glass of tap water.

"It's a date," he said, walking back to the bedroom to get dressed, giving her a view of his ass.

She exhaled loudly. "Damn, that's fine."

A low buzz surrounded her, and she panicked. *FUCK, AN EARTHQUAKE!*

False alarm; it was J's driver pulling into the underground parking lot. The booming bass seemed to not have any other percussion with it, just a rolling throb that shook the building and kicked the bejesus out of her solar plexus. Within seconds, a chorus of Russian abuse was pouring out of the other apartment.

"The boys are here; I gotta bounce." J grinned. "Come over here and give me a kiss that'll last a week."

Kara walked to him and laid her head on his chest. His hands reached down and cupped her ass, and he kissed her forehead, nudging her head back with his chin. She looked up and he kissed her lips hard, pressing his face against hers and making her hangover scream.

"Okay, Mrs. J, that's gonna last me the week. I am gonna head down to the car. Can you come unlock the laundry stairs?"

Fuck, that's right. Kara rolled her eyes. He had to go into the underground garage via the small outdoor stairs in the back to avoid photographers. She grabbed her keys in one hand and took J's hand in the other and led him out the door, in her T-shirt and yoga pants.

J wrapped his arms around Kara's waist and made it hard to navigate the narrow path that led to the small backyard behind the apartment building. She unlocked the security door to the laundry and the garage and held the door open. He kissed her once more before heading down the stairs. She closed the door quietly and turned to walk back to her apartment. She jumped when she saw the man sitting in the tree in the backyard of the house behind her building. She gasped and put her hands to her chest.

"You fucking scared me," she hissed at him.

He pointed a long-lens camera at her and started snapping off rapid-fire photos as Kara ran back inside.

✳   ✳   ✳

"He's gone, as far as I can tell," said Billy, coming inside the apartment an hour later. "But just in case, let's hold hands and grab ass as we walk to my car."

"Okay, thanks," said Kara grimly, waiting by the door. "The damage is done anyway."

"I know, right?" laughed Billy. "What the fuck are we? The Scandal Sisters?"

"How did the guy know what was going on?"

"They probably trailed Jimmy J here," Billy explained.

Kara shook her head.

"I didn't expect my first big tabloid break to appear next to some old Russian lady's underpants on a clothesline."

"Breaking news, K-Dub. Always be vigilant. Also, you could have controlled that better and made quite a bit of money, honey."

"Well, you knew I was seeing him," Kara protested. "You could have set the photographer up, too. We could have both made money."

"I don't set up my friends."

Kara gave him a death stare.

"Well, not without their consent."

"Fine. You have my consent. Set a sister up."

"Sure thing. But first you have to get dressed. Hurry up so we're not late to your actual job as a stylist."

It took nearly half an hour before Kara settled on a vintage sleeveless zip-front denim jumpsuit with rhinestones around the flared hems as suitable work attire for the day.

As they walked out to the street, Kara peered cautiously from tree to tree through her sunglasses, but there didn't appear to be any more photographers waiting. She could see Billy's convertible sports car double-parked on the street, its backseat loaded with garment bags and shoe boxes for the shoot.

"The magazine got you all this?" Kara asked.

"I'm a very important journalist," he replied. "The images to go along with my story must be perfection."

At the car, Billy spun her around and planted a long, cartoony kiss on her lips.

"Girl," she laughed, pushing him away and waving her fingertips at his shorts and tight T-shirt combo, "in those nine-inch-inseam shorts, *nobody* is ever going to believe you're my boyfriend."

"You'd be surprised, darlin'." He opened the door for her and kissed her again before she got in. As the door closed, he made eye contact with the photographer who'd been watching their every move from behind an SUV across the street. Billy winked, and walked around to his side of the car.

✳ ✳ ✳

"I wonder if the valet will reject my car today," Billy joked as they approached Amber's.

"There ain't no valet for a photo shoot," sniffed Kara. "It's a production day on her show, so there's gonna be trucks and shit everywhere. We are gonna have to unload in the driveway and then find our own parking. So it's just as bad."

"That's worse," huffed Billy. "I hope you taped your soles."

Sure enough, a TV van blocked Amber's triple driveway and a series of BMWs littered both sides of the street.

"Fuck this." Billy double-parked next to the van. They dragged the wardrobe bags out of the backseat of his car, laying thousands of dollars of clothes on the road like cheap groceries. Billy popped the trunk and whipped out the spindly metal pieces of a portable clothing rack, assembling it with one hand while waving irate neighbors by with the other.

As soon as it was upright, Kara started hanging the various bags from designers and stores.

"How'd you even get me this gig?" she asked. "I have no idea what she's looking for, you know. This could be a disaster."

"Calm down, for fuck's sake," snapped Billy. "You're a stylist now, but you'll be a reality star by this afternoon and your stylist résumé won't matter anymore. It's my master plan. Now watch the clothes while I go park."

As Billy peeled off to find a spot on the street, Kara smiled and thought about how much he'd changed in just two years from the pushy new kid in town she'd met backstage at *Tomorrow's Teen Star*. She'd been assisting the show's stylist, dressing one of the contestants. Kara hadn't realized that the kid was gay till she barged in on him and Billy in the middle of a hot makeout session.

"Damn, you're pretty," Billy had said without skipping a beat. "Are you the stylist?"

"Stylist's assistant," the contestant had countered snottily. "She's basically a delivery girl. Don't worry about her."

Billy had seen the sting on Kara's face. He pushed the kid away, took the clothes from Kara, and dropped them on the floor in front of the kid.

"You'll have no trouble dressing yourself, then, future superstar," Billy had quipped, leading Kara out of the dressing room.

As the door had closed behind them, he said loudly, "Fuck that guy. If you wanna make some real money, let's out the douchebag to the tabloids."

They didn't need to out the kid. His nervous performance on TV that night ended his teen star dreams. Billy and Kara celebrated with margaritas at Marix, and had been friends ever since. At first he wanted to mastermind her transition into a celebrity stylist, but now Billy wanted to make her a reality TV star.

When he returned, they hauled the rack up to the same oak doors that Nicola had walked through just a week before. Amber's affable and enormous bodyguard, Jenkins, opened the door.

"Oh, hey, Billy," he said warmly, stepping forward and embracing him in a bear hug. "Hey, Jenkins," mumbled Billy into Jenkins's huge chest.

"You must be Kara," smiled Jenkins, extending a meaty hand that engulfed hers.

"I am. It's a pleasure to meet you."

"The pleasure's all mine," laughed Jenkins. "Step back, you two, I got this." Jenkins reached out with one hand and lifted the clothing rack up into the air as if it weighed nothing.

"What's the scene like inside?" asked Billy.

"Same bunch of losers as always," sighed Jenkins. "But hey, I need a little favor today, if you don't mind."

"Anything, my man," said Billy.

"Amber had some people over last night, and once again . . ."

". . . someone stole shit?" Billy finished.

"Yeah, and you and I know who it was. Can you make a few calls today while you're here? Amber doesn't believe me that he's the thief and I need to put a PI on him before he sells the shit. If I'm not too late already."

"Sure—what did they get?"

"Well, apart from the usual, they've started hitting her jewelry. Man, they're getting ballsier. This time, they took a watch that Pablo Vassar gave to her in Vegas last month. . . ."

"No fucking way," exclaimed Kara. "I saw that watch on TV. It was worth nearly a quarter million dollars."

"That's the one," boomed Jenkins angrily. "And any second now, it's going to be worth a pound of heroin to the luckiest dealer in Hollywood if we don't get to it first."

"I'll have your answer ASAP, Jenks."

"Appreciate it." He wheeled the clothing rack through the kitchen, where a team of Mexican women were cooking and cleaning, and an assortment of tiny dogs were barking incessantly in a child's play-pen in the corner. "Take the clothes to the back bedroom on this floor, and I'll tell Amber you're down here."

Kara hung all the dresses and laid out the shorts, tops, and jeans on the bed. On the floor, tens of thousands of dollars in shoes were grouped by color. Today, Billy was freelancing for *Right Now Weekly*, the glossy weekly fashion tabloid. Officially, his assignment was to wrangle Amber through a photo shoot that captured Amber and her home in a variety of seasonal looks. The magazine would then have a "brand-new exclusive" shoot with Amber to run for every season of the upcoming year. His unofficial job was to listen out for any careless celebrity gossip that Amber spilled so he could sell it to the highest bidder among all the tabloids. For the past week, he and Kara had visited scores of designers and compiled clothing that said Halloween, Thanksgiving, Winter Wonderland, Christmas, Spring Pastels, and Easter, not an easy feat in July.

Kara was just finishing Summer Sensation when Amber bustled in, clearly naked beneath a pink satin robe, her blond hair in curlers.

"Hey, whore," she rasped. "I'm Amber; what's happening?"

"I'm Kara." Kara extended a hand, which Amber ignored, collapsing onto the bed on top of the pile of swimsuits that Kara had just organized.

"What's all this shit?" Amber waved a lazy hand in the general direction of the clothes.

"You're shooting a year's worth of looks for *Right Now Weekly*, today," Kara explained. "You're gonna be busy."

"Fuck that," Amber drawled. "I told them I would only wear my own clothing lines, so I don't need any of this."

Kara looked at the floor, unsure of how to answer. She was grateful when Billy appeared in the doorway.

"Hey, bitch." He planted a wet kiss on her lips.

"Hey, faggot," said Amber, falling backward onto the mountain of swimsuits. "I am not wearing any of this shit; you must be smoking crack."

"Girl, this isn't a catalog shoot for your child labor Penney's line." Billy smirked. "This is going to be the year you claw your way back to the top. Just do as I tell you, season by season, and you'll be selling your shit at Bloomingdale's again. We agreed on this."

Amber rolled her eyes and hugged her knees tightly to her chest.

"You're not wearing panties again," chided Billy.

"Oh, can you see my vagina?"

"No, I believe that's your asshole."

Billy pushed her off the swimsuits.

"Let's figure out your first look. Our photographer and your TV crew are both ready to roll. This is going to be on your show, not just in the magazine, so don't blow it for me."

"I'm too stoned," Amber moaned. "Let's do this tomorrow. I forgot, I have a friend coming by later, I can't do this."

"Give me your purse," Billy whispered to Amber.

He opened the small LV she handed him and pulled out a small brown glass vial. Handed it to Amber. "This usually works for you, dear."

"What the actual fuck do you think you're doing?" Amber barked, springing to her feet while closing her hand around the bullet. "I don't do drugs in front of strangers."

Billy didn't react.

"There's the bathroom." He nodded toward the door in the corner, turning to help Kara salvage the tangled pile of swimsuits on the bed.

When Amber reemerged, she chose sexy nurse as her Halloween outfit and stumbled out into the living room that was bedecked in pumpkins and fluffy toy black cats. When the photographer started clicking away, she writhed in the short candy-striper dress as if she were in a hip-hop video.

"Honey, you're being too sexy for the tabloids," the photographer said impatiently.

"I'm a sexy nurse, you crackhead," she slurred, sniffing several times. But she dialed down the squirming and duck-facing as the camera flashed rapidly.

"Did you get it?" she asked eagerly. "Is it time to move on?"

"Sure," deadpanned the photographer, a stocky woman in her midforties. "We can make it work."

"Good; next I wanna do Fall Fabulous."

"No," said Billy. "Thanksgiving is next."

"Fuck that; I can't do two holidays back-to-back," Amber spat. "We're doing Fall Fabulous."

The entire crew looked at their feet. Billy realized he'd lost this one.

"Okay, everybody, next up is Fall Fabulous, out in the garden by the tree."

He pointed at a eucalyptus that had been covered in fake red and yellow leaves.

"Oh, and I'm wearing my own clothes for that one," Amber sniffed, stomping from the room.

Almost an hour later, the photo crew was still waiting for Amber, pacing nervously around the camera and lights. The TV crew seemed used to it, laughing and shooting the shit. Billy was about to go find her when she appeared in the doorway clad in a cheap-looking red minidress with feathers on the shoulders. An enormous gold cross hung between her breasts.

As both crews silently moved into place, Kara ran up and whispered in Billy's ear. His eyes widened and he snapped at Amber. "You look like Little Red Riding Whore. Go change."

Amber tugged silently at the hem of the dress. "It's vintage," she eventually purred.

"Is there a problem?" asked the photographer.

The TV director looked hurriedly at his crew, making the universal sign to keep the cameras rolling.

"Kara," said Billy dramatically, seeing the cameras turn onto him. "Can you explain the problem with this 'vintage' dress?"

"Honey, you can't wear this," she began.

"You're fired," sighed Amber. "Please leave. Jenkins!"

Kara realized this was her moment. She stepped forward and grabbed Amber's arm. "Listen to me, you crackhead," she snarled. "This is the same fucking dress that Michelle Monaco was wearing when she stepped out of the limo and flashed her labia at the paparazzi."

Amber started laughing. "So what?" she guffawed. "Nobody was looking at the dress, everybody was too busy staring at her damn pussy. That thing looked like two baby rats fighting over table scraps." She paused, looking at the crew, who feigned silent laughter. The director beamed at her, excited to be getting some reality TV gold.

"I noticed the dress," said Kara firmly. "And I'm styling this shoot, and I'm saving your ass from an embarrassing Whose Pussycat Wore It Best feature. Now get your fucking ass back to the dressing room." She grabbed Amber by the shoulder, spun her brusquely around, and marched her inside, followed by the TV crew, back into the bedroom.

"Jesus fucking wept," Kara marveled from inside Amber's huge walk-in closet. "Your wardrobe is like a Halloween superstore of tabloid scandals!"

"What do you mean?" asked Amber, genuinely intrigued for once. "This is just the spare closet. There's two more closets upstairs."

"There's the dress from Zia Zandrian's DUI, and that blue one is the same that Anna Parker wore when her boyfriend OD'd in her arms, and that one there is what Donna Hart had on when she made out with that homeless guy on Sunset. Why the fuck do you have all these super-identifiable clothes?"

"I dunno, bitch," moaned Amber. "People just send me shit."

"Honey, fashion is like a fucking hypodermic." Kara bristled. "Use once and toss. There's no need for all this chintz to be cluttering up your house."

"You're a cunt," said Amber.

"And you're a stupid crackhead who can't dress herself for shit," Kara snapped back. She could hear the TV crew whispering about bleeping out their swearing. But no one asked them to tone it down.

"Love you, mean it," laughed Amber, sitting on the bed. "Listen, you wanna come work for me?"

Kara stopped dead. *What is happening?*

"You're a hot bitch," said Amber. "Are you also a hungry tiger?"

"I'm neither," said Kara, not sure what Amber was talking about.

"Good. You start Monday. Fix my closet."

"You want me to work for you?"

"Yeah. I pay five hundred a day, but only when you're here. You in?"

"Uh, sure," Kara spluttered. "Can we seal it on Snapchat?"

Amber nodded and Kara whipped out her phone and started filming.

"This my new boss bitch," she said, holding her phone at the perfect angle. Then she pointed the lens at Amber, who mumbled, "Hey, bitches, fashion team represent."

They both reviewed the footage. Amber gave her a thumbs-up and Kara tapped AMBER BANK FASHION SQUAD and posted it.

"You gonna follow me?" Kara asked.

Amber looked at her like she'd been asked if she was a leper. Billy burst in. "We are about to break for lunch, and we are behind schedule. I need a Fall Fabulous look right fucking now or I'm going to lose my shit."

"Calm down, kwaaaaan," Amber drawled. "Miss Bitch here is going to dress me right now, and we'll be out. I just want this shoot to end. We'll hurry. Can you get my hair magician? Bobo can fix my curls while Miss Bitch puts my new dress on." Billy disappeared.

Kara pulled a floor-length golden-silk sheath dress off a hanger.

"What about this?" she asked.

"Fuuuuck," sighed Amber. "If you're sure no bitch has died, puked, or flashed her cooch in it, I'll wear it."

Billy returned with Bobo, the trans Amazonian black hair stylist, who had a satchel overflowing with hairspray in one hand and a hair dryer in the other.

"Are we having a hair emergency?" the stylist vamped in a deep voice, flicking at a thick, shiny purple weave and pointing at Amber.

"No, I'm just trying to save time. I told you, Bobo, I have a gentleman coming by this evening so I need to get done on time."

Bobo turned and grimaced at the TV crew in the doorway.

"What are you doing that for?" asked Billy, suddenly alarmed as a TV camera pushed into his face.

"Bobo doesn't approve of my friends," sniffed Amber.

"Gurl, I like plenty of your friends," Bobo boomed. "I just don't know why you keep invitin' Paul Stroud around."

Kara and Billy exchanged bemused glances.

"Why, Bobo?" said Billy with a smirk. "What's wrong with Paul Stroud?"

"Oh, gurl," Bobo hooted. "Don't you know? That dude has gassed more innocent bitches than the state of Texas."

CHAPTER 13

BILLY SPENT TOO MUCH OF his alone time in the bar of the Montage. He could make two martinis and four sodas last several hours while he scoped out the celebrity interactions and made small talk with the makeup artists and stylists who made Hollywood go round. He almost always picked up at least one story to sell to a tabloid, and sometimes, he picked up one of the stylists, too.

Today's scene at the bar was typically Monday sleepy, rich, and Beverly Hills boring. The faces were all taut and even, the nose jobs all vaguely similar. Even though nobody there was famous, they all still wore sunglasses inside.

A ruggedly handsome burly guy walked into the bar and took a seat on a couch. Billy took a sip of his martini and sized the newbie up. He didn't fit in. He was dressed in total hipster cowboy. Jeans, T-shirt, and boots meant to look like a day on the range that Billy quickly identified as Rag & Bone, A.P.C., and Frye, respectively. His short sleeves revealed thick forearms dusted in thick blond hair. The bearded blondish guy was into some heavy texting. His eyes hadn't left his phone even while taking a seat. *Get your mind out of the gutter*, Billy reminded himself. *It's a workday.*

Billy finished his martini and decided to go talk to the interloper when he spied Gaynor coming out of the ladies' room on the other side of the lobby. She had on a floor-length chinchilla coat, her face framed by a tumble of blue-black curls resting on the soft fur.

She crossed the elevator lobby in four long strides and pushed a button. Billy watched intently as she stepped inside and selected her floor, trying to memorize the level of her finger when it hit the button.

As soon as the door closed, Billy left the bar and also called an elevator. When he got in, he tried to text Nic. No service. He tried to guess where Gaynor had gone.

This is Gaynor, he figured. *Penthouse only*. He pushed the six.

When he got there, the hallway on six was deserted; it had low golden lighting and a whispering mechanical hum. As he stepped out of the elevator, he heard someone rummaging in a purse down the corridor to his left.

Then he heard a door open, and some rustling. He moved quickly around the corner, hoping to see a door swing closed, but was greeted by an empty hallway. The door had closed already, but the hallway was only forty feet long, with just one door on each side. He cautiously crept down the hallway. Room 614 on the left, 615 on the right.

Billy pushed his ear up against the door of 614 and was greeted by silence. Moving across the hall, he cupped a hand up to the door of 615. He heard a woman's laugh, definitely not Gaynor's, but oddly familiar. He squinted as he tried to place it, and kept listening for any further sounds. None came.

He stood in the hallway, trying to decide what to do. There were no housekeepers on the floor at the moment. He had only a hundred bucks in his pocket, but that would be enough for bribes if one turned up.

It was 1:11 p.m. He still had time to sell a story to a tabloid for the Monday newsstand deadline if one landed in his lap. He returned to the bar and took a different seat, this one facing the elevator lobby, in case Gaynor chose to exit that way. The bearded guy was still there, just as engrossed in his phone. A beer now sat on the bar in front of him.

"A good time for another martini," Billy said to himself. He ordered his drink precisely, with a smile, and within minutes he was nursing a very dry gin martini with lemon twist and no olives.

The bar area was buzzing with low conversation, and Billy surreptitiously scanned the crowd for anything at all that could be sold as a story. It was a sea of old money and artifice but no star power. At the end of his scan, he happened upon the handsome stranger again, who was now staring right back at him.

Billy raised an eyebrow at the guy, who returned a short wave. *Focus, Billy, focus; no time for this right now.* It was okay to fuck like a whore on rent night, but not to be a whore when it actually was time to make rent.

He glanced at his phone. There was a text from an editor asking if he had any breaking news. It must be a slow week.

He was disturbed a few seconds later by a thickly accented voice beside him.

"Can I join ya, mate?" the stranger asked.

"Uh, sure, yeah, of course," Billy said with a laugh.

"I'm Donnie," the guy said, extending his hand. "What's your name?"

Billy stared into his green eyes, noted laugh lines extending out at the edges and a mop of golden-blond hair that was about three months past its haircut due date. Donnie's rusty beard was shot with a few gray hairs. Billy guessed the guy was probably pushing forty.

"So," said Donnie as he took his seat. "What brings a handsome man such as yourself to a boring place like this on a sunny Monday afternoon? You meeting somebody?"

"Not exactly," said Billy, trying to place the guy's accent. "I have some work to do and this was the most convenient place for a martini."

"A thirty-dollar martini," corrected Donnie. "I come here because it's quiet and they have Guinness on tap."

"Fifteen-dollar Guinness," Billy countered. Donnie smiled broadly.

"You got me there, mate," laughed Donnie.

"Let me guess," said Billy with a grin, "you're a New Zealander!"

Donnie's expression darkened. "Fuck you, mate, I'm an Aussie!"

"Same thing, right?" Donnie's sour visage told him it wasn't. "I've heard Australia is beautiful," Billy fumbled, trying to get the dark look off Donnie's face.

"Relax, mate, I'm just fuckin' with ya." Donnie took a sip of his dark beer. "And tell me if you want to drink your drink in peace and quiet and I'll leave you alone."

"Hey, no, this is fine." Billy was disarmed by the stranger's handsome face. "But I may have to bolt at any minute. Don't be offended if I do."

"Hmm," said Donnie pensively. "Drinking alone in a hotel bar, and may have to run suddenly."

"Yes, that's me."

"Intriguing. You don't look eager enough to be a hooker, you're not carrying a camera so you're not a tourist or a paparazzo, and you're not dressed right for actor or agent. I'm trying to figure out your story."

"I told you my story," Billy said.

"No, mate, you told me *a* story. I'm trying to figure out the truth."

"Are you always this borderline creepy annoying when you meet people?"

"I've been told that that's the case, yes." Donnie took another swig of his beer.

"It's off-putting," scolded Billy.

"Just making small talk, mate. I'll volunteer why I'm really here—I'm a gofer. I go for things. And this bar is the most central location I can find. So I just wait around here until I get called. There's a chance I'll have to vanish like smoke at any given second, too."

Bingo, thought Billy. *I've landed a live one.* "Who do you gofer for?" Billy asked, attempting to sound more blasé than he felt.

"Couple folks," Donnie said dismissively. "Gofers don't tend to talk much about their jobs. Comes with the territory."

"I get it," said Billy, dejected. "Is your boss upstairs?"

"I don't have a boss," Donnie said affably. "I work for meself. Which is how I'm allowed to drink Guinness in the early afternoon."

"Cheers to that." Billy raised his glass to the strange intrusion to his afternoon.

Donnie had just ordered them another round of drinks when Billy excused himself to the bathroom. As soon as Billy was out of sight, Donnie whipped out his phone and pushed a speed dial. He got voice mail. As usual.

"Seamus! It's me," he said. "I'm with that Bill guy at the Montage. Can't figure out what he's up to here. I think he's tailing someone, but he's cagey. He's a flirty little fucker, too. I'll keep on it. Text me with any guidance. Cheers, mate."

A few seconds after he hung up, he received a string of texts from Seamus.

Hey, Bluey, can't pick up right now. Text me. Has he mentioned Nicola?

Bluey shook his head. He'd never seen Seamus like this over a woman before. He'd pulled plenty of medical records in the past, and checked many more police records, but this time, Seamus had him checking out her friends, too.

It was a fucking minefield. Nicola lived with some girl who banged rappers, her best friend sold stories to the tabloids, and her boss was one of the most outrageous publicists in Hollywood. Red flags everywhere, and Seamus was refusing to see any of them.

Bluey had lifted Nicola's prints from his SUV while she and Seamus were out on the yacht. He discovered she'd been detained in a stolen car at sixteen. Her then-boyfriend took the rap for that one. Her most recent boyfriend was in jail for running meth, but they'd broken up and she'd left town before his trial. Bluey assumed that was why they'd broken up. In modern America, this amounted to no big deal.

Hasn't mentioned her. He's staking someone out.

That's worrying, Seamus texted back. **He could sell this whole thing to the weeklies. I know it's his job, but I need you to find out if he'd ever sell Nicola out.**

On it. He's playing it close to the chest.

Flirt back. Nothing wrong with that, right?

Nothing except the fact that he's a dumb kid lol.

Just make sure he's got Nicola's back.

On it, not literally! Gotta go he's back

Okay

Billy had barely taken his seat again when the elevator doors pulled open and Helen Powers stepped out, her million-dollar mane fanning out from the dark sunglasses hiding half her face.

Fuck, that's all it was, thought Billy. That was the laugh that he'd heard through the door of 615. Helen was Gaynor's client, so it made sense that Gaynor had gone to meet with her. Billy was crestfallen. It had been a generic client meeting. And Helen was using the public exit. Billy was bummed. He'd been hoping for a sale.

"Why the long face, mate?" joked the Australian. "You got a hard spot for old Helen, do you?"

"Huh?" said Billy, confused. "No, I'm gay, as if you couldn't tell."

"Well, so's she, so you're almost a perfect match."

"So the story goes," said Billy. "Nobody's ever been able to prove anything."

"That's due to the massive smoke screen that her team blows around her," Bluey said. "She and her superstar girlfriend wove quite a web in Hollywood when they reached the big-time. They each got the arranged marriage to other superstars, the film career, everything, and those marriages both lasted conveniently just under ten years. The women are still together."

"What are your sources?" asked Billy way too quickly.

"I knew you were a reporter," laughed Bluey. "Gotcha."

"I'm not a reporter," said Billy.

Bluey let it hang in the air uncomfortably.

"Okay, I am." Billy dropped his guard. He'd never see this guy again, and Donnie wasn't going to give him any dish anyway now that his secret was out.

"Who are you trailing?" Bluey asked.

"I'm not sure," Billy said honestly. "Something's up with a big-name publicist. It might turn out to be a big story, or it might turn out to be ammunition or collateral."

"Who do you work for?"

"I'm a free agent. I pitch to all the weeklies on Mondays and sell to the highest bidder."

"So you sell any big stories recently?"

"I'm trolling the Montage bar at lunchtime on a Monday. Does it look like I've sold any stories?"

"I don't know," said Bluey, looking at his watch. "Maybe you like to sell a fuck ton of stories, not just one."

"Nah, it's a really slow week," Billy said. "I haven't sold a thing. If I don't hear something soon, I'm gonna be living on finger food at events for the week."

"Well, I hope you hear something soon, mate." Bluey sipped his beer. "I'll need to push off in a little while. I'm not super interested in the whole celebrity thing. I mean, look at all the people working as actors on TV. How many of them are you going to be hearing about in six months? It's all bullshit."

"That's gloomy," said Billy. "And sadly accurate."

"Yeah, I don't really care too much for stars. Though I do like some eye candy. Like that Seamus guy, he's hot."

"He's dating my friend," quipped Billy.

"He's not gay," said Bluey.

"I have female friends," scoffed Billy. "Der."

"So is that going to be in your magazines?" Bluey probed.

"Hell, no," Billy said defiantly. "Friends are off-limits. That's her business, even if she's stupid for dating an actor. I mean, they're fun to fuck, but for God's sake, don't date them."

"Hear, hear!" As their glasses clinked, a riot of noise poured in from the front of the hotel doors. They looked up to see Max Zetta getting out of an armored SUV. The hotel security guards were scrambling to hold back the screaming paparazzi, their cameras sending blasts of silver light through the entire lobby.

"Fuck," exclaimed Billy, digging in his pocket and throwing two twenties on the bar.

"Nice talking to you, Donnie," he said, turning and rushing to the elevator lobby. As he called the elevator, he noticed that Donnie had followed him.

"What are you doing?" he asked exasperatedly as the elevator doors opened.

"Having some fun, mate."

They both stepped into the elevator.

Billy pushed the six and they ascended in awkward silence. They stepped out onto the hallway, and Billy walked rapidly to the far end, Donnie at his heels. He wanted to be able to pretend to be leaving when Max hopefully came to this floor. "Don't say anything," he hissed to his unwanted accomplice.

The elevator bell rang. As the doors opened, Billy suddenly grabbed Donnie and pushed him against the wall, kissing him. The Aussie played along and ran his hands theatrically up and down his back. Billy could hear footsteps approaching and then pause right by them.

"For fuck's sake," a familiar voice said disdainfully before stepping around them. "Get a room, you fags."

Continuing the kiss, Billy shifted slightly so he could stare after

Max as he walked to Room 615. He produced a key from his pocket and opened the door.

"Jesus," he heard a familiar Colombian accent say. "You kept me waiting. Now get your holy fucking ass in here. Get on your fucking knees and pray for forgiveness, my son. I'm not happy."

CHAPTER 14

KARA PUSHED HER WAY INTO the usual mayhem of Amber's kitchen. A salty old Guatemalan woman whose name badge read Concepcion barked orders in Spanish to the other housekeepers while smoking a cigarette and ineffectually blowing the smoke out the window above the sink.

Kara threaded her way through their midst, stepping over small dogs and freaky short-legged cats, all prowling in hope of a dropped morsel of the home-baked kale chips one woman was making.

A cadre of production assistants clustered at the bottom of the mirrored staircase that led up to the bedrooms.

"Hey, you guys, I'm Kara. I'm here to work on Amber's wardrobe. Do you know where she is?"

The PAs all looked at one another and laughed.

"What's so funny?" asked Kara. "She told me to be here at ten thirty."

"Poor you," scoffed a dreadlocked woman in a puffy vest. "They make us get here at seven, and Princess never rises before noon."

"You're kidding, right?" said Kara, alarmed. To her dismay, all of the PAs shook their head in a desultory group no.

"Well, fuck that, I'm gonna go wake her up."

The PAs sprang into electric-shock action, snatching up their coffees and rushing out of the room. The dreadlocked woman stayed behind, thrusting a sheaf of papers into Kara's face. "Did you sign these releases?" she barked.

"I ain't signing nothing," said Kara. "I'm just here to work on her wardrobe."

"Oh, wait—you were here Sunday. You already signed your releases then. We're good. We're gonna send a film crew up with you."

"I don't think so," said Kara with a tight smile. "I gave you guys that scene on Sunday because of the magazine. You're gonna have to ask Amber."

"Honey," purred the woman, twirling a dreadlock in her fingers, "Amber works for us. She does what we tell her. And if you're going up to try to wake her, we are going to film it."

"Well, you better be quick, sister!" Kara sprinted up the stairs.

Kara locked Amber's bedroom door behind her just as she heard the crew on the steps. The room glowed in dark pink light courtesy of the chiffon rose curtains that hung in the windows. Amber was sprawled nude across the top of her covers, looking like a sex doll dropped from a great height.

The air was warm and humid and smelled of perfume and ashtrays. A pink satin eye mask covered the top of Amber's face. Kara needed air. She moved to open a window and got a great view of Amber's vagina. *If I had a dollar*, she thought. Amber's legs were open impossibly wide, one bent back at an odd angle. She was snoring like a train.

The footsteps of the production crew stopped outside the door. Kara waited for them to knock but heard whispers instead.

She gripped Amber's shoulder and shook her lightly. "Psst," she whispered. "Amber? It's Kara. I'm here to do your wardrobe. Wake up."

The snoring didn't falter. Kara jostled her harder, and the snoring got louder. Amber sounded like Kara's grandpa. She shook her harder, and Amber's head lolled from side to side, her ropy platinum curls bobbing above her pink pillow. Her snoring oscillated into a whine. She sounded like an excited pug.

A staccato rap beat on the door.

"Kara, please open the door," a man's voice barked.

"Yep, be right there," Kara yelled, looking at Amber for any sign of consciousness.

"Kara, if you cost us this shot, you can say good-bye to ever working in reality TV again," the man threatened.

"I ain't working in it now, bitch!"

Kara angrily tore back the pink curtains. Sunlight washed over Amber's naked skin, but she didn't move. Kara lifted the sleep mask from her face. Amber's eyes were open, but her pupils were rolled up into her skull.

"Jesus Christ, she's overdosed," Kara whispered, her hands flying to her mouth. She grabbed a half-full glass of water on the bedside table and hurled it into Amber's face. Amber spastically came alive, flailing and pawing at her face.

"OH MY FUCKING CHRIST WHY DID YOU JUST THROW VODKA INTO MY EYES?"

Amber lurched out of her bed and bounced off her dresser into her private small bathroom. She twisted the cold faucet on and cupped her hands under the stream. Without hesitating, she started hurling handfuls of water into her eyes.

"I'm fucking blind," she sputtered angrily. "I can't even see who the fuck you are."

The pounding on the outer door got louder and louder.

"Kara, let us in right fucking now," the producer yelled.

"Kara?" asked Amber, pressing her face into a huge fluffy pink towel. "Who the fuck is Kara? Who the fuck is in my room? HELP! HELP!" Amber started screaming.

Kara backed away to the far corner of the room, in case Amber kept a gun in her bathroom.

"I'm Kara, you fucking idiot," she yelled. "You hired me to come fix your wardrobe. We met on Sunday."

Amber finished wiping her eyes and slowly lowered the towel. "Oh, hey, bitch," she said. "You nearly fucking blinded me."

Amber's eyes were all red and bleary. Her wet blond curls straggily stuck to her cheeks.

"What the hell is going on in there?" bellowed the producer.

"Go fuck yourself, bitches," Amber sulked at the door. "Hey, bitch, come help me clean up."

"Girl, you're naked, and wet. There's not much to clean up."

"You have a point," said Amber, walking slowly from the bathroom, waving her hands around as if they were divining rods. "If I was my vaporizer, where would I be?"

"I ain't your drug dog."

"Amber, what's your ETA?" the producer snapped through the door.

"Ten minutes, promise," she said in a baby-girl voice, flipping double birds at the door. "Be right out."

She spied her vaporizer pen and lurched for it, holding down the button with its neon-blue light, sucking on it like a baby piglet at the teat. She exhaled a pungent plume of steam. "That's better. Now sit on the toilet, bitch," she instructed Kara. "Talk to me while I shower to keep me company."

✳ ✳ ✳

An hour later, Amber was finally camera ready. She took her meetings with the producers as if nothing untoward had happened. Kara began her wardrobe purge in the first of two spare bedrooms that Amber had converted into closets. All four walls featured two racks of hanging clothes, one above the other. In the center of each room, a custom dresser was filled with lingerie, jewelry, accessories, and the occasional forgotten bullet of coke.

Poring over the racks of clothes, mostly unworn and still tagged, Kara exhaled loudly. At least two million dollars' worth of clothing hung unused in that room. The hanging rails were packed so tightly that it was almost impossible to remove a single item. Kara thought back to the tiny bedroom that she had shared with her stepsister, Olive, and how when they'd hit puberty they'd prayed to be the same size so they could share all the clothes in their tiny dresser. She wrestled a bunch of dresses from one of the racks so she could start working. She laid the stack on top of the dresser, and nearly fainted from sticker shock.

The top dress still had a $22,000 tag from the Gucci store. Amber had paid for this one. She picked up the pearl-strapped black mini-dress and held it up to herself. She walked over to the mirror and posed with the dress in front of her. It was fucking exquisite.

"You like it that much, huh?" Amber asked from the doorway. "Fine, it's yours."

Kara jumped and threw the dress back onto the counter.

"I, uh, no, I just started, this is a huge job."

Amber laughed, picking up the Gucci from the dresser and handing it back to her.

"Girl, I don't even remember buying this, so I'm hardly going to miss it. Keep it."

Kara put the dress to the side of the pile. She'd ask Amber if she was serious later. Maybe.

"I forgot what your job was," Amber slurred.

"I haven't started yet . . . bitch," Kara answered, not taking her literally. "You were gone all of ten minutes. I'm still figuring out my plan of attack."

"What are you going to attack?" Amber asked, clearly confused.

Kara realized that Amber really had no memory of hiring her.

"I meant, I am still figuring out how I'm going to clean this shit out of here. I think I'm going to start on the clothes you've already worn too many times, and we'll sell those and split the profits. Then we can go through the stuff you've never worn. Some of it is dated."

"I knoooow," whined Amber, her memory jogged. "But if I keep it a few more years, I'll have the best collection of vintage in Hollywood and all the hungry tigers will be so fuckin' jealous."

"Right," said Kara patronizingly. "Riiiiight. So, do you want to donate it or sell it on eBay?"

"I don't even know what you're talking about," Amber sniffed. "I figured we'd just put it in the trash. I don't want no fucking starlets turning up in my dresses because they got 'em for twenty bucks at Out of the Closet."

"Well, that's not what I meant," said Kara patiently. "We can either sell them and give the money to charity, which is good press for you, or we can donate them to a women's charity, or something like that."

"I also don't want a bunch of battered bitches shopping at Walmart in my clothes. Are you retarded?"

Kara nearly walked out. She took five deep breaths. "Amber Bank, you're the most offensive troll I've ever met," she said with slow deliberation. "Is this the real you, or are you playing me? Because I've never met a more appalling person than you right now."

Amber slumped against the door. "I'm sorry. You're right. I should leave this bitch in front of the cameras. I don't give a fuck what you do with the dresses. I just don't want to look bad in photos. I know that's shallow. I know I sound like the worst person ever. It's just . . . I just . . ."

"You just what?"

"Well, I need you to do something else today."

"I thought you were going to show me the real you."

"I will, I promise, I'll be myself. If you do this one thing for me."

"That's not how it works, Amber," Kara said firmly. Amber was worse than a five-year-old.

"Oh my God, I fucking know how it works." Amber was suddenly angry. "Here's what I need you to do. I have to go do the *Ellen* show this afternoon. I hate doing that show. So I need you to come with me. And I need to ask you an even bigger favor."

"Bigger than going to a TV taping with you? I dunno . . . ," Kara joked.

"I'm serious, bitch," Amber snapped. "I want you to be my coke sponsor."

"Yeah, no, mama, I don't want that job," said Kara brusquely. "I'm here to sort out your damn clothes, not to be your fucking sober coach."

"Please," wheedled Amber. "I don't even know why I do it all the time. I'm ADD. It doesn't even do anything, but I just keep doing it." Amber stood there silently, shaking her head. "What? I just opened my fucking heart to you and that's all you can do? Judge me?"

"Oh girl," Kara said drily, "if I was judging you, your white ass would know it."

Amber took this as a positive response.

"So you'll do it?" Amber grinned broadly. "Great."

✳ ✳ ✳

Kara hated herself for being bullied into the limo as it headed over Laurel Canyon toward the Valley. At each bend of the serpentine climb, Amber complained about carsickness. Kara sat facing backward, feeling just as nauseated.

"This is when I start freaking, this is when I start wanting the coke," Amber said suddenly.

"I'm just going to say this over and over, in my role as your coke sponsor," Kara said. "It doesn't do anything for you."

"It makes me feel like I'm confident; it makes me feel like I'm interesting."

"I thought you said it doesn't do anything for you because of your ADD?"

"Right, and I have my Adderall so I'm good there, but there's just something about it, if I snort a line, I don't feel any different but I think it gives me confidence," Amber said, with no affectation to her voice. She sounded like a scared kid.

"You're the guest, they want you there, and you're always on that fucking show," said Kara. "If you sucked, they wouldn't have you back."

"I've never done the show without coke. But I can't risk it; I got pulled over with some a while back and I passed it off, but if I get caught again, I'm going to jail."

"I recall," said Kara. "Amber, look me in the eye. Are you carrying right now?"

Amber nodded slowly.

"Hand it over," Kara said deliberately.

Amber pulled her huge Birkin onto her lap and began rummaging around in its depths. She produced a pink plastic bullet full of coke and showed it to Kara, who snatched it from her hand, lowered the window, and tossed the bullet out onto Laurel Canyon.

"What the actual fuck did you just do?" snapped Amber.

"Give me the rest," said Kara evenly. "Either give me all of it, or hand me your purse."

Amber's shoulders slumped. She dramatically threw her fourteen-thousand-dollar purse onto the floor of the limo at Kara's feet. As Kara reached for it, Amber snatched her phone from its depths and unlocked it. Kara suppressed a laugh. Of course her code was 1234. Amber busied herself with checking her Google alerts and ignored Kara.

For the next ten minutes, as they climbed higher and higher up the winding road in its perpetual traffic, Kara rummaged through a mountain of makeup, pot wax, vaporizers, joints, papers, phone chargers, old phones, and dog collars, producing six one-gram baggies of coke in various stages of consumption.

"Is this everything?" she said eventually.

"Like I fucking know," Amber said angrily. "Maybe. Probably. Don't hold me to it."

"It better be," said Kara, tossing the baggies out the window. "Is that what a coke sponsor does?"

"I don't know, I guess," said Amber openly. "All the other ones just told me not to do it. That didn't work, so I guess you're onto something."

When they reached the security gates at the soundstage, Amber freaked out for real.

"I can't do this," she said. "Can you call and cancel?"

"It's a live taping, Amber," said Kara. "You can't let Ellen down. You can do this. You don't need the coke. It's just a Dumbo feather—you don't need it."

"Oh, the flying elephant?" she asked. "You mean he didn't need that feather to fly?"

Kara rolled her eyes. "Did you even see the movie? He had those big ears all along."

"I fell asleep, I forget." Amber fished a vaporizer out of her purse. She started puffing it like a cigar, filling the limo with wisps of sweet ether.

"Easy, tiger," Kara said. "We're getting close; you need to be on fire for Ellen."

Christ, it's like a hotbox in here, she thought, opening the window and seeing a visible cloud of pot vapor rise out into the smoggy afternoon air.

"It's fine," Amber slurred, "I can handle my pot, see?" She took another huge hit, and the car rolled into the security lane.

A half an hour later they were sitting in their backstage greenroom. Nobody had bothered them since a PA had dropped them off. Amber was passed out across a love seat, her head thrown back, her mouth wide open. She was snoring like a train.

Kara took a photo and sent it to Billy and Nic. Billy responded immediately.

I could probably sell that for you. It'd be worth $25 to the Cleveland Plain Dealer.

Really? Kara responded.

Nah j/k

Kara opened her Snapchat. She looked around for a suitable background, but the room was budget-hotel bland, plus orchids. She briefly considered including Amber in the footage she wanted to shoot, but decided against it. She looked at her followers list, and noticed that Amber still hadn't accepted her request.

She grabbed Amber's phone from the top of the Birkin and unlocked it. She opened Amber's Snapchat and accepted herself as a friend. Then she did the same on Amber's Instagram and Kik. Amber had told her she didn't have Facebook, but the app was on her phone. Kara opened it and learned that Amber's Facebook pseudonym was Princess Queen Tiger, with a matching profile photo of a tiger wearing a tiara. She sent herself a friend request, accepted it on her own phone with her other hand, then switched Amber's phone off and dropped it back into her purse.

A harried-looking woman with a headset and a clipboard came into the room and introduced herself as Kate, the pre-interviewer. She took one look at Amber asleep on the huge leather couch.

"And she's high again," she observed, resignation in her voice.

"Yep," Kara said bluntly. "She's out."

The pre-interviewer, a woman in her early forties with a short shag haircut and a striped shirt under a puffy vest, shook her head. "Great. Fucking great," she muttered. "What the fuck am I supposed to have her talk about on air? Wait—will she be fine to do this?"

"Search me," said Kara. "I'll wake her up, but I figure it's best to let her sleep for a bit longer."

"She needs to be in hair and makeup in twenty minutes."

"Okay, I'll wake her in ten."

"Who are you, anyway?"

"I'm her friend; I work for her. I'm redoing her wardrobe."

"Are you on the show?"

"Yeah, I guess," Kara lied. "I just started shooting."

"Okay, good."

Kara looked at her quizzically. The woman picked a walkie-talkie from her belt and spoke into it. "Kate for Bob. Kate for Bob."

"This is Bob," the walkie crackled.

"We've got a greenroom situation. Bank is high and passed out, but we have her newest cast member here with her. I say we do a duo interview."

Kara stood suddenly, shaking her head and waving her hands. "No fucking way," she said.

Kate clicked off her walkie. "Come on, it'll be easy."

"No, this isn't going to happen," Kara said urgently. She shook Amber awake. As her eyelids parted, Kara was in her face.

"Bitch, wake your shit up right fucking now," she yelled. "You need to get on this show or they're going to make me go on with you. We both know that ain't gonna happen."

"That's a great idea," Amber mumbled, her eyes closing again. "We can be like BFFs and we can be all funny and shit, I'm down." She fell back on the couch.

Kate picked up her walkie. "This is Kate for makeup. We'll have two for the Amber segment. I'll bring them up in ten minutes."

Kara was suddenly glad she'd shoved the Gucci dress in her purse.

CHAPTER 15

LATER THAT NIGHT, AND NOT terribly far away, Nicola was blessing her GPS for its skillful navigation of the landmark-free dead zone of the San Fernando Valley. At the GPS's behest, she turned left and right, past an endless stream of liquor stores, check-cashing places, and empty restaurants.

She had no idea where she was, geographically or emotionally. It was time for the second date.

The GPS told her that four more nondescript blocks would scroll past her before she reached her appointed destination. The Valley confused her, with its vastness and lack of anything you actually wanted to look at. She blew a kiss to her phone. Without its guidance, they'd find her corpse by a freeway on-ramp being devoured by crows.

She took a quick look at her eyes in her rearview mirror, lit by bursts of headlights and flashing neon. She had deliberately done very little to her appearance. Seamus had promised her this was to be a low-key dinner date. No need to dress up. She'd been relieved to pull on her favorite Jordache jeans and her red Converse Chucks. Nicola had topped it all off with a hoodie, but then Kara vetoed it. "You've jumped from second date to married ten years," she had scolded. Its replacement—a slate-gray cashmere Theory sweater with a deep V-neck—was jumbled on the passenger seat. It was still 85 degrees at 7:55 p.m. She didn't even know why Kara had made her bring it. Thank God she had worn a silk tank underneath.

She slowed down midway along a dim block of Woodman. Bluey had warned her that the restaurant sign was small and easy to miss. The GPS lady was telling her she'd reached her destination, so she just parked and got out.

Checking her phone for the street number, she approached a black storefront. She spied a tiny Itokin Valley Sushi sign, the size of an envelope. Despite the closed sign on the door, it wasn't locked. She pulled it open and stepped into the saddest restaurant she'd ever been in.

White plastic chairs surrounded tables covered in red-and-white dropcloths. A gray-haired Japanese sushi chef appeared behind the bar, and bowed.

"*Arigato gozaimasu,*" he said cheerily. An older Japanese woman emerged from a curtained doorway beside the sushi bar.

"Good evening, Miss Wallace," she said. "It's lovely to meet you. My name is Yumiko. I'll be serving you tonight."

"Hi, Yumiko," smiled Nicola, copying her bow. "Nice to meet you, too."

"May I have your car keys, please?" Yumiko asked. Surprised, Nicola handed her keys to Yumiko, who slipped them into a pocket of her kimono.

"Follow me, please." Yumiko bowed again. She turned and walked down the curtained walkway, to a screen door with paper insets. Yumiko slid the door into a recess in the wall. Seamus was sitting at a low table in the middle of an incongruously sumptuous room, decorated with stark red, white, and black wall hangings.

"Hey, Dayton." Seamus beamed. "Glad you could make it."

"I'll be back with your first courses in a short while. Please call with the bell if you need anything," said Yumiko, bowing and exiting the room backward.

"Thanks, Yumiko," said Seamus, clumsily bowing and standing at the same time. As the door clicked closed behind them, Seamus put his hands on his hips and looked Nicola up and down.

"Get over here," he said huskily.

Nicola stepped forward, and he wrapped his arms around her and pushed his thick, soft lips against hers, lingering for a second before breaking the kiss.

Nicola muttered, "fuck that," and pulled him to her again, inhaling deeply. He smelled so good to her, no cologne, just the warm musk of his skin, just as she remembered from the yacht. It was driving her crazy.

Seamus chuckled as they kissed, and grabbed playfully at her ass. She responded by cupping his ass with one hand and rubbing the other hand up and down the side of his hips.

She broke the kiss.

"What are you laughing at?" she said accusingly, her brows knitting slightly.

"I'm not laughing at anything! I'm laughing because I'm happy. I wanted to do that, too, but I was being polite."

"Fuck being polite," Nicola said, squeezing his ass. "If I'm going to drive to the Valley, you're going to make it worth my while."

"And I plan to, my love, I plan to," Seamus said in a corny old-timer voice. "Can I interest you in some sake?"

"Hmm," said Nicola slowly. "You could interest me in some beer. Sake tastes like nail polish."

Seamus looked disarmed, as if he should have known this already. He rang the bell. Yumiko slid the door open almost immediately.

"Two large Sapporos, Yumiko, *arigato*," he said.

"My pleasure," Yumiko said, closing the door quickly, locking it again.

"Sit, please," Seamus said, motioning to the low table.

Unsure as to whether to sit opposite him or next to him, Nicola stumbled on a cushion. Seamus caught her arm and pulled her to him. "One more for luck," he said, and they kissed again.

Nicola pulled Seamus's top lip in between her teeth and bit down slightly. He groaned into her mouth, that same deep wolf growl he'd done on the yacht. He pressed his crotch against her lower stomach and she could feel that he was getting hard. She ended the kiss, moved carefully backward, and took her seat on a huge red satin cushion.

The bell rang, and Yumiko appeared with their beers.

"This dinner is going to be torture," Nicola said with a smile after the door closed again.

"Yes, it is." Seamus sat opposite her. "Thankfully this is the best sushi in Los Angeles, so you won't mind waiting."

I dunno, thought Nicola to herself. After they'd gotten out of the crate inside the truck on Saturday, she'd been so flustered by the turn of events that she had just wanted to go home. But after Bluey dropped her back at her apartment, she'd been relentlessly horny. She'd masturbated in the shower as she washed off the sunblock. A short, powerful orgasm had come rocketing out of nowhere almost as soon as she held the shower head between her legs, and later in bed, she got off again, remembering Seamus's fingers trailing her bikini line in that ocean cave. Part of her regretted not taking it further, and another part of her was happy to have waited. But she knew that tonight was not going to end that way.

"What's the deal with this place, then?" she asked. "Best sushi in LA and completely empty on a Monday night?"

"They're always closed to the public on Monday night," Seamus explained, sipping his beer. "They open up to certain customers, for private dinners like this, if they are asked, politely."

"Aha, so this is where you bring all your dates?"

"No, love, this is normally where I bring all my *mates*; we take over the front room and we can talk as loud as we want, we can talk about whatever the fook we want, and there's no chance that someone at the next table will sell the conversation to the tabloids. There are places like this all over LA. They're mainly in the Valley these days, but there are new places popping up in downtown and the east side, you know, as restaurant owners start to learn that working this way is much more lucrative than selling a story to a tabloid once a year."

Nicola desperately wanted to ask Seamus how much he paid to have the restaurant open for him, but thought it would be gauche. Gaynor had taught her all about gauche.

"So on a regular night, is this place packed?" she asked instead.

"Yep," Seamus said, cracking open an edamame pod and offering it to her. "There's a line down the street. You'll see. Mizuro-san is the master. I've never had sushi like it."

"Why did I have to give my keys to Yumiko?"

"Bluey moved your car so that nobody can plate you. We think this place is still safe, but after Saturday, we just can't be too careful."

"Being famous sure makes things complicated."

"I like you, Nicola. If you get ID'd by a magazine, your world will be turned upside down, and we'll be finished. You'll walk. It's not fun. It's just a measure of respect, you know. I just want this to be as normal as possible, under the circumstances."

"Under the circumstances," she repeated. "Well, you're off to a good start. This is almost like a normal date, I guess." Yeah, if a normal date involved one of the biggest stars in the world buying out LA's most exclusive sushi restaurant for the night.

"I do want to apologize for how Saturday ended," Seamus began, clearly nervous all of a sudden. Nicola was taken aback. She cocked her head and smiled at him.

"You don't have to apologize," she said seriously. "First dates, for me, are always historically awful. At least yours was just weird at the end. It was pretty great for the most part."

"You're kind," Seamus said earnestly. "Well, if you won't let me apologize for screwing up the date, please at least let me thank you for putting up with all this ridiculous bullshit. Believe me, I wish it were easier." He picked up a chopstick and slowly twirled it in his fingers. "I wish we could just go down to the pub and have a couple beers and share a few yarns. . . . I mean, you know, just shoot the shit."

"It's not that big of a deal," said Nicola.

"That's what you say now," he said, and then stopped.

"That was a half sentence," Nicola said.

"Aye, it was, it was," said Seamus, breaking eye contact and looking at the table. "I don't want to get ahead of meself here.

"Is there anything that you're not a fan of, sushi-wise?" he asked, switching topics.

Nicola thought for a second. "Uni, I guess," she said. Then she flashed back to her lunch with Gaynor's kids. "I'd also prefer it if all the food was already dead when it reached our table."

"So you've been to Kazu, then, eh?" Seamus laughed, before ringing the bell to signal to Yumiko that it was time to start bringing their food.

✳ ✳ ✳

They exited through the back door into a small parking lot, where Seamus's black Lexus SUV was parked. The night chill had finally arrived. Seamus pulled the unlocked passenger door open and helped Nicola up into her seat.

"If you're cold, your sweater is on the backseat."

Nicola turned, and sure enough, her gray V-neck was folded neatly in the dim light. That Bluey was good at his job.

Seamus leapt nimbly into the driver's seat.

"So where to now?" she asked.

"Well, it depends on what you want to do next," he said playfully.

"Seamus," Nicola said very seriously. "I'm tired. I think it's time for you to take me home, or to my car. . . ."

His face fell. "Okay, uh, sure!" He failed to hide his disappointment.

"Ha!" she laughed. "Just fuckin' with you. Sorry. Let's go to your place. I really think it's time for this flirting bullshit to pay off one way or the other."

Seamus laughed a huge belly laugh.

"You cheeky monkey," he roared. "I got another suggestion, since once again, a normal idea like going to my actual house isn't an option."

He sped out through an alley and turned back onto Woodman, which managed to get even more depressing as they drove. Slowing outside a decrepit single-story hotel, Seamus declared, "Here we are."

An incomplete neon sign announced that it was the BURBANK MOT R INN. Lit by the fuzzy blue light of a kidney-shaped pool in the corner of the parking lot, it looked like somewhere to bring a hooker, not a date.

"My mother always told me to never go to the Bates Motel with suspicious movie stars," joked Nicola.

"Your mother was right," Seamus laughed.

"Mothers always are." Her laugh cut off as Seamus guided the SUV down the alley behind the building.

"Uh, Seamus . . . ?" Nicola said tentatively, noticing her Tercel was already in the parking lot.

"Trust me," he said, pulling up to a single door in the back of a long wall that was tagged with overlapping, derivative graffiti. He stopped the car so that Nicola's door was lined up with a door in the wall.

"You're kidding, right?" Nicola asked uncertainly. "Like, if I Yelp this place, right now, the first thing I'm going to read is a bedbugs advisory."

"Appearances can be deceiving, m'dear," Seamus replied, putting the car into park and getting out. He opened her door and gave her his hand. Helping her down to the street, he put his arm around her and opened the motel's back door.

Nicola stepped into an elegantly appointed room. Polished cement floors gleamed under the glow of an array of Jonathan Adler lamps, all set to low dimmer. A Cali king bed covered in white linen dominated the room. It was scattered with rose petals. Candles burned on low mid-century tables, their scent subtle and masculine.

"What the hell?" Nicola spun in the center of the room.

"Did you really think I'd bring you to a fleapit?" Seamus chided softly, placing his hands on her hips and gently nudging her toward the bed.

He turned her around and loosely wrapped his arms around her waist, letting his hands fall onto the top of her ass. He gazed down into her eyes and softly kissed her lips.

"Were the rose petals too much?" he asked with a half grin.

"Little bit," Nicola replied. "But the candles smell so good, I can forgive you."

She stood on her toes and kissed him again. She felt his hands lift her shirt, and suddenly his warm, callused palms were rubbing her stomach, and then they roamed around to her back. He unhooked her bra deftly, kissing her deeper and deeper all the while.

Suddenly, Nicola heard the SUV engine roar from the other side of the wall, and then drive off. Panicked, she broke the kiss.

"Your car," she gasped. "It's being stolen . . . oh wait . . ." She slumped against him. "It's Bluey, right?"

"You're learning," he said, taking her by the hand and leading her to a low table in the middle of the room, where a bottle of Cristal was resting in a silver ice bucket. He popped it open and poured them each a glass of champagne.

"This is another one of these secret hookup places for celebs, isn't it?" she asked. He nodded and half-smiled.

Raising his glass, he met her eyes.

"To finally meeting a real girl," he said, his green eyes boring into hers, flickers of gold from the candles dancing around his pupils.

Jesus Christ, he's fucking handsome, Nicola thought. She took a huge gulp of her champagne and ran her fingers behind his belt buckle. She led him over to the bed and undid his belt, and then his pants.

"Hey, what about kissing me?" Seamus pleaded.

"You're such a girl," Nicola said, kneeling down. She tugged his jeans down to his knees and could see that his hard-on was already tenting his simple white boxers. She reached up and grabbed it through the fabric, and Seamus made that same guttural groan he'd made earlier when they kissed. It rumbled Nicola again. She slowly pulled his boxers down. His cock sprang free, and Nicola leaned forward and grabbed it with her hand. She made eye contact with Seamus.

"Oh my fookin' God," he whispered as she slid her mouth down on him, and slowly, they moved together as he sat down onto the bed and lay back.

"Bloody hell," Seamus moaned as she worked him over. "Bloody hell."

It became a mantra. The harder Nicola worked, the more Seamus moaned "Bloody hell" over and over. As she felt him start to tense up, Seamus reached down and cupped her face.

"Get up here and kiss me," he said. Nicola stood and surveyed him, lying back on the bed, his shirt pushed up, his pants around his knees, and his erection throbbing against a nest of curly hair.

"Nice," she said with a comical nod of her head.

"Take your shirt off," he instructed.

"What about my bra?" she asked. "You only got halfway with that."

"You do the top, I'll tackle the bra and jeans."

Nicola pulled her shirt over her head in one swoop. She shook her head to get the hair out of her face, and her bra, unfastened at the back, slipped off one shoulder and then the other. Seamus sat up and leaned toward her.

"Wait—I have to get my shoes off," she said, bending down and undoing her Chucks, pulling the laces loose through the eyeholes.

"Watching a woman unlace trainers should not be this hot," he gasped. "Look what you're doing to me."

Nicola shucked off her shoes and stood up to see Seamus pointing at his hard-on. Why were men always so damn proud of their boners? He pulled his shirt over his head and pushed his pants down with one foot, and then the other. He'd already kicked off his shoes. Wearing nothing but white socks, he stepped toward her and reached for her breasts, cupping them in his rough hands. His thumbs lightly brushed her nipples and he kissed her, deeply. She felt her knees go wobbly and she leaned into him. One of his hands slowly traced a line down to her stomach. She expected him to unbutton her jeans, but instead, he slipped his fingers down inside her underwear, where they stopped as soon as they touched her pubic hair.

"What?" she said into his mouth.

"You've got pubes," he said, into hers. "I fookin' love pubes, and nobody in LA has 'em."

"I'm a woman," Nicola said, grabbing his cock. "I don't need to look like a little girl."

With that, Seamus plunged his hand down and began playing with her. Nicola moaned deeply as Seamus started to kiss her rhythmically, moving his hand in unison with his tongue, working her over top and bottom. *This can go on all night*, Nicola thought. *All fucking night*.

Seamus slowly laid her onto the bed, then grabbed the ankles of her jeans and yanked them off. He began rubbing himself against her and she forced her eyes to stay open, to not break his gaze.

"What's this? We're playing Just the Tip?" she joked. He laughed out loud.

"I love that game," he whispered, pushing the head of his cock just inside her. "Everyone's a winner."

Nicola lifted her hips, feeling him slide farther into her.

"Not yet, lassie," Seamus said breathlessly. "I gotta . . . I just gotta . . ."

He dropped suddenly to his knees and buried his face deep into Nicola's crotch. He began to eat her with alternating softness and ferocity. One minute, he would gently be licking at her inner thigh, breathing deeply onto her, the next he'd be plunging his tongue deep, his hands caressing her legs and her body. It was overload, and Nicola felt waves of warmth start breaking all over her.

"You're sweet, of course you're sweet," Seamus groaned from between her legs, pushing his face hard against her. After a hazy eternity, just as Nicola could feel her orgasm building deep inside her stomach, he stood up and reached for the nightstand. He ripped a condom open with his teeth and slid it on.

Staring into her eyes, he bent forward and started to kiss her. With each kiss, she felt him slide farther inside her. She clenched her muscles around him, and he groaned. She felt his balls finally hit her ass, and they began to rock together, very slowly. He began thrusting, short, slow thrusts, his furred belly rubbing against her smooth one. She locked her legs behind his back and drew him tightly to her, taking over.

She mirrored his short thrusts with her own tightly controlled bucking. "Bloody hell," he began again. Propping himself on one arm, he watched himself slide in and out of her. His eyes rolled back in his head, and then back to hers.

"You have no fucking clue," he whispered. Nicola smiled at him. *Really?* Her view wasn't too bad, either, as sweat started to bead on Seamus's bouncy dark curls and his green eyes glowed in the candlelight.

✳ ✳ ✳

After they were done, the second time, Nicola excused herself and went to the bathroom, pulling her phone from her jeans pocket as she went. As she closed the door, she leaned back against it and read her texts. Billy was looking for her, and Kara was with J.

The drought is broken, she texted Billy.

Mama just got done right, she texted Kara.

She turned on the sink faucet to cover the sound of her peeing, and hoped that at least one of her friends would respond. Neither of them did. She flushed and washed her hands, then headed back into the motel room.

As she stepped through the doorway, she caught Seamus stuffing his phone back into his jeans pocket.

"We both did some texting, huh?" He rolled onto his back and put one arm behind his head. She couldn't stop staring at his thick legs and his defined chest. He had told her he was working out for a movie. If that was the case, all men should work out for movies.

"I'm sorry, love, but I have got to eat you again; get up here now," he said as Nicola walked toward the bed. He lay back and she got on all fours and crawled up his length, until his face was below her crotch. As she lowered herself onto his face and sat upright, he grabbed her ass to help her rock back and forth, and he watched her eyes close in ecstasy.

✳ ✳ ✳

At the end of the alley outside their room, Bluey sat in the SUV, a Trenta Starbucks red-eye in one hand, and a small pair of high-powered binoculars in the other. Movement at the other end of the alley caught his eye. A man with a backpack was looking into the darkness of the alley, then over his shoulder. Up and down, up and down. Bluey set the coffee into the cup holder and put the binoculars up to his face. With his other hand, he opened the glove compartment and took out a small pistol. He switched the binoculars to night vision and squinted to focus better on the face that sprang into detail.

He didn't recognize the intruder as any known paparazzo or reporter. The guy walked into the darkness of the alley, and after several more furtive glimpses over his shoulder, he undid his fly and started pissing against the building. Bluey relaxed, putting the safety back on the pistol. As the guy finished and shook off the last drops, Bluey put the gun back in the glove compartment and picked up his coffee, taking a huge swig. It was only 11:11, and it was going to be a long night.

CHAPTER 16

DOWNTOWN LA WAS ITS DESERTED, grandiose self. Billy paid a homeless guy wrapped in an LA Kings blanket five dollars to "watch his car" and hustled along Broadway toward the party. He pulled out his phone. It was 11:15 p.m. and Nic had finally responded to his pleas for company. She was with Seamus. He'd be hitting the party alone.

The intersection at Broadway and Seventh was a ghost town, and Billy started seeing imaginary zombies hiding in doorways and heard voices in the rustle of the falling leaves. Downtown LA was good practice for the zombie apocalypse. After surviving the bullying that comes with being obviously gay at a young age in Dayton, Ohio, Billy knew the zombies would be a cinch. As long as he had Nicola at his side, just like she'd been since second grade.

He took his phone out of his pocket again and sent one last text, a group message to Nicola and Kara.

OK, bitches, in case you get done shagging I'm putting both your names on the list, this is gonna be a big one. Come! Free phone!

Waves of camera flashes bounced up Broadway. Fuck, there was a red carpet in front of a step and repeat backdrop for the latest Samsung Galaxy phone. He hoped there'd be a side entrance. He zipped his YSL black leather jacket up and tugged on the waist of his Topshop black jeans, pausing to nervously rub the top of each of his tan Zara boots against the back of his leg. He walked up.

The throng of photographers waiting at the red carpet all turned to check him out at once. The disappointed looks on their faces when they realized he was nobody depressed Billy.

Drawing closer, he saw a mob scene around the check-in desk. He threaded his way lithely through it and waved at his friend Solstice behind the desk. She jumped up and reached through the throng and pulled Billy the remaining few feet to check in.

"Baby doll," she squealed. "Thank God, you're here."

"Sweetheart," Billy replied, kissing the back of her hand.

"My fucking feet are killing me," Solstice hissed into his ear. "We're almost at capacity and the fucking fire marshal is circling like a fucking buzzard. Get your ass inside immediately before they shut the carpet down."

Billy groaned in sympathy. "Hey—you have Nicola Wallace and Kara Jones on the list, right?"

"Yeah, baby, but the list won't matter if that fucking fire marshal can't be paid off, so tell them to hurry." She handed him a bright pink wristband to put on. "And don't worry, I'll send all three of you a phone tomorrow."

"Okay, thanks." Billy smiled, squeezing her hand. "Solstice, you're the best. Can I sneak in or do I have to suffer the carpet?"

Solstice winked at him, and snapped her fingers at an enormous security guard at her side. He waved Billy back into the side door. Billy turned to blow a kiss, but Solstice had resumed her battle with the frothing sea of desperate hopefuls who, even though they were on the list, were just not A-list enough to risk a fire marshal–mandated party shutdown.

Billy slipped through the doorway and quickly attached the wristband to his wrist. There was another security guard watching the elevator, and one blocking the staircase.

"What's better, guys?"

"Take the stairs," said one of the guards. "People keep stopping the elevator so they can do blow in private."

Billy gave a knowing look to the guards and turned to the staircase.

After five long flights of hard marble stairs, he heard the elevator ding, and one of the guards chuckled and the word "sucka" floated up the stairwell.

Billy emerged into a smoky lobby. An intern in a borrowed dress nodded at his wrist and another behemoth security guy stepped aside to let him into the party. Billy could see the place was truly brimming with people, and for once, it was packed with stars, not wannabes.

Of course it was packed: it was a smartphone launch party. So what if it was Monday night? All the stars would receive a phone for attending. A thousand-dollar phone. Actors would do circus tricks for free shit. *Fucking disgusting.* Billy made a note to call Solstice tomorrow to thank her and make sure she remembered to send that phone.

The party was like the MTV Movie Awards. Rock stars and rappers mingled with movie stars while agents and publicists hovered nervously around their charges, their faces blank with bored responsibility. They were all strangers. Billy took a deep breath and snagged a drink from the tray of a woman in a bikini and a space helmet, and headed out onto the roof deck.

A wall of cigarette smoke and perfume washed over him as he made his way to the parapet of the building. Turning his back on the madness, he looked down at LA sprawling below him to the south. *Los Angeles, you're a dirty old whore, but you come alive at night*, he mused. Taking out his phone, he did a series of selfies with the dirty old whore as the backdrop.

Putting his phone away, he was surprised to see Ethan Carpenter being dragged off by a man in an impeccably tailored, impossibly bland black suit. Just before they were swallowed by the crowd, Ethan spotted Billy and held his phone up to his ear and mouthed "call me."

The guy who was dragging him swiped Ethan's hand down, and turned to shoot Billy a filthy look. It was Jon Weatherman, the gay agent with a reputation for his hot temper, and the notorious lengths he'd go to in order to keep his clients closeted and working.

Weatherman held fast to the old-school logic that the public still wasn't able to buy an out, gay actor as anything else, and he notoriously told his closeted clients to save the coming-out party for their syndicated TV days.

Fuck those two. Billy sipped his drink angrily. It tasted like bathroom cleaner, a foul concoction of vodka and the energy drink that was the cosponsor of the party. He felt his phone vibrate and he pulled it out eagerly, but his face fell when he read Kara's text.

Sorry gurl, me and my fiance are getting busy.

Billy grimaced as he polished off his drink in one huge gulp and swiped another from a passing bikini astronaut. A woman's voice rose angrily to his left and the crowd parted. Controversial teen star Kiri Anderson was losing her shit at her long-suffering boyfriend, Joe Peralta, a former nobody whose career had suddenly skyrocketed due to two things—a fluke role in a surprise blockbuster, and some artful plastic surgery that elevated his bland face to leading-man material.

"You are a fucking slut," Kiri bellowed, trying to swat a tiny fist at Joe. "Who haven't you stuck it in? Have you fucked this whole party?"

"Calm down, baby, let's go get some air," Joe said, smiling to the onlookers as if nothing was wrong, even though he was gripping Kiri's wrists tightly in his hands.

Billy grabbed his phone and started videoing, keeping it close to his chest like he was texting so he wouldn't get caught.

He pushed closer for better footage, and the crowd surged forward as everyone tried to see what the hell was causing Kiri's meltdown. Just who *had* Joe fucked? Billy tripped and fell against Kiri's back. She elbowed him in the chest and turned and barked, "Watch it, asshole!" Her face was right in front of Billy's phone.

Kiri spun back around and hurled her cocktail into Joe's face. She tried to make a dramatic getaway but the crowd blocked her.

She looked wildly from side to side, searching for an exit. Billy's phone screen filled with a stark closeup of Kiri's dilated pupils and a huge rock of cocaine lodged just inside her right nostril.

"Get that fucking thing out of my face, you disgusting cocksucking faggot," she sneered, snatching for Billy's phone. He stepped aside, and she missed, tripping into the guy next to Billy and pinballing through the crowd, which ate her up in a split second.

Joe stood wiping the booze off his face with his sleeve, and the party resumed around him.

Billy filmed the rest of Joe's cleanup, until he spied Kiri's team flood out onto the roof. He could hear their angry chatter over the music. They wanted to find the guy who'd filmed it. *Time to go.* He slid his phone into his pocket and headed toward the doors leading to the fire escape. He barely made it five feet before he felt a hand clamp onto his shoulder. He turned and faced the blandly handsome and overly Botoxed face of Kiri's feared publicist, Owen Trinsk.

"Do I know you?" Billy asked innocently.

"I doubt it," spat Trinsk, sounding much angrier than his motionless face indicated. "I would like to have a word with you."

"G'ahead," Billy said, looking around as if searching for a friend.

"How'd you like one of these new phones?" the publicist said coldly, holding up a boxed example of the phone the party was launching.

"I dunno," said Billy. "I just got a new phone, and it's a two-year contract. I'm kind of stuck with it, but thanks, that's generous of you."

"Give me your fucking phone," the publicist hissed. "Or I'll destroy you."

"Get your fucking hand off me right now." Billy pried Owen's fingers off his shoulder. "Or I will knee you so hard in the nuts that your string of underage Mexican girlfriends won't be in danger of getting pregnant anymore."

"How fucking dare you." Owen's eyes widened as far as they could, veins starting to stand out in his neck and temples.

"Nice talking to you," said Billy, breaking away and pushing madly through the crowd. He tried the fire escape. Of course it was locked. There was a long line at the men's room. Behind him he heard Owen yelling at people to "not let him escape." Billy ran for the bathroom line, a hand pressed to his mouth.

"Move it, I'm gonna puke," he bellowed. Rolling their eyes, they all stepped aside. He rushed to the bathroom door and started beating on it. "Hurry up, man, I'm about to puke my guts up, fucking hurry!"

The door unlocked and opened inward. Billy fell in with it. He spun and met eyes with Ethan Carpenter, who pushed the door closed and locked it. A barrage of fists started beating on it as soon as the lock clicked.

"What the fuck have you done now?" Ethan asked.

"Hang on a sec," Billy said, leaning over and planting a peck on his cheek. Then Billy pulled his phone out and rapidly e-mailed the movie file to himself and cc'd Nicola. He paused to make sure it was sending, then clicked it off and put it back in his pocket.

"Uh, hi," Billy said, straightening and flashing his brightest smile.

"I've missed you," said Ethan.

"That was a stressful fucking weekend, dude," Billy said.

"Yeah, it was, *dude*," said Ethan snottily. "It was so bad for you, I can't imagine."

"Oh, come on," said Billy seriously. "You need a fucking reality check. That's not how you go about a first date."

"I bought you clothes and flew your ass to Vegas, Billy."

"Two things I'm very capable of doing for myself, thanks."

"You don't know how hard it is for me," Ethan whined.

"You're right, I don't," said Billy. "Because I'm not a closeted super-star with a billion-dollar franchise resting on my bankability as a teenage heartthrob. I get it. But you don't have to be a dick about it, fucking smoking meth when you don't get your way. You're thirty-one; you're not a baby."

"Wow. Why am I even helping you?"

"Dude, I saved your life, I got you to the hospital, and I did not sell your story. I think it's safe to say that I still have credit with you."

"If you weren't so hot, I'd punch you out right now," said Ethan with a flash of the fake cheesy grin that Billy had seen on everything from billboards to lunch boxes.

"You're gonna catch some shit if that agent of yours sees us together, right?"

"Remember one thing," Ethan said coldly. "Those assholes all work for me. They can push the line, but if they cross it they're fired. I've made them all so fucking rich, and it's not enough, but I'm at the point where I can fucking destroy them and they know it."

"So they're all just desperate to milk you while they can?"

"So?" Ethan sniffed haughtily.

Billy checked his phone and breathed a sigh of relief when he saw that the movie file had sent.

"Ethan," he said seriously. "I need one favor. I need you to take my phone and get it out of here. Kiri and Joe just had a spectacular fight and I got it all on video. Her people are going to beat me up to get ahold of this, and I know they won't even touch you."

"Oh, so you need me now, *and* you trust me?" Ethan crowed.

"I'm calling in a favor," Billy said, handing his phone over to Ethan, who slipped it into a pocket inside his jacket. "It's the least you could do."

"Wait—so you'll come get your phone off me, maybe later tonight?" Ethan said hopefully.

"Yes, I will."

"Okay. I'll be home by one, same building on Wilshire. Go to the doorman and tell him you're there to see Montgomery Clift and then add that your favorite movie is *The NeverEnding Story*, and he'll let you up."

"Uh, okay, sure, that makes sense," Billy said patronizingly. "Let's get out of this bathroom. Together or separate?"

"Kiss me first," Ethan said, grabbing Billy's crotch. Billy groaned and submitted to the kiss. *Of course he has coke mouth*, Billy thought, sighing. He shared Nicola's disdain for drugs, and Ethan was embodying his every reason for hating them.

"Okay, let's get out of here," said Billy, pushing the star away. "You ready? Let's get out together."

They stood back and Billy opened the door. Kiri's team blocked their way. Ethan looked them up and down, then turned to Billy.

"That was fucking disgusting, you fucking loser," he yelled, and disappeared into the crowd.

Kiri's publicist grabbed Billy's arm. "Come with me or I'll break your fucking arm," he spat.

"Hey, man, calm down, I'm just really fucked up," Billy drawled. "What's your problem? Hey, help, this guy is trying to get me to suck his dick, come on, HELP!"

Billy felt the pressure on his upper arm increase, and the publicist wrapped his other hand around Billy's wrist.

"I'm about to twist your fucking elbow so hard, I will tear every tendon in your arm. You need to shut up right fucking now."

"Yo, Billy, 'sup, my man," said a reedy voice in Billy's ear. He turned and found himself staring into the violet eyes of MC Dee, the shock rapper whose latest album had been number one for the past month. He immediately felt the pressure on his arm slacken. *Can tonight get any weirder?*

"'Sup, Dee," he said nervously.

MC Dee reached down and disengaged each of the publicist's hands from Billy's arm.

"Why the fuck you manhandlin' my guest at my party?" Dee demanded.

"Just playin' around, Dee, just playin around," the publicist said with syrupy fakeness.

"Well, that ain't cool, son," Dee said. "Now it's about time you went back to your own little coke whore and left me and my boy to have some fun."

"Hey, man, of course, no problem," smarmed the publicist. "Let's set up a lunch; might be good to see what we can do together."

"Was I unclear?" the rapper asked. The publicist's brows knit quizzically.

"I'ma spell it out for you, you dumbass Ivy League dog fucker," Dee said in his best rap voice. "Get the fuck away from my friend. If I see your Botoxed face again tonight, you're gonna have a lot worse than a twisted elbow. *Vamos*, nigga. *Vamos*."

Dee draped an arm around Billy's shoulder and led him toward the roped-off VIP area.

"Uh, thanks for that, dude," he said. "I'm not sure I understand what just happened."

"Just looking out for my homies," Dee said.

"But we haven't met," said Billy.

"We have now." Dee swiped two cocktails from a passing tray. He handed one to Billy and raised his own in cheers.

"To men who can keep secrets," Dee said. They clinked their glasses and Billy downed his entire drink in one chug. Dee was clad in his badass white rapper uniform of saggy jeans and a white singlet, with leather gauntlets on each wrist. Shards of light from the mirrorball glanced off his shaved head. He turned those violet eyes on Billy again, and winked.

"How do you know I can keep secrets?" Billy asked.

"Well, that's *my* secret to keep, Holmes. I heard you're trust-worthy, to the right people. And I just helped you keep your elbow in a *functioning* state. So I figure I'm the right people. And I figure you up to payin' me back."

"I'm sorry, Dee, I am not following you at all." Billy felt Dee's hand graze his ass by way of explanation.

"I'm going to give you a card. It has a phone number on it.

You're going to call this number tomorrow morning, and you'll come to the address that I give you. We're going to have a fun afternoon."

Billy's eyes widened as he finally understood that the most homophobic, misogynistic rapper in the world was hitting on him.

"You could have just *said* that you wanted to fuck," he said blithely.

Billy doubled over as Dee sucker punched him in the solar plexus, and all the air vanished out of his lungs.

"You dumb fucking faggot," Dee said loudly enough for the party of girls at their table to hear. "You say shit like that to me again and I'll fucking shove my AR-15 up your ass. Now let's be cool and drink some goose."

Billy's eyes were watering. "I need to get out of here," he said.

Dee gripped his wrist and pulled him into a chest bump. "Call me tomorrow, Billy," he whispered.

When they parted, there was a business card in Billy's palm.

Billy stumbled over the low velvet rope that somehow kept the desperates out of the VIP area. The squelchy bass music was deafening and he was nauseated from Dee's punch. In the lobby, a fire marshal was already yelling at people. Billy scooted around the drama and dashed headlong down the staircase, panicking the whole descent, waiting to hear footsteps behind him.

As he neared the bottom floor, he paused and waited. He could still hear the melee from the street but could not discern any individual voices. He peeked around the corner and saw only the security guards. He slowly walked the remaining steps and pushed out the side entrance. He leaned in and pinched Solstice on the ass. She turned slowly.

"I knew it was you," she said with a disappointed look. "You getting out before the exodus?"

"You're getting shut down?"

She nodded. "Any second." She looked him up and down. "What's wrong, poodle? You look beat to shit."

"That wasn't fun," he said. "But if you are getting paid based on media hits, this is going to be good for you."

"What do you mean?" Solstice asked, suddenly alarmed.

"Wait and see," he teased. "Nothing bad, but your media hits are going to go through the roof."

She rolled her eyes.

"Get out of my sight," she sighed.

"Love you, bitch." Billy looked over his shoulder every fifty yards of the walk to his car.

✳ ✳ ✳

The doorman did not bat an eye as Billy repeated Ethan's ludicrous instructions. He called an elevator, and Billy got in. When the doors opened at Ethan's floor, the star was standing there naked with his arms spread.

"I see you made it out alive."

"I see you don't currently have my phone," said Billy. "Or at least, I hope you don't."

"It's over there, you jerk." Ethan stepped forward, his even honey-brown skin glowing in the dim light. "Now come here and give me a hug."

"Dude, you don't even want to know what happened to me after we parted," Billy said. "Kiri's team tried to break my arm, and then MC Dee punched me and I may have cracked a rib."

"Oh, he made a move on you?" Ethan sniffed. "Fucking Crystal, I'll kill her."

"What the fuck are you talking about?"

"You're so dense, Billy," said Ethan. "Crystal is Dee's publicist. She must have told him that you're a good down-low date."

"So he's totally gay?" Billy marveled. "MC Dee? The guy who sings 'Your Pussy Is My Pussy' and 'Adam and Eve'?"

"I guess," purred Ethan, suddenly annoyed. "I'll call Crystal tomorrow. She ain't pimping my man out, 'cause I ain't sharing you. Get into bed."

"Ethan, I think I seriously cracked a rib. I can hardly breathe, much less suck your dick."

"That's okay, baby," cooed Ethan, unbuttoning Billy's shirt. "Let's spoon. Since you have a broken rib, I get to be the big spoon."

Billy, his phone, and the scandal it contained were being held hostage by last week's potential scandal. Billy tried to sigh in dramatic irony, and his busted rib spasmed, making him flinch.

"C'mon, my bruised baby," Ethan cooed in a baby voice. "Let me make everything all right."

CHAPTER 17

HOW COULD A DAY THAT began with waking up in a movie star's arms have turned to shit so quickly? Sleeping in was definitely the first mistake, and the countless anxious texts from Gaynor, Billy, and Kara hadn't sweetened the deal.

Seamus had rolled out a volley of sweet, fat, slow kisses in his final attempt to get her to stay with him all day. She tried to clear her mind and enjoy the fuzzy, salty taste, but she had left him lying naked on the bed, with an adorably sad expression on his face and his morning wood tenting the sheets.

She had brought a small overnight bag, but Seamus had presented her with an outfit that he assured her was "no big deal"—so she stepped out into the dusty Valley morning light in a bright pink Victoria Beckham fitted strapless dress and some black patent Italian leather pumps. She felt slightly preposterous as she made her way across the empty hotel parking lot to the Tercel, its deep turquoise color sparkling in an odd way. Bluey had obviously had it washed.

Opening the door, she realized the whole thing had been detailed, by both the smell and the lack of Starbucks cups in the back. An iced Venti Americano sat in her cup holder, beads of sweat collecting on its plastic skin. By the time she turned her key in the ignition, she was not surprised to see that she also had a full tank of gas, though she was torn over who to be appreciative of—Seamus or Bluey.

She hit home on her GPS and was horrified to see that the relatively short drive back across the Hollywood Hills was going to take her fifty-five minutes. No point arguing with the GPS gods. She resigned herself to a slow journey back over the long, squat mountain range that separated Hollywood from the rest of the world.

Risking driving tickets for an hour by texting, Nicola learned that Kara was still banging J, apparently all over their apartment. Billy had been involved in another big scandal that would make him rich, and Gaynor wasn't coming to the office today. Oh, and a new intern was starting. And there was a photo shoot that needed covering. With Paul Stroud.

"Omagod, *buenos días*," cawed a raven-haired young woman sitting at the usually empty desk right by the front door, rushing to her feet. "I'm Alicia, I'm your new intern."

"Hi, Alicia," smiled Nicola. "Welcome aboard."

After they shook hands, Alicia just stood there, a plus-size vision in black tights and a flowing black chiffon shirt over a lacy and very visible bra. She shifted her weight from one overstuffed strappy red sandal to the other. Nicola looked down at her dress, wondering if she'd spilled coffee down it.

"Is there a problem?" she asked, still a little panicked.

"Girl, you look even finer in person than on TV." Alicia smiled with admiration. "I saw you on *ET* with Paul."

"Oh, thanks," said Nicola awkwardly. "That was just a work thing, I wasn't meant to get photographed."

"Bitch, please," laughed Alicia. "If you don't want to get photographed, don't walk down the carpet in the arms of a megastar!"

"You know this is a publicity firm, right?" Nicola said coldly, walking to her own desk and setting her purse down. "It's our job to take our clients to events. And it's not my fault if Paul put his arms around me on the carpet."

"Bitch, why you defensive?" Alicia blurted. "I told you, you pretty, and then I told you, you prettier-R-L than on the TV. Now you're bitching me out because it wasn't your fault! What wasn't your fault? Bein' pretty? Please. I just gotta know one thing."

Nicola softened and smiled. "Sure, Alicia, what?"

"Is he a good kisser?"

Nicola paused. "Why are you working here?" she asked very politely. "Do you want to be a publicist, or are you doing this to meet the stars?"

"Oh no, Miss Nicola, I wanna be a publicist. I love the way Gaynor tells us at church about the things she does for the celebrities, all the charities and all the great things."

Nicola raised her left eyebrow and fought to suppress laughter.

"Well, okay, then," she began. "The first rule of publicity is that you never kiss and tell, and you never let your clients kiss and tell. So whether something happened or not, I can't tell you either way."

"You banged him, huh?" laughed Alicia conspiratorially, returning to her desk and plopping her chin onto a chubby fist.

"Second rule of publicity," Nicola said sternly. "Stop saying banged."

"Fine, whatever," sniffed Alicia. "Listen, I can't do nothing. My computer won't turn on, and neither will yours."

"Why did you try to turn mine on?" Nicola asked suddenly.

"I wanted to look something up on Pinterest," Alicia said, as if that was the obvious answer.

Nicola took the security key from her purse and inserted it into her computer, and pressed the power button. Its loud chime filled the office and startled Alicia.

"Hey, how'd you get it started?" she blurted as Nicola quickly put the key card back into her purse.

"It's tricky, you need to do it the right way," Nicola said absently. "Hey, can you open all that mail and sort it into piles for me to go through? Thanks."

"Hey, I ain't yo mail lady," Alicia said loudly.

"No, Alicia, you're my intern. Which means you do what I ask, without question. You're basically below a mail lady, but if you play well with others, this could be the best thing to happen to you. I'm not a bitch; I just want the mail opened while I check the voice mail."

Alicia tried to stare her down and failed. She silently lifted a huge pile of mail to her desk, and began to slowly tear envelopes open.

Nicola was about to start listening to the office voice mail when her cell phone rang. It was Billy. She hit the talk button.

"About fucking time, Nicola," Billy started. Nicola sat down. This was going to be a long call.

"I'm well, thanks, how are you?" she said blithely.

"Save it," Billy spat. "Have you listened to my messages? Where the fuck were you last night? Have you checked e-mail?"

"No, on a date, and no," Nicola replied. "It took me a half hour to read all your texts, so all I can assume is you went and got very drunk someplace last night, and I figured I could call you during a break in my actual job that pays me money."

"You want money?" The edge in Billy's voice scared her. "Check your fucking e-mail right now. Are you alone?"

"No," Nicola replied.

"Then put your headphones on while you watch the video."

"Okay, I'm putting you down," Nicola said, laying her phone on the desk. She plugged in her headphones and found Billy's e-mail. She clicked on the video, and almost immediately, her jaw hit the floor. Just after Kiri's final "fucking FAGGOT," Nicola hit pause and moved her face closer to her screen, examining Kiri's wildly dilated pupils and also the huge rock of coke that was caught at the back of her nostril.

She pulled the earbuds out of her ears and picked up her phone.

"Um, amazing," she said.

"Right?" Billy asked. "Is my publicist there? I need to figure out how to sell this."

"You know Gaynor's not really your publicist, right?"

"If she helps me sell this, she'll get her ten percent," Billy said. "Come on, hook a brother up."

"What's in this for me?"

"Okay, fuck it, *you* sell it then, I'll give *you* ten percent. I don't fucking care. What do you think I should do?"

"Can you give me a half hour? Did anyone else film this? Did anyone take phone photos or hear her saying faggot?"

"People were shooting pics, and there were eyewitnesses. A couple blogs are on the heels of the story, and there are pics of her crying at the party after our little exchange."

"Okay. Good, this is building interest. We just have to figure out if we sell it to a TV show, or a magazine with an online presence. Or we offer it to her people for buyout."

"Scratch that one," sniffed Billy. "That little coke whore is calling me a fucking faggot in the video, in case you missed it. I ain't doing a buyout. She can kiss her career good-bye. I want an agency to license this after the exclusive so it can keep making us money from VH1 clip shows until we're old."

"All right, bitter party of one, I'll figure out how to make you rich in a little while. I just got into the office."

"What? That's late."

"Thanks for pointing that out, and yes, I'm aware."

"Did you sleep in?"

"Yes, but not in my own bed; now I really need to go."

"I didn't sleep in my own bed, either," said Billy enthusiastically. "Let's grab lunch and share diary entries."

"I can't," Nicola groaned. "I have shit to do here, and then apparently I'm working a photo shoot this afternoon that may run late. I don't have time for stupid things like a private life."

There was a knock at the office door, which was always kept locked. Nicola looked over at Alicia, who was playing a game on her phone, oblivious to the knock. "Psssst," hissed Nicola, pointing at the door.

"What?" humphed Alicia, not looking away from her game.

"I gotta go," Nicola said into her phone. "I'll call you in an hour."

Nicola ended the call and stood up. "Alicia," she barked. "Open the door!"

"Fuck, okay," Alicia grunted, pushing herself clumsily up from her chair. "Why we even gotta keep all these damn doors locked for anyway?"

Alicia let out a long, slow whistle that subtly included a string of Spanish. Nicola looked up and saw her taking an intricate floral arrangement and a Cartier bag from a delivery guy. Alicia put them on her desk and then signed for the delivery. Nicola reached into her purse and pulled out the key to Gaynor's office.

"Here," she said. "I'll open Gaynor's office and we can put them in there for her when she gets here."

"They for you, dumb bitch," Alicia said pleasantly, dropping them on Nicola's desk.

The flowers were a tight abundance of orchids, succulents, and strange pale pink lily things in a square white clay vase. There was nothing on the card except her name. The Cartier bag was small. Nicola eyed it suspiciously.

"What you scared of?" Alicia reached for the Cartier bag. "Cartier don't bite!"

Nicola snatched it from her. There was just a small jewelry box inside. She swallowed nervously, taking it out of the bag and setting it on her desk.

"Thass it?" howled Alicia. "Come AWN. You gotta open it now."

"Alicia, you have a mountain of mail to open, and I really need a coffee. Can you please run out and get me an iced red-eye?"

"I see what you're doin'," Alicia huffed, dragging on a red padded jacket. "You arready keepin' secrets."

Nicola handed her twenty dollars.

"Get yourself a coffee, too, Alicia," she said politely. "Thanks!" The intern finally left her in peace for a minute.

A second later, Nicola's phone buzzed with an incoming text. She looked at her phone. It was from Seamus.

Do you like them?

Nicola took a deep breath and slowly undid the satin ribbon that held the Cartier bag closed. She reached in and pulled out the tiny jewelry box. She flipped the lid back to reveal a pair of diamond earrings, single stones set in gold, with long, flowing gold chains encrusted with diamond dust hanging down from each. They sparkled weakly under the dull fluorescent light. Nicola couldn't imagine how they'd look in sunlight. Did Seamus send this package standard to every conquest? Was this something that Bluey did every morning after? Or was this something new for both of them?

She reached for her phone and responded to Seamus.

They're beautiful, Seamus. You shouldn't have. I mean it. The flowers would have been enough. But thank you. So very much.

She stared at the earrings again, running a finger along the trails of diamond crumbs that sat below each rock. She suddenly wanted to put them on right away; then just as suddenly, she wanted to send them back.

She carefully put the earrings into her purse, into a zipped side pocket, and then set the flowers on the corner of her desk, beside her laptop.

I can still feel you on my lips, Seamus wrote back.

Nicola reached up and massaged her upper right arm through the sleeve of her blue shirt. She felt the gentle pain of the bruises that Seamus's grip had left there.

I can still feel you everywhere, she typed.

Rematch? he replied in a split second.

Sure. Working tonight but free tomorrow.

You're not free anymore. See you tomorrow. Thanks again for last night, Nicola. I don't do this all the time. You're special to me. Big smiles here. XO

Jesus. Nicola exhaled loudly. What the fuck was going on? She'd made a few promises to herself when she moved to LA. Number one was "don't fall for an actor" and now *this* was happening. Every ounce of common sense told her that she was getting played, that this was what rich and famous people did: they charmed people easily, and then they discarded them. She sat at her desk for ten minutes, wondering if she should end it with Seamus on the spot.

A knock at the door interrupted her mental battle. "Alicia?" Nicola called out.

"Nope, mate, it's Bluey," came the reply. "Open this fuckin' door, will ya, mate? This shit weighs a ton. Hope yer hungry."

She was surprised to see Bluey holding a large white box. He strode into the office, set the box on the coffee table, and turned to her.

"How you doing today?" he asked cheerfully.

"I'm good, thanks," Nicola replied. "Do you ever sleep?"

"I get enough beauty sleep for this face."

"Thanks for gassing up my car. And making it cleaner than it's ever been."

"Eh, don't mention it," said Bluey with a dismissive wave. "That your desk there?"

Nicola nodded, and Bluey took the lid off the box, presenting a three-course meal on very familiar plates. They were from The Ivy. Bluey took the small plate, a shrimp cocktail, and placed it on Nicola's desk. He reached back into the box and pulled out a set of silver cutlery wrapped in a napkin, and set that beside the appetizer.

"Dig in," he admonished.

"Bluey, what the fuck are you doing?" Nicola asked, smiling.

"I was supposed to bring you breakfast this morning, but you slept late and then you bolted, so I wanted to make up for it."

"Bluey!" she gasped. "No. You don't have to do stuff like this, and neither does Seamus."

"I know that," he said affably. "Now sit down and fucking eat so I can get out of here. I'm double-parked out front."

"There's spots under the building."

"I know, but I love double-parking in West Hollywood. It fucks everyone off. It's a small price to pay for inconveniencing these entitled motherfuckers."

He bent and removed the entrée, a huge chopped salad with grilled chicken and grilled shrimp. He placed it on her desk. He then produced a bottle of sparkling water and a glass and set those beside the salad. He took the dessert—a small crème brûlée with blueberries—and put it on the coffee table. He picked up the box and bowed to Nicola.

"Dig in, mate," Bluey said, heading toward the door. "Am I seeing you tonight?"

"You didn't see me last night," Nicola retorted.

"Incorrectamundo," Bluey laughed. "I saw you. That you didn't see me means I did my job well. So, am I seeing you tonight?"

"No, Bluey. I have to work late tonight. Some photo-shoot thingy."

"Ah, that sucks, matey," he said. "Anyhoo, I am gonna make like a fart and blow and see if I didn't get a ticket."

"What about the plates?" Nicola exclaimed.

"Keep 'em, I guess," Bluey said. "I'm sure we paid for them." And he was gone.

Nicola sat down and unwrapped her cutlery. She took the top off the sparkling water and took a swig from the bottle. She looked at the vaguely Mediterranean patterns on the dishes that were now hers to keep. She speared a single shrimp and plopped it into her mouth. This was all a bit too much. But it wasn't terrible.

Laughter and machine-gun Spanish echoed down the hallway outside, and Gaynor's key slid into the lock. The laughter stopped when Gaynor and Alicia saw Nicola eating on a full set of dinnerware from The Ivy at her desk.

Predictably, Alicia broke the silence.

"Bitch, if you didn't want to order my lunch too you just coulda said so," she said, placing the iced red-eye on Nicola's desk.

"*Ay yay yay!*" squealed Gaynor, clad in neon-orange satin tights and a huge fake fur over a tight black dress. "I told Paul to send you something nice, and the flowers would have been enough," she said loudly, touching a finger to the orchids on Nicola's desk.

"I thought you weren't coming in today," said Nicola, her hand covering her mouth. "Who's Paul?"

"Stroud, you silly girl, Stroud," laughed Gaynor. "Did you forget already? Señor Gassy Ass!"

She burst into a loud cackle.

"Why would Paul send me flowers?" Nicola asked, dabbing at her mouth with her napkin.

"So that things weren't awkward at the shoot today."

Nicola decided it was easier to let Gaynor be wrong for once.

"Right. Well, it worked," said Nicola, stuffing another shrimp in her mouth. "I can't wait to see him."

Gaynor stared at the food on Nicola's desk.

"You're making good choices, Nicolita," she sniffed with admiration. "I didn't know The Ivy had started doing delivery. Eh, I guess everyone has to make ends meet. But give that dessert to Alicia. You can't risk it."

"Thanks, I love pudding," said Alicia, moving with surprising speed toward the hapless dessert. As she was returning to her desk with the dessert balanced between her fingers, she paused and looked directly at Gaynor.

"He sent her jewelry, too, she just doesn't want to tell you."

"No, he did not," snapped Nicola. "And please clean that dessert plate when you're done. It's mine."

✳ ✳ ✳

Eight hours later, the photographer had captured Paul Stroud in every room of his house, and Nicola was sitting on the couch as a mousy woman in her late fifties finally began interviewing him. The questions were resoundingly bad and mundane: "What do you like about acting?" and "What was your design mission with this house?" Paul answered each one as if he'd been asked for his recipe for peace in the Middle East.

When Nicola had arrived at the house, Paul had acted like he and she were old friends. He had hugged her warmly and taken her around and introduced her to the photographer and his crew, and then to the reporter. The reporter's eyes had blazed with recognition, and then disappointment.

"Oh, so you *are* the girl that Paul took to the premiere," she deadpanned.

"I am," said Nicola. "I'm his publicist, and I accompanied him to the movie."

"Why didn't you say anything the next day?" the reporter asked, still hoping for a story of some sort.

"Why bother?" Nicola said with a smile. "A publicist taking a client to his premiere isn't a story."

"That's why I pay her the big bucks," said Paul with fake sincerity. Nicola elbowed him in the ribs.

The reporter smirked and made an illegible note in her notepad. Nicola distrusted her already.

The interview was still going an hour later. Neither the reporter lady nor Paul seemed to mind. Nicola was falling asleep on the couch, and had resorted to dramatically pinching herself to stay awake.

"We've got time for two more questions, you guys," she said dejectedly.

"Oh no," said the reporter. "I have another page of questions! The magazine will kill me if I don't get them all answered."

"It's fine, Nicola," Paul said calmly. "I don't have any plans for tonight."

Nicola looked at her phone. It was nine thirty p.m.

"Okay," she said with a sigh, giving in. "You have a half hour. This ends at ten."

"Thanks," said the reporter.

"See why I pay her the big bucks?" Paul said. Again.

She felt her phone buzz in her hand.

Did you try to get Gaynor to sell my video?

Fuck, with all the diamonds and the shrimp going on today, she hadn't done anything with Billy's video of Kiri.

"Hey," she interrupted. "Sorry, I forgot your name, but I have something to show you."

The reporter looked like a dog receiving a treat as Nicola flicked at her phone, looking for the video. She located it and hit play, holding her phone in the direction of the reporter and Paul.

As the video progressed and the sounds of last night's party filled Paul's empty house, the reporter's face went into complete shock.

"Oh em eff gee," she said, not realizing that it was just sad at her age. "This. Is. Everything. Who the fuck owns this footage?"

"A friend. And he's looking to sell it."

"Send it to me," the reporter said.

"Uh, no," snapped Nicola. "Do you have a card? I can give your details to my friend and they can call you."

The reporter reached into her purse, an imitation Louis, and pulled out a nondescript logo-free card. *She's a freelancer*, thought Nicola. *Ugh*. She handed the card to Nicola. "Can I see it again?"

Nicola was about to replay the video when Paul butted in.

"Hello; if this is to end by ten, we'll really need to get back to the interview," he whined.

"Sorry, Paul, you're completely right." Nicola texted Billy that she was waiting for an offer. Then she sent the footage to Gaynor and asked her to send it to *Access* and *ET*.

The reporter, typically, had saved some scandalous questions for last, and Nicola was able to finally step in and end the interview.

Nicola ushered her out unceremoniously, and then did a quick sweep of the house to make sure everything had been put back in place after the shoot.

Paul appeared in the living room doorway as she gathered her purse.

"What's the rest of your night look like?" he said, propping himself against the door frame on one elbow.

Nicola sighed.

"It looks like my pillow, and my sheets, and my comforter," she joked. "I'm really wiped; it's been a long day."

"Me, too," said Paul, with sudden seriousness. "You have no idea how hard it is to come up with all those answers. It's really tricky, but I'm good at it."

"That you are, Mr. Stroud," said Nicola, heading for the door. "That you are."

Paul moved to block her way.

"You don't have to drive home right away," he said softly.

"I do, Paul," said Nicola firmly.

"You can't tell me you didn't dress in that sexy outfit because you want an early night."

"That's true, I can't. But I can tell you that I didn't choose this dress at all. It's just a dress."

"I had a great time last week," said Paul with a wink. "I was hoping we could maybe throw down again."

"Not tonight," Nicola smiled, opening the front door. "I had fun last week, too, Paul." She waved as she began to close the door. "It was a gas."

As she walked down the dark Hollywood Hills street, Nicola's phone rang. It was Seamus. She answered it immediately.

"Hey, Ohio, how's it going?" Seamus said.

"Cute," said Nicola. "I just finished work; we just wrapped a shoot at Paul Stroud's place."

"Wait—you went to his house again?"

"Seamus, he's our client. It was a shoot. Yes."

"He hit on you, didn't he?"

"If you can call it that," Nicola said with a sigh. "He should have said I'm just too lazy to jerk off and you're here so how about you service me?"

"I hope you brought your gas mask."

Nicola burst out laughing. "So everyone but me knew about him?" She got her keys out and got into her car.

"Where are you headed tonight, sweetheart?"

"To sleep," Nicola said. "What about you?"

"I slept a lot today," Seamus replied. "I'm actually gonna check out a little party, nothing major. I'm saving myself for dinner tomorrow, if you're still up for it."

"I am, I am, we can . . . ," Nicola said, turning her key in the ignition and getting no response. "Fuck."

"We can probably manage that," laughed Seamus.

"No, come on," Nicola said, trying the key again and again.

"What is it?" Seamus said, alarm in his voice.

"My poor car won't start. Won't even turn over. Shit," Nicola said.

"You outside Stroud's?" Seamus asked. Nicola said she was. "Okay, Bluey's not too far away; I'll send him to get you and take you home. Don't go back inside that douche's house, just wait in your car and Blue will be along in about fifteen. You'll be in bed asleep soon enough, my dear."

"Dude, I have Triple A," Nicola protested. "Triple A Premier, even."

"I won't hear of it," Seamus said. "Text me when you get home safe."

"Okay, thanks," she said, resigned to it. "You be safe, too. And see you tomorrow."

She hung up and sat there in the dark silence. After a few minutes, she noticed the old-lady reporter walking quickly back to the door of Paul's house. She knocked gingerly, and Paul opened the door, shirtless. He wrapped an arm around the reporter's back, and pulled her to him, kissing her on the lips.

Nicola smiled a wry grin. The reporter must have heard the rumors, and she was still willing to cop a face full. Who said tabloid reporters didn't know how to sniff out a story?

CHAPTER 18

THE DING OF THE ELEVATOR ricocheted like a birdcall around the cement cavern of the parking lot of Seamus's Beverly Hills condo complex. Seamus stepped into bright fluorescent light and spotted Bluey waiting, as usual, in the red zone in front of the elevator doors. He waved comically at him, then got in the car.

"Hello, boss," Bluey said warmly.

"Hey, Blue," Seamus responded, roughing up Bluey's already messy hair with his hand. "Did you get Nicola home okay?"

"Yeah, mate," Bluey replied, pulling the car toward the exit gate. "She was a sleepy girl. Didn't look like she got much shut-eye last night."

Seamus laughed. "That makes two of us," he said.

"Three of us, you fucking arse," Bluey said with mock severity.

"You never sleep," Seamus said. "Captain Redundant."

"You have a point," Bluey said absently, pulling the car up onto the street. He paused, checking for paps on bikes. Certain the street was empty, he made a slow left.

"How about that fucking cunt Paul Stroud?" Seamus said. "He was lucky to get Nicola once, the fuck if I'm going to let him disrespect her like that again."

"Would you like me to send him a warning?"

"Hmm. Maybe. Not yet. Lemme talk to Nicola and see where she is with him. He's her client, of sorts."

"He's a fucking tool," Bluey said curtly. "Farting in women's faces. What a fucking douche."

"Maybe we'll send him a little message that he needs to treat all women a bit better," Seamus said. "No need to single out Nicola. Let's do a public service. Shut the fucker down."

"Nicola said that after she turned him down, he called the reporter who did his interview back and banged her."

"Wait—he's farting into the face of the press right now?"

"I'd say so," laughed Bluey.

"Maybe he does have a purpose after all," Seamus roared. "Let's leave the fucker be. There are a lot of journalists I can think of who deserve a face full of fresh fart."

Cresting Coldwater Canyon, they could see the lights of the Valley spread out below them like grains of dirty sand. Halfway back down to Valley level, Bluey hung a right and wended the massive car through a narrow, sleepy street.

"Is there a valet?" Seamus asked as they slowed down and Bluey checked the address on his phone.

"Don't think so, boss," Bluey replied. "Want me to drop you at the gate and then park?"

"Nah, let's park and walk. My legs could do with it. I've been a slug all day."

They parked beyond the house and walked back. The houses they passed were shrouded in darkness. It was nearly midnight.

"I can't even hear any music," Seamus whispered as they reached the metal door set in an imposing cement wall. Before Bluey could knock, the door swung open, and he was pulled into a bear hug by a gigantic black man.

"Hey, Landis," Bluey said into the man's chest. "Good to see you, too."

"Landis," said Seamus, shaking the guard's hand. "Good to see you, man."

Landis gave Bluey a noogie and pushed him away.

"Thanks for coming, gentlemen," he said, returning to the temporary desk by the door. A closed-screen surveillance system had been set up, with two monitors showing multiple angles of the street outside. Beside that sat a plastic filing box full of cell phones, each one in a Ziploc with half a playing card taped to it.

"Want us to check our phones?" Seamus offered.

"You guys are fine, thanks for askin'," Landis said, sitting down and surveying the monitors. "Head on in, have fun."

This generic rent-a-mansion was familiar to Seamus, though he was sure he'd never been there before. Probably saw it on a reality show, he reasoned. It was built into the hillside, and the backyard was in the front.

The grassy lawn around them was lit by a scattering of eerie white orbs that pulsed and changed color in time with the faint music drifting from the house. Actors, musicians, and lowlifes huddled in small groups around the light balls. Clouds of pot vapor dissipated in the night air.

"Let's do this," Seamus said, walking toward the house. Bluey lagged behind him, watching the heads turn as Seamus passed. He was the biggest star at the party, and he'd become a target before too long.

They pushed into the kitchen, and were accosted immediately by Amber, her tiny boobs spilling out of a scarlet Herve Leger minidress.

"Oh my gawd, you guys," she bawled, wrapping her arms around Seamus. "I just got here, we shoulda carpooled!"

Amber threw an arm around Bluey and drew him and Seamus into a weird group hug.

"Come closer," she whispered, and they all put their heads together. "You guys wanna get high, right?"

Bluey shrugged. "I'm the driver," he said without a trace of regret; otherwise Seamus would insist on a cab. "And I have a big day tomorrow, so I can't sleep through it."

"I'm down," Seamus said. "Whatcha got?"

"Like you need to ask," Amber said. "You want pills or the real thing? I have both tonight."

"I'll take a pill to start," Seamus said. "We can revisit the other options later."

Bluey shot Seamus a look. But it was ignored.

Amber reached into the pocket of her half jacket and pulled out a red Target prescription bottle. Seamus made out the OXYCODONE in bold at the top, and Amber's real name.

"You get prescribed in your own name?" he said, his eyebrows knit in concern.

"It's the safest way to carry," she singsonged, popping the lid and removing three pills. She seductively placed one in Seamus's mouth, one in hers, and handed Bluey the third.

"In case you change your mind," she quipped. He dropped it into his jeans pocket. Amber grabbed someone else's drink off the counter and took a swig. Seamus followed suit.

"Whose fucking house is this anyway?" asked Seamus.

"Who knows?" Amber laughed. "It's a production location for that reality show. They've wrapped but they paid for it for another month. So it's a party house for a few weeks. Then the production will pay for it to be all fixed up and tidy. Cool, huh?"

"Or depressing," laughed Seamus. "Your choice."

Bluey looked around at the vaulted ceilings and the high-tech decor. He raised an eyebrow at Seamus. They both knew this place was going to be nothing but a drug den for the next month. The repair bill was going to be enormous.

"Hey, Amber," said Bluey seriously. "Who's here? Is it safe or are there any bigmouths?"

Amber switched immediately into business mode. "There's a couple hungry tigers upstairs in the drug room, but I told Courtney to get them too fucked up to remember anything. I gave her five Oxys to make sure that they're unconscious by midnight. I'd say that everyone else is using, and therefore trustworthy."

"Thanks, copilot," Bluey said with a smile. "I'm gonna go do a lap and reconnaissance the shit out of this place and then we can all relax."

"Thanks, mate," said Seamus as Bluey vanished into the house.

Amber turned to him and put her arms up onto his shoulders. She leaned forward, and Seamus could see down her red dress. Her almost-flat breasts were exposed, and her nipples were hard. Amber followed his gaze.

"I'm fucking freezing is what's happening there," she laughed.

"I can see," Seamus said with a whistle. "You could put someone's eye out with those things."

"There's a couple rooms in the back," Amber said suggestively. "We could head there and warm up before our pills kick in."

"Hmm," said Seamus, putting his fingers to his scruffy chin. "While that is a lovely idea and a generous offer, I'm going to pass."

"What?" Amber said, annoyed. "What is your problem? You're such a fuckin' tease."

"Not tonight, love." Seamus put his hand on her shoulder and moved her back from him.

"You suddenly got a girlfriend?" Amber said, an angry edge creeping into her voice. "That mousy bitch from my party? Are you fucking kidding me?"

"You're funny," Seamus said genially. "I just got here. I want to check things out and get a drink that isn't someone else's. Let's catch up a little later."

"Suuuuuure," Amber said eagerly. "Just so you know, I have plenty more Oxy, but if you get serious, I have a bunch of clean shit and some pure white. Don't tell anyone."

"Your secret's safe with me," Seamus said, nudging her conspiratorially and heading back out to the front lawn.

Stopping by one of the bars flanking the pool, Seamus poured himself a tumbler of Johnnie Walker Black and ambled away from the crowd. Staking out a solitary spot between the pool and the far wall, he turned and surveyed the crowd.

Maybe 150 people scattered across the huge lawn, many of them clustered on a Moroccan rug ringed by heat lamps. A clutch of starlets in similar shiny short dresses and matching straightened hair were sneaking glances at him and gossiping, probably making bets on who would be taking him home later.

This fucking sucks, he thought. There was no point in even coming to these things anymore. The parties were more of a habit than the pills. The one he had taken was starting to work, making things less alien and giving the party a velvety, comfortable aspect. He breathed a sigh of relief, took a swig from his Scotch, and tilted his head back, feeling the opiate's numb warmth wriggle its way from his fingers to his toes like a wave of sweet nausea. He swallowed hard and took a deep breath.

You're such a fucking loser, he thought. *What a joke you've become.*

He became lazily irritated at himself. It was his normal first port of call when he used, but this time, it was intensified. He thought about Nicola, about how she made him feel. Bluey wanted him in rehab. As the effects of the Oxy got stronger, Seamus drifted from Scotland to Hollywood. *I have a stupid fucking job. I never wanted it. I was a nice guy in Scotland. I'm a nice guy now.* He stared into his drink. *You're a self-pitying junkie acting like a nice guy*, his brain spat.

He closed his eyes and stood like that for a time. Nobody came to bother him; even though the groups of C-listers were eyeing him like big game, a sixth sense must have told them that there was no point approaching him until he settled into his high. Seamus eventually opened his eyes and took another deep breath. His vision was blurry. That was a good thing.

You're still a fucking donkey; you're faking the world.

"Fuck off, won't you?" he snapped at himself and walked back inside, searching for Bluey. He wanted to leave. He groaned when he entered the living room and saw the stripper pole. Did every fucking party house have a stripper pole? A trio of wasted guys were sprawled on the couch while the teenage daughter of one of rock and roll's elder statesmen listlessly threw herself around the pole, one breast hanging out of her dress. Sporadically, a balled-up dollar bill would be tossed at her. Each time, the starlet smiled with her eyes half closed and slurred, "Make it rain, baby."

Seamus followed a staircase up to the second level of the house.

The corridor at the landing split in two directions. Seamus wobbled on his feet as he pondered his next move for a minute, and realized he was higher than he thought. *I hate you*, he thought sharply. He lurched toward the door closest to him and pushed it open. A California king bed was buried beneath a pile of winter coats and jackets. It was still summer. Junkies feel the cold. At one corner of the bed, Courtney Hauser sprang up as if electrocuted.

"What the fuck?" she yelled, throwing a black jacket back onto the pile. "Oh, hi, Seamus." She smiled suddenly. "I didn't know you were here."

"Looking for your jacket?" Seamus arched his eyebrow knowingly.

Courtney was a well-known thief, and anyone who left cash or drugs in their jacket pockets was going to regret it.

"Yeah," Courtney replied, wrapping her bony freckled arms around herself. "I got really cold all of a sudden." She walked toward him and licked her lips.

"I have the funniest idea," she said.

"Which is?" he asked, already backing away from her.

She lifted her dress, revealing a haphazardly shaved pussy. He winced at the sight of the nicks and the bruises on her inner thigh.

"Aw, come on, Courtney," he said, stepping back. "Have some pride."

"Don't be so boring," she purred, lifting her dress even higher. "You know you wanna fuck me on top of everyone's coats."

She put one hand between her legs and started playing with herself. Seamus turned and walked unsteadily out of the room.

"Fuck you, you dirty Irish cunt." Courtney's rusty voice scratched his ears.

"I'm Scottish," Seamus said as he headed down the hall.

He bumped into Amber and Bluey on the stairs.

"I need a fucking espresso," said Seamus gruffly. "I'm way too high for this fucking party."

"Coke's just gonna make it worse, mate," cautioned Bluey.

"I actually meant fucking coffee," snapped Seamus.

"I didn't," said Amber gleefully, pulling a bullet out of fuck knew where. She handed it to Seamus, who deftly tipped and twisted it and pushed it up his nose.

"Yep. An actual coffee . . . ," Bluey said.

Seamus felt the coke hit. His eyes widened immediately, and he almost looked like himself again. He felt like more of an asshole.

"This party is all kinds of fail," he said to them.

"Really?" said Amber rapidly. "I think it's kinda cool. Why don't you like it? It's really fun. What can we do to make you happy? Hey—I was talking to Jamie and Ellery outside; they're doing mushrooms. Want some? I can get some for you. I hear they're really strong. Want me to go get some?"

Seamus and Bluey rolled their eyes at each other.

"Sure, Amber," said Bluey. "Why don't you run along and see what you can get for Seamus?"

Amber took off down the stairs like a startled cat.

"Jesus," marveled Seamus. "How much fucking coke did she snort?"

"Less than you, boss," said Bluey with a smile. "Less than you."

Seamus leaned back against the wall and started laughing. "You gonna lecture me, Blue?"

"Not right now, boss."

"Where can we hide out?" Seamus suddenly looked weary, and older than his thirty-four years. "I wanna chill for a minute, then make our escape."

"Follow me," Bluey said, guiding him up the stairs to the top level of the house.

"Is this a shooting gallery?" Seamus asked as they reached the top. "Because I'm not in the mood for that kind of shit, either."

"No, that's downstairs where we just were," Bluey said. "There's just a bunch of guys up here nodding off; at least it's quiet."

"Eh," said Seamus. "I think I might be done. Are you fine to drive? Because I'm happy to call a car."

"I'm good, mate," said Bluey. "Lemme pound a bottle of water and we can be out of here in five minutes."

"Good deal," said Seamus. "Let's head down to the kitchen."

A series of caterwauling screams pealed up the staircase.

"SHE'S FUCKING OVERDOSING," screamed a woman's voice. "GET THE FUCK OUT OF MY WAY."

"Holy shit," said Bluey, pushing his way past Seamus. "Stay there, mate. I'll sort this out."

The screaming spread like wildfire, and Seamus was surrounded by a group of junked-out guys he recognized from series dramas. "Hey, Seamus," several of them slurred, offering him fists to bump and hands to shake. Seamus frowned. In Hollywood, there was never a bad time to network.

He pushed through the pack, following the sound of the commotion. The screaming was coming from the bathroom, but a press of bodies prevented him from seeing inside. The crowd parted deferentially as he drew closer, and he saw Ellery Stone half naked, being held under a cold shower by some dude he recognized from somewhere.

"Someone get me some fucking adrenaline, or some speed or some meth or something," the guy screamed, his voice breaking in panic.

"WHAT THE FUCK ARE YOU DOING TO ME?" Ellery bellowed, twisting and fighting the guy as cold water stung her skin. Her top had come undone and her fake boobs pointed skyward. "AM I DYING? THIS FUCKING HURTS. JOHNNY, GET ME THE FUCK OUT OF HERE."

"What did you take?" the guy demanded. "How many Oxys? Or did you shoot?"

"WHAT THE FUCK ARE YOU TALKING ABOUT?" Ellery

spluttered as water filled her face. "I ATE SOME SHROOMS AN HOUR AGO. WHY THE FUCK ARE YOU HURTING ME?"

"You lying whore," the guy screamed, and slapped her hard across the face, sending her head smashing back into the tiled wall. Seamus had seen enough. He stepped in and grabbed the guy by the back of his shirt and lifted him like a wet puppy. He tossed him onto the toilet and snapped the water off. Ellery crumpled into a sobbing pile on the shower floor. Seamus pulled a towel from the rack and wrapped it around her as he tried to get her to sit up.

"Come on, love, we'll fix you up," he said.

"HOLY SHIT YOU ARE NOT SEAMUS O'RIORDAN!" Ellery bellowed into his ear.

Bluey pushed into the room, sending people flying into the walls.

"Holy fuck, boss, I'm sorry, I was trying to stop some dumb bint from calling the cops and the ambulance. Do you want me to call Dr. Brownstone?"

"No, Blue. It's fine. She's just frying her brains on mushrooms, and I guess someone gave her some pot, too. She's totally fine; it's that dumb fucker boyfriend of hers who lost his shit. We need to get her dried off and comfy and she can hopefully hallucinate in peace."

Bluey lifted Ellery from the cold floor and carried her along the hallway. He barged through a closed doorway and yelled at someone to get out, and two guys and two girls emerged, pulling on their clothes. Seamus followed, and saw him laying her on the bed with the towel over her. "Where's Amber?" he asked. "We need to get her some dry clothes."

"You're made of stained glass," Ellery cooed, touching a finger to Bluey's face.

"I'll go get her," Seamus said, turning and leaving.

✳　✳　✳

Half an hour later, the party drama had been forgotten. Ellery was upstairs quietly enjoying her trip, and Bluey, Amber, and Seamus were still in the kitchen. Bluey watched Seamus pour three tumblers of Johnnie and set them on the marble countertop.

"How about another pill, missy?" Seamus said to Amber, who promptly produced two more pills. Seamus and Amber swallowed them with whiskey, and Bluey looked Amber up and down, wondering where in that tiny dress she was keeping all these drugs. They stood in silence for a while, until Amber felt her phone vibrate.

"Hey, you guys, be right back, just have to go let my friend in."

As her platinum-blond hair bounced out the door, Seamus looked at Bluey and sighed deeply.

"I'm too old for this shit, Blue," he said.

"I hear ya," Bluey said. "But we all have bad nights."

"Naw, man, it's worse than that," Seamus continued. "Look around us. Why the fuck are we here? Who are we friends with here?"

Bluey was surprised by the tone in Seamus's voice.

"Do you want employee or friend?" Bluey asked softly.

"Friend." Seamus knit his brow and met Bluey's gaze.

"Seamus, it's fucking time to quit."

"Can we do it after this movie?"

"There'll be another movie right after this one, boss."

Seamus stood quietly. Bluey noticed his knuckles whitening as his grip on his whiskey glass tightened.

"It's just," Seamus began, "I mean, I'm just, this whole thing . . ."

"Okay, boss, it's okay," Blue said with thinly veiled force. "After this movie, we're going to the clinic. It's time for this to stop."

Seamus grabbed Bluey's arm tightly and stared into his eyes.

"Thanks, man. Thanks. I'm tired. I'm tired of it."

Bluey saw Seamus's eyes lose focus, and he could tell that Seamus's second pill was kicking in. He put an arm around his friend and scoped out a place to weather the initial high. He spied Amber coming back through the door leading a beautiful black woman by the hand.

"Hey, you guys," Amber said brightly. "I want you to meet my new bitch and costar!" She paused dramatically. "Seamus, Bluey, this is Kara."

Bluey shook Kara's hand, then Kara turned to Seamus, her eyes widening as she saw how fucked up he was. She dropped her hand to her side.

"Kara, hi, lovelytomeetyou," Seamus slurred.

Bluey led him over to a chaise longue beside the kitchen window and sat him down. He watched as Kara leaned in close to Amber and started whispering in her ear. Amber turned and glanced down at Seamus and then nodded and kept whispering. Bluey made a mental note to investigate Kara in the morning, and then he groaned out loud as the penny dropped.

Kara Jones. She was Nicola's roommate.

He wrapped both arms around Seamus's shoulders, hauling him to his feet and heading toward the door.

"Just gonna get our boy some air," Bluey said with false lightness. "We'll be right back."

He didn't stop moving until he had Seamus safely buckled into the backseat of his SUV.

CHAPTER 19

"OH MA GAWD," ALICIA YELLED as Nicola walked through the door of the office. "You look ah-MAY-zing today!"

"Huh?" Nicola juggled her coffees and purse as she locked the door behind her. "You've been watching too much Bravo."

Gaynor was bent over Alicia's desk, scrutinizing something intently. She straightened slowly, her hair a tumble of processed curls today, and dramatically gave Nicola a once-over, complete with fluttering eyelashes.

"*Mija*, it's a miracle," she bellowed. "Somebody got some last night."

"Yes, some sleep," said Nicola, a blush starting on her cheeks.

"Return to facing me, right now," purred Gaynor. Nicola placed her coffee and her purse on her desk and turned to face her boss. Gaynor walked slowly toward her, waving a fingernail in a curious pattern, pointing at different parts of Nicola, and making odd clucking sounds as she did.

"No, pussycat, you've had sex, I can tell," she insisted.

"Your radar is off, Gaynor," said Nicola with a smile.

"Then why do your cheeks look like poison apples?"

"Because you're humiliating me in front of Alicia," Nicola countered. "I was in bed, alone, asleep, as soon as I got home from Paul's house."

"You were at Paul's house, that's right!" squealed Alicia. "How did it go?"

"Yes, Nicola," said Gaynor knowingly. "How *did* it go?"

"The shoot went off without a hitch," Nicola said, taking her seat at her desk and sipping on her coffee. "They got everything they needed."

Gaynor would not be deterred.

"*Mi Nicolita*, I haven't heard a word from Señor Stroud since around ten p.m. last night, and he is still asleep. I thought you were with him."

"Not me, Gaynor, not me," Nicola said with a smile.

"Stop lying, *coño*. It's ugly on you." Gaynor splayed her red talons on Nicola's desk. "You can't tell me that he didn't try to hit on you."

"I never said that." Nicola laughed. "He totally hit on me, and I declined. That doesn't mean he slept alone."

Dawning horror crept across Gaynor's face.

"No . . ." She exhaled dramatically. "No . . . Nicola, come into my office. You have to tell me everything."

"Oh ma gawd," Alicia said, eyes widening as she started to stand and follow them.

"YOU STOP!" Gaynor bellowed, presenting the palm of her right hand to Alicia. "You have mail to open; we have to discuss a client in private."

"No fair." Alicia sat back down like a bag of dropped garbage. "I want to hear."

"Then be a good intern, dear," said Gaynor with horribly fake kindness. "And when you become an assistant publicist, you will get to hear. Trust me, there'll still be scandal."

"Oh, fuck me, I'm missing out on scandal," Alicia grumbled as she reached for the pile of mail on her desk and balefully stared at the two women walking down the hall away from her.

Nicola recounted the story of the shoot as Gaynor alternately feigned yawning or nausea.

"Then my car broke down and Seamus sent Bluey to drive me home."

"Of course he did. I don't know how Seamus got ahold of that one, or what he has over him, but he's the best celebrity minder in this whole fucking town. If we could clone him, we'd make billions."

"He's a really sweet guy," said Nicola, nodding.

"He's got you fooled, then," said Gaynor darkly. "He'll do whatever it takes to protect Seamus. You think he's just a bodyguard?"

"Isn't he?" Nicola asked, surprised.

"*Pendejita*, Bluey lets Seamus live the life he wants to, gives him freedom that few stars can have. You never see the bad pics in the magazines. You guys got hit on Saturday; there were photos, no?"

"I guess so," Nicola said. "They would have gotten us heading back to the yacht on the speedboat."

"Well, the magazines are out today, and nobody has anything on Seamus's new girl. Don't you think this is weird?"

"Huh, I guess you're right." Nicola pondered how the photos could have been held back, and wondered just what Bluey had to do with it.

"Okay, enough about your private life," said Gaynor, and Nicola was shocked to be getting off so lightly. "But first, there's one more thing."

"Yes?"

"Sign him as a client. Sign him for us. If you land Seamus O'Riordan as a client, you will instantly become a senior publicist in this agency. This gentleman is your fast track to the top. Don't tell me you're in love and that this is pleasure, not business, because that's bullshit and you know it. You're giving him something; make sure you take something in return."

"You make me feel like a prostitute with alarming regularity," Nicola said matter-of-factly.

"Don't sound so American," Gaynor scolded. "I thought you weren't hung up on sex."

"I'm not hung up on sex at all," Nicola said loudly. "I am a bit hung up on the fact that after I blew Paul you gave me two pairs of thousand-dollar shoes, and now you're offering me a pay increase if I can turn a one-night stand into a client. Listen to yourself."

"*Mira,*" Gaynor began slowly. "We are publicists. We get our hands filthy and we roll around in dirty laundry all day, every day. And when we do a good job, we get rewarded. Whether it's a press release, a smoke screen, or a blow job, it doesn't matter. We keep our clients happy, and we keep their scandals out of the tabloids and out of the courtrooms at all costs."

Gaynor took a breath and quit the theatrics.

"You did a good job; you deserve a reward. Don't be so goddamn fucking old-fashioned and treat your pussy any differently from your hands. You'll have a good time, and you'll be successful. It's not like I'd ever ask you to have sex with someone that you don't want to."

"Gaynor, I'm not going to monetize every single date I go on for the sake of this agency," spat Nicola. "I'll never go near Paul Stroud's stinky ass ever again, and now that I've fucked Seamus I'll probably never see him again. The last thing I need to do is hook up with another celebrity, ever."

Alicia interrupted, beating the shit out of Gaynor's door until Nicola opened it.

"You guys," she wheezed breathlessly. "Sorry to interrupt. I have the building manager on the phone. I don't know what he's talking about, but there's some sort of truck in our parking space or something and it's blocking the driveway."

"Fucking Omar," said Gaynor angrily. "He's like an ingrown hair in my ass. He's fucking crazy. My car is there, your car is there, that's it."

"I didn't drive today, I took a cab," said Nicola.

"Okay, you guys, WHATEVER," said Alicia, waving her hands by her thighs for emphasis. "He asked you to go to the parking garage right now. And he sounds pissed."

They stomped down to the parking garage, where a wiry Armenian gent in his late fifties was swatting his hand on the back of a flatbed truck as it pulled away.

"You are inconsiderate ass-monkey," he yelled at the truck as it lurched away. "Get the fuck out of my building and never come back here."

He turned and stormed toward Gaynor and Nicola. "What the fuck, Gaynor?" he yelled. "You can't just have a tow truck blocking people in here at lunchtime. You have to call first."

Gaynor walked up to the red-faced building manager and ran the back of her finger up and down his cheek.

"You can blame me for a lot of things, you cranky bastard," she said softly. "But this time I don't know what you're talking about."

"Don't bullshit me," he spat, pointing a gnarled finger at the black BMW 1 Series sedan that was parked in Nicola's spot.

"What?" shrugged Gaynor. "That's not ours; she didn't drive today, so somebody has taken her spot."

"The guy said it's a delivery for Nicola Wallace," Omar ranted. "Last time I checked, that's her standing right there."

"It's not mine," said Nicola, noticing an envelope on the car's windshield. She gulped, walking toward it. She tugged the envelope out from beneath the wiper and opened it. There was a single sheet of paper inside, folded into three.

She could feel Gaynor and Omar staring at her as she unfolded the sheet of thick paper.

THIS ONE WON'T LET YOU DOWN.

HAPPY WEDNESDAY.

STILL ON FOR DINNER TONIGHT?

SEAMUS XXX

She felt her blood boil.

"I'm very sorry, Omar," she said in a measured cadence. "I didn't know this was going to happen. I'm sorry if it caused any problems."

"Problems," bellowed Omar, relieved to be able to continue his rant. "I had Fleur and Rhiannon from Pilates Solutions on the second floor screaming at me. They couldn't get their cars out and they had some big-budget client that they were late for as a result. And now they're telling me that it's my fault that their chakras got out of balance and their client isn't able to relax around them."

"Oh no, it's a first-world catastrophe," said Gaynor with a wink. "Listen, Omar, text them that we're sorry and that by the time they get back, there'll be some chakra-balancing gifts waiting for them, with our apologies."

"What about me?" said Omar without skipping a beat.

"I can ask my fat intern if she'll give you a hand job," said Gaynor casually, already walking back toward the stairs.

"Fuck you, Gaynor," spat Omar. "Why are you always such a bitch?"

"Baby, maybe you should put a little honey out from time to time?" she purred. "When you act like a crying *puta* all the time, it's hard to feel anything for you except hostility."

"I'm nice to you," Omar protested. "I cover all your tracks."

Gaynor froze and shot Omar a death stare so intense that Nicola had to look away.

"Oh, Omar, I forgot to tell you . . . ," Gaynor said, equal parts sugar and steel. "That fur coat your wife wanted? It came in this morning, but it was the wrong size, so I sent it back. I don't think they make her size anymore. Too bad, huh?"

The color drained from Omar's face. He looked from Gaynor to Nicola and back again.

"But I told her . . . ," he began.

"You communicate with her?" Gaynor turned from him, but

kept talking. "Communication is key in a relationship. I'm sure you'll have no problem explaining why she's no longer getting a fur coat."

"Gaynor, please . . . ," Omar pleaded.

"Nicola!" Gaynor commanded. "Come on. Back to the office. And please hand me that note."

Nicola shared a look of commiseration with Omar, and then sheepishly followed her boss back inside.

As soon as they got in the stairwell, Gaynor spun around.

"Is that car a gift from Seamus?" she asked breathlessly.

"The note is vague," said Nicola, still annoyed. "But it's from him, yes."

Gaynor enveloped her in a big hug, her vinyl skirt squeaking. "This is amazing, I can feel it. You need to sign him immediately."

"NO, Gaynor," Nicola barked. "I have to call him right now and have it taken away. Don't cancel the fur coat."

Nicola went to the ladies' room on their floor and locked herself in a stall. The bathroom was empty. She called Seamus's number and got his voice mail. Before she could leave a message, he texted her.

In meeting can't talk. Did your gift arrive?

Nicola looked down at her left fist. She was clenching it so tight the knuckles were bulging, striped red and yellow. She breathed deeply and unclenched her fist.

Seamus. Take it back. This isn't how this is going to happen.

The little bubble that meant he was typing began immediately.

Nicola. I got it free. Please accept it. It's not a big deal. Let me buy you dinner tonight and we can talk about it.

It is a big deal. It's inappropriate. This is not what I want. Please take it back. I will make you dinner at my place. Tonight. 8 p.m. Nothing fancy.

Are you sure?

Y

OK. Sorry. I think I understand. I'll have it removed. Your old car is at the mechanic's. I'll have them rush it and get it to you asap.

Thanks. I will pay for repairs.

We'll discuss over dinner. See you at 8.

CHAPTER 20

NICOLA BARELY RECOGNIZED HER APARTMENT. After a frantic flurry of texts, Kara and Billy had called in stylist favors from every store on Beverly Boulevard. They'd transformed her home from WeHo working-girl basic to Dwell summer Hamptons. If people in the Hamptons had Russian neighbors with loud TVs.

Her bedroom was a candled oasis, a loaned fluffy comforter and mountain of pillows stacked against the headboard. She had lied to Gaynor, saying they were dining somewhere else in the Valley, just to put her off the scent in case she planned to have them papped.

Deciding that the living room and bedroom looked good enough, she returned to the kitchen, where the smells from the oven indicated that her family-recipe meat loaf and baked potatoes with rosemary and garlic were cooking perfectly. She began to gently warm the gravy on the stovetop and she tipped the scratch-made salad dressing onto a bowl of kale, strawberries, and slivered almonds. Dinner was almost ready.

Her plans to wear jeans and a White Stripes T-shirt had been bludgeoned to death by Gaynor, who had insisted on styling her. The simple black dress could have been common-folk fashion if not for the Miu Miu tag. *Fuck you, Gaynor,* she smiled. *I'm going barefoot.*

She set the small table carefully, working around an orchid that was doomed if it didn't go back to the store. Setting the water glasses down, she glanced around and couldn't shake the irony that this generic West Hollywood rental was about to host one of the world's biggest actors. "What the fuck am I doing?" she whispered to herself as she walked to her bedroom to finish getting dressed.

Seamus was still twenty minutes away. She stepped into her tiny en suite and brushed some light powder on her face, added a smidge of liner to the corners of her blue eyes, and dabbed on a tiny amount of nearly nude lip gloss. She shook out her chestnut hair, pleased with the way the curls fell around her face and almost touched her shoulders. *Near enough, good enough*, she smiled to herself, heading out to begin putting the finishing touches on her evening.

A popping, hissing sound came from the kitchen. She bolted out of the bathroom. The gravy was boiling over, spattering the entire stovetop.

"Oh, for fuck's sake," she sighed, plucking a pink gingham apron off a hook by the stove and pulling it over her head. Boiling gravy splashed onto her arm as she lifted the pan from the heat. Tears welled up in her eyes as she looked at the red welt on her skin. She shook her head, furious at herself for being so . . . herself. She was way more nervous than she should be.

Calm the hell down. He's just a guy. And if a night in an 1,800-dollar-a-month first floor apartment with popcorn ceilings, vertical blinds, and deafening Russian television through the wall didn't scare him off, nothing would.

As she rubbed her thumb across the reddening scald on her arm, a gentle knock rapped on her door. *NO NOT NOW*, her mind screamed. She walked to the door just as she heard Seamus's voice waft to her ear.

"Hello, Nicola, it's me," he announced in his smooth burr.

Despite his unmistakable voice, she still put her eye up to the spyhole in her door and saw him standing there, transformed by the fish-eye lens, looking vaguely circular but still stupid handsome in a simple blue-and-white plaid shirt and jeans. Nicola stepped back and opened the door.

Seamus stepped inside and closed the door quickly behind him. He smiled a wolf's smile.

"Ohio, uh-oh, I know I'm in trouble, but can we talk about it after we find out if I can get that dress off without undoing the apron?"

✳ ✳ ✳

Over an hour later, Nicola, dressed only in her underpants and the apron, finally served their dinner.

Seamus walked out from her bedroom, his hair a curly mess, wearing his boxer shorts and his unbuttoned shirt.

"Sit at the table," Nicola smiled. "It'll be right up."

Seamus sat down. He put a hand up to his face and took a deep breath.

"Goddamn, you smell so great," he said.

"Oh, Christ, would you go wash your hands?" Nicola scoffed hypocritically, since she'd just been taking a deep breath of Seamus's scent from her apron while the food heated up in the microwave.

"I'm good, lady boss," Seamus laughed. "So what's this you're serving?"

"Well, this is pure Dayton, Ohio, right here," laughed Nicola, sliding Seamus's plate onto the table. "It's meat loaf and taters, a dollar dinner as my mom would say, and I cheated and made a California salad, too."

"Dollar dinner, huh?" said Seamus. "It smells great, so get over here and let's eat."

"Well," smiled Nicola, sitting down with her own plate, "in Dayton it's dollar dinner. In LA, all of this somehow cost eighty bucks at Whole Foods, but I will never tell my mother that."

"See? Things *are* different in LA." Seamus laughed, taking her hand across the table. "So . . . you wanna have our big serious talk now, before we eat?"

Nicola paused and swallowed, then met Seamus's gaze.

"Sure; it's not that bad. We just need a few ground rules."

"Okay, lay 'em on me," Seamus said, sitting back and looking at her, an *almost* innocent expression on his face.

"For a start," she began, "a car is not an appropriate gift after three-ish dates. I know it's the thought that counts, and I know you probably get offered free cars the way I get offered free cheese samples at Costco, but that doesn't change anything."

Seamus nodded, still holding her hand.

"And this is the sort of dinner we should be having," she continued, her voice wavering a little bit. "I'm not backwoods. I'm not a redneck. I just don't think that I'm ever gonna truly connect with someone over a hundred-dollar steak at the Four Seasons. I'm simply not wired that way."

"If I may interrupt," said Seamus quietly. "That's precisely what I like about you."

"Seamus, I don't even know how to handle that yet," Nicola said with clear honesty. "I'm just getting started in this town, and I don't know all the rules. I don't know all the weird Hollywood physics yet, but I do know that being linked to you in any way would change my life, and probably not for the better."

"Ouch," Seamus said, putting his free hand over his heart.

"You know what I mean," Nicola continued. "I'd go from assistant publicist to celebrity girlfriend in the blink of an eye, and that's not something I'd ever bounce back from, professionally. I have done a lot of thinking about this—and yes, I do see it from your side also. You've become successful in your field, and your private life is gone. I realize it's not easy for you, either, and so far, this has been fun, and yes, we have a connection, but the car today just made me aware . . ." She trailed off.

"Nicola, tell me what I need to do, and I'll do it," Seamus said. "You don't know me that well, I agree. I know that. And as much as you can imagine my love life, the truth is so much worse. I was attracted to you immediately, but not for any reasons you might guess."

Nicola rolled her eyes, and Seamus furrowed his brow. "You know I'm uncomfortable with compliments, and I know one is coming," she explained.

"It's not a compliment, then," Seamus said with a warm smile. "It's a fact. You're funny as fuck and you're down to earth, and you surprise me in good ways. Over and over. So I just wanted to help you out since your car died . . ."

"You did help; you had Bluey bring me home, and that was enough."

"Nicola, I'll say it again. Just tell me what to do; what can I do that makes you comfortable and makes you want to be around me?"

"Eat your food," she began. "It'll get cold."

He obediently picked up his silverware and started cutting his meat loaf.

"We've been on three dates, ish," she began. "They've all been weird, in their own way. Until tonight. This is what I'm comfortable with, and this is the most comfortable I've been with you. I like this. I'd do this again. But I haven't been to your place, and I don't really know where you live. We've done fantasy dates. I feel like I'm on *The Bachelor*. And the car today just showed me how vast the gap between us is."

Seamus took a deep breath, then placed a piece of meat loaf in his mouth.

"Holy shit," he said. "This is fuckin' delicious. You really made this yourself?"

"Yeah, I did," Nicola said, blushing slightly in the candlelight. She cut a chunk of her own meat loaf and ate it. "You're right, it's pretty good. My mom would be impressed."

"Listen," said Seamus cautiously. "My career, my public stuff, that's just my job. You have your job, I have mine. The fame? That's ripples on a pond that I can't control; they do their own thing. But I don't subscribe to it. I don't give a shit about it. I'm not even going to bullshit you here. I'm not an actor. I'm a lucky bastard. I can repeat a few lines of dialogue from memory in front of a green screen, and get paid millions of dollars. It's almost offensive. And I plan to walk away from it, just not yet. But my job is not the sum of who I am and it's not what I'm going to be doing for the rest of my life."

Nicola looked at him seriously. "No?"

"No," he said, shaking his head broadly. "And before you ask, directing is not what I really want to do. I want to make this money for a while longer, and then vanish. I want to have a wife and kids. I wanna be a dad. And I want to vanish to the Scottish Highlands and have a nice stone house and maybe a small farm, and probably do something there for the locals, just be part of a small community. It's how I grew up and it's the thing I miss most."

Nicola stopped eating and put her fork down.

"You don't believe me, do you?" he asked simply.

"I don't *dis*believe you," she said slowly. "But if that's what you want, why are you sending me diamond earrings and a new car?"

"Because I can," he said simply.

"It still feels like our timing is off. I feel like you're still a bit more into me than you should be at this point in our dating life."

"Maybe that's true," he said, slightly forlornly. "And I think you feel it, too, but I can also see that it's not fitting in with your plans to conquer Los Angeles."

"Seamus, a man cost me my hometown. I need to have walls."

"Do you want to tell me what happened?"

"It's not a fun story. It's kind of *Jerry Springer*."

"I promise not to throw a chair at you."

"Okay." Nicola pulled the apron up around her like a coat. "Long story short, my boyfriend of five years, the guy I planned to marry, turned out to be a meth dealer. I don't even know how long he was dealing for. He was good at secrets. Apparently."

"Meth's an idiot's drug."

"They're all idiot's drugs, Seamus," she whispered. "My dad was a great guy, a musician. But he was also a junkie. He left when I was eight. Died when I was fifteen. It sucks . . ."

Seamus reached over and squeezed her hand.

"Anyway, Tony, my boyfriend, had been dealing meth for a while. And he got my little brother, Robert, hooked. All of this happening right under my nose, and I was so busy being a publicity assistant at WDTN in Dayton, I just didn't even know."

"How'd you find out?"

"Billy, of course. We've been best friends since we were in second grade. He moved out to LA . . . Billy came home for a visit, and I still don't know how he found out; he won't tell me. But before I even knew it, he'd gotten Biscuit—that's what I call Robert—into a program, and he'd called the cops on Tony. He and my mom sat at the kitchen table and told me. I was devastated. So devastated. My whole life went up in flames in an instant. And then they told me they were both in favor of me coming back to LA with him." She paused, and then confessed, "It was the darkest time of my life. I was so young when my dad left, and he was a stranger by the time he died—so somehow those times weren't as horrible as this one. When I felt like a complete fool."

"Jesus, Nico . . ." Seamus put his palm up to her cheek.

"That's what my dad called me," she said softly.

"You told me that on Saturday. Do you want me to stop calling you Nico?"

"No, it's comforting. In a weird way."

"So you just left on the spot?"

"Kinda sorta. I called the station and offered them two weeks, but my boss had gone to high school with my mom and he knew what had gone on. He said I could leave right away if I wanted, and he gave me one hell of a reference."

"So that's how you ended up at Huerta?"

"Not exactly. I think it may have helped Gaynor notice me. But we met through Billy. Gaynor has four desks that she'd basically fill with chimps if they'd work for intern pay. Her giving me a job wasn't that big of a deal. But we somehow hit it off."

"And you're obviously good at what you do."

"And how would you know that?"

"I know what it takes to make a good publicist."

"And what might that be?"

"Nerves of steel and balls to match."

"I don't think I have either of those."

"People rarely think that about themselves. Trust me. You're strong."

They ate in silence for a long time.

"I can't believe I just told you all that while wearing panties and an apron," Nicola finally said, attempting to sound light, and failing.

"I'm honored by your trust, Nico. It means a lot."

"Only Billy and Kara know," said Nicola. "I don't know why I even told you. I guess I wanted you to know why I can't just go wild and date you. I . . ." She sighed a little. "I wanted to marry Tony. I would never have moved. I would have lived my whole life in Dayton. The worst part of it was, I was so blind. Tony *knew* I hated drugs, and he knew how much I love my brother. He deliberately fucked me over in the worst way possible." She shook her head a little. "I'm not ready to just be someone's girlfriend after a couple dates. I'm honestly not even sure I'm ready to be somebody's girlfriend ever."

Seamus looked hurt and then tried to mask it with a smile.

"I like you, I do," Nicola reassured him. "Against my better judgment," she added, and smiled wanly.

"What if we just take this one step at a time?"

"What does that mean for you?" she asked.

"Okay, I'm going to be honest as fuck here, since you were," he began. "It means I'm going to like you as much as my heart wants to, but we'll just keep it casual. We'll see what happens."

"Thanks," she said. "I'd like to react to you as a friend, and a lover, and see how much fun we can have. I'd like to just have fun for now."

"You have no idea how special you are; just the fact that you're asking for this, it's amazing," he said earnestly.

"See?" she said. "That is you moving too fast."

"I'm just being honest," he said softly. "This dinner—no other girl I've ever met has done this. This is what I've been craving since I left Scotland. As you know, LA isn't much of a framework for a normal life once you get famous."

"Well, I can guess," she said. She took a breath, and asked, "Do you really think you can do the one day at a time thing?"

"I can, I think," he said. "If you want to date other guys, you obviously can. But I'll tell you now, I'm kind of sold on you, so if it's all right with you, lady boss, my heart won't be into dating other women too much. And I'm planning to change a few things to make my stupid life a bit more of a better fit for you . . ."

He paused. She waited for him to continue, but he didn't.

"That would be your choice." Nicola took another bite of meat loaf. "I'm also currently not seeing anyone else, but it still feels premature for you to be changing your life or for me to be locked down. The car felt like I was being locked down. Or bought."

"I'm sorry about that," he said. "That's not how it was meant." He exhaled slowly. "Are we at the end of our serious talk now?"

She nodded with exhaustion. "Yeah, I think that's about it," she said. "To recap. We are just starting out dating. We are keeping it light. We are having fun. It doesn't always have to be so emotional, right? And once in a while, we are going to split the check at dinner. Cool?"

"Yes," he said, squeezing her hand. "I accept your terms, you ballbuster." He laughed and looked relieved when she did, too.

"Ballbuster?"

"I'm just giving you shit," he said. "And I'm going to warn you—when a Scotsman likes someone, he will give them a lot of shit. So if it's fun you want, you better get ready."

"I'm ready." Nicola smiled.

Seamus picked up his glass of pinot.

"To us, and our keeping-it-light future," he said. She clinked her glass against his.

"Erm . . . ," he said. "Um . . . before we revert to small talk, there's one last thing I'd like to clear with you."

"Okay," said Nicola apprehensively.

"I had Bluey take your car to my mechanic to get it fixed. And he went a little crazy, and what's done is done, but your car will be returned to you later tonight, and I won't hear of you paying me for it; it's my treat. It's the last thing I'll do until you give me another green light. Okay?"

Nicola wondered what on earth they had done to the car, but she nodded slowly. "Okay," she said. "That's very kind of you. Thank you."

"Phew," laughed Seamus, polishing off the rest of his wine and getting up to refill his glass from the bottle. "So now we can get onto the fun light stuff? 'Cause I'm sweatin' bullets up in here."

"Yes, please," said Nicola as he refilled her wine. "Let's finish our dinner and get back into the bedroom."

"Can you keep the apron on?" Seamus said, running his hand under the front of the apron and caressing her nipple.

"You like dress-ups, huh?" she asked.

"Certain things have been known to work," Seamus teased.

"With your other women?"

"That, or in my mind," he laughed. "I think it's time for dessert now." He pulled her upright and started to kiss her again, running his hands inside her undies and cupping her ass.

Nicola started to return his kiss when she heard Kara's key slide into the lock and the door opened.

Seamus scrambled behind her and used Nicola as a modesty shield.

"Oh, holy shit," Kara said, stopping short when she saw them. "I'm sorry, so sorry, I been texting you for hours; I figured you guys were out or asleep."

"It's fine, we're about to hit the hay," Nicola said, not noticing a strange look pass between Seamus and her roommate. Kara played it cool as Nicola stood in front of Seamus in order to conceal his hard-on.

"Listen," said Kara hurriedly, "I'ma go catch a movie."

"Oh? Okay," said Nicola, before clumsily adding, "Kara, this is Seamus. Seamus, this is Kara."

"Hey, Seamus, nice to meet you," Kara said with a broad grin that Seamus could not read. "And I hope you understand, but I'll shake your hand next time." She began to back out of the door, then paused. "And Nicola, you can keep the apron."

CHAPTER 21

FOR A FRIDAY, IT HADN'T been too bad. Nicola had sailed through Gaynor's morning theatrics and Alicia's parakeet chatter floating on a post-date cloud that she hated herself for. So cheesy. She was just glad that Seamus had refrained from sending her flowers, a catered meal, or a car.

The Tercel now drove like a sports car. As she effortlessly passed cars on Beverly and wove around the traffic with a new confidence, she suspected that Bluey had had the entire engine replaced. The tires also looked suspiciously wide and new, and somehow, a Bose stereo had been made to fit where her old AM/FM cassette system had been.

Tonight was a Huerta Hernandez girls' night out. Gaynor confided to Nicola that she was finally considering signing reality stars. "They've got to be easier on the old *coño* than these big movie-star motherfuckers," she'd groaned. Thus, she'd shifted her sights to Amber, and possibly even Kara. She'd set up a table at Freddy's, and announced loudly to her disgruntled staff that only she and Nicola would be going.

"If any of you other bitches show up and use my name, my list to get in, you'll be working at Ontario Mills by Monday," Gaynor had declared at the morning meeting. Nicola, staring down at her notepad, felt six pairs of hateful eyes boring into her. Then she felt a kick under the table and heard Alicia whisper, "Bitch."

Kara had decided to go full Afro "to give Gaynor the Studio 54 vibe," so it was impossible for them to share the bathroom mirror while they got ready. Tonight's full Afro was over two feet across.

"Our next place will need a wider bathroom mirror, K."

"Honey, I want our next place to have studio lighting, two sinks, and a GoPro mounted above a six-foot mirror." Kara laughed, whipping her hair with a vintage 'fro comb she'd bought on eBay.

"I'd settle for a security building with less Russian television."

"I'm thinking we can probably move in a couple of months." Kara paused work on the 'fro and leaned out the bathroom door. "They're offering me semiregular status on Amber's show."

"But are they gonna pay you?"

"There's more chance of them paying me than Amber paying me."

"I thought she offered you five hundred a day?"

"She offers everyone five hundred a day," Kara said ruefully. "But she don't write the checks. Her mom does. And her mom didn't hire me. I don't care. I'll sell that Gucci dress if I have to. The show says they'll pay me a thousand a week during season. We really need to move."

"Well, the checks need to come in first." Nicola made a hurry-up gesture. She needed the mirror, too. "This dump is eighteen hundred. We'd need to pay around three thousand a month for something nice, and we just don't have it. I don't want all my money to go into rent."

"Why don't you let Billy set up a photo with Seamus? That would be a nice bonus. . . ."

The look on Nicola's face froze Kara in her tracks.

"Whaaaaaaaa?" Kara said earnestly. "It's gonna happen sooner or later if you keep on dating the fool. You may as well make money on it."

Nicola shook her head. She hadn't told Kara too many details of the dates, only that Seamus was fiercely protective of things.

"Look," she began, "Seamus goes all-out to keep his shit private. . . ."

"Yeah, sure he does; it's so private to star in blockbusters and be out at parties every night doing . . ."

"Why the hell do you care so much about me dating Seamus all of a sudden?" Nicola snapped. "I'm not asking you to justify why you're banging Jimmy J!"

"I don't give a shit about Jimmy J," Kara said. "I don't even need him anymore, now that I got on a TV show."

"Why are we even fighting?" Nicola sighed. They'd never raised their voices at each other before. "I get it. You want to move. I want to move, too. And when we can afford it, we will get a better place. But right now, I need the mirror. And a hug. If your damn hair will permit it."

"I'm sorry I got all ghetto on your ass, N. Come here and hug a bitch." They hugged gently, beneath Kara's huge cloud of hair.

"Now gimme five more minutes of mirror time."

※　※　※

Nicola walked back to her room and plonked onto her bed to wait.

Fuck. She hadn't called her mother this week. She picked up her phone and dialed. Her mom answered on the first ring.

"There's my girl," Mauve Wallace said brightly. "I was getting worried."

"Hey, Mom, sorry; my week got away from me."

"What's this one's name, then. Not the same one from TV?"

Nicola rolled her eyes. "No, Mom."

"I took a picture of you from the TV and I took it to CVS and they made it into a photo for me. I put it on my nightstand."

"Mom, how's Biscuit doing?" Nicola asked, using the nickname she'd called her little brother since he was born. He'd been the hardest thing to leave behind.

"He's good, peanut; he's still doing his meetings and he's sober as a judge. Probably more sober; you know how the judges are these days."

Nicola laughed.

"Oh, peanut, I got those shoes you sent me, they're beautiful, thank you so much. I love them. But I didn't have anything to wear with them, so I'm gonna go buy myself a dress tomorrow. Aunt Vonnie is gonna come with me."

"Mom, you're supposed to sell them on eBay. You could probably get like eight hundred bucks for them. They're fancy."

"Nicola Wallace! I know what Louboutins are. I'm from Ohio, not the moon."

"Sorry, Mom."

"I'm keeping them, baby. When else am I gonna have shoes like this? Aunt Vonnie and I are gonna take ballroom dance classes so we can meet guys. I'll wear the shoes to the graduation dance. I took 'em down by Louie's shoe repair and he says he fixes those red soles all the time."

Nicola whistled. Her neighborhood was changing.

"Anyways, Mom, I gotta go. We're all heading to Freddy's for a girls' night out. With my boss."

"Oh, I saw that place on *Entertainment Tonight*. That boy from that pop band got drunk there before he crashed his Lamborghini. I'm sure it's not that dangerous. You have such a glamorous life, peanut. I'll tell Biscuit you said hi. Freddy's. I can't believe you're going to Freddy's."

"Mom, it's a work event. Think of it as unpaid overtime. Love you, bye."

"Bye, sweetie."

Gaynor had sent Nicola home with four complete outfits for tonight. All of them were too short, too shiny, and too generic for her. Nicola had gone with Joan Jett classic—faded skintight Dsquared2 jeans, a neon-blue T-shirt, and a vintage pink blazer. A pair of new red Chuck Taylors sealed Gaynor's disapproval.

"*Madre de Dios*," squalled Gaynor as Nicola climbed into the limo. "We're not going to a Lilith Fair revival; what the fuck is this? I sent you home with ten dresses and this is what you wear?"

Nicola ignored her, startled by the presence of Alicia in the back-seat. "Hi, Alicia, you look pretty. Gaynor, you remember Kara?"

Kara and Gaynor exchanged quick hellos. Kara gave Alicia's outfit—a skintight black dress and opaque black tights and black pumps—an approving smile, which faded as she panned up to Alicia's penciled-in eyebrows and brown lipliner around pink lip gloss. Her hair was pulled back into a strict ponytail. She looked like a hefty Mexican dominatrix.

"Well, Nicola," Gaynor continued. "I was going to tell you that tonight, you forget about Seamus, but looking at you, it looks like you've forgotten about men in general."

"Is this going to go on all night?" Nicola asked as the car turned onto Santa Monica Boulevard. "Because it's already boring. I'll make you a for-real bet. I bet I get hit on more than any of you."

"What are we betting for?"

"Up to you." Nicola stared down Gaynor.

"Okay, lady gay." Gaynor ran her tongue over her lips like a lizard. "If I win, I get to dress you for a month. I'd like to make a woman out of you."

"Sure," smiled Nicola. "And if I win, I get two days off where you don't call me once. No emergencies. No excuses."

"I don't care what you ask for, Nicolita. You won't win. The way you're dressed, the only people who will hit on you are that butch DJ and maybe a half-blind gay valet who thinks you're *un hombre*. I'm safe."

Alicia let out a squawk when the car drove past the red carpet that extended six feet from Freddy's door to the gutter.

"Hey, we missed it," she exclaimed.

"We are going in the back, girls," Gaynor announced. "We do not want to look desperate."

"But I wanna get papped," Alicia whined.

"Then get famous," Gaynor snapped. "For now, it's the maids' entrance for all of us."

The limo pulled into the tiny lot behind the club.

"This is not a fun night," Gaynor said seriously. "We are here to be seen. Do not be a disaster, do not be a hungry tiger, and do not do a single fucking thing that will cause me a headache tomorrow. This is work. Make it work."

"Yes, Mom," Nicola said with a smile.

"One last thing." Gaynor waved a silver-clawed hand threateningly at all of them. "If you ask for bottle service, you're paying for bottle service. Alicia! How much does bottle service cost?"

"More than my pussy can make in a month," she droned, repeating a morsel of advice that she'd heard all day.

Gaynor nodded, satisfied.

"*Vamos, chicas,*" she said as Nicola opened the door and they all piled out of the car.

A dead-eyed woman let them in via the club's rear door and hustled them down a dark, narrow corridor. As they neared the doorway into the main room of the club, Gaynor kissed Kara on the cheek.

"Welcome to the club, *mija,*" she said. "The Huerta Hernandez club. Enough drive-bys at Bootsy's. Tonight, let's make it real."

Then Gaynor actually hugged Kara. Nicola's eyes widened in disbelief. Gaynor's eyes met hers and rolled comically. She shoved Kara into the melee on the dance floor. She turned to Alicia and Nicola.

"*Trabajo, putas!*" she cawed, wrapping her arms around their shoulders and leading them onto the dance floor.

Nicola was not surprised to see that, like most of the exalted Hollywood clubs that tourists fantasized about getting into, Freddy's was just another repurposed small deli on the Sunset Strip.

Banquettes lined both walls, a RESERVED sign perched on each table. The narrow area in the center doubled as a dance floor and a holding pen for the nonfamous. Only three of the eight banquettes were occupied, each fiercely guarded by a uniformed hostess in a matching skintight black minidress, spike heels, and flint eyes.

Amber was already there. She rose above the crowd, dancing on their table, platinum hair glowing above a minuscule red glittery strap dress. She waved enthusiastically when she spied Gaynor. She grabbed their table hostess by the shoulder and yelled something in her ear. The hostess's demeanor changed immediately. She smiled broadly at them, unlatching the velvet rope and ushering them in.

"Good evening, ladies," she said with forced enthusiasm. "It's a pleasure to have you tonight. My name is Marta; I'll be taking care of you. Anything that you want." She paused, locking eyes with Nicola. "Anything at all, I'll be happy to get it for you."

Gaynor leaned close to Marta and said something to her in Spanish. Marta's eyes narrowed in annoyance; then as Gaynor kept talking, they widened and she broke into a grin. Nicola knew Gaynor had just instructed her to bring a Grey Goose bottle filled with water, in exchange for professional head shots.

"Of course, Ms. Huerta, anything you wish," Marta said, vanishing into the crowd.

"Nicolita, the bet was for men. That bitch don't count," Gaynor cackled, pushing Nicola onto the banquette.

Nicola found herself sitting opposite Amber.

"Hey, Amber," she said, blowing her a kiss across the table. "I'm not sure if you remember; we met at your birthday."

"Well, hello, you." Amber didn't take her eyes off her phone. "Who are you dating tonight? Seamus O'Riordan or Paul Stroud?"

"Very funny," Nicola deadpanned. "Paul's a client, and I have no idea what Seamus is up to tonight."

"Really." Amber thrust her phone into Nicola's face. "He knows exactly what you're up to. He just texted me."

Blinded by the light from the screen, she could barely make out the texts, but the name at the top did say Seamus. And some hearts. Amber pulled the phone back before she could read anything.

"Oh, calm down." Amber ran an icy hand along Nicola's blazer. "I'm just giving you shit. It's fine. Everyone falls for Seamus when they meet him. We've all been there."

Suddenly, the energy in the room changed. The din of conversation stopped and every head in the crowd spun to face the bar. Nicola followed suit. Falling-apart pop tramp SaraBeth Shields and her drug-dealer-turned-manager stood in front of the bar, on the last step before the dance floor.

SaraBeth looked more run-down than runway, a huge gray men's trench coat pulled around her anorexic frame. At least she'd gone and had her hair and face done, Nicola noted. SaraBeth scowled at the crowd, pulled the trench tightly around her, and darted across the dance floor, heading directly for the banquette next to theirs. Her manager stood in front of the velvet rope, inflating himself like a pigeon, though Nicola couldn't tell if his goal was to block cell phone photos, or make sure he was in them.

SaraBeth fell into her booth and resumed texting. Three feet away, her manager pulled his own phone from his black jacket pocket. They were texting each other. He leaned and whispered to their hostess and she reacted like an electrified cat, darting off toward the bar. SaraBeth rolled her eyes, then resumed angrily stabbing at her phone.

Alicia started trembling. Gaynor gave her an elbow jolt to the ribs and sternly mouthed, "Keep it together." She hyperventilated and continued staring at SaraBeth, her eyes like satellite dishes.

"Señora Huerta," Alicia stammered. "All my high school life, I wanted to be SaraBeth Shields."

Gaynor gripped Alicia's upper arm.

"So, then, like now, you need to raise your game."

"Señora, no, you don't understand. I even did an interpretive dance

228

to her song 'Poison Love' for my sign language class. They said it was too sexy. And now she's right there. *Dios mío*, I love her so much."

Gaynor released her grip on Alicia's arm. The naked joy on the young girl's face softened her heart.

"Don't get your hopes up," she began gently, "but maybe later we can talk to her."

Alicia did a little happy dance and then suddenly slumped onto the banquette, shaking her head in shock.

Marta appeared through the crowd with the water in the Grey Goose bottle and mixers in glass carafes. She set the tray on the table and poured "shots" for them.

"*Mujeres!* Shots!" Gaynor trilled, pointing at their host. "You too, Marta!"

Marta's eyes rolled as she poured water into a fourth glass and held it aloft.

Six glasses clinked loudly, catching SaraBeth's attention. "*Salud*," yelled Gaynor.

"Da fuck?" Alicia spluttered. "How do you make a shot so weak? This just tasted like water!"

Gaynor's lips thinned, but she didn't break her smile.

"Do you want to spend the night waiting in the limo, *chonchis*?"

Alicia theatrically threw her head back and shot the rest of the water, slamming her glass down so hard that Gaynor flinched.

"Alicia, once again I will remind you, real vodka is seven hundred and fifty dollars a bottle." Gaynor pursed her huge red lips. "That bottle of water is costing me a hundred dollars. And head shots. Behave, or I'll make you refill it in the bathroom."

Before she left, Marta handed a tall glass of actual vodka and soda to Amber on top of the banquette. Alicia watched the transaction with open hostility.

Nicola was scoping out the room. Gaynor had told her that from now on, a monthly trip to Freddy's was a big-game safari for the agency, and she wanted Nicola to "start bagging rhinos."

She spied Brian Gregory and Saul Gold at a booth across the narrow room. Their unlikely Hollywood bromance had blossomed on a just-completed buddy comedy. Imaginatively, Brian had played the handsome jock with the sick sexual fetish for grandmothers, and Saul was described in the casting script as "nerdy off-sider." Nicola watched Saul fawning over Brian. It was a role he was apparently comfortable with in real life, too.

"Aw mah GAWD!" Alicia had seen them, too.

Strangley enough, Amber seemed just as excited. The blonde tapped Nicola on the shoulder and motioned to the whole table to lean in.

"Listen, you bitches," she said nastily. "This ain't a fuckin' funeral. I want dancing, I wanna see shots, and I want the whole club to see our panties. Even you, intern. If we're fucking hot enough, Brian and Saul will send us over a full bottle of actual booze. It's better than this by-the-cup service."

Amber lithely clambered up onto the vinyl seat and spread her arms wide over the dance floor. People actually cheered. She raised her drink in the air and then downed it in one long gulp.

"Wooooohooooooo, bitches," she yelled, inaudible over the music.

Gaynor pulled her phone from her purse and began to check her e-mail. Kara popped up next to Amber, shaking her ass in her denim micro shorts, immediately filming a Snapchat. Alicia began to follow suit.

"Not you, not yet," Amber barked. "Just me and the costar for the first two songs."

Alicia sat back down, crestfallen. Nicola looked at her and gave her a smile.

"This part of the evening is business," she yelled into her ear. "Do you wanna come to the bar and get a real drink?"

Alicia looked at her balefully. "Really?" she said cautiously.

"Sure," Nicola smiled. "Hey, Gaynor, I can expense a couple drinks, right?"

Gaynor looked up, stone-faced. "If you sign clients, you can expense a lot of drinks. Until then, you're on a two-drink maximum."

"Perfect, let's go," Nicola said, taking Alicia by the hand and leading her out of the booth.

"Gurrrr." Alicia abruptly stopped moving on the tiny dance floor. "I gots to pee."

The restroom sign pointed up a small staircase to their right, and Nicola grabbed Alicia's hand. Turning toward the stairs, she walked right into Brian Gregory.

"Hey, rocker chick," he said with his trademark goofy smile, running a hand through his wheat-blond hair. "Where are you in such a hurry to get to?"

"Oh, hi," said Nicola. "Nowhere exciting; my friend needs to use the bathroom."

Gregory peered over her shoulder and gave Alicia the once-over.

"Oh shit, rocker chick," Gregory said loudly. "Didn't realize you were into the ladies. It's all good; come by the table later and we'll do shots."

Nicola began to protest, but before she had a chance, Brian had moved past them.

"Oh ma gawd," she heard Alicia say behind her. "You talked to . . ."

Nicola yanked Alicia's hand so hard, she nearly toppled her.

✳ ✳ ✳

The four-person bathroom line had not moved in ten minutes. The two girls ahead of them were banging on the bathroom door, and yelling at whoever was inside. A security guard finally came and said he'd clear the men's room for them. He disappeared into the restroom for a minute and returned, waving the first two women in.

"I'll get you two in next," he said to Nicola and Alicia, blocking the door to the line of men that was forming.

The women's room door finally pulled open and the host of a basic cable fashion show spilled out, wiping her nose. Nicola grabbed the door and pushed Alicia inside.

"Lock the door." A girl in a pink low-cut and ill-fitting minidress was bent over the sink, doing a huge line of coke. Nicola locked the door as the woman slowly stood upright. It was SaraBeth.

"Thanks, bitch," she drawled in her southern twang. She leaned close to the mirror and looked at her makeup. She picked at a skin flake near her mouth, then started lifting up sections of her hair and inspecting her extensions. Nicola fought to suppress a grimace at the sight of the scabs she could see on SaraBeth's scalp. How could this be the same girl whose first CD had been a guilty pleasure at every party and club when Nicola was twenty-one? She did quick mental math. SaraBeth was twenty-two. Nicola felt sick to her stomach.

"How'd y'all get such purty hair?" SaraBeth said, looking right at Alicia in the mirror. "Lookit yer hair! It's so thick and natural looking. Who did it?"

"I did it myself," Alicia said nervously, looking around to make sure SaraBeth was talking to her.

"That's your own hair?" SaraBeth marveled. "I'm so jealous, I can't stand it." She moved toward Alicia and reached out and ran her fingers along her thick black ponytail. "It's beautiful."

"Hey, Alicia," Nicola interrupted, "don't you need to pee?"

"I'll kill you," Alicia spat, ducking into the tiny room's single stall.

SaraBeth extended a hand to Nicola. "What's your name, darlin'?" she asked.

"I'm Nicola." She shook SaraBeth's hand. It was small and very cold. SaraBeth pulled Nicola's hand up to her face and inspected her nails.

"These nails are amazing," she marveled. "I can't have nails; I bite them clean off."

"Try acrylics," Nicola said, trying to wrest her hand away from the pop star.

"I can chew through the wall of a barn when I'm nervous," SaraBeth said quickly. "I'm always nervous. Look at my nails! Look how disgusting."

She extended a flattened hand in front of Nicola's face and Nicola saw that the nails were bitten way below her fingertips, and the corners were red and crusted with dried blood.

"Hey, would you like a bump?" SaraBeth asked, pulling a packet of Parliaments out of a purse sitting in a puddle of water by the sink. She fished inside, retrieving a brown glass vial of cocaine. She unscrewed the cap and set the vial on the sink. She carefully took a cigarette from the pack and turned it upside down, and tapped the vial until some coke fell into the recessed filter tip. She extended it to Nicola, who just stared at it, not bothering to hide the disgust she felt welling up inside her.

"What?" SaraBeth drawled. "I know it's ghetto, but I ain't got no nails."

She moved the cigarette to her nose and snorted the coke up out of it in one noisy, congested breath.

"See? It works," she said, refilling the cigarette tip. "Want one?"

"No, not after seeing what it's done to you," Nicola said as the toilet flushed. She entered the stall as Alicia exited, locking the door behind her.

Nicola heard another snort from SaraBeth and felt herself wincing in anticipation even before Alicia spoke.

"Hi, SaraBeth," Alicia stammered. "I'm Alicia. I love your songs. Oh mah gawd. That one about the bad boyfriend, that's the fuckin' jam, I fuckin' love it. . . . Wait—why you putting your damn cigarette in your nose? Oh mah gawd, is that coke?"

"For fuck's sake, you stupid wetback," SaraBeth drawled. "Hey, pretty dyke," she called to Nicola. "Can you fucking tell your maid to back off?"

Fuuuuuuck, Nicola groaned, pulling up her pants just in time to hear a loud thud. The stall door shook inward, the latch nearly pop-ping off its screws. A garbled noise followed it.

She flushed and pulled the latch back and the door fell in. Alicia had her hand tightly around SaraBeth's throat. Both Alicia and SaraBeth met Nicola's eyes, but only SaraBeth's were pleading for help. One of SaraBeth's hands clawed toward Nicola for assistance. Nicola brushed it off and pushed past her, and began washing her hands in the sink.

"SaraBeth," she said slowly. "This is my friend Alicia, you racist coke whore. You owe her an apology."

"Fuck you both," SaraBeth wheezed. "You've really fucked up here. You're nobody. You don't know who you're messing with."

"Alicia," Nicola said slowly.

"Yes," Alicia said tentatively.

"Don't leave any bruises and don't knock her out."

"Gurl, I'm smarter than that," Alicia said with a laugh. She sud-denly let go of SaraBeth, who struggled for purchase on Alicia's arm but failed and fell backward, her skull smacking loudly on the edge of the toilet bowl. She crumpled lifelessly on the floor.

"Oh mah . . . ," Alicia began.

"Don't!" Nicola snapped. She nudged the inert form on the floor with her foot and it moved.

"Ow, my fucking head," SaraBeth whined. "Get me a fucking doctor, you dykes."

Nicola looked into Alicia's eyes and winked.

"Yes, of course, we'll do it right now."

Nicola looked at SaraBeth's coke vial, still sitting on the counter. She pulled a pink bandanna from her back pocket and wrapped it over her hand before picking up the vial. She unscrewed the lid and tipped all of the coke onto the counter.

"Wha the fuuu?" Alicia marveled.

Nicola said nothing. She took a cigarette from the packet and scooped coke into the tip, and then she dropped it on top of

SaraBeth's leg. She took her cell phone out of her pocket and took photos of the coke, the moaning pop star, and then one of the entire room. She nudged SaraBeth again.

"What, you fucking bitch?" she drawled.

"I'm going to send help," Nicola said with measured anger. "But if you do anything to my friend, these photos I just took will be all over the Internet."

The faded pop star groaned.

"Gurl, you're my hero," Alicia gushed as they opened the door. An angry crowd of women who needed to pee bitched them out as they passed. Nicola grabbed the security guard by the arm.

"You have an overdose in the women's room," she said tersely. "And it's SaraBeth."

Nicola took Alicia by the shoulders and pushed her in the direction of their booth. "Tell Gaynor what happened," she said as she pushed her adrift into the dancing crowd.

A man's hand on her shoulder spun her around. Brian Gregory's handsome face leaned in to her ear.

"Hey, rocker chick, did you have some nice fun with your lady friend upstairs?"

"What the fuck is it with you?" She pushed him away.

"Damn, relax," he said with another easy grin. "I know you're not a dyke, I'm just giving you shit."

"Hilarious." Nicola started to walk away. "What's next? Maybe some cancer jokes?"

"Oh no, you have cancer?" Brian asked, suddenly concerned.

Well, that confirmed it. He was as dumb as she'd heard.

"Brian, I'm straight and I'm cancer-free," Nicola said sympathetically. "And I'm going to go sit with my friends."

"After this dance." Brian took her hands and started bobbing his knees in and out in vague time to the music. Billy called this "straight guy dancing" back home.

"I haven't seen you around," Brian said, his lips brushing her ear.

"Around what?" Nicola said coldly.

"Hey, listen," Brian said. "Just thaw it a little bit. Give me a chance; I know I got off on the wrong foot here."

Nicola shrugged. "Okay," she mouthed over the deafening bass drop. She felt her phone vibrate in her pocket. She pulled it out.

How's your night, Ohio?

She smiled and kept on dancing with Brian while she texted back.

Yours is better than mine, I promise.

She spied Gaynor staring at them from the booth. She made a hand motion that was like signing an autograph. *Gaynor wants his autograph?* It took her a second to realize Gaynor wanted her to sign him as a client. Nicola rolled her eyes, then remembered their bet. She gave Brian a quick kiss on the lips.

"What the fuck?" He was grinning when she pulled away.

"Nothing." Nicola smiled. "Just felt like it."

Brian leaned in and pushed the hair back from Nicola's neck. He started kissing her very gently, right at the edge of her pink blazer. His lips toyed with her skin, his tongue occasionally licking her lightly.

Nicola leaned in as his arms encircled her waist, his thumbs hooking inside the back of her jeans. He pressed his crotch against hers, and she could feel him growing hard against her. His hands moved to her wrists. Suddenly, he tugged her hands behind her back and bit down hard on her neck. Nicola screamed and ripped her arms free. She grabbed the front of his T-shirt and pulled his face an inch from hers. He eyed her hungrily.

"I could tell you liked it rough," he rasped as he got closer to her.

"Does it get you off?" Nicola said, the pain in her neck blinding her.

"Yeah, bitch, it does," Brian growled, baring his teeth at the end for good measure.

"Good," snarled Nicola, drawing her fist back by her hip and then punching him in the nuts as hard as she could. He dropped like a sack of potatoes in a sea of shocked onlookers.

236

"Rough enough?"

Nicola stormed back to her booth, one hand covering the reddening bite mark on her neck.

"You set me up again," Nicola yelled in Gaynor's face. "Why the fuck don't you warn me about these fucking monsters? He is a literal vampire!"

"*Ay*, I didn't think you were his type; this time I would have warned you. He is very rough with his women; the only way to deal is to tie him up first, and then it's okay."

Nicola wondered if Gaynor knew what every Hollywood star was like in bed.

"Anyway, did you give him your card?"

Nicola turned away, shaking her head in disbelief.

"Give me your card," Gaynor said gently, her hand extended. Nicola pulled one from her purse, pressed it into Gaynor's palm, and Gaynor vanished.

Kara pulled Nicola up onto the banquette, a quizzical look on her face. Nicola shook her head; she didn't want to talk about it. Amber stopped waving the Grey Goose bottle in the air and sidled up to her.

"You sure have a knack with the guys," she said, unable to mask the venom in her voice. "You're zero for three. Maybe it is time to try women."

Fuck this shit. Fuck this night. Nicola dropped down and sat on the couch. Across the table, Alicia glared at her.

Amber danced off onto the main dance floor, vanishing into the crowd. Kara was dancing by herself on the banquette, and began to wave her arms the same way that Amber did.

"Are you in trouble, too?" Alicia yelled.

Nicola smiled. "Get up and dance, girl," she yelled back.

Alicia shot to her feet with alarming speed, and in a split second was shaking her ass with surprising feline grace. Kara moved just far enough away from her to not be in the same photo frame and kept on dancing.

Nicola pulled her phone out of her pocket. Her home screen was covered in texts from Seamus.

Are you OK?

Want me to come get you?

Nicola?????

Hey no pressure but if you're having a bad night I'm doing nothing we can fix this.

Hello?

She read the texts with a small smile growing on her face.

Sorry. I had to fend off a vampire

Um OK

"Excuse me, miss."

Nicola looked up to see Perry Pruitt, the newly divorced half of a famous reality TV couple. His Midwestern good looks glowed even in the dim club lighting.

"Miss?" Nicola scoffed. "I'm Nicola. You don't have to be so damn polite."

Perry laughed. "Well, I have a question for you," he said. "Is your friend up there single?" He looked quickly at Kara and back.

Nicola thought about Jimmy J, then nodded vigorously. "Yes, she's single; she's very single," she said. "Here," she continued, sliding out of the booth, "go dance with her."

Perry nodded thanks and stepped up onto the seat, extending his hand to Kara. Her face lit up and she shook his hand. They started dancing close.

Nicola pulled out her phone. He had texted her back.

I didn't know you were into role play

At least he was being flirty, and not all wah-wah feelings. She decided to play along.

You don't know I'm into a lot of things

I'm intrigued

Fuck it, she thought, and typed, you should be.

You free tomorrow night? Wanna do a little role play?

She waited thirty full seconds before texting.

Y

"Nico, Nico, Nico." Gaynor burst through the crowd. "You win the bet. That *coño estúpido* is very sorry he bit my staff. He is sending us some real drinks to say sorry. And then he will be in on Tuesday to meet with you. Of course, Hollywood's most notorious S and M pig wants a dominatrix as a publicist!"

Nicola took a deep breath and smiled wanly as Marta arrived with a tray of actual alcoholic drinks and poured a round of shots for them all.

As they raised their shots in the air, the doors at the back of Freddy's burst open, flooding the room with the flashing red lights of an ambulance.

In an instant, camera-phone flashes joined the siren's red blasts, and everyone in the club turned to the staircase, at the top of which Amber Bank was attempting to carry the listless body of SaraBeth to safety while giving good face to all the amateur paparazzi in the crowd.

Nicola glared at Alicia.

"Did you fucking tell her?" she bellowed.

Alicia shrugged, grinned, and kept on dancing. Kara sprang from the top of the banquette and raced through the crowd. She bounded up six steps in two leaps and positioned herself at SaraBeth's ankles, helping Amber carry their prize while making sure she moved slowly enough to be in more photos.

Amber's perfect grin faltered as she shot a death stare at Kara. Nicola saw it and smiled. Amber clearly did not enjoy sharing the spotlight with her new costar.

Gaynor had a strange expression on her face that it took Nicola a few seconds to recognize. It was pride. She was proud of them both.

Perry appeared by Nicola's side.

"I guess it's time for me to clear out," he said dejectedly.

"Oh no." Nicola touched his arm. "Just hang out here for a minute. Kara will be right back."

Amber and Kara struggled to elegantly descend while carrying all eighty-five pounds of unconscious SaraBeth. Amber's heel wobbled on a step and she faltered, banging the top of SaraBeth's head into the railing. A loud "oooooh" rose from the crowd, and the flashes from the cell-phone cameras merged into an almost constant spotlight. Amber did her best concerned-but-still-sexy face and soldiered downward into the crowd. Kara's face never changed.

"Both of them are geniuses," Gaynor muttered into Nicola's ear. "They're both gonna need a good publicist after this."

CHAPTER 22

BILLY PULLED INTO THE RITE Aid parking lot at the corner of Sunset and Fairfax, parking as far as he could from the cluster of homeless guys congregated by the Dumpsters. Why was West Hollywood so much sketchier than downtown, even at eleven a.m. on a Saturday?

His phone dinged. It was Kara.

Rough morning. Gonna be ten late. Sorry, sweets.

Ten minutes? Yeah, right. If Kara was anything less than a half hour late, for anything, it was a miracle.

Billy snuck in through the kitchen of The Griddle. He spied an old friend, Anson, who'd apparently transitioned from actor to waiter, working tables. He marched up and kissed him on the lips.

"Any chance of a table, bubba?" Billy winked, looking through the windows on Sunset, where a huge crowd of hungry hipsters waited.

Anson nodded at a vacant two-top against the bloodred wall.

"Take that, quick."

Billy casually sat down and put his backpack on the other seat. Anson sauntered over and poured coffee into his waiting cup.

"You eating alone today?"

"Naw." Billy blushed and looked away. Anson's eyes had always slayed him. Big brown beauties ringed by long black lashes popping against his dark brown skin.

"How's the acting going?"

Anson deflated. "You know, auditions. Auditions. More auditions. I've been up for best black friend, black husband, black basketballer. Basically, imagine any character too minor to even give a name, and then add the word black in front of it. That's what I've been up for, but so far, no bites."

"Don't fret," Billy said gently. "This is that part of your career you'll recall in your memoir as the time you almost threw in the towel, before your big break."

Anson picked up Billy's hand and kissed it. "Thanks, sir," he said softly. "Hey, listen, I better serve these other folks or I'm gonna be swamped in shitty Yelps."

"Before you go," Billy said suddenly. "I'm looking for a paid source here. Sell out a few celebs, pay the rent."

"You're the third person to ask me, and I only started here two weeks ago."

"Oh," said Billy, slightly crestfallen.

"Don't worry, B," Anson laughed. "I thought they were setups, so I told them to fuck off. I always say yes to you. What do I do?"

"You wait on a celeb, you eavesdrop like a Russian spy on rent night, and you call me. Boom."

"I still have your number," Anson said. "Be nice to have a reason to use it again."

In his short time in Hollywood, Billy had developed a network of contacts at all of the tabloids, entertainment websites, and blogs. Each week, he sold enough scandal tips and photos to pay the rent on his tiny WeHo guesthouse and the lease on his Audi A4, but not much more. It was time to monetize his access without turning into a reality star, or worse, a celebrity blogger.

Only one tabloid had managed to link him to the Ethan Carpenter Vegas scandal. Billy had insisted on an in-person meeting, and he had been shocked at how easily he'd been able to manipulate the giraffe-faced editor into killing the story in exchange for some "additional details" about the Kiri coke scandal (which had already earned him twenty thousand dollars).

The woman he'd met, Sandra Sandstein, had been easily bluffed into believing that Billy had been at the hospital as a reporter, not a sex prisoner. Billy had been shocked when she revealed that she was the executive editor, and not an associate. She quickly revealed that her job was on the line if she didn't start breaking stories. Billy told her he could bring her five stories a week. He regaled her with tales of the parties he accessed easily, and tidbits of information that she could easily develop into cover stories if Billy agreed to be her on-record unnamed "source."

She'd offered him a three-thousand-dollar-a-week retainer on the spot, and told him she'd pay more if he could convince a celebrity to work with them to stage stories. Every weekly had a starlet who'd cooperate on fashion stories and inside tips—except Sandy's. Billy immediately thought of Kara and set up this brunch. He just wished he'd remembered to be a half hour late.

Anson had refilled Billy's coffee three times before Kara, in dark jeans, a floor-length shearling coat, and face-hugger sunglasses, plopped down at the table, her hair bundled in a vintage silk scarf.

"Gurl," she sighed, resting her head on the Formica.

"Is that hungover talk for 'I'm sorry I'm so late'?"

"No, it's hungover for you're lucky I'm not a lot later." She flagged down Anson. "Make it a red-eye, baby."

"What time did you get in, dear?"

"Five, I think," she said. "We were at Freddy's till it closed, then I went to an after-hours at Amber's. It got pretty crazy." She paused, her eyes visibly widening behind her glasses. "Actually, the whole night was insane."

"I'm all ears," Billy said, leaning forward.

✳ ✳ ✳

Ten minutes later, Billy was closing a deal with Sandy Sandstein on the phone.

"So that's ten grand for the SaraBeth story, and it's definitely a cover?"

Kara ripped her sunglasses off and mouthed, "Shut the fuck up!"

Billy kept nodding, nodding, listening. He covered the phone.

"Can you get photos?"

"Everyone who was there has photos."

"Anything unique?"

"Nicola took some, but you know she won't sell them. She says they're insurance. Alicia told me she took some on her phone over Nic's shoulder."

"Have Alicia text them to me."

"You'll have to pay her and guarantee she won't get busted."

"Deal."

Billy went back to his conversation with Sandy, and Kara picked up her phone to text Nicola for Alicia's number. Her phone was covered in texts from J, but her lips were still tingling from making out with Perry all night. She needed to end things with her rap lothario. He had gone from sublime to ridiculous way too fast.

Billy ended his call and looked at her.

"Anything else last night? Sorry, the SaraBeth stuff was major. Needed to sell it."

"Tons of stuff. Nicola got bit by Brian Gregory."

"I know."

"I saved the best till last. I hooked up with Perry Pruitt."

Billy smiled and nodded.

"Honey," Kara purred. "You look like the cat that got the cream."

"You're a series regular on Amber's show now, right?"

Kara nodded apprehensively. "Ish . . ."

Billy downed his entire cup of coffee in one gulp and sat in silence. She could practically hear the gears whirring in his brain.

"Got it," he said at last, ready to outline his grand plan. "Baby gurl, we are going to make you a star."

Kara slowly sat bolt upright and theatrically dragged her huge sunglasses down her nose, exposing some seriously bloodshot eyes.

"Blech." Billy waved his hands in her face. "Put the glasses back up. My eyes."

"Can it, queen." Kara pushed her glasses over her eyes. "Now get back to the story about making me famous."

"*Spyglass* wants me to manage a celebrity for them. They want someone who will do fashion stories. Boom, you're a stylist. They want someone on TV. You're Amber's new off-sider. And they want story lines that we can play out in real life. So now you're about to bang Perry Pruitt, and you'll be his first celebrity date since his dingbat wife left him on the final season of their reality show."

Kara looked like she wasn't getting it.

"So I'm doing all this for free? For exposure?"

"No, you nutjob," Billy crowed. "I don't know how you'll get paid, but you'll get paid. Everyone says they don't pay for stories, but everyone pays. We just have to figure out with them if you're getting a regular retainer or if you get paid per story."

"Looks like I'm ordering pancakes *and* waffles today, kwaaan." Kara extended her hand. "I don't care if you're my manager or my pimp, we're shakin' on it."

They shook hands, and then Kara jumped up and sprinted around the table and hugged Billy.

"Ow, I shouldn't have done that." Kara winced. "My head." She walked back to her seat in slow motion. "So when do we start?"

"I'm meeting Sandy on Monday," Billy said. "When are you seeing Perry next?"

"Whenever he calls; I ain't gonna chase him."

Billy sat for a second, sipping his coffee; then he nodded decisively.

"Got it," he exclaimed. "Let's start it off with a scandalous breakup with Jimmy J."

"How do I make it scandalous?"

"You tell me. What's the worst breakup that ever happened?"

"I got dumped via text once. It sucked but I felt so *Sex and the City* that it was okay."

"Eh, who the fuck cares about *Sex and the City*? We need something that works right now. We need something to go viral."

He pointed at Kara's phone.

"Unlock it!" he barked. "I need to go through your pics. We are making a breakup meme." Kara took her phone, held her thumb on the home button until it unlocked, then passed it over. Billy started scrolling.

"We have a winner," he announced after poring through a shocking number of sexts on Kara's phone. "Also, side note, how many photos of your vagina do you actually need? Wait. Don't answer that. Can I use this photo?" He turned the phone toward Kara.

"That's his O-face," she said. "He wanted to know how he looks when he comes."

In the photo, J was biting his lip, his cheeks were puffed out, and his eyes, gazing skyward, were slightly crossed.

"I dunno, Billy, this seems kinda cruel . . ."

"Wait, do you like him?"

"No, but this is just some dude who picked me up in Pavilions. I knew him a day before he proposed. It's been silly, but he hasn't been horrible to me."

"You know, he has proposed to three other women in the past month," Billy said.

"Get the fuck out of here." Kara nearly knocked over her coffee. "Why the fuck didn't you tell me?"

"I just found out," Billy said. "I pitched him as a story to the magazine and they said that they'd been contacted by three women who wanted to sell their wedding photos. Same story—they're all attractive black girls who aren't in the business. I guess his biological clock is ticking. Sorry to break it to you, but it's not you he wants, it's the babies you'd make."

"Ugh, what a jackass," said Kara. "My first marriage proposal and it's not even legit."

"Let's make a meme, baby," Billy said.

Using a meme generator app on his phone, Billy added a spiral of blues and pinks behind J's head, and the text HEY PUSSY PLAYA. NOT MARRYIN' YA. SEE YA LATER.

After they stopped laughing, Billy wiped his eyes, texted it back to Kara, and told her to send it to J.

He responded immediately.

What kind of fucking joke is this?

Kara did not pause before replying.

Maybe one of your other fiancées will marry you. We're done.

Kara hit send, then silenced her phone and turned it facedown.

"Now what?"

"Now the magazine *somehow* intercepts this meme. Then we contact the other three women and have them go on record. You can't go on record, and you'll have to pretend to be horrified that J leaked your text. The producers of Amber's show will try to lock you down to a contract as soon as the magazines hit. So we need to have your next steps in place by then."

"And they are . . . ?"

"Perry Pruitt," Billy said. "Obviously. He will call. Set up a date. He'll suggest one of those out-of-the-way places in the Valley, but miraculously, you'll get papped."

"We will?"

"Yeah, because I'll send the photographer. Girl, we are in business. You're about to be a reality TV star."

"Fuck it." Kara shrugged. "This is more fun than organizing wardrobes."

CHAPTER 23

FOR THE SECOND TIME THAT morning, a loud banging at the door woke Nicola.

"Kara, are you home yet?" she called. Silence.

She looked at her alarm clock. Twelve thirty. She'd been surprised she could fall asleep again so easily after her first unwelcome caller—Jimmy J had tried to kick the door in an hour earlier, not believing that Kara wasn't home. She had opened the door just a crack, and J had burst in. After checking Kara's room, and the bathroom, he had stood in the middle of their living room, rapping under his breath and dancing from side to side.

"Hey, J, you need to go."

"I'm thinking of my next move so smooth," he'd rapped. "That bitch done made a mistake."

"Well, that bitch ain't home, and this bitch needs some sleep." She'd guided him gently through the door, closing it on his ass as he left, still rapping.

This time, a delivery man was visible through her peephole.

He handed her a box addressed to her by name only. There was no address on the box. Curious. She signed for it and stepped back inside. She heard her phone ding in her bedroom.

Did you open it?

Seamus. Of course.

About to

She laid the large brown box on the dining table and grabbed a knife from the sink. Carefully slitting the sides of the box and center seam on the box top, she pulled the flaps open. A handwritten note sat atop violet tissue paper.

Hey, Nicola! Sexy fun times await. Nothing serious, my pretty woman. Let's have a laugh. A car will pick you up at ten p.m. Follow the driver's instructions. We'll have a . . . ball. Non-creepy fourth-date-appropriate. Love, Seamus xoxo

Opening the tissue paper, she removed a gorgeous olive-gray knee-length Anna Sui trench coat. Seamus was off to a good start.

Well?

So far so good.

Next she pulled out a pair of gross red patent-leather stripper heels and a white Lycra minidress with cut-out panels at the sides. Her face fell.

Dude, a hooker fantasy?

Seamus didn't miss a beat.

I'm a movie star, pretty woman. Trust me on this one.

⁂   ⁂   ⁂

It was 9:40. Kara still hadn't come home and had been infuriatingly cryptic in texts. Billy had been equally vague. They were somewhere together, and it felt weird that she hadn't been invited. Nicola spanked herself on the wrist.

"No mo' fomo," she admonished herself, and looked at herself in the mirror. The white dress was a cheap Halloween costume. She gave it one last spin in the mirror and pulled it up over her head.

"I can't do this." She tossed it onto the floor.

In the bathroom mirror, she surveyed the results of her makeup battle between good girl and evil. She'd gone heavy on the eyes, kohl rimmed and smoky, but the rest of her face was almost bare. She rethought her lip gloss and dabbed a rosier pink on her lower lip. It worked. She shook her curls around her face. She looked at the time on her phone. "Fuck," she muttered; somehow it had become 9:55.

She stood in front of her mirror in her lavender La Perla lingerie. She kicked off Seamus's hideous whore shoes and pulled on the silver strappy Louboutins.

"Fuck it." She pulled the trench coat on over her lingerie. It was 10:01 p.m. She grabbed the tiny Gucci clutch that Gaynor had wanted her to take to Freddy's, locked her front door, and walked out to the street.

A limo was waiting for her with the door open. She stepped inside and shut the door. The driver didn't speak to her, but started driving.

The nondescript limo with its unseen driver stopped at the corner of Santa Monica and Highland. The screen between the back and the driver's seat lowered.

"Miss Tiffany, this is your stop. Please step outside and wait here for your appointment."

Nicola opened her purse.

"There'll be no need, Miss Tiffany. Your fare has been paid."

"Well, at least let me tip you," she said.

"That won't be necessary, Miss Tiffany," the driver said, getting out and coming around to open her door. "Have a good rest of your evening."

Nicola got out and straightened her coat. The limo slowly rolled off into the crawl of Saturday night Hollywood traffic. Nicola felt alone and vulnerable. She felt the chilly night air on her bare legs and shivered.

The only humans she could see were an old couple waiting at a bus stop on the other side. She stared at her phone, willing a text from Seamus to appear. She looked up and down the street again and decided that she'd call a cab in five minutes and go home. This was lame.

"Excuse me, miss," said a familiar deep brogue. "I'm looking for a little fun tonight."

Her eyes blinded from staring at the bright light of her phone screen, she knew it was Seamus in the driver's seat of the black Maserati that had pulled up.

"Are ya?" Nicola deadpanned. "It'll cost ya."

"Get in; I got cash."

Nicola sauntered over to the open passenger-side window and leaned her head in.

"Lemme get a look at ya!" She sized up Seamus and made an exaggerated show of approval. She unlatched the door and got in.

"My name's Willie," Seamus said.

"Nice to meet ya, Willie," she said, extending her hand. "I'm . . . uh, I'm Tiffany."

"Hey, Tiffany," Seamus said, steering the car out into the sea of traffic. "I think we're alone now."

Nicola laughed. "So what do you do for a living?" she asked.

"I'm a groundskeeper at a local school," he said seriously.

"Do the kids call you Groundskeeper Willie?" Nicola asked, barely able to keep from laughing.

"Among other things, the little fuckers," Seamus said.

"Nice car for a groundskeeper," Nicola sniffed.

"It's a private school," Seamus said, making a left off Santa Monica onto a side street. Suddenly, a cop siren wailed behind them and the car's interior filled with flashing red and blue light.

Seamus said *fuck* under his breath as he pulled over. Nicola rapidly checked the buttons on her coat and pulled it down over her legs, crossing her ankles demurely. The cop car pulled up behind them and flooded the Maserati with blinding light. They sat silently until the cop appeared at Seamus's window. As soon as Seamus rolled down the window, the cop's eyes went wide.

"Good evening, officer," Seamus said.

"Good evening, uh, Mr. O'Riordan," the cop said. "Do you know why I'm pulling you over?"

I'm about to be charged with prostitution, Nicola panicked. *Great.*

Her mom would love that. She pushed her fingernails hard into the palm of her hand and took a deep breath.

"I do not know, officer," Seamus said affably. "I sure wasn't speeding."

"You made an illegal left turn, sir," the policeman said.

"I can't turn here?" Seamus said, honestly surprised. "I do it all the time."

"Saturday night cruising laws, sir," the officer said, pulling out his ticket book. "I'm going to need to see your license and registration."

Nicola exhaled, a long, slow breath of relief, and shot the cop a wan smile. He smiled back.

"Evening, miss," the cop said.

"Evening, officer."

Five minutes later, Seamus was stuffing the traffic violation into the glove compartment, and they pulled back onto the road.

"Sorry about that, Tiffany," Seamus said.

"Your price just doubled, Willie," she replied huskily, opening the bottom two buttons of her coat and slowly crossing her legs. Seamus looked over at the newly exposed inner thigh.

"I'm good for it," he said, swallowing drily. Seamus deftly threaded his way through the streets of Hollywood. He absently reached across and ran the back of his knuckles up along Nicola's thigh. She pushed his hand away.

"Payment up front," she said, looking out the window.

"I said I'm good for it," Seamus laughed, placing his warm, callused palm on her knee as the car turned off Los Feliz, up into Griffith Park.

"You're bringing me into a park," Nicola said curtly. "At night."

"I can't take you home," Seamus said. "The wife is home."

"Even if this is just a front seat handy, you're still paying the full amount."

He laughed as they plunged into the pitch dark. After a winding mile or so, she saw a boom gate blocking the road ahead. And out of the dark, Bluey materialized, and swung it open.

"Perfect timing," Seamus said as he barreled through the gate. Nicola looked in the rearview mirror and saw Bluey closing it behind them.

They continued up a deserted road, and the Griffith Observatory rose out of the ground ahead of them, behind its now-empty parking lot. The building was illuminated by floodlights. Seamus drove right up to the front.

"You bring whores to the observatory?" Nicola laughed.

"Come on, Tiffany," Seamus said, getting out of the car and coming around to her door.

He helped her out and stood expectantly in front of her, arms open wide.

"I don't kiss on the lips." Nicola strode brusquely away across the lawn toward the main building.

"Follow me," Seamus said, catching up to her easily. He led the way to the right side of the building and disappeared down an old stone staircase, past a deserted restaurant patio, and around behind the building's back corner.

Nicola checked to see if Bluey's car had followed them. Seamus's car sat solitary in the parking lot. She took a deep breath. Bluey had secured the area. They wouldn't be bothered. She unbuttoned her coat and pulled it open, revealing her lingerie, and followed Seamus.

When she found him, on a terrace at the back of the observatory, with all of LA sparkling below in the distance, she grinned. His pants were unzipped and he was already rock hard. He whistled as he looked her up and down.

"Where's the dress?"

"What dress, Willie?" She walked toward him and took him in her hand. He gently gripped her arm and pulled her hand away.

"Tonight's about you, Tiffany."

He reached inside her coat and grabbed the sides of her underwear, and slowly pulled it down. He started kissing her on the center of her chest, and as he pulled the panties lower, he kissed a line down her belly until he buried his face in her crotch, breathing deeply.

She stepped out of her lingerie, leaving it on the ground. He slid the coat off her and turned to lay it on the concrete wall that separated them from the cliff below. Then he turned back and grabbed her under the armpits to lift her effortlessly and set her down on top of the coat. Nicola sensed the forest dropping below her, a feeling that made her not want to look down. Seamus grabbed her hips, and they kissed. He moved down her neck to her chest, and she began to lean back over the abyss. Her head fell back, and she had to open her eyes. All of Los Angeles, a black-and-light constellation of spiraling dots, spreading out beneath her in every direction, stopped by haze, or the deep dark of night and the Pacific.

"This is beautiful," she sighed.

"So is this," Seamus said, staring at her hungrily. He kneeled, still firmly holding her hips, and begin kissing the insides of her knees. Switching from leg to leg, he worked his way slowly upward. He alternated deep kisses with light flicks of his tongue as she began to lose her mind. She grabbed his curly hair with both fists, and he let out one of his basso growls. She pulled him closer to her, wrapping her legs around his neck and crossing her ankles.

Secure in his arms, her legs tight around him, Nicola let herself fall back again, the twinkling lights of Hollywood blurry and upside down, and the smell of bark and sage rising up the canyon.

Seamus's breathing got louder, and Nicola realized that if he got carried away and let go of her, it would be bad. She felt her orgasm warming inside her. Seamus groaned loudly, his hot breath against her, and that was it. She grabbed his hair and clung to him even tighter, trying to stare at Hollywood. She couldn't fight the waves anymore, and her eyes closed as she finally relaxed against him.

A strong arm slid around her lower back, and another scooped her shoulders, pulling her onto the parapet again. Nicola sat there with her breath coming in jagged pants. She fought to get her brain to function.

Raising her head slowly, she saw Seamus standing in front of her, sliding on a condom. His cheeks and forehead were shiny in the moonlight.

"How about now, Tiffany?" he whispered. "Now do you fuckin' kiss?"

Nicola nodded, and he stepped forward. He wrapped his arms around her back and roughly kissed her with passion that was new to them. He kissed her so hard she was pushed back over the abyss, his strong hands making sure she wouldn't fall. As they kissed, she felt him gently pushing against her, his head teasing her as he began to rub back and forth, and suddenly, with another loud growl, he slid all the way inside her.

Without warning, he rapidly let go of her back, and Nicola let out a short yell as she fell backward. He instantly grabbed her around the thighs, and began to fuck her.

"Oh my God," Seamus said over and over. "I wish you could see what I can see."

Nicola wrapped her legs behind his back for safety, and relaxed, her arms reaching out into space.

"This is fucking magic," he panted. She raised her head. He was staring at her with a naked, open expression she couldn't place. "Nicola, you don't know what you do to me."

"Shh," Nicola said. "I'm Tiffany, and you're on the clock. Get to fuckin' work."

Seamus smiled his trademark half smile, strengthened his grip on her thighs, and started delivering long, slow thrusts that gradually sped up again. He freed one hand and ran it across her stomach, her chest, and up to her neck. He grabbed the back of her head, lifting her off the wall completely, and fell into the rhythm that Nicola recognized as his pre-orgasm.

She wanted to kiss him, to feel his rough, hairy chest against her, but he was miles away. She stared at his closed eyes and the sweat-tipped ringlets of hair that bounced around them. He bit his bottom lip as he started to come. She felt her own orgasm rocketing through her. He let out a roar and pulled her upright, crushing her against him, his moans loud in her ear as he shuddered. They held each other for a minute, catching their breath.

"Hey, can I get down?" she whispered after a while. "This wall is cold."

"Oh my God, I'm so sorry." He lifted her down and put the coat back over her shoulders.

She cocked an eyebrow as he removed the condom, and then pulled a Ziploc from his pocket, placing it inside.

"Really?" she asked.

"I can't be too careful," he said ruefully. "I'm ninety-nine-point-nine-percent sure nobody knows we are here, but the last thing I need is for some paparazzi to be selling my sperm on eBay."

"Yeah, because that's normal." Nicola picked up her panties from the ground. "Here, I'm not putting these back on," she laughed. "Toss 'em in the baggie, too."

"I have a change of clothes for you in the car," Seamus said.

Nicola stopped to look at him. He looked just like a regular, considerate guy, not a movie star. He held her hand as they walked back around front.

There was an overnight bag in the trunk of the car, as promised. Seamus handed it to her, and Nicola squealed with delight. Inside were square-cut underpants that she slid on immediately, distressed jeans, and a Clash T-shirt. She took off the coat, standing there in her mismatched bra and panties, and held the shirt up.

"You like it?" Seamus kissed the top of her head. "It's vintage, 1978, baby."

"Get out of here." Nicola whistled as he nuzzled his stubble in her neck. She pulled the shirt on, then shook out the jeans.

"I'll need your help for this part," she said.

"I am not normally a fan of helping you get your pants on." Seamus chuckled as Nicola placed a hand on his shoulder and shucked off her Louboutins. She stepped into the jeans, and then back into her shoes.

"I knew you wouldn't wear those stripper shoes," he said.

"Yeah, you need to learn the difference between hooker and Hot Topic."

"Oh, I know it well," he smiled. "Clearly you've never been to Edinburgh."

She pulled her coat back on.

"So what do you usually do with your hookers at this point in the evening?" she asked.

"I kill them and throw the body over the wall," Seamus said in such a cartoony American accent that she burst out laughing.

"That actually concludes the *Pretty Woman* portion of our date," he said softly. "How d'you feel about a sleepover?"

"That would be lovely," Nicola said. "Your place or mine?"

"Well," he said slowly. "That depends on how long you want to cling to your fantasy of a regular date. I'm happy to go to your place, I like it there, or we can go to the stupid high-security glamour flat that my agents rented for me, just as long as you promise to think of it as a nice hotel, and not a reflection of me personally. Nothing there belongs to me. I'm only there until I start work on the next movie."

"Hmm," Nicola said, pressing a finger to her chin. "We have less chance of being interrupted by an irate rapper at your nice hotel. Let's do that."

Seamus raised an eyebrow but didn't ask. He pulled out his phone and sent a short text, which Nicola assumed was to Bluey, and then he opened her car door for her.

"Tiffany, I want to thank you for an awesome night," he said.

"Thanks, Groundskeeper Willie," she laughed.

He handed her an envelope, and closed her door and walked around to his side of the car. It contained a wad of Monopoly money. She laughed and pressed the cash against her chest.

"Wow, Willie." She smirked. "I'm gonna buy Boardwalk."

"Mayfair, darlin'." He smiled, taking her hand. "Let's get you a hotel on Mayfair."

CHAPTER 24

EVERY COMPACT PARKING SPOT IN the Kings Road parking structure—and part of the ones on either side—contained an oversize SUV. Billy scaled higher and higher in his A4, cursing with comical abandon at the self-centered assholes who parked that way. He was going to be late for his breakfast meeting with Sandy Sandstein. At Hugo's, of course.

His phone rang. It was Nicola.

"Oh, hey, remember me?" Billy asked. "Your best friend you haven't talked to since Friday?"

"Your name's Jimmy, right?"

"Hardy har. You better have a good excuse, or even better stories. I called you like a zillion times yesterday!"

"I know, Billy boy, and I'm sorry. I had a very Seamus weekend."

"Is that a good thing or a bad thing?"

"You know," she said slowly, "you're gonna hate me, but it's decreasingly a bad thing."

"Ah, fuck," he said. "I knew it. I fucking knew it. You know this is a disastrous move, right?"

"Says the antidrug antifame guy who's still fucking the biggest closeted meth head on the tween circuit?"

"Yes, but that's different. I'm not going to fall in love with Ethan."

"And I'm not going to fall in love with Seamus," she said. "This is just fun, and he's surprisingly non-Hollywood."

"Okay, so let me get this straight. You've dated on a yacht, in a private restaurant, at a secret motel, and this is normal?"

"Well, on Saturday he rented out the observatory so we could fuck!"

"You went to Santa Ana?" Billy almost hit a car coming down from the dreaded rooftop parking area.

"No, you airhead, the fucking Griffith Park Observatory." She laughed.

"Girl, we are overdue for drinks." Billy finally pulled into a vacant space just inside and safe from the blistering sun.

"Tonight," Nicola said. "You, me, and a bucket of Moscow Mules."

"I was supposed to see Ethan," Billy protested.

"Yes, you *were*," Nicola said breezily. "But now you're seeing me. He can sit in his closet and smoke meth till you get there."

"Fine, fine. Gotta go make the doughnuts. See you later!"

He hung up and chose to jump down the smelly stairs instead of taking the gross elevator. Both options reeked of piss, but the stairs felt less prisonlike. Reaching the street level, he pushed through the security doors and exited onto Kings Road, looking for his lunch date.

Sandy cut quite a figure standing outside Hugo's, all drooping shoulders, mom jeans, and off-the-shoulder eighties workout shirt. Rhinestones spelled out CHOOSE LIFE. She was checking her BlackBerry and stealing furtive glances at every passerby.

She saw him crossing Kings Road and slouched toward him, embracing him in a hug that felt like it was in slow motion. He struggled to extricate himself.

"Sorry I kept you waiting."

"Oh, don't worry, sugarplum," she said, her voice making him queasy. "I've been breaking news and taking names."

"Well, I have lots more of both for you. Let's get a table."

After rejecting the first three tables their server offered them (too out of the way, too dark, and bad energy), Sandy decided that the central location of the fourth was "just right."

She then tortured the guy with a list of her food allergies and sensitivities. He suggested the vegan quinoa salad. By the time Sandy was done modifying it, it was basically a Big Mac. The server, exhausted, looked at Billy.

"For you, sir?"

"Chop salad, add chicken," Billy said with a wink.

The server burst out laughing as he wrote it down. "Thanks, man." He extended his hand to Billy. "I'm Oscar. I've seen you around."

"What was that?" Sandy asked with a paranoid edge when Oscar had gone. "Some secret gay thing? Was that code? Oh my God, have you hooked up? You're into black guys? Oh, wait." She paused. "Is he one of your sources?"

"A lady never reveals her sources," Billy said in an exaggerated drawl.

"Not even to meeeeee?" Sandy wheedled.

Especially not to you, you hideous beast, Billy thought as he took a sip of his water.

"So, what can we do with the SaraBeth story?" she asked.

Billy looked at her with dead eyes.

"I've been texting you about this since Saturday," he said exhaustedly. "You haven't answered yet. I have a source who was there, and who saw it all. She can't go on record, but she'll talk."

"Right, for ten thousand dollars." Sandy frowned.

"Yes, and if you don't agree to it right now, I have to connect her with the *Star*. Time's a-wasting!"

"Why are you breaking my balls, Billy?" Sandy wailed.

"Hey, Sandy, no sweat; if you don't want it, she can take it elsewhere."

"No, you cheeky thing." She batted her eyelids slightly out of sync. Billy realized she was flirting with him. "I just like a little foreplay before I get fucked hard."

"Ten thousand is a steal." He ignored her. "Did you bring contracts?"

Sandy hauled her denim purse onto the table and withdrew a sheaf of papers. The top one was a contract headed SARABETH SHIELDS OVERDOSE COVER STORY $10,000. The one beneath it agreed to pay Alicia four thousand dollars for her iPhone photos.

She handed Billy a pen. He signed them both, and they spent the next few minutes in silence as he connected Kara with a *Spyglass* reporter, and forwarded the high-resolution photos to Sandy's art director.

Their food arrived just as Billy was getting done.

"Where were we?" he asked while Sandy took a sip of her water.

"Well, basically, I want to offer you a job," she said, a trickle of water running down her weak chin.

Billy's eyes widened a little bit.

"This is a job interview?" he asked cagily.

"No, silly, I'm already offering you a job," Sandy said. "We want you just for ourselves. You'd be like our roaming news director, out in the field, sending us all your stories."

"I dunno." Billy stirred his salad with his fork. "I mean, Kara's going to pay me a thousand commission just for connecting that call. I can probably do better if I stay freelance."

Sandy's basset face froze. She narrowed her eyes and leaned in toward Billy.

"I can offer you two twenty a year, guaranteed bonus, and you only have to be in the office Mondays and Wednesdays. I want to lock your pretty self down."

"But I'm not a journalist," he sputtered.

"Ugh, who is?" Sandy said conspiratorially. "I studied communications and had a sociology major, and like, what good is that? I worked as an assistant in New York for ten years, and I mean, where was my lucky break?"

"I'll take it, then," Billy said.

"Thought you might." Sandy seemed very pleased with herself. "So today's your first day at work. How about you spill some stories?"

Billy flicked through his phone until he found the Master J breakup meme.

"Billy, a meme is not a story."

"It is when Jimmy J's fiancée found out he'd proposed to three other women and that's how she dumped him."

There was so much half-chewed food inside Sandy's mouth when it fell open that Billy had to look away.

"Can you get it on record?"

"Not from the woman who sent it, but we can definitely get the other three."

"Okay," said Sandy thoughtfully. "We can probably fit it into this week's issue. Can you come into the office after this and get the story up and running?"

"Uh, sure," said Billy. "I don't understand why you're not more into it, though; Jimmy J is a huge star and this is deliciously humiliating."

"You aren't a journalist, darling; you don't know the rules."

"What the actual fuck are you talking about?" he asked sweetly.

"We don't cover black people," she said brightly. Billy coughed in surprise. "Don't be naïve. It's not racism," she continued. "They just don't sell for us."

Billy shook his head. "*They* don't, huh?"

Oblivious, Sandy stabbed at her salad. Billy saw Oscar approaching.

"Well, then you're not going to like the star I've arranged to be our *Spyglass* celebrity," he began.

"Oh God, I should have warned you not to get a black person," Sandy said, rolling her eyes.

Billy hoped that Oscar hadn't heard her. Oscar stood behind Sandy and flipped her off. He'd heard.

"Listen," said Billy, "you want this one. She's young and beautiful, and she's just been added to Amber Bank's reality show, and she knows everyone."

"Will she pin my book on Pinterest?" Sandy asked.

"Will that make it okay that she's black?" Billy asked incredulously.

"Will you pin my book?"

"I'm not on Pinterest."

"What?" Sandy squawked.

"I have a penis. Pinterest is a housewife site. Not into it."

"That's hilarious." Sandy smacked a palm on the table for emphasis. "Every gay I know is on Pinterest."

"Every gay I know is on Scruff," Billy countered. "I'll promote your book there."

"Oh, so you will promote it? Great, thanks," Sandy gushed. "I had a lot of interest but I decided to self-publish, so every little bit helps. So, will this girl promote my book?"

"If it's a deal breaker, sure." Billy hated Sandy more every second.

"Great, well, let's start brainstorming her."

"No need. She just dumped Jimmy J and is about to be dating Perry Pruitt. I've scheduled them to get papped together on Wednesday night."

"Oh my God, we have to make sure we get those pictures!"

Billy gripped the table for strength.

"The pap will be working for us," he explained.

"Oh, phew," Sandy said with a theatrical eye roll. "That was close."

Standing on the corner of Kings Road and Santa Monica, Sandy was explaining how to get to the *Spyglass* office.

"I've already been there," Billy said, starting to walk away.

"Before you go, I have to call my boss from the car. I have two things to ask you about."

"Okay."

"Crystal Connors told me that Gaynor Huerta is your publicist. What's up with that?"

"Gaynor's a friend. She helped me out of a tight spot recently, but she's not my publicist."

"Oh, that's weird." Sandy was clearly confused. "Crystal said that you might know something about Gaynor and Max Zetta."

Billy's poker face kicked in. *Spyglass* was on to his story.

"She's his publicist," he said. "That's about all I know."

"I heard she's more than a publicist to him."

"Ugh, that's gross," Billy said. "I haven't heard anything. But then again, I probably wouldn't hear anything. Is this a big story that you'd do? Aren't they a bit too old for *Spyglass*?"

"Oh my God, you are such a *newb*." Sandy cracked up so hard she bent double. "You're pitching me a black girl cover star, but you don't think old people sell magazines? Heck, even old people outsell blacks at the newsstand."

"What was the other thing you needed to ask?"

"I hear you know a lot about Seamus O'Riordan."

"I know he's hot, and I see him at parties from time to time, but that's about it. Did you want anything specific?"

"Billyyy, don't treat me like I'm stupid."

"I couldn't possibly." Billy smiled. "But I don't have anything on Seamus. I haven't even seen him out for a few weeks now."

"That's exactly what I'm talking about," Sandy said as if she was talking to a child. "He was spotted with a mystery woman a week ago, and there's a high price on her head. Very high. Bring that in and we can start talking bonus pay."

"Okay, I'm on it, boss," Billy said.

Sandy consulted the chunky black G-Star watch on her wrist. "Okay, fun's over, we need to get back to the office. You have six pages to fill and the clock's a-ticking."

※　※　※

As soon as Billy got into his car, he called Gaynor.

"*Pendejo*, I don't have time to bail your faggot ass out today" was her opening remark.

"The shoe's on the other foot today, *abuelita*," Billy responded. A howling cackle came from the phone.

"Gaynor, this is serious," he said. "I just had lunch with Sandy Sandstein from *Spyglass*—"

"Stupidest. Woman. Ever," Gaynor interrupted.

"No arguments there," Billy said. "But listen, she started asking me if I knew anything about you and Max Zetta. She said that Crystal is spreading some rumors."

"What did you tell her?" Gaynor was suddenly all business.

"I said I didn't know anything," Billy said. "Because I don't know anything."

"Good. Thank you, *mijo*," she said. "I have to go now. I know you have my back."

She hung up. Billy realized he felt bad for her. Since they'd met, she had helped him, and more important, she had helped Nicola. *Crap*, he thought. *I've become protective of Gaynor fucking Huerta.*

✳ ✳ ✳

Inside Sandy's Prius, a similar phone call was taking place.

"G'day, Sandy."

"Bluey, your accent is so sexy, I can't stand it," she said.

"So how'd your lunch go?"

"I did what you asked," she said. "I pushed for info on Seamus and this mystery woman, I offered him a lot of money, and he didn't bite."

"Hmm," Bluey said. "Are you telling me the truth?"

"Oh my God, of course I am. I want my end of the deal so bad."

Bluey sighed into the phone. "So, he did not say one word about Seamus or who he's dating?"

"Didn't you hear me the first time, maaate?" Sandy's Australian accent was almost as awful as her regular one. "He said he didn't know anything."

"Okay, thanks," Bluey said.

"You're welcome, maaaate. So now, tell me where Seamus will be sitting reading my book, and I'll send a paparazzo over to get the shot of him reading it. Make sure he holds the cover so that a photographer can get it clear in the shot."

"Got it, Sandy," Bluey said. "And you remember our side of the deal, right? If you ever print a bad photo or story about Seamus, he will go on *The View* and say your book is the worst thing he's ever read. You got that?"

"Loud and clear," snipped Sandy. "You don't have to be such a J-E-R-K about it."

"Yes," Bluey sighed. "I do. Bye, Sandy."

CHAPTER 25

THE FALLOUT FROM THE JIMMY J story was much better for Kara than it was for J. *Spyglass* hit newsstands on a Wednesday. By Friday, the story and the meme had spread like wildfire. J had already lost thousands of dollars in bookings, and Kara had been offered a contract to stay on Amber's show as a permanent player. The following Wednesday, *Spyglass* had a cover inset of Kara at dinner with Perry Pruitt, and just this morning, two weeks later, Kara had been offered a holding deal to shoot a pilot for a spinoff show.

Nicola and Billy had been behind her negotiations the whole time. When the production company asked for Kara's publicist's phone number, she'd automatically given Nicola's name. They'd signed the contracts this morning at home and she had just given them to Gaynor, who was now barreling out of the lunchroom waving a champagne bottle above her head.

"Listen up, bitches," she declared to the army of disgruntled interns at their desks around the copier. "This is how you do it. Miss Wallace has been working here for under a year, and she just landed another celebrity client. As of today, Huerta Hernandez represents Kara Jones, and she was signed by Nicola Wallace."

"Who the fuck is Kara Jones?" A blond girl in jeggings and an oversize T-shirt glowered into her phone.

"You won't be asking that after two months of Huerta Hernandez magic, Desiree," Gaynor snapped. "Also, in two months, you'll still be cleaning the lunchroom, smartass."

She tore the cork from the bottle. "Nicola, bring your cup over here."

Nicola took her foam coffee cup full of champagne back to her desk. Gaynor had promised her an office when she had either five clients or three "big" ones. For now, she still sat near the entryway, across from Alicia, who had apparently spent her SaraBeth photo money on hair extensions and a lot of clothing at Torrid.

The past two weeks had been comparatively quiet for her. Billy and Ethan had settled into a weird rhythm, and Billy swore he wasn't just using Ethan for stories. Either way, he'd been working at *Spyglass* and busy most nights. Nicola had signed Brian Gregory as her first client. He'd come to the office and tried to bully her down to a $1,500 monthly rate. Behind him, Gaynor had made a whip-cracking motion. Nicola had stepped up and put her face right into his.

"Listen, you talentless hack, if you think I'm going to put out fires for your stupid ass for fucking minimum wage, you can walk right now."

Ten minutes later, he signed a contract paying Huerta Hernandez ten thousand dollars a month, with a one-year guarantee, and Gaynor was talking bonus and promotion with Nicola.

Seamus had been in and out of town. He was prepping to start his next movie, so it made perfect sense that he needed to fly to Japan for one day to meet with his kung fu instructor, then do some green-screen tests up north outside San Francisco. They'd squeezed in some dinners at his studio rental, as Seamus called it, and one charmingly low-key night out on a funky boulevard in Highland Park. She hated to admit to herself that she missed him.

She was still sipping on her champagne when the door opened and Seamus himself walked in.

"What the fuck are you doing here?" Nicola gasped, spitting champagne all over herself.

"It's a lovely surprise to see you, too." He grinned, sweeping her up in a big hug.

He went to kiss her and Nicola gave him her cheek, her eyes darting toward Alicia, who was about to burst like a cherry bomb.

"I came to say hi." Seamus pulled back. "I was driving by and there was a vacant meter on Beverly and it still had the flashing green light, so I, uh . . ."

"You can stop," Nicola said, still in his arms.

"OH MA GAWD," Alicia blurted out, standing up. They pulled apart, laughing.

"Alicia, this is Seamus, and Seamus, this is Alicia." Seamus nodded in Alicia's direction. Alicia extended her hand and shook hands with the air, a glazed expression of shock on her face.

"Can you please let Gaynor know we have a guest?"

Alicia just kept nodding. Nicola wasn't sure she'd heard anything.

"So, uh, this is unexpected." Nicola shuffled her feet like a nervous schoolgirl. She willed them to stay still. She knew every single girl in the office was staring at her.

"Yeah, I was actually going to call you, but then, you know, the empty spot right out front."

"Totally unplanned."

"Listen, Nicola, if this was planned, I'd have a bunch of flowers."

Alicia collapsed in her chair. "OH MA GAWD."

They both yelled "Alicia!" at the same time.

"Sorry," she muttered, fixating on a piece of junk mail on her desk.

Gaynor's office door opened and the usual sounds of bustle and chaos got closer.

"Nicolita, you brought a friend to work today." She swanned over in a white pantsuit and fuchsia heels.

Nicola began to introduce them.

"We've met before," Seamus interrupted graciously, kissing Gaynor's hand.

"A gentleman always remembers." Gaynor was blushing. "Even if he's lying."

Seamus raised an eyebrow.

"The first time I met you was poolside at the Montage," he said. "After that, I've talked to you probably ten times." He paused. "I think I actually saw you last week at the Montage again, but you didn't answer when I called."

Gaynor's face fell for a split second, but she recovered with a tight smile.

"Ah, *mi guapo*," she purred. "I must be getting old if I'm too involved in my own drama to hear the call of a handsome man."

"You're a busy lass," Seamus said. "I'm sure you had something better to do."

"Did you come to take Nicola away for the afternoon?" Gaynor said, quickly changing the subject.

"What? Um, sort of," Seamus sputtered. "How did you know? Did you talk to Crystal?"

"My darling, if I can help it I *never* talk to Crystal. That was just small talk."

"Oh." Seamus laughed. "Well, guilty as charged. I did come to ask Nicola out, but I hadn't planned on an audience. Is there, uh, somewhere we can talk?"

Gaynor rolled her eyes. "But of course; take my office. I can stay out here and . . . oh, never mind, just go."

✳ ✳ ✳

Nicola pulled Seamus into Gaynor's office and then closed the door behind them.

"Where are you taking me?"

"No beating around the bush then, eh?" Seamus said, and Nicola saw that he was nervous. Very nervous.

"I . . . uh . . . well, as you know, the movie starts shooting next week, in Ojai," he said. "And I'm just going to say it. This is what I hate about my job. I'm a homebody. I like being in one place. And I hate being pulled away just when I meet someone who is . . . who is . . ."

"Who is someone you're dating," Nicola said with a smile. "Go on."

"Would you come up and stay with me?" Seamus said, blinking twice before making eye contact.

"Seamus, I can't," Nicola said, shocked. "I have a job. I have clients now. I'm just getting busy."

Seamus reached out and put a finger gently on her lips.

"I know, Nicola, so please hear me out."

She nodded.

"This is a huge leap for us as a couple, and I know that. It's too early and it's too much and it's too fucking everything, but this is the nature of my job. This is why actors rush into shit all the bloody time. I'm not saying that I'm rushing into anything, but to be completely honest, I like you. I like you in a way I haven't liked anyone, for years, since I started doing this ridiculous job, and if I go away for three months, even just to Ojai, I may as well forget about it. And you. And I don't even know how you feel; I don't know if you're on the verge of liking me or of kicking me to the curb. So it feels like there's a gun to my head and I don't know what to do or how to play this." He paused, looking right into her eyes. He was out of breath, panting and staring at her, spent.

Nicola wasn't sure what to say. "Seamus, Ojai is only like an hour away."

"I know," Seamus said quietly. "I'm also not here to pressure you into saying anything at all, or coming to a decision right now. I've done some thinking and I have what I think might be a compromise of sorts."

"Okay," Nicola said hesitantly.

"Just come with me for preproduction. See how it feels. Take a couple days off. We'll have a villa all to ourselves. I'll have to do a couple quick photo shoots, but you can go shopping or whatever. You can bring Billy or Kara if you want. It's a big villa. What's the word for a big villa? Anyway, I'm rambling."

Nicola reached out and punched him affably in the right shoulder.

"What the fook was that?"

"That was me being awkward as fuck," Nicola said. "Let me talk to Gaynor. That was probably the worst invitation I've ever received, so of course I'd like to say yes." Seamus's smile lit up his entire face.

"Okay, gotta run, the meter's nearly out." He leaned over to kiss Nicola. She burst out laughing.

"You didn't put any money into the meter?"

"I didn't have any change," Seamus said.

"They take credit cards, Seamus."

"Are you fookin' crazy?" He laughed. "Those things are so easy to hack."

"*Ay*, your life."

"*Ay* my life indeed," he said. "Now come here and give me a little kiss and I'll be off."

Nicola walked Seamus to the elevator. As soon as it closed behind him, Gaynor stood up from her perch on Alicia's desk.

"You're going to Ojai, Nico," she said.

"Oh shit, you could hear through the door?"

"No," said Alicia. "She had her phone on conference the whole time!"

Gaynor rapped her diamond knuckles on Alicia's desk.

Nicola rolled her eyes.

"Of course you did," she sighed. "I'm an idiot."

"You're not an idiot," Gaynor said firmly. "So go. Put yourself on the map as a publicist in this town."

"Gaynor, he wants a girlfriend, not a publicist," Nicola said, exasperated. "I can't just pack up and go to Ojai."

"Yes, you can," she said. "You won a bet for some days off. Just go with him."

She pushed Nicola toward the elevator and added one last order. "Take Kara, not Billy."

CHAPTER 26

BILLY SQUIRMED IN HIS SEAT in Ethan's loaner Lexus LFA as it lurched and pitched its way up the labyrinthine streets of the Hollywood Hills.

"Have you driven a sports car before?" Billy asked.

Ethan shot him a death glare. "Didn't you see my last movie?"

"Honey, I'm not going to rely on *Wheels of Fortune* for any sort of reality," he said with a sneer.

"Good point," said Ethan, his face illuminated by the LFA's futuristic console lights.

"Why didn't we just drive your car?"

"I wish we had," Ethan sighed. "But Lexus is paying me to drive this around. Crystal insisted."

"How about we just stick it in first and creep up the hill?" said Billy. "I don't want us to Matthew Perry into someone's front yard."

Billy rubbed his palms together. They were sweaty. He was nervous. He felt like a debutante. He'd never gone to a Velvet Mafia party as someone's date before. He wasn't nervous about that part, but he was wary of the added attention, and how it could destroy the anonymity that was crucial to his tabloid business. He had decided to play it safe in a simple white Ralph Lauren jacket over a white T-shirt and contrasting black J Brand jeans that fit him perfectly. He glanced at the streetlights playing across Ethan's shimmering purple Vivienne Westwood suit and wondered if he'd played it too safe.

"How big is this goddamn parking lot?" Billy asked as they neared the crest of the Hills.

"Honey, nobody but the A-Gays get to park on premises." Ethan touched a hand to his chest, indicating that he was an A-Gay. "Don't you know anything? Everyone else takes a shuttle from the parking lot at Hollywood and Highland."

Tonight's party was at Robert Flanger's house. This was ground queero of the closeted Hollywood scene, dating back to the late 1960s. Since then, Flanger had helmed a string of blockbuster franchises, but was currently in career free fall. His parties, and his casting couch, however, were still legendary.

The car rounded one last corner and stopped at an imposing metal gate that completely hid the house behind it. Two security guards in nondescript black suits approached the car. They smiled when they recognized Ethan.

"Good evening, Mr. Carpenter, Mr. Kaye," said the larger guard. "Welcome."

Ethan nodded. The massive metal gate swung inward, and Ethan tapped the accelerator, sending the car lurching unceremoniously into the long circular driveway. The gate closed behind them.

The valet was eyeing the car hungrily as they exited. Ethan tossed the keys to him.

"Good luck with it," Ethan said. "And don't fucking scratch it."

The house was an ornate 1920s chalet, flanked by huge oaks. Light spilled from stained-glass windows on the first level, and the house itself spread grandly across the entire hilltop. As they walked up the path toward it, Ethan spun Billy around by the shoulders.

"Notice anything?" he asked.

Billy shrugged, not sure what Ethan was asking.

"Can you see any other houses?"

Billy did another circle and his eyes widened.

"Wow, you actually cannot see any other houses from here."

"Nope," explained Ethan. "That's why Robert bought it, back in the sixties. Back then, it was impossible to photograph this house. These days, someone can get pics of the front from anywhere down there"—he gestured toward the distant lights of Hollywood and downtown—"but nobody can shoot the backyard except from a drone or a chopper. This is the most private house in LA. He doesn't even have neighbors to sell him out."

Holy shit, thought Billy. *What the hell am I going to see tonight?*

A butler in an impeccably tailored suit opened the main door for them.

"Good evening, Mr. Carpenter," he said smoothly. "I'm so glad you are able to join us tonight. My name is Joe, and I'll be taking care of you tonight."

"Hi, Joe," Ethan said, shaking his hand.

"I see you've brought a guest," Joe said, bowing in Billy's direction.

"Yes," Ethan explained. "This is my boyfriend, Billy."

Billy flinched at the word.

"Hello, Billy," Joe said drily. "Mr. Carpenter, I hope you understand, but I'm going to have to ask your friend to sign our standard nondisclosure agreement, and also to surrender his cell phone."

Billy quickly looked at his phone. The screen was filled with notifications of texts from Kara asking about the party, who was there, and whether it was men-only or could she crash it? He had definitely noticed a change in her since they launched the *Spyglass* project. He hoped he hadn't created a monster. He quickly powered down his phone and handed it to Joe, who took it and vanished behind a curtain just inside the hallway. He returned moments later with an NDA and a pen.

Billy scanned the letter. He would be liable to "prosecution and US$5 million penalty" if he were to speak of what he saw that night. Standard Hollywood stuff. He couldn't resist misspelling his full name, so tonight, he was Wilhelm Koye, and his signature looked nothing like the one on his driver's license.

The house was shrouded in darkness. Thousands of candles

burned weakly on every surface, and the quiet throb of silky disco filled the air. Billy struggled to identify any of the people there as their faces flashed from candlelight to silhouette and back again. All of these guys were flickering ghosts. The fucking NDA hadn't been necessary. At all.

Muscly young men in square-cut Speedos passed lithely through the crowd, handing out cocktails and cleaning up empty glasses. Ethan grabbed two vodka sodas from a passing tray and handed one to Billy. They clinked glasses, and Ethan draped an arm around Billy's waist, leading him through the living room and out to the rear yard. Billy noticed heads turning as they passed, feeling both exhilarated and uncomfortable.

Billy could not believe the backyard. The mountain rose dramatically at the rear, a black wall of solid privacy shielding a clipped lawn and pool area also lit by countless candles. Groups of men chatted on the lawn, occasional ripples of blue light from the pool washing over them.

Ethan led Billy to an empty corner of the lawn, by the craggy stone of the mountain.

"Let's stand right here," Ethan said. "I need a few drinks before we talk to anybody."

Billy realized Ethan was nervous. "Do you even know anyone?" he asked.

"Depends what you mean by 'know.' I've met a bunch of these people at awards shows, and I've talked to a few of them at these parties, but I'd guesstimate that you're the only person here I actually know. Who actually gives a shit."

"Are you okay?"

"No. I don't belong at this party. I'm a fucking joke here." Ethan pulled away and walked two steps, clearly waiting for Billy to follow. When he didn't, Ethan turned back to him, a pained expression on his face.

"Look at these assholes! Everyone here is a major someone. I'm just a pretty boy from the 818 who got lucky. I make stupid movies for little girls and boys. They don't respect me and they ain't rushing to sign me. Those guys over there?" Ethan pointed at a group of older men in khakis and button downs, all smoking cigars. "They run studios and networks. My managers keep me in the closet but force me to suck up to those guys at these parties, in hopes that I'll book a blockbuster."

"I thought you were an A-Gay, Ethan. Calm down and we'll go talk to them."

"Are you fucking crazy?" he wailed. "It's a fucking caste system." Ethan caught himself as his voice rose. "It's all timed. I am in the 'arrive between ten and ten thirty' slot. The big stars get the eleven p.m. slot; they arrive when the party is perfect. It's orchestrated. Walking in at ten twenty-five, people know my station. My movies grossed more last year than any other actor you'll see tonight, but I'm still an early time slot."

"You're overthinking it." Billy squeezed his shoulder.

"No, I'm fucking not." Ethan poured his drink down his throat. A near-naked waiter materialized and replaced his empty glass with a full one. A second later, Robert Flanger himself drifted out of the same darkness.

"Ethan Carpenter," he said in his whisky-oak voice. He planted a kiss on Ethan's lips. "I'm so glad you could make it tonight."

"Of course," Ethan said, suddenly gracious. "Robert, please meet my boyfriend, Billy."

Flanger sized up Billy with a grin. "Billy, it's my pleasure." They shook hands and Flanger turned back to Ethan, immediately forgetting that Billy existed.

"Good box office on the last few pictures, Carpenter," he said.

"Yes," said Ethan, all business. "Right now, we don't know which sequel to do first."

Flanger's eyes lit up.

"I got the script for the space zombie sequel today—they want me to commit," he said. "Have you read it yet?"

"That's what I'm supposed to be doing tonight," Ethan replied.

"Me, too," smiled Flanger. "I think we would enjoy working together," he continued. "But I loathe doing sequels. What do you think I should say?"

"I think you should say yes," Ethan said. "I'd be honored to work with you. And if you sign on, we can band together to iron out the more idiotic things in the script. The first one was terrible when they brought it to me."

"I know," Flanger said. "I passed on it. Stupidly."

"Well, let's do this next one together and make it better than the first one," Ethan said eagerly.

"Yes, I think I shall," said Flanger. "I'll call my agent in the morning and say yes. Anyway, how rude," he said, turning back to Billy. "You've brought your boyfriend here, and we've done nothing but talk shop. Please, gentlemen, enjoy your night, and Ethan, let's get a lunch on the books for this next week to discuss our vision for the sequel."

They all bowed and Flanger made his exit, heading toward the next group of men on his circuit.

"See?" Ethan said as soon as he was out of earshot. "It's all so perfectly choreographed. That desperate old fag needed that discussion and didn't want to have it in front of anyone too major. He basically just pissed territorially on me in front of the head of the studio over there."

Ethan drank his drink in a single gulp.

"Dude, you need to just learn to be in the moment," Billy said.

"You sound like my fucking acting coach," Ethan snapped. "Actors are only in the moment when they're working. Otherwise we are insecure and panicked. Deal with it."

※　※　※

The party unfolded exactly as Ethan said it would. Five of the biggest actors in the world had arrived within seconds of one another, and all were inside the party by eleven thirty. Flanger ran a tight ship. Billy caught only glimpses of them before they were swallowed by the flickering darkness.

He leaned over to Ethan and whispered, "You know what? You may not be as crazy as I thought an hour ago."

"Of course I'm not," Ethan sniffed. "*I'm* actually not crazy at all, it's my circumstances that are crazy."

"I'd say it's about fifty-fifty." Billy gave Ethan's arm an affectionate squeeze.

"Well, what changed your mind?"

"Just watching what's going on," Billy said. "Clearly there's two different A-lists here—the marquee name list, and the old gay money list, and even they don't openly accept each other. And you're right, you're a pariah."

"They figure that I'll be done in six months," Ethan said with smug defiance. "I got lucky with the first movie, and I know that. Test audiences loved me, so they had to go back and expand my role with stuff picked up off the cutting-room floor. I'm a realist. I know that the only thing separating a successful actor from a janitor is a stroke of luck."

"I'm not sure if you're a humble visionary or just another bitter actor."

"Bit of both, I'd say," Ethan said in a bad English accent.

"You're not ready for Shakespeare, love." Billy watched Ethan survey the crowd, a fragile look of disdain on his face.

"Hey," Billy said, wrapping an arm around Ethan's cold shoulders, "this party sucks. Wanna take a lap and then leave? Is that an acceptable thing to do?"

Ethan smiled and planted a quick peck on his lips.

"Sure," he said with a wan smile. "That would be . . . acceptable."

Ethan grabbed Billy's hand and pulled him toward a small stone pool house. "You wanna see where most of the superstars in Hollywood got their start?"

"I thought we were leaving."

"We are. But this is gay Hollywood history."

Nearing the pool house, they were joined by Flanger.

"And where are you gentlemen headed?" he asked, as if it wasn't obvious.

"I was going to show Billy the pool house."

"Oh, so modern of you, so early in a new relationship." Flanger's eyes glinted at the news. "So is it three-way only or do you play separately?"

"Hey, now," Billy said defensively. "We haven't had that discussion yet." This boyfriend talk was starting to get on his nerves. While he hadn't seen or suspected any drug use by Ethan for at least a week, he also knew he'd never date a user.

"Oh, I'm so sorry," said Flanger, clasping his hands together melodramatically. "Will you forgive my assumption?"

"It's fine, of course." Ethan tried to smooth things over. "I just wanted Billy to see the most legendary pool house in Hollywood."

"This should be on those pesky Hollywood tours," Flanger said perkily, his ego appeased. "This has been ground zero for the superstar gays since the sixties. I bought it from a producer who'd been hosting parties since the Jimmy Dean days, and I was more than happy to continue the tradition. Back in my day, I bedded some of the world's most bangable . . . I mean, bankable stars on the pillowed floor of this humble pool house."

As they got to the doors, Flanger made a little show of peeking through the small pane of glass on the door.

"Looks like it's empty," he whispered conspiratorially, throwing the door open to reveal a gaudy beige leather mid-century sectional couch and a sunken living room. An enormous flat screen hung on one wall, images of gaudy eighties-era porn lighting the walls. It was totally an orgy room.

"Oh my God, I'm at the gay Playboy Mansion." Billy laughed.

"Well, thank you, dear boy," Flanger said, scratching absently at his skull. "I'm trying to remember the last impromptu orgy that happened here. No one has any fun anymore. My goodness, I swear it was the nineties. And you wouldn't believe who that was, even if I told you."

"Why don't you try me?" Billy smiled.

"I thought you'd never ask." Flanger playfully grabbed at Billy's butt. "Relax," he snapped at Ethan. "I know, I know, you're boyfriends, and you don't want your first three-way to be with ugly old me. . . ." Flanger paused, waiting for the boys to disagree. The silence was deafening.

"So, let's set the scene. It's 1994. That miserable imp Cobain had just sucked on the shotgun, and all of those little actors who loved him were devastated. They brought their heartache up to my party. And their heroin. They all holed up in here and I got very Nancy Reagan. Nothing kills a party like heroin. So I barged in here, thinking I was breaking up a shooting gallery. Whoa, Nelly, was I wrong. I walked in on six of Hollywood's hottest stars, completely naked, and finding more traditional ways of forgetting their pain."

Ethan had heard this story before, and started checking his phone, but Billy was enthralled.

"Look at you," Flanger said. "You want me to name names, don't you?"

"That's up to you, Mr. Flanger," he said. "I'm entertained already."

Flanger leaned back, and like a town crier, began.

"The first person I saw, on his knees and naked as a jaybird, was—"

The door at the back of the pool house, obviously the bathroom, swung open, derailing Flanger completely. Ryan Powell, the hot movie star hailed as the new Redford, walked into the room, adjusting his shirt.

He locked eyes with Billy and smiled.

"Oh, hello there, gentlemen," Powell smirked. "Didn't mean to interrupt."

Flanger pretended to faint against a wall.

"Catch me, Ryan, I'm falling."

Then a handsome Australian walked out of the bathroom. The same one Billy had chatted up in the hotel bar at the Montage.

His eyes widened when he saw Billy, but he didn't acknowledge him.

"Well, Mr. Powell," Flanger said obsequiously, "I see you've already made a friend."

"Hey, Bob," said the actor. "Robert Flanger, this is Bluey."

Flanger and Bluey nodded affectionately at each other.

"I know this Australian criminal," Flanger said.

"How ya going, Bob?" Bluey greeted him amiably.

"Well, I'm apparently very remiss, socially," Flanger vamped. "Please introduce yourselves—Ryan Powell, Bluey, this is Ethan Carpenter and his boyfriend, Billy."

"Hey, Ethan." Ryan stepped forward and wrapped Ethan in a hug.

"That's funny," said Billy, "because I've met this guy before." Billy spread his arms to hug Bluey. And received a handshake instead.

"Hey, Bob, we don't want to interrupt anything," Ryan said with a knowing look. "We'll leave you boys to it."

As the men all exited the pool house, Flanger fanned himself theatrically.

"I daresay there'll be nothing to interrupt," he said, looking hopefully at the younger men.

They made polite excuses about another party and headed back through the yard to the house.

They were intercepted by Joe the butler at the front door as they were about to make their getaway.

"Mr. Kaye," he said smoothly. "I have your phone and belongings here—if you could just step into my office to sign for your phone, I can hand it over. You can wait for him up front, Mr. Carpenter."

Billy followed Joe behind the curtain, into a small, immaculate office. When Joe turned to face him, he was furious.

"Wilhelm, is it?" Joe seethed through clenched teeth. "I have been informed that you are a reporter for *Spyglass*. Additionally, I know that you gave a false name on your NDA. I'm sure it was just a matter of haste and excitement, so I've prepared a new form for you to sign. I trust that will not be a problem."

"I'm not going to lie to you, Joe," Billy said. "I don't plan to sell a single thing I saw tonight. But a lawyer once told me to *never* put my real name on an NDA at a party."

"There are parties, young man, and then there are *parties*," Joe said imperiously, holding a pen above the new contract.

"This one also includes an admission that you may have lied to gain entrance to the party, but you're now willing to accept a ten-million-dollar penalty for any leaks traceable to you."

Billy noticed that the new contract that Joe had prepared was an inch thick. The previous one had been a single page.

"I'd need a lawyer to look at that before I sign it."

"Of course, if you have one with you, or can get one here within a half hour. Otherwise I'll be forced to call the police and have you arrested for entering our premises under false pretenses. Mr. Flanger is very good to the local constabulary, and they, in turn, are very good to him."

"Gimme the fucking pen." Defeated, Billy scrawled his name and initials wherever Joe pointed as he flipped the pages.

Task complete, Joe stood upright and fished Billy's phone out of his pocket.

"It's been a pleasure to have you here tonight, Mr. Kaye."

Billy pushed through the curtains without looking back.

✳ ✳ ✳

They had barely driven five hundred jerky yards from the gate when Ethan pulled the car into an empty driveway.

"Are you going to fucking tell me how you knew that Australian guy or not?" he yelled.

"Ethan," Billy said exhaustedly. "There's nothing to tell."

"You're kidding, right?" Ethan spat.

"No, I'm just tired; can we go back to your place and cuddle?"

"Sure, right after you tell me how you know that guy."

Billy took a deep breath.

"I was on a stakeout at the Montage. He chatted me up. We made out in a hallway. He said he'd call me but he never did. Full story. You probably don't believe it."

Ethan laughed. "Oh yes, I do believe it. And I believe that whoever you were stalking knew you were there and hired him to get you off the scent."

"Whatever do you mean?"

By this time Ethan was laughing.

"You're the gossip columnist and I'm telling you this? That *dumb Australian* works for Crystal. He does the dirty work for a couple of the really fucked-up celebrities on her roster. He makes sure that none of her clients get in trouble, or if they do get in trouble, he makes sure the trouble goes away. After Vegas, Crystal threatened that she was going to start making me pay for his services, too. That's why I'm on my good behavior with you. Now tell me who you were stalking?"

"Max Zetta, meeting some woman at the Montage."

Ethan screwed up his button nose.

"That's not Bluey's beat at all. Thought you were going to say Seamus O'Riordan. That's who Bluey mainly takes care of."

CHAPTER 27

GAYNOR EMERGED FROM THE ELEVATOR doors outside Huerta Hernandez, a wriggling pugwawa puppy in one arm, an eighties Fendi baguette in the other. Despite her vintage gold pantsuit and the enormous faux fur collar on her floor-length black suede Jagger jacket, she looked like her battery pack was fading, and it was only ten fifteen.

As the doors slid closed behind her, she turned in slow motion, and groaned.

"*Madre mía*, why are quaaludes illegal?"

She slammed her palm against the elevator call button and the doors opened. Her boys, Patrick and Sylvester, stood there, tracing patterns on the floor with their feet.

"My darlings, if you try to escape one more time today, I will call Grandma and see if she wants you to visit her in Colombia."

Two pairs of sweet almond eyes widened in terror.

"She told me she wants you boys down there for a month, so you can learn your roots."

"Mama, no . . . ," Patrick began. Sylvester lifted his finger to Patrick's mouth. "Shush, *hermano*, let me handle this one."

"Mother, we are sorry, we were just messing with you."

Gaynor looked at her sons, the loves of her life. Two monsters who knew exactly how to manipulate her the same way she played the press. She'd raised them too well. They were just like her.

"I'm gonna play the card today, boys," she rasped. Their eyes widened.

"Yep. Today is a red card don't-fuck-with-Mama-she-hasn't-slept day. What happens if you cross that line, *mis angelitos*?"

"You send us to Grandma for a month," the boys said in unison.

Gaynor closed her eyes and took a deep breath.

"Today is so bad, it'll be two months."

※　※　※

Gaynor bashed three times on the office door with her elbow, knowing she was interrupting Alicia's early morning ritual of instant coffee, online quizzes that told her which fictional character she was, and Pinterest.

"Da fuck?" she heard Alicia say loudly. There was another loud thud, and some yelling.

"Alicia, you slow *coño*, get your sweaty ass out here and help me get this fucking thing inside."

After some more shuffling noises, the door slowly opened, and Alicia peered through the gap.

"Did you even go home last night?" she gasped, before spying the twins behind their mother. "Oh, fuck, sorry, of course you did."

Gaynor thrust the dog at Alicia.

"Please take Fuchi."

"Dogs belong outside, Gaynor," Alicia said, stepping back in fear.

"This dog will be feasting on your fucking ham hocks if you don't take it in five . . . four . . . three . . ."

"I'm scared of dogs. A dog bit me once when I was—"

Gaynor pushed Fuchi into Alicia's chest and walked away. The dog slipped onto Alicia's belly, which saved it from falling. She gingerly put an arm around it, and the dog licked her arm.

"It's licking me, argh."

"She likes you. Good. Don't sit on her and don't let her piss on anything. Keep the boys in the conference room until lunchtime, and do not disturb me. Send Nicola in as soon as she arrives."

"Gaynor, I'm your intern, not your nanny!"

"I thought you wanted to be an actor?"

Excitement flickered across Alicia's face.

"Yes, Señora Huerta, oh ma gah, you know it's my dream. Do you have some acting for me?"

"Yes. Act like a fucking babysitter." She slammed her office door behind her.

"We heard what you said to our mom," Patrick said. "And we're not kids."

"Hey, it's not personal," Alicia said, herding the boys into the conference room. "I just don't get along with kids and kids don't get along with me."

"It's probably your makeup," Sylvester said. "You really aren't doing yourself any favors with that harsh look."

Alicia turned and stared at the boys, her hands on her hips.

"That was a low blow, kid," she said, hurt registering on her face.

"It wasn't meant to be," Sylvester said. "You're being a stereotype. You're much prettier than you're letting yourself be."

"Kick back, Casanova." Alicia swatted at Sylvester's coiffed hair with a black-nailed hand.

"He knows what he's talking about," said Patrick. "Mom let him work with a big hair and makeup artist last year for the Oscars. He knows all the tricks."

"I ain't looking for a makeover." Alicia opened a small cupboard and pulled out a stack of screener DVDs. "Here's a bunch of blockbusters for you two to watch. Let the TV babysit you like all good American children."

Alicia turned to make sure the HDMI cable from the Blu-ray was connected to the TV. She heard the conference room door lock behind her. She rushed toward it, nearly tripping over Fuchi, her fellow prisoner.

✳ ✳ ✳

Gaynor splayed her elbows across her desk, letting her forehead hit the leather desk protector. Its cool hide felt good against her skin, and she pressed down hard, the pressure on her skull relieving the pain inside it. She took a deep breath.

Beside her, her phone pinged. She scrabbled her nails across her desktop until she located it. Dragging it slowly under her hair, she raised her head just enough to be able to see the screen. It was from Billy.

You OK today?

She rolled her eyes behind her sunglasses.

I will be. Gracias.

She shook her head. *When did this strangely ethical tabloid reporter and I become a team?* He had come into her consciousness like a gnat, calling her for comments on various scandals like so many other reporters in Hollywood, setting traps that she could see a mile off. However, this one was getting behind the curtain and digging up real dirt. She had demanded to meet him, and it all fell into place. His broad, handsome face was open and beguiling. He didn't look like all the cookie-cutter pool boys that littered the Beverly Hills power gay circuit. Something else that set him apart from all the other garbage pickers, Gaynor soon learned, was that he was trustworthy and followed his own weird moral compass.

Before long, he and Gaynor had developed a perfect symbiotic relationship. He'd bring major scandals involving her clients to her, and she'd either pay him to be quiet or give him an even better story on someone else's client in exchange for him killing the story about her own. She grew to enjoy him. He always made her laugh, and never wasted her time.

Gaynor was accustomed to calls at any time of the day or night over her thirty years as a publicist, but when she saw Billy's name pop up on a call at ten p.m. last night, she knew it would be bad.

"*Ay, mijo*, shouldn't you be dancing on a box in some awful gay bar?"

"Gaynor, we need to talk."

Her stomach shrank as Billy confirmed that *Spyglass* and possibly other magazines were onto her affair with Max Zetta. He had seen their files. The lawyers had approved them to go into print the following week.

"*Pinche* fucking rags," Gaynor had hissed. "They have no proof."

"Gaynor, they do. Everyone does. You've been sloppy. I've seen you myself."

"Are you selling me out? Billy!"

"No. I was chasing a story, and it turned out to be you. I still didn't know what was going on until I got to see the *Spyglass* files. They're talking cover story."

"Why are you telling me this, then?"

"To help you. I still owe you from the Ethan Carpenter mess."

Gaynor heaved a sigh of relief, grateful for Billy's weird karmic credit.

"Okay, *mijo*. *Gracias*. Tell me this—does anyone have pictures?"

"No, but all the agencies are on high alert. You can't meet or see him outside of a red carpet."

"Billy, I know my job. I know the situation." She paused, overwhelmed by a desire to tell Billy everything. She forced it down. "And *mijo*, you don't need to know the whole story, but it's not an affair."

"Hey, I don't care what you do with your clients. I'm not here to judge you."

She clenched her fist, nails digging into her palm.

"I know. Maybe I'm judging myself. Mr. Kaye, you've saved my ass again, and I thank you. And one day, in the future, I will make you my mother's margaritas and tell you all, and you will laugh your bubble butt off. Is it a date?"

"We have a date, Ms. Huerta. We have a date."

Gaynor had been up all night figuring out what to do.

Nicola was shocked when she opened the door. Gaynor's face was pale beneath her makeup, and she looked old and frail.

"What the hell happened to you?" Nicola pulled the door closed behind her.

"I get that a lot," Gaynor said, attempting a laugh. "I have something to take care of. It won't be easy, and it might cost us a client. A big one."

"Can I help?"

"Sign Seamus." Gaynor gave a wan smile. Nicola knew she wasn't joking.

"Gaynor, I can't, it's too weird," she began. "I'm off to the film set with him and Kara tomorrow. He says phone service isn't great up there, but call me if you need me."

"Nicolita, I know. That's not what I wanted to see you about."

"Oh?"

"Yes. I have been hearing some things and I wanted to warn you."

Nicola was confused.

"You've done a good job with Kara. You and Billy have put her on the map. She'll get her spinoff. But you've made an enemy."

"I don't think Jimmy J will give me too much trouble," Nicola said, making gang signs with her fingers.

"It's not that loser," Gaynor spat. "It's Amber. Her former publicist called me this morning. He wants her back. He is trying to use you as leverage to have her fire us and go back to him. Amber is jealous of you and that makes her dangerous. She is a cockroach. She has survived being a teen star, more overdoses than a Berlin restroom, and several stints in the loony bin. You've made her costar eclipse her, and now Seamus is taking you to the set of his movie, and she claims he was supposed to take her."

Nicola exhaled loudly. "I'm not sure what you want me to do," she admitted candidly. "Do you have any advice?"

"I don't, Nico. I don't have any. Amber is a tenacious bitch and an awful enemy. I have your back on this. Just keep your front covered. Now take my boys to the mall while I make some calls."

Nicola began to protest, but the look on Gaynor's face stopped her dead. She'd never seen her look so defeated.

"Okay. Text me when you want me to bring the little angels back."

✳ ✳ ✳

Gaynor sat at her desk, unmoving, for nearly half an hour after Nicola left. She took a deep breath and told herself to snap out of it. She needed to rip this Band-Aid off. No matter how much it was going to hurt.

She pressed speed dial six. Two rings later, Max answered.

"Hey, you gorgeous Spanish mama," he drawled. Gaynor moved the phone away from her ear and regarded it as if it stank.

"Max, I'm Colombian," she sighed. "Listen . . ."

"Gaynor, I hope you're on your way," he interrupted. "I got us a bottle of hundred-year-old Scotch and I'm ready and waiting."

And half the bottle's probably already gone, Gaynor thought.

"Listen, Max, I won't be able to make it today."

"You better be joking," he snarled. "We have a fucking deal, Gaynor."

"Max, I have the boys. They tortured their sitter and she quit last night, and it's just not going to be possible today. I'm stuck here."

"They're fucking adults; leave them alone," Max said angrily. "I have everything set up. You only have to come here for an hour."

"Max, please try to understand. I will come next week, we can reschedule this; you know I'm always happy to help you out."

"Listen, you fucking whore, this is part of the deal; this is why I pay you so fucking much money every month."

Gaynor took a deep breath. He was already drunk.

"Max," she said quietly, "I'm your friend; please calm down."

"My friend? You're not my friend," he roared. "You're a dirty wetback whore and I pay you twenty thousand dollars a month so you can keep me out of the fucking tabloids? Get me on Fallon once a fucking year? I can get that shit for free. The twenty thousand is for this other stuff and you know it. Do you put down whore as your occupation on your tax returns, or does the IRS just automatically assume publicists *are* whores?"

"Max, we've never fucked," Gaynor said deliberately, fighting to keep her temper under control.

"You know what I mean," he yelled. "And I'm the boss here. You *work* for me. So you don't get me all ready for my afternooner and then try to call it off. If you don't show up right now, I'll just call a fucking escort service and find an honest woman to come get me off."

"Now that I'd love to hear," Gaynor said ruefully. "How would you find the right whore? Is there a Yelp for people like you?"

"How fucking dare you, you fucking illegal cunt. Listen." He paused, breathing heavily into the phone. She heard glass clink in the background after he took a deep swig of whisky. "Tell me right now, yes or no, if you're coming to see me, or if I'm about to fire you as my whore, I mean, as my *publicist*, and before you answer, just know that if I fire you, I will be represented by Crystal within five minutes."

"Max," Gaynor said, as if speaking to a child, "you and I both know that you need me, and that we've made a good team for nearly twenty years. Someone's on our trail. We need to cool it. I can tell you've had a drink, so please have some water and maybe just lie down for a minute. Let's talk when you sober up."

"So that's a no," he said tonelessly. "Gaynor, you're fired. I'll have my manager sever our contract immediately. And while I have you here, go fuck yourself, you broke-down spic. I fucking hate you."

Gaynor gently set the phone back on her desk. Her hand was

shaking as she raised it to her eye and wiped away the angry mascara-filled tear that spilled down her face.

She poured herself a shot of Galliano. *Santa María, why do you hate me so?* She downed the shot, took two deep breaths, and willed her fingers to stop shaking.

CHAPTER 28

THE POST-MAKEOVER TERCEL EFFORTLESSLY HIT eighty-five miles an hour as Nicola and Kara sped over a mountain pass just north of LA and descended into the nowhere land of Valencia, all neon chain restaurants and big box retail. The bones of the roller coasters at Six Flags loomed ominously over the dusty afternoon.

"Oh look, it's Ohio in the desert." Nicola surveyed the endless generic freeway landscape spreading out to the brown rise of desert mountains.

"Well, only if you got some In-N-Out in Ohio." Kara laughed, pointing at the big red arrow to their left.

"You know what I mean," Nicola said. "This could be fucking anywhere. It's always surprising how quickly LA turns generic."

"You don't need to drive up the 5 for that to happen, gurl," Kara quipped. "Just drive over Laurel Canyon."

"The Valley is weirdly unique," Nicola replied with a half smile. "It's like the machine that makes LA work. I don't hate it."

"You didn't grow up in it, then," Kara said pointedly, remembering the boring weekends of her youth in North Van Nuys: Friday and Saturday nights at either the Galleria or the Fashion Square, days cruising the strip malls of Ventura Boulevard. "This stuff never changes. It's all chains and big box and soul-destroying sameness. At least you had . . . I dunno. What did you have?"

"The quarry? The county fair?" Nicola said. Her phone buzzed again on the center console. "Wanna take a bet about who is blowing my phone up?"

"I don't even need to look. It's gonna be Gaynor, mainly, Seamus next, then Billy and maybe your mom. Do you want me to look while you're driving?"

"Sure, thanks."

"It's Gaynor, but there are a ton of texts. She says it's code red."

"Put her on speaker."

"Nicolita, you couldn't resist answering." Gaynor's jubilant voice filled the Tercel. "You're gonna be a good publicist."

"Make it quick, boss. You're breaking the rules."

"Even better, you're a bitch now. Anyway, listen, something bad has happened to our former client, Mr. Zetta. He got drunk and wrapped his car around a traffic signal on Little Beverly yesterday. Got out of the car and yelled like a crazy person at the crowd that gathered."

"Oh dear." Nicola could barely suppress a smile. Couldn't have happened to a nicer bigot.

"Oh yes, Nico. If you want to see it, just use Google. It's everywhere. So, for once, we are not saying 'no comment.' We are only saying one thing. Please repeat after me: Max Zetta is no longer represented by Huerta Hernandez."

"Max Zetta is no longer represented by Huerta Hernandez. But Gaynor, in an hour I will be turning my phone off."

"I bet you another day off that you don't."

⁂ ⁂ ⁂

As soon as they left the freeway, the countryside opened up and they followed a winding highway through fields of strawberries and other green crops. The Ohio flashbacks got stronger. They turned onto the road to Ojai, and were swallowed up by oak trees and bursts of sunlight as they drove along a stream. Nicola turned off the AC and opened her windows, taking a deep breath.

She felt a million miles from LA, and some of the tension drained out of her shoulders. She felt it palpably leave her body. Seamus had told her that they had a masseuse on set. She had laughed and called him a pampered bitch. She regretted it now. She'd assumed she could just ask Seamus for a backrub. Like a normal boyfriend. And he could stop learning how to sword fight aliens, and put the production of a $200 million blockbuster on hold. Like a normal boyfriend.

Eh, you've dated worse, her brain chided her. *You're in Hollywood now. This shit is normal.*

Nicola tried to meditate as she drove, forcing thoughts to fly away like birds while she enjoyed the scenery in silence. After a while, she noticed that Kara was filming her.

"Hey, what are you doing?"

"I've been watching your face," Kara said. "Whatever you're thinking about, you've been kind of half smiling to yourself and shaking your head."

"Wanna guess?"

"Oh, I know what you're thinking about." She laughed, switching off the camera. "You thinkin' 'bout Seamus."

"I am, I am," Nicola confessed. "It's all stupid wrong and I keep going back for more."

"So you're admitting that you finally like him, huh?"

"No," Nicola said sheepishly. "I'll admit that I'm still trying to NOT like him, but it's getting harder. He works so hard at being charming, he's so fucking earnest with me, and he just seems like he might actually be the person he says he is."

"Humph." Kara rolled her eyes. "We've talked about this. He's an actor. A big one. So he's a bullshitter and he's incredibly skilled at giving people what they want. I've told you a hundred times to keep your distance."

"Every time he turns the works on, I have your voice playing in the back of my head," Nicola says. "I'm not sure who to listen to."

"Me, durr," Kara said seriously. "I grew up in this town, I got the Hollywood street smarts on my side. Never trust an actor."

"Oh, but rappers are okay?"

"I never trusted J," Kara said. "You know I didn't."

"So why did you agree to come this weekend again? To watch out for me?"

"Don't be like that," Kara said, looking at Nicola. "I'm accompanying my best friend on a weird weekend adventure. The fact that we won't hear from Gaynor or Amber, and we're staying with the biggest star in the world, is just gravy. I wanna show you the shitty art galleries and handicraft stores of Ojai while your lover is off doing movie star crap. And just maybe get a little footage for my pilot."

"Do I have to be in it?" Nicola sighed. "Publicists are not supposed to be on camera."

"You'll barely be in it," Kara promised. "This is all sizzle-reel stuff. Me being on location for a legit movie helps sell the pilot. I just need to show them what we do."

"Nobody sells a reality show without making someone look like an idiot."

"Are you calling me an idiot?"

"I'm sorry," Nicola said. "I may actually just be a little nervous, but it's not about Seamus. Not sure what's up."

"My mama said to always listen to your intuition."

"My intuition wants me to turn around and spend the weekend shopping at the Grove."

They reached Ojai, and Nicola was surprised by the wave of disappointment that washed over her. She had expected something magical. But it was just a single strip of the stores rich people frequent, in the midst of rolling hills. Expensive clothing, dodgy art, sushi, and nouvelle cuisine. They drove through it in a minute, and the GPS sent them up a winding country road back into the mountains, turning onto an unmarked driveway sandwiched between towering walls of oleander, pink and white flowers everywhere.

After almost a mile, a guard's building made of huge rocks appeared in front of them, blocking the road.

Nicola wound her window down to speak to the genial Burl Ives–ish guard, but before she got a word out, he greeted her by name.

"Miss Wallace, welcome to Prairie Blossom," he said. "And I see you have Miss Jones with you."

With a smile, the guard handed two sheets of paper and a pen to the girls.

"If you'd both be so kind as to sign this NDA," he said. "It's a standard form—you can't shoot anything from the movie and share it online, and you can't reveal any plot points or costumes or anything. The usual stuff."

The guard waited patiently for the signed papers to be back in his hand. He then asked for their driver's licenses, photocopied them, and meticulously stapled them to their NDAs.

"Thank you, ladies." The guard smiled genially. "I now own you both." He handed them another paper.

"Here's your map of Prairie Blossom," he said. "I'll let Mr. O'Riordan know you've arrived. He's asked that you drive directly to your accommodations, in the Hammond Building. Just follow this road all the way to the main area and you'll see a sign directing you to the house on the right. Park out front and Mr. O'Riordan will meet you there."

"Thank you, sir." Nicola smiled as the huge metal gates creaked inward and they sped off along the dusty road through the oleander.

A turn pushed them through a break in the hedge, and both girls gasped as the estate spread out below them—a huge Roman-inspired collection of terra-cotta mansions and smaller buildings nestled among groves of olive trees. An emerald polo field was surrounded by medieval bleachers and dwarfed by a life-size prop spaceship, smooth and silver with razor-blade wings, that was crashed into the grass.

"That's one hell of an alien DUI," laughed Kara. Nicola shook her head. It was going to be a weird weekend.

The signs to the Hammond Building appeared just beyond the polo field. Nicola slowed as she took a blind corner into a driveway that wrapped around an ornate round fountain, water spilling down into a lily pond. She killed the engine to park behind Seamus's truck. A wood door opened in the house and Seamus, clad in gym shorts and nothing else, bounded out.

"I'm sorry, gurl, but holy fuck, he fine," Kara said, fanning herself.

"Keep it in your pants, sister."

Seamus was at her car door before she could get her seat belt undone. He threw it open with a gentlemanly flourish and kneeled before Nicola.

"Welcome to my kingdom, m'lady," he said, in his poshest English accent.

Nicola grabbed his hand and was hauled out of the car and into his arms.

"Why, my lord, your estate is every bit as . . ."

He shut her up with a kiss. He'd been working out and he smelled just the right amount of clean and manly. *Stop it*, her mind screamed. *You're acting like a fifteen-year-old.*

"Get a mansion," Kara barked at them, and they broke apart laughing.

"Hey, Kara, how are you?' Seamus asked, and Nicola noticed an odd tension in his voice. She looked from him to her friend and saw them locking eyes.

"I'm good, O'Riordan," Kara said, looking away. "Hey, Nic, can you pop the trunk?"

Nicola bent and tugged several times at the trunk latch on the driver's side floor until it finally released with a slow creak. Both women walked to the trunk to get their bags, and Seamus waved them away.

"Ladies, please head inside. I will take care of your bags."

Kara shrugged, quipped, "Okay, Jeeves," and headed inside. Nicola turned to Seamus.

"Lemme help," she said. He shook his head and leaned in and kissed her forehead softly.

"Our room is the big room at the top of the stairs. Head on up."

Nicola gave in and walked inside.

✳ ✳ ✳

Seamus grabbed the two huge suitcases and set them on the ground. He pulled them both behind him along the pressed sand path between beds of lavender.

As he walked into the main living room, he saw Kara sitting on the couch.

"Your room is just through here," he said, nodding toward the hall at the rear of the vaulted room. "Which bag is yours?"

"The green one," Kara said, without looking at him.

Seamus grabbed the green bag and began to pull it across the tiled floor. As he got near Kara, he glanced up the stairs to make sure Nicola wasn't around.

"What's your problem today?" he whispered.

"She likes you," Kara said bluntly. "And I don't think you've been entirely honest with her."

"You don't know what we talk about," Seamus said defensively.

"So you told her about being at Amber's after hours?"

"No," he said. "What exactly do you mean?"

"I'm not an idiot," Kara said. "And neither is she. And I was fine with this while it was just her first movie-star fling, but you're working her over and she's falling for it. Either you come clean to her, or I'll do it for you."

"I can take care of my own relationship," Seamus whispered

angrily. "You don't get it. She's the first woman I've actually cared about in years. And I fucking care a lot."

"Good to know," Kara said, springing up from the couch and walking toward her room. She paused suddenly and turned, grabbing her suitcase from Seamus's hand.

"Listen," she said, pausing. "You seem all right. For an actor. Deep down you're probably a good guy, but you and I both know that fame fucks you up, and I know what that party was, and I was disappointed to see you there."

"You were there, too," he said, his eyes narrow.

"I'm being paid to be Amber's best friend," Kara said condescendingly. "You're going to be seeing me at a lot of places I wouldn't normally be at."

"Kara, if you've already made up your mind about me, that's fine, but you're also not the one I'm dating. I appreciate you caring for Nico, I really do, but I'm just going to have to ask you to trust me on this. I won't disrespect her."

Kara began to walk away. "Like you said, I'm not the one you're dating. Just be honest with her, please."

⁂ ⁂ ⁂

The master bedroom was an open, airy space. Heavy, dark beams crisscrossed the roof, and a stretch of glass doors opened onto a balcony that wrapped around the whole room. Nicola stood on the balcony, the warm wind filling her head with the smells that she already associated with California: the sage, the manzanita, and the jasmine. There was another smaller Tuscan house across the way, and behind that, olive groves stretched away up the mountains behind them, catching the afternoon sun.

The high-pitched hum of a leaf blower drifted in through the window, reminding her that this was California, not Sicily, followed by a billowing cloud of dust and scarlet bougainvillea petals from behind the smaller house. A maintenance man armed with the leaf blower appeared. Nicola watched as he blew the fallen petals off the stone path that ran around the house, letting them fall on the manicured lawn. It had bugged her since she moved out here, the way that nobody raked up the litter when it landed. Like most of LA, it was a temporary fix.

Her reverie was broken by the sound of Seamus opening the door behind her, then the feeling of his arms wrapping around her waist.

"Not bad, eh?" he whispered, nuzzling his face in her hair and kissing her neck.

"It's not bad," she said. "Reminds me of our farm in Tuscany." She waved her arm toward the huge rocket that glinted in the distance. "Especially the spaceship."

He laughed and turned her around. She lifted her head to kiss him and was surprised when he pulled her to his chest and hugged her hard, his arms strong around her, not venturing down to her ass. He kissed the top of her head, keeping his lips there, resting softly against her scalp.

"I missed you," he said softly, and immediately he felt her tense up. "Thanks for coming," he added. "We're going to have a great weekend."

She lifted her face from his chest and kissed him passionately, her fingers twined in his black curls, changing the mood. He lifted her off her feet and carried her back into the bedroom without breaking the kiss. As they got near to the bed, Seamus spun and let himself fall backward with Nicola on top of him, landing on the bed without breaking the kiss or their teeth.

✳   ✳   ✳

The maintenance guy killed the motor on the leaf blower as he approached the cars parked outside the villas. Looking around furtively, he walked to the side of the driveway and leaned the leaf blower up against the thick trunk of an old oak. He quickly pulled a

Galaxy from his pocket and took photos of the Tercel and the front of the villa that Nicola and Seamus had been on the balcony of just seconds before.

The eagle has landed. Car trace successful. SOR and mystery girl inside. Not being as careful as usual. Await advice what to do next.

CHAPTER 29

BILLY SPED UP THE HIDEOUSLY narrow switchbacks of the Hollywood Hills, alternately blinded by the glare of the sun and then by its absence, praying that there weren't any oncoming cars at each hairpin corner.

He hadn't meant to answer the call from the blocked number a half hour earlier, but his finger hit the wrong button. He'd been annoyed, until he heard Robert Flanger's mellifluous voice.

Billy had immediately panicked, imagining some sort of further punishment for the whole fake-NDA thing. He was wrong.

"If you're not too busy, I suggest you come up to my house right now," Flanger had fairly purred. "We have fallen face-first into a particularly juicy scandal featuring one of our most homophobic actors. Personally and professionally, you will benefit greatly from coming here now. I hope you can make it."

Intrigued and relieved, Billy had thanked Flanger, reconfirmed his address, and hit the road.

The ornate wrought-iron gate swung open as Billy drove up, and as he turned into the horseshoe driveway, Flanger strode toward him and extended his hands warmly.

"Come here, my boy," he said, gesturing for Billy to come toward him. Billy got out of the car and walked into Flanger's embrace.

"My goodness, you got here fast," Flanger said, hugging Billy for longer than Billy thought necessary.

"Yes," he said into Flanger's shoulder, "you said I needed to hurry, so I drove like SaraBeth Shields on the wrong way of a freeway."

Flanger released him from the hug and smiled warmly. *Jesus,* wondered Billy. *What the fuck is this scandal?* Flanger was hopped up like a kid at Christmas.

"I wish more young people had your tenacity." He motioned for Billy to go inside. As Flanger pulled the door closed, Joe the butler emerged from his curtained office cubbyhole.

"Hello, sir," he said warmly. "It's good to see you again."

"Okaaaaay." Billy stopped in the middle of the foyer. "This is weird. I was basically marched out of here like a criminal two nights ago, and now I'm like a long-lost son returning home?"

"I must apologize for that mix-up," said the butler, "but I hope you understand the nature of these parties and the freedoms they offer necessitate extra precautions."

"Yes, Billy, we read you wrong," Flanger said, closing the door behind him. "I hope you don't mind, but we did do a thorough background check on you, and I'm happy to say that you passed with flying colors. For a tabloid man, you do seem cursed with a conscience."

"Your background checks reveal that I have a conscience?" Billy said, one eyebrow raised.

"Well, it does seem that you're very protective of your social circle, even though all of Hollywood is dying to find out who Seamus O'Riordan's secret girlfriend is."

Billy stopped dead and turned to Flanger.

"Okay, how the fuck did you find that one out?"

"It doesn't matter," said Flanger. "You're gay, you understand the risks and the costs, and in this town we had to become very cunning to survive and keep our lucrative careers safe. It takes a village to be Rock Hudson, my boy. Yes, times have changed, but a taste for cock can still terminate a career. I'm sure your boyfriend has made you acutely aware of this."

"Point taken," said Billy. "And yes, I do try to have some decency in what I report, and I take care of my friends."

"That's why I called you here. Our guests of honor will be here shortly." Flanger and Joe exchanged knowing half smiles. The secrecy was driving Billy mental.

"Can you give me any info before they get here?" he said, settling into one of the oversize dark brown leather chairs by the windows.

Flanger took the chair opposite him with a Mona Lisa smile.

"I'd like nothing more than to *debrief* you," he said lecherously, waiting for Billy to respond to the flirt. An awkward second passed, and Flanger resumed his monologue.

"Max Zetta has long been a bigoted sack of hateful shit," he said, his perfect diction making the obscenity sound almost polite. "He has humiliated gay crew members, he has attacked gay staff members, he has donated money to antigay causes, and he has extolled the virtues of traditional marriage at the expense of gay equality."

"Yes, Mr. Flanger, I know all that. And?"

"Well, it seems that yesterday, Mr. Zetta downed a bottle of whisky for breakfast and wrapped his car around a pole in Beverly Hills. Things only got worse when the cop who got there, a lovely gent by the name of Harrison, was a bit too obviously gay for Mr. Zetta. When Harrison tried to help him from the car, Zetta swung a fist at him, which missed, but still counts as aggravated assault. He then unleashed a tirade about not wanting a dirty fag to touch him."

"Okay," said Billy, slightly annoyed. "I saw all of that on YouTube about five minutes after it happened."

"Well, Harrison had to arrest poor Mr. Zetta, of course," Flanger continued. "The entire drive to the police station was faggot this and cocksucker that. So of course, our policeman friend impounded Zetta's belongings. And . . . hmm . . . copied his laptop onto one of those miraculous little USB memory things. They can hold so much! The contents, young man, will be very interesting to you."

Joe appeared in the room with a glass pitcher containing iced tea and slices of lemon and orange. He poured glasses for both men, and then stood and formally addressed his boss.

"Sir, your guests are about to arrive."

"Perfect, Joe, thank you," Flanger said. He raised his glass and tipped it toward Billy. "Cheers, good sir. A toast to the end of one of the great bigots of our time."

Billy held his glass back.

"I thought it was bad luck to cheers with nonalcoholic drinks."

"My dear, who ever said this was nonalcoholic?" Flanger cackled and clinked his glass against Billy's. As Billy sipped, the unmistakable scent of bourbon tickled his nose.

"So, just a regular afternoon pitcher of old-fashioneds?" He laughed. "We're going to get along just fine."

Billy heard Joe welcoming folks out in the main hall. A swaggering CHP officer with black hair, blue eyes, and heavily tattooed arms walked into the room. Billy nearly tripped on his own feet as he stood to greet the cop. His stomach dropped when Bluey entered the room behind him.

"Hey, Billy," Bluey said amiably, walking toward him with his hand outstretched. Billy ignored it and turned to Flanger.

"So that's your fucking background check? Seamus's kangaroo? Wow, I feel really validated."

"I told you he wouldn't be too bloody happy," Bluey said.

"Shouldn't you be in Ojai wiping Seamus's ass?" Billy spat.

"Got the weekend off, mate. Maybe you and I can grab a drink."

Billy walked up to the cop and shook his hand. "I'm Billy," he said.

"I know," said the cop. "I'm Harrison."

"Okay, everyone," Flanger said with a giddy edge in his voice. "Let's all let bygones be bygones. We have a laptop set up in the kitchen. Let's go see some filth. It's almost too delicious."

Bluey handed a memory stick to Joe, who stuck it in the waiting MacBook on the kitchen counter. The men crowded around it.

"Have you seen what's on here?" Billy asked Harrison, deliberating positioning himself by the cop's side in front of the laptop.

"I took a quick look at some stuff," Harrison said, waving a tattooed forearm at the laptop. "There's one folder I found that's the one you want. It's hidden inside a folder of photos of his grandkids. It's called JC."

Bluey looked Billy in the eye.

"So you know the deal, right, mate?" he said affably. "We are going to sell these, and we are going to destroy Max Zetta."

Billy thought about Gaynor and shifted uncomfortably from one foot to the other.

"I'm already conflicted," Billy said, and all the men turned to look at him. "His publicist, Gaynor, has done some real solids for me, and this will really fuck her."

"I have a great idea," said Flanger. "Call her right now and tell her to fire him as a client. Trust me."

"No need, mate," said Bluey. "He fired Gaynor two days ago. He's talking to Crystal but they haven't signed, so if anything it'll become my problem." Billy silently thanked his lucky stars that Gaynor has listened when he warned her. But he was still nervous about what he was about to see.

Bluey began to click through the contents of the memory stick.

"They ain't pretty," warned Harrison. Flanger clapped his hands like a seal.

Bluey clicked on the folder marked JC, then on a subfolder titled EASTER. He highlighted all the images and then clicked Open. The screen filled with images that made all five men gasp.

In the first image, Max was dressed as Jesus, in the center of a nondescript hotel room. He had a crown of thorns on his head, and a dirty robe on. In the subsequent photos, he masturbated furiously on the bed.

"Who fucking shot these photos?" Harrison asked.

"They're all self timer; the camera position hasn't moved at all," Bluey said, clicking through the photos.

"He has a JESUS FETISH," Flanger crowed, spilling his cocktail on Billy's back. "All these years we thought it was a God complex, but no."

Bluey clicked on the next folder, and they all made disgusted noises at photos depicting Zetta masturbating—still in Jesus drag— onto a Bible.

"This is so fucked up," Billy said.

"No, my dear," Flanger said, barely able to contain himself. "This is karma, and it's delicious."

Bluey clicked on another folder titled CHRISTMAS.

"This should be good," he muttered.

These photos were the first ones to feature another person. Zetta was dressed in a loincloth and a wig, and even though it was supposed to be Christmas, he was sporting some fake bloody wounds on his wrists and ankles, and he was kneeling before a woman dressed as the Virgin Mary. She held a black veil to her face, only her hands visible. Bluey clicked through the photos, and they watched Zetta move from rubbing the woman's feet to lying on the bed with his head in her lap, at which point, once again, he started masturbating.

They were near the end of the photo set when, in one photo, the woman's hand was placed on top of Zetta's head, a huge emerald ring on her right hand.

Billy grabbed the counter to steady himself. Harrison grabbed him.

"Hey, kid, are you okay?"

Billy stayed in his arms.

"Yes, what is it?" asked Flanger, intrigued. "Spit it out!"

"Um . . . I, uh . . . I know who that woman is," he stammered. "We can't sell these. We can't. Oh fuck, Jesus, fuck."

"That's what she said," Harrison quipped, proud of himself.

"Son, who is it?" Flanger implored seriously.

"It's Gaynor. I'd know that gaudy-ass seventies ring anywhere."

"Well, that's why we're all here." Flanger put his arm around Billy. "To protect the innocent. We shall weed out the photos that she's in before we send them anywhere. They haven't gone anywhere yet, have they? Harrison? Bluey?"

"No, sir," said Harrison.

"Well . . . ," said Bluey.

Billy grabbed Bluey by the collar of his shirt and shook him.

"Who the fuck did you send these to, you dirty fucking drug dealer?" he yelled. "Did you send these to Seamus?"

Bluey looked from Flanger to Harrison and finally made eye contact with Billy.

"No, you drama queen," he said, pushing Billy's arms away. "I sent them to my actual boss. I sent them to Crystal."

CHAPTER 30

KARA WOKE FROM HER NAP nestled into the finest linens she'd ever felt against her skin. She stretched like a cat, lethargically. When she grabbed her phone to switch it off silent, she saw the screen was full of texts. She thumbed through them. Perry Pruitt, the reality show producer, then an all caps CALL ME from Amber, and a string of increasingly urgent texts from Gino, the paparazzi agent she'd dealt with for the Jimmy J photos. She felt her insides freeze. What if they wanted their money back?

She called Gino's number. He answered immediately.

"Kara *mia*," he purred. "So lovely for you to call. How's Ojai?"

"What's wrong?" she said, sounding every bit as panicked as she was trying not to sound. "Wait—how do you know where I am?"

Gino chuckled into the phone. "A little birdie told me that you were on a certain movie set this weekend."

"Damn, you're good at your job," Kara marveled. "Well, maybe I am and maybe I'm not, but even if I was, I signed an NDA so I can't send you any photos of the set."

"It's not the set I want, bella." Gino was suddenly all business. "Remember how much you got paid for that shitty meme and a few other snaps from your phone? If you get me photos of Seamus and Nicola Wallace, I'll get you five times as much."

Kara froze at the mention of Nic's name.

"I can't, Gino; she's my friend. They don't want this to get out."

"Kara, if I'm asking you about it, it's already out. Don't be a silly girl. If you don't make this money this weekend, somebody will. I promise you."

Kara took several deep breaths.

"I need a minute on this. Let me talk to Nic and see what she says."

"NO," Gino roared. "If you mention this to Nicola, I will finish you."

"Hey, man, fuck you," Kara began.

"Fuck me? No, it's definitely a case of fuck you, you pathetic loser. If you jeopardize this, I'll call Amber back and you'll be off the show so fast your fucking 'fro won't stop spinning for a week."

Amber, Kara seethed. Of course Amber had sold her out.

"I don't deserve to be spoken to this way," she sniffed. "I haven't done anything wrong."

"Yet," Gino cautioned. "Look, either you take the photos yourself, and you get to control the situation, or we get that cooperative gardener to try to get the nude shots through the bathroom window. But if you tell them—if we even *suspect* you've told them—the only way you'll ever get into Freddy's again is if they hire you as a bathroom attendant. Are we clear?"

"So, a shot of them together, outside, fully clothed, will shut you up?"

She could hear Gino grinning on the other end of the line.

"It will do more than shut me up; it will make you rich."

"Fine. You'll have it by Sunday," Kara said tersely and hung up. At least that bought her some breathing time.

Her phone dinged as two more texts came in.

Call me.

Right fucking now.

Both from Amber.

She called.

"Oh, hi, bitch," Amber said brightly.

"You're fucking kidding me," Kara began.

"Oh, so you've already talked to Gino? So we're all good?"

"Amber, you know I can't do this."

"Kara, what I know is that you can't not do this. Do you remember who you work for?"

"She's my friend. She's my roommate. And she's my publicist."

"So she's about to be my publicist, too. And let's face it. You and I are cut out to be celebrity girlfriends, but Nicola is clearly not. She's definitely a behind-the-scenes girl. This thing with Seamus isn't going to work. You and I both know that the sooner it's over, the less it's going to hurt her."

"Why do you even care, Amber? Are you jealous?"

"Of a girl in love with Seamus?" She laughed. "Do you even know how many of his girlfriends I've outlasted? Your hillbilly friend won't know what hit her when Seamus gets bored of her."

"Amber, you two are just friends, right?"

"You wouldn't understand," she sniffed. "Listen, I gotta be somewhere. Tell your friend not to get too attached. And make sure you get the shot. Byeeee."

Her phone rang as soon as Amber hung up. It was Robyn, her producer on Amber's show.

"Gurl, this is big," Robyn began. Robyn made hyperbole sound like understatement. Always. "We need you to get some footage this weekend."

"Did you even read the NDA I sent you? I can't shoot shit."

"You're so lucky you have me, you really are. I'm the best. I didn't just read the NDA, I read between the lines. You can shoot whatever the hell you want that isn't movie related. You can shoot Seamus, off set. You can shoot Tom Kendall, who signed onto the movie yesterday and was just papped in Ojai."

"Nice!" Kara licked her lips. Kendall was fine.

"So, I just talked to the director, and if you get footage with either of them, we can use it in the spinoff. Is that big enough for you or are you holding out for fucking Taylor Swift?"

"I can't hear you." Kara struggled out of her comfy bed. "I'm getting ready to go meet Tom Kendall."

✳ ✳ ✳

Kara peered up the staircase. The door to Nicola and Seamus's room was ajar, and the only light was the setting sun. Both cars were still parked out front. They must have gone for a walk.

She threw her HD camcorder into her Herschel backpack and took one last look in the mirror over the leather couches. She'd pulled her hair back behind a vintage Pucci headband, and she looked bangin' in black Dior hot pants and a raspberry sheer tank. She slipped on strappy Vuitton cork wedges and made her way out the door.

In the gathering dusk she could see lights glowing from above the polo field, the spaceship glinting brightly, workmen still clambering over its surface; a welder was sending an arc of sparks shooting from one of its wings out into space.

She could smell food cooking and figured it was coming from somewhere by the polo field, so she began walking. The klieg lights around the field filled the dusty road with an eerie blue glow. The dusk chill gave her goose bumps and she picked up her pace.

Behind the bleachers that would be full of extras in alien costumes in just a few weeks, Kara spied the telltale white tent of catering. Her tummy rumbled, and she realized she hadn't eaten since yesterday. She could see people sitting at the long tables, laughing and eating their dinner. Nicola and Seamus were sitting with a small group of men and women, and as she drew closer her heart leapt. Tom Kendall was sitting with his back to her, right next to Seamus.

Suddenly grateful for the chilly air and the fact that she wasn't a sweaty mess, Kara skirted the catering tent until she could approach in full view of Tom. Seamus saw her first and waved her over, and she sashayed up to them, a huge smile spreading across Tom's face. She saw Nicola roll her eyes and put her head on the table. *Bitch.*

"Hey, guys." Kara stretched, one arm over her head. "Man, I passed out. Thanks for not waking me."

"We woulda needed a fucking atomic bomb," Seamus roared. "Everybody, this is Nico's friend Kara."

"Hi, Kara," the table chorused. Kendall stood and extended his hand.

"I know you from somewhere, don't I?"

"That's entirely possible," Kara demurred, waiting for Nic to move aside so she could sit opposite Tom. "But I don't know you. Yet."

She slid onto the bench across from him and set her backpack on the table.

"What's good to eat?"

"Uncle!" Nicola yelled, smacking her fist into the table. Kara kicked her hard.

"Everything's good," Tom said eagerly. "You wait there, I'll get you a plate."

As he walked over to the buffet, Kara stared at his muscly thighs beneath his torn khaki shorts, and the golden skin of his belted arms.

"It's so beautiful here," she said softly, to nobody in particular.

"Hey," Seamus said, raising a beer to her. "Did you bring your camera? I wanna say something."

Kara pulled a Canon out of her backpack and turned it on, pointing it at him.

"You rolling?"

Kara nodded.

"I would like to thank my guests this weekend for coming up to Ojai and making my job less boring. So, here's a toast to the girl I'm not dating, Nicola Wallace, and her friend Kara Jones, who Tom isn't dating, either." Seamus paused, and laughed. "Yet."

Kara shifted her focus to Tom at the buffet and zoomed in. As if he sensed the camera, Tom turned and waved, and gave her a free version of a smile that usually cost twenty million dollars and a lot of back end.

Many bottles of wine later, Seamus pulled his phone from his pocket and looked at it, his brow furrowed.

"Hey, you drunks, it's time for Nico and me to call it a night. I have an early fitting, and I cannot have a hangover for my second swordsmanship lesson."

"Excuses, excuses," called Tom as Seamus took Nicola's hand and helped her off the bench.

"Is everything okay?" Nicola asked as they reached the edge of the tent.

"Dunno, love." Seamus held his phone up to her face.

It was a text from Bluey.

Mate. I'm with Billy at Gaynor's. Can Nic call real quick?

"Holy fucking shit." She patted her pockets. "I left my phone up at the house."

Seamus flicked his screen and hit dial, handing it to Nicola. Bluey answered before it rang once.

"Bluey, hey, it's Nicola. What's going on?"

"Oh, hey, mate, keep your shirt on. I'll get Billy."

After some rustling and what sounded like muffled laughter, Billy came on the line.

"Well, you picked the right day to take off work," he began.

"Billy, is everyone all right?"

"Everyone except Max Zetta," he laughed. "That bastard sure hated gays, but he loved the Lord."

"Billy, you're not making sense," Nicola said impatiently, and Billy settled down to business, telling her everything. Seamus stood patiently, watching Nicola's face transition from shock to laughter and back again. This was going to be a good one. Finally, she spoke again.

"So what the fuck are you going to do?"

"We have a call with Crystal in one hour, and we've come up with an offer she won't be able to refuse."

"I wish I was there." Nicola regretted saying it as soon as she saw Seamus's face fall.

"No you don't," Billy said. "Now go make love to your movie star."

Seamus wrapped his arms around her as she lowered the phone, and Nicola rested her head on his chest.

"Do you wanna know what's going on?"

"Not unless you absolutely need to tell me right this second."

"I don't. I'm happy just like this."

"Nico, I know we agreed to try to keep things normal, but I figured that here, on a movie set, we could maybe just bend the rules a little bit."

She met his gaze. He looked like a sad puppy. She thought about his offer.

"You're right. It's probably pointless to resist."

"Good." He released her from the hug and took her hand, leading her into the darkness below the bleachers. "When was the last time you fucked in a spaceship?"

CHAPTER 31

"GAYNOR, YOUR HOUSE IS EVERYTHING." Billy sprawled in a balloony purple beanbag chair, rubbing his bare feet on an immaculate and expansive white flokati rug.

"What can I say? The seventies made me happy." Gaynor punctuated her sentence with shakes of a martini shaker. She poured one for Billy, then turned and pointed the shaker at Bluey.

"Nah, mate, I'm good with the cerveza," he nodded.

"Australians, I'll never understand them," Gaynor groaned, pouring a martini for herself. With a spoon she dropped four plump green olives into each and handed one to Billy.

"Do you have little skewers for the olives?"

"Use your tongue." Gaynor flicked her tongue at Billy. "It's sexier."

"Gurl, are you ever gonna leave Studio 54?"

"*No sé, mijo.* Can you give me one good reason?"

Billy took his martini and gently swirled the icy, viscous gin around in the heavy glass. The three of them sat silently, listening to the gentle thump of the disco music wafting from speakers that were nearly as tall as Gaynor.

Gaynor pressed a button on the intercom on the wall.

"Alicia, how are my little treasures?"

"Patrick is watching *Scarface* and Sylvester is giving me a makeover," came the tinny response. Gaynor smiled. After the boys had left Alicia locked in the conference room so long she'd peed her pants, she'd sent Alicia on a commercial audition this morning, and by this afternoon, she had a willing babysitter.

Billy took another sip of his martini and watched as Gaynor, in zebra tights and a zebra-print halter top, skipped barefoot back to her spot on the red leather sofa. He had dreaded calling her to tell her about the photos, but Gaynor had not been ruffled at all.

"You've taken care of it, *mijo*?" she had said.

"I tried, but Crystal got to them before I did."

"Of course she did, but don't worry. This is good news."

Billy had explained the whole scenario, and Gaynor had remained calm.

"*Mijo*, I'm set for a cut and color with Mr. Ray at six. Can you have Bluey arrange a phone conference with the dragon lady for nine tonight? We can have some cocktails at my house and put her in her place."

✳ ✳ ✳

The meeting at Flanger's had turned into everyone on their cell phones, and Harrison had gotten bored. He had deflected offers from each of them to drive him back to Beverly Hills and called an Uber instead. Once he was gone, they had figured out an attack plan. The solo photos of Zetta were being sold, whether Crystal liked it or not, and it was up to Billy to negotiate the fate of Gaynor and the photos she appeared in.

As the meeting drew to a close, Bluey had come up and put his arm around Billy's shoulders.

"Mate, I'm really sorry we got off on the wrong foot."

"I am, too, I guess. There are worse ways to get bullshitted than by kissing a dumb Aussie at the Montage."

Bluey burst out with his loud belly laugh.

"Let's go grab a beer. You and I need to work out a unified front or our respective bosses will claw each other to death."

Flanger and Joe had exchanged identical eye rolls as they bade the men adieu.

⁂ ⁂ ⁂

"Crystal's changed her mind," Bluey announced at eight forty-five. "She's coming here in person. I just texted her the address." Gaynor and Billy exchanged drag queen looks of horror.

"I'm gonna need a drop cloth." Gaynor stood and stalked toward the kitchen. "I don't wanna get blood on the Warhol."

"Well, you better be quick, Gaynor; she says she's just around the corner."

Gaynor returned with another martini glass, not a tarp. She set about rinsing out the shaker at the wet bar in the corner of her living room. She filled it and the glass with ice, and as they were chilling, the doorbell rang.

"Be a lamb, would you?" Gaynor nodded at Bluey, who sprang out of his yellow beanbag chair and headed for the door. She hurriedly prepped the martini, and this time made two skewers of four olives each, dunking them into the gin just as she heard Crystal's heavy heels clomping down the hallway.

"*Ay, los zapatos!*" Gaynor cried. "Take off your damn shoes. This isn't Neiman Marcus."

Crystal sailed into the room like a miniature Karl Lagerfeld, all black suit, gold chains, and huge dark glasses, her colorless hair not moving an inch. She surveyed the room—the beanbag chairs, the red couch, the mirror ball, and the blue lacquered coffee table—and seemed at a loss for words. Billy felt his scrotum shrivel when her impenetrable dark glasses stopped at him.

"How the fuck do you manage to be everywhere?" she barked at him. "You're like the fucking Forrest Gump of scandals."

"Just lucky, I guess." Billy stood, extending his hand. Crystal veered in the other direction and snatched her martini from Gaynor.

Bluey came in behind her and resumed his perch in the yellow bean-bag. *He looks like Big Bird in his nest,* Billy thought, smiling.

"Gaynor, it's Friday night and it's been a long week. Are we going to fuck or just finger each other tonight?"

They sat beside each other on the couch, and Gaynor clinked her glass against Crystal's.

"*Mira,* this is nothing; let's let it be nothing."

Crystal sighed, and seemed even smaller. "I like that idea. Tell me your plan."

"My plan? It's simple. Flanger is determined to sell the photos. He is willing to delete the ones I am in. You and I have both done these things, to keep the clients happy and out of the tabloids. I think that for old times' sake, we can just let it go."

Crystal laughed, a cold, hollow sound that reminded Billy of a crow.

"That's a good scenario for you, but it's as satisfying as a tit fuck for me."

"Crystal," Billy interrupted, "you're gay. Don't you want to see this fucking homophobe go down? How can you represent him after what he said, how he thinks?"

"Listen, cornhusk, if the gays and the homophobes in this town didn't work together, you wouldn't have a movie industry. I don't give a fuck about his politics. I give a fuck about what he pays me to stay famous. Speaking of which, Ethan Carpenter has decided to give heterosexuality another chance, so you're single. Now go find a new fucking lover on Grindr and let the experts handle this one."

Billy blew her a kiss. "You should write for Hallmark," he cooed.

Gaynor stood up, turning to face Crystal.

"Once this scandal hits, you can name your price with Max. He will be forced to pay you whatever you ask. Nobody wants this job anymore. He's so tiresome."

"My dear, I've already told him that there's some shit up ahead on the freeway. I've set his rate at fifty thousand dollars a month for the next six months. I've hired him two full-time fetish hookers and a sober coach who's willing to dress in the Shroud of Turin if he asks. I've promised Flanger that Max will be the Grand Marshal of next year's West Hollywood Gay Pride in exchange for the dick pics staying private. I'd say I've contained the worst of it. So tell me why it wouldn't at least give me something to laugh at if I let the pics of you go public, too."

"I don't know why you just can't be nicer," Gaynor sniffed, getting off the couch and pulling open a drawer within the top of the coffee table. She removed a small stack of black-and-white eight-by-tens. She held one in front of Crystal's face for a second, moving it just in time to avoid being sprayed by the gulp of martini that flew from Crystal's mouth.

"Where the fuck did you get that?" she seethed.

"Bianca Jagger gave it to me in 1979. She told me it would always be my get-out-of-jail-free card in Hollywood. And I haven't had to use it until now. If you weren't such a bitch, I wouldn't have had to use it at all. Now, is that good enough of a reason for you to kill the pics I'm in?"

"You fucking win. I don't care anymore. And Gaynor, thanks for that. I really do think I might throw up."

As soon as Crystal gave in, the mood changed. Gaynor poured herself an Amaretto sour and plonked onto the couch next to her, promising to send her Zetta's files. They began to banter like an old couple, and Billy realized that both of them loved the charade of animosity, but behind it was a surreal shared history that almost passed as friendship.

An hour and two martinis later, Crystal air-kissed Gaynor, waved at Bluey, flipped a bird at Billy, climbed back into her clunky boots, and left. Immediately both men turned to Gaynor.

"What the fuck was in that photo?" they said in unison.

"Trust me, boys, you don't want to know."

Bluey and Billy both turned their most effective pleading stares on Gaynor. They reminded her of her twins.

She let out a big breath.

"Have you ever heard any rumors about Crystal's client Avery Beckner?"

Bluey rubbed his stubbly chin. "He bedded every hot actress in Hollywood, from the late sixties until he got married in the nineties."

"Right, so you're on the right track," Gaynor cackled, warming to the game. "So ask yourself, after all those beauties, why did he marry such a plain Jane as Lee Pierce?"

"I'm not sure." Billy shook his head. "Come on, what is it?"

Now it was Gaynor's turn to look like an ecstatic child.

"It's poo, darling," she bellowed. "Poo! Avery likes it, and Lee doesn't mind."

Both men made puking sounds.

"But, mate, what was in the photo?"

"Oh, you know, just little old Avery back when he was dating his America's sweetheart costar from that sci-fi movie. With the costar. And a glass table."

"Okay, enough." Billy gagged. "We don't need to see the photo."

CHAPTER 32

"HI, MOM, I WAS ABOUT to call you."

"Sure you were, Nicola, and I've got a used bridge to sell you."

Nicola took a seat under a tree outside an Ojai boutique selling children's clothing at prices children could never afford.

"So what's new, Mom?"

"Don't play games, Nicola. Biscuit told me you're dating a movie star."

"Fucking Billy!"

"Don't cuss, peanut. At least he's keeping us in the loop, missy. So why don't you tell me where you are?"

"Okay, Mom. I've been seeing Seamus O'Riordan, and I'm in Ojai."

"I'm not sure which one he is. Biscuit showed me a photo, though; he's handsome enough. . . . Wait, did you say Ojai?"

"Yeah, Mom, why?"

"Oh, Nico! That's where the bionic woman lived with her lovely dog. I used to dream about living there when I watched that show."

"This is where she lived? How the hell do you even remember things like this?"

"Oh, I assure you, it was a big deal. Everybody wanted to live in Ojai in the seventies."

"Well, they come here to die now. It's like Florida with oak trees."

"So is it serious with this boy, then?"

"No, Mom. We're just dating. And he's not a boy, he's a man."

"Whatever you want to call him, I'm sure he's a step up from Tony. He treating you good?"

"Yes, Mom. He's very kind. He . . . uh . . . yeah, actually, he treats me good."

"Nico, it's okay to trust someone again."

"Let's not get ahead of ourselves, Mom. How's Biscuit doing?"

"He's doing so well. He got his one-year sobriety medal thingy and he's real proud. I told him that if we save up, he and I might come visit you next year. How would that be?"

"I'd love it, Mom."

"Maybe we could meet your movie star boyfriend!"

"Mom, you're breaking up. Are you still there? I can't hear you. Love you. Good-bye."

Nicola put her phone back into her purse and looked up and down the main drag of Ojai. She couldn't imagine the bionic woman sprinting along this dusty two-lane highway unless she was trying to get the hell away from the society matrons who cluttered the side-walk with their strollers and their dogs while they window shopped and gossiped.

She pulled her phone back out and texted Kara, whom she hadn't seen since dinner last night. Some girls' weekend this was turning out to be.

Her clock and the sun beating down on her told her it was almost two p.m. Seamus was in sword training until five and they'd ar-ranged to meet back at the house then. Nicola couldn't remember the last time she'd been bored like this.

She got up and headed back to her car. There was a pool some-where on Prairie Blossom, and she decided to find it.

✳ ✳ ✳

The sun was lower in the sky when Nicola woke up, wrapped in a towel on a lounge beside an azure pool. She blinked behind the vintage Ray-Bans that had been her mom's until she stole them, and surveyed Prairie Blossom. The estate rolled out in every direction around her, rising into the hills, and bees buzzed in the heat haze over the valley. There were no signs of life. One of the spaceship's metal fins rose incongruously behind the terra-cotta roof of the main house, a sprawling mansion of oranges and reds.

She looked at her phone. It was dead. Crap. She'd forgotten to charge it last night. Standing, she let the sun warm up her skin. It felt glorious. She stuck a toe into the pool, happy to find that it was still deliciously warm. *Fuck it*, she thought, and dove back in. She swam all the way to the other end underwater, surfacing to a view of the mountains around her. Maybe her mother hadn't been wrong about Ojai.

She dipped her head back into the water, wringing it out with both hands as she stood. She got out and let the air dry her skin. She decided to walk back in her wet scarlet ASOS bikini. She pulled on her Prada slides, threw her towel over her shoulder, and put her shorts and tank inside her purse with her phone. It was after five. She looked at the road that she had taken to the pool. It wound down through an orange grove, around the polo field and the catering tent, and then back to their guesthouse. Probably take her ten minutes to walk. Another road extended to her right, and around several barns. It would probably be shorter, or she could at least cut through the field behind their house.

The road was little more than a worn, dusty trail by the time it hit a pair of old wooden barns where the owners pressed olive oil. Nicola could smell the scent of wood-soaked oil on the afternoon breeze. There were wildflowers amid the grass by the corner of one of the barns, and she walked over to pick a small bunch, either for Seamus or for her hair, she wasn't sure which yet.

As she drew close to the barn, she heard a woman's voice. It was Amber's. Maybe that's what that traitor Kara had been doing all day. She sidled up to the barn and peered through a crack. She fought to suppress a loud groan.

Inside the barn, Seamus and Amber were leaning against an old truck, drinking beers. They were standing about five feet apart, laughing about something that one of them had said. Amber looked like she was about to saunter into Freddy's in a tight pale-blue dress with a printed sheer overlay. What the hell was she doing here?

Seamus looked at his watch.

"Listen, Amber, I gotta get going. Nico's gonna be waiting back at the house. Thanks for coming up today. You really hooked a brother up."

Amber moved closer to him.

"Of course, handsome," she purred. "Anything for you. Here, lemme give you a few more, you know, just in case."

She dragged her purse off the hood of the truck and pulled out a pill bottle. She began to open it, and then thought better of it, tossing the whole bottle to Seamus, who caught it deftly in his right hand.

"One for the road?" she asked.

"Sure, why not?" Seamus twisted the cap and poured two pills into his hand. He handed one to Amber, and they each washed them down with the last swig of their beers. Nicola pressed her face against the rough wood of the barn, feeling it scratch her cheek, anger rising up inside her. She wanted to run back to her car and leave. She wanted to throw up. She couldn't do either quietly enough.

Fuck this, she thought, pushing herself off the splintery wood. She moved slowly, in shock, along the wall toward an open door. She could still hear them talking but couldn't make out words over the blood buzzing in her ears. She grabbed the edge of the doorway and pulled herself into the barn.

"What the *fuck* is going on here?"

Seamus spun, dropping his beer bottle in the dirt. Nicola saw him tuck the pill bottle into his pocket.

"Nico, what are you doing here? I'm just about to head back to the house. . . ."

"What am I *doing* here? What am *I* doing here?"

"Hey, Malibu Barbie, 'sup?" Amber drawled, a smile flickering at the corner of her lips.

Seamus turned to Amber.

"Can you please leave us alone?"

"Of course, doll." She began to walk toward Nicola. "I told you, you wouldn't be able to hack it."

As she drew closer, Nicola flicked her foot and tripped her, sending Amber plunging to the dirty barn floor.

"What the actual fuck, you wretched beast," Amber screamed. Nicola stepped toward her and clenched her fists.

"Get the fuck out of here or I will kick your sorry junkie ass to death right here, right fucking now."

Amber scrambled to her feet and headed for the door, dirt smearing her dress, hands, and legs. She paused at the door and blew a kiss to Seamus.

"Call me, sugar," she cooed. "And bye, loser."

She was gone.

Nicola turned to Seamus and was shocked to see that he was leaning against the car, crying.

"Nico, come here, please come here," he sobbed. "I can explain; I can explain everything."

Nicola didn't move. The pain in her chest was too great.

"Show me the pills," she said, her voice breaking.

Seamus reached into his pocket and retrieved the bottle. He tossed it to Nicola. OxyContin. Prescribed to someone named Jill Overton. She tossed it into a far corner of the barn.

"Can you explain lying to me? Can you explain why you omitted to tell me that you were a junkie when I told you about why I had to leave Dayton? About my stupid ex-boyfriend who got my little brother hooked on fucking meth? When I told you how much I *fucking hate drugs*?"

"Nico, please, just listen. It's a pill habit. It's just prescription pills. It's just Oxy!"

"Sure, because hillbilly heroin is so much better than the other kind."

"No, it's not. You're right. But it's just as hard to quit, and I've been trying to quit."

"That definitely explains why you're using that reality show cockroach as your drug mule on our weekend away. It looks like you're doing a great job of quitting."

"Please call Bluey, please. He will tell you. He's tried to get me off it twice. I just never have ten weeks off to do it for real." His crying went deeper, into loud wrenching sobs. Nicola thought she was going to throw up.

"Seamus, I'm leaving. I'm going home. I can't," she stammered. "I really . . . fuck. I just can't believe I was so fucking dumb."

"No, Nicola, please stay and we can talk. You'll see. I didn't tell you because I've been working to quit. And I planned to tell you once I had an escape plan in place. I swear on it. Nicola, I love you. I love you more than I love anyone."

"Those words really mean a lot when they're coming from someone who just downed a couple of Oxys. You're fucking high. Thanks for this moment that I'll fucking treasure forever."

Nicola had a sudden out-of-body feeling, seeing herself in her red bikini and slides, yelling at a movie star in a dusty barn. She angrily hurled her purse to the floor and pulled out her shorts and tank, dragging them over her wet swimsuit.

"I need to get out of here, Seamus. And I need to get away from you." Her breath caught in that telltale you're-gonna-cry way and she blinked angrily to stay the tears.

Seamus went to move to comfort her and stumbled.

"My God, you're so fucking high. Why did you have to get fucking *high* this weekend? Oh my God, are you *always* high?"

Seamus looked at her with guileless honesty, and she felt a pang in her heart.

"I didn't want to go cold turkey in front of you," he said simply. "I'm maintaining. I thought I'd packed enough but I hadn't, so I called Amber when Bluey didn't answer."

"You know that's the fucking problem, don't you? You're like a fucking two-year-old, with an army of nannies bringing you drugs. This sucks." Nicola's voice started breaking. "You're *this* close to being a good guy." The tears started. "You were *this* close to being someone I could fall in love with."

"I still am, Nico." Seamus opened his arms and took several steps toward her. "I'm gonna clean up and we can get back on track."

"No, Seamus," Nicola said, a new fire in her voice. "We don't have a track. You can get as clean as you want. I don't care. You're an actor and a junkie, so you'll always be a goddamn fucking liar."

Seamus collapsed cross-legged on the dirty floor, his face in his hands.

She turned and sprinted from the barn.

CHAPTER 33

THE TERCEL SCREECHED TO A halt on a dusty road hidden between oleander hedge walls on the far side of the huge estate. Nicola looked at her knuckles gripping the steering wheel, circles of white tension. She breathed deeply and willed her fingers to relax. She killed the engine and sat in silence, swirls of dust spinning outside the windows.

She looked at her phone, plugged in but still only at 24 percent power, for the millionth time in thirty minutes. No word from Kara. Her green suitcase had exploded all over her bedroom, and it still didn't look like she'd been back to the room since last night. She punched in another furious text.

Kara. I'm leaving. I'm gonna wait for half an hour, but if I don't hear from you, I gotta go. Sorry.

Her phone rang just as she hurled it onto the passenger seat. Billy.

She debated answering it for a second and then held it up to her ear.

"Sunshine," he chirped. "How's your day?"

"Yours is better," she said tensely. The tone in her voice chilled Billy. He hadn't heard it in a year.

"Seamus is a junkie," he said coldly.

"Now you fucking tell me. I just found out myself. While I was standing wet, and in a bikini, and he was doing Oxy with that scuzzy bitch Amber."

"Fuck, baby. Fuck. I'm so so sorry. Bluey literally just told me. I guess he's been trying to get his ass into rehab. For you."

"Too fucking late, Billy. He's had a month to tell me. He knows the whole story with Biscuit. He fucking knows. And he lied."

"You coming home, punkin?"

"Yes; I need a hug, Billy."

"You're only seventy-five miles away. I'm ready."

"I have to wait for Kara, who's off fucking Tom Kendall and has been MIA for nearly twenty-four hours."

"Oh shit, that's great!" Billy nearly screamed before catching himself. "Okay, back to you, back to you—man, that Seamus is a dirty dog."

"Thank you."

"Are you okay, babe? Seriously? Do I need to send a helicopter?"

Nicola took a long breath and pushed it out in a deep whistle.

"Yeah. Yeah, no permanent damage. Feeling stupid won't kill me."

"You're not stupid. And from what I heard, he was ninety-eight percent legit with you. Bluey already has him booked into residential rehab as soon as he's done with this movie."

"Wait—how the fuck do you know so much about Bluey?"

"We have a lot to talk about when I see you." Billy chuckled. "He and I helped Gaynor avoid a disaster last night. It was kind of thrilling."

The phone vibrated. It was Kara.

"Gotta go. Kara's alive." She switched calls.

"Gurl, what's the dramurgency?" Kara sounded like she'd just woken up. "Did someone take your photo?"

"What? No. It's code red. We need to leave right now. Do you want to ride with me back to LA or not?"

"Are you mad at me? Did I do something wrong?"

Nicola shook her head. Why did everything have to be about Kara?

"No, of course not. It's Seamus; we broke up, I need out."

"Where are you? I can be at the house in ten minutes."

"See you there."

✳ ✳ ✳

The evening sun was pulling behind the mountains as Nicola parked again in front of the guesthouse. Her stomach sank at the sight of Seamus's truck. Kara had texted that she was in her room packing. She hadn't mentioned seeing anyone else. Nicola clenched her eyes closed and open in an attempt to banish the tension headache that was forming across the front of her brow.

"Grow the fuck up," she hissed at herself, walking inside.

The house was in darkness except for Kara's room. She headed in. The tornado of clothes had vanished, and Kara was sitting on top of a hurriedly overstuffed suitcase.

"Hey, help me zip this up while you tell me what the fuck is going on."

Nicola grabbed the zipper and started yanking it.

"I'll tell you in the car. Long story short, Seamus is a junkie."

Focused on closing the bag, Kara forgot to act surprised.

"Oh, he told you, huh?"

Nicola sprang back as if she'd been electrocuted.

"You fucking knew?"

Kara's shoulders dropped. "Not a hundred percent, but I suspected."

"I can't fucking believe any of this." Nicola yanked the zipper closed and dragged it off the bed, knocking Kara to the floor. She tried to wheel it out to the car but it kept listing from side to side, knocking into the walls. "FUCK," she yelled again.

She hurled the suitcase on top of hers in the Tercel's trunk and returned to the living room. This was going to be a fun ride back.

Kara was standing in the hallway. She was shaking.

"Nic, I confronted him yesterday. I saw him at a party the other night, and I wasn't sure. I told him if he didn't tell you this weekend, I was going to. I promise."

They stared at each other in silence, their heavy breathing the only sound in the room. A text hit Nicola's phone, the ding ringing out in the dark. She turned her phone over. The text was from Billy.

I just got offered photos of you and S from this weekend. There's a security breach on set. You're not safe. Get the fuck out of there.

Nicola slumped against the door frame.

"What now?" Kara asked timidly.

"There's a paparazzo somewhere around here. We've been papped. Billy just told me everything."

Kara, mistaking the panic on Nicola's face for accusation, thought she had been caught.

"They forced me to do it," Kara wailed. "Please don't hate me. But I didn't do it yet."

Nicola froze.

"What the fuck . . . ?" she said bloodlessly. "You were going to sell photos from this weekend?"

"I said I'm sorry; let's get the fuck out of here. We can talk about it on the drive home. It didn't happen."

Nicola pulled her phone out and texted Billy.

They fucking tried to get Kara to take pics but she says she didn't. We are all clear.

Billy responded immediately.

Nope. There's a pap on location right now. Watching you. I just talked to agency.

Nicola felt dizzy. She put her hand on the wall behind her just to feel if it was real.

"Oh, get over it," Kara said, smiling blithely. "You can't be so basic as to believe you could do this in a bubble. This is a career maker for both of us."

Nicola couldn't speak. She drew her right hand into a fist. She wanted to smash Kara's face in.

Before Nicola could start swinging, a scraping noise came from upstairs, and they heard a door creak open. Amber's voice drifted down to them.

"Uh, you guys, I need your help. It's Seamus. I think he's overdosed."

Without thinking, Nicola rushed up the stairs. Even in the dim light, she could tell that Amber was pale as a ghost. She shoved her out of the way and hit the light switch. The room flooded with light and she saw Seamus unconscious on the bed. White vomit flecked his chest and cheeks. A trickle of blood ran from his inner elbow. Amber had shot him up. For a split second, Nicola considered punching her fucking lights out instead of Kara's.

She ran to Seamus, poking her fingers inside his mouth to clear his airway, and turned his head sideways. He groaned loudly and his eyelids fluttered.

"Seamus." She grabbed his chin, holding his face in front of hers. "Stay with me. Wake up. Kara, get the *fuck* up here."

By the time Kara entered the room, Nicola already had one of Seamus's arms around her shoulder.

"Help me get him down the stairs," she barked. Kara kicked off her heels and dove under Seamus's other arm.

"Oh, thank God you're here. I just didn't know what to do," Amber said, relief in her voice.

"Shut up and get out of my way or I will kill you with my bare hands." The look in Nicola's eyes said she meant it. Amber retreated to the balcony.

"Don't go near the window, you fucking moron!" screamed Nicola. Amber stepped back into the room and wrapped the curtain around herself. She started to cry.

"Seamus, I need you to help me, I need you to walk," Nicola implored. Seamus groaned and tried to stand. The momentum was enough for them to get him up and walking. When they got him to the stairs, Nicola carefully placed his hand on the banister and stood in front of him, both hands pressed against his chest.

"Okay, one at a time, O'Riordan. Don't fucking fall on me." He groaned again, his eyes almost open. And step by step, all sixteen of them, they made it to the living room. Seamus stumbled on the step down to the driveway, nearly pitching them all onto the trunk of the car. Kara disentangled herself from his armpit and opened the rear door. They clumsily tumbled him inside.

"Ride with him, Kara," Nicola instructed, rushing around to the driver's side. She heard Kara get in beside Seamus as she turned the engine.

"Slap him as hard as you can if he nods off. And call 911. Have an ambulance meet us at the gate or even on the long driveway. Google wherever the fuck the Ojai emergency room is."

The Tercel sped off into the dusk, spitting rocks back at the house. In an upstairs window of the smaller guesthouse across the way, a photographer leaned out to catch his last shots of them pulling away.

CHAPTER 34

THE DRIVEWAY THROUGH THE OLEANDERS had never seemed this long before. Dark had fallen, and Nicola started to think she was trapped in an Alice in Wonderland maze of green leaves. The only sounds in the car were Kara talking to 911, then yelling at Seamus, and the occasional deafening slap across his face.

"Fuck," Kara yelled suddenly.

"WHAT?" Nic glanced in the rearview mirror. Seamus's eyes were open and moving.

"My camcorder. I left it on the counter at the guesthouse."

"Not now, Kara," Nicola seethed. "Not fucking now."

Suddenly the bushes flanking the road began to flicker with red. *Good, the ambulance is here already*, Nicola thought as she rounded a curve in the road and the guardhouse came into view. She was wrong.

News trucks and private cars blocked the road past the guard building. Nicola's stomach fell. The news of Seamus and his onset photo scandal had broken. The press had arrived in full force. In the distance, she could see people scurrying and training their cameras on the Tercel.

"Kara, lay Seamus flat, now. NOW!"

Screeching to a halt at the guardhouse, Nicola yelled at the guard.

"Sir!" she called urgently. "I have Seamus in the back; we need to get him to the hospital and I need a diversion, *now*."

The guard's eyes widened as he took in the scene in the back of the car, Seamus deathly pale and barely conscious, his head in Kara's lap. He looked hurriedly at the crowd in front of the boom.

"Okay, ma'am," he said, and rushed back to the other side of the guardhouse. He waved his arms at the paparazzi and said, "Hey, everybody, listen: there has been an incident on set, and they're doing a press conference right now at the main house. I'm going to open the gate here and let you all in; I'll just need to see your driver's licenses before I can let you in."

There was a mad scramble as all the photogs and crews rushed back to their vehicles. The guard walked back inside, turned, and winked at Nicola, and then raised the boom over the exit lane. Nicola fishtailed the car slightly and sped past all the parked cars and trucks. She was almost past the line of cars when a black Escalade pulled in front of her, blocking the road.

She stopped inches from the SUV. A middle-aged man in camo shirt and pants got out, holding an HD camcorder on his shoulder.

"Where you headed in such a hurry, girlie?"

Nicola wound down her window.

"Move your fucking truck, asshole," she yelled.

The guy swung the camera's flash into her face, blinding her.

In the distance, she heard an ambulance siren getting louder and louder. She blindly swung for the video camera, aware that he was filming everything. She didn't care. Her fingers gripped fabric and, with all her might, she hurled the photographer backward. He fell, and the video camera flew from his hands. Blinking away the blinding circles of white light in her eyes, she heard the ambulance stop in front of her before she saw it.

"Over here," Nicola yelled.

Kara waved her arms beside the car. "Follow me," she yelled. "You're gonna need the stretcher. Opiate overdose."

One of the EMTs pulled open the ambulance doors and started unloading the gurney. The other one walked up to the guy with the video camera as he tried to get to his feet and pick up the camcorder at the same time.

"Sir, I'm going to have to ask you to move your truck."

"I'm going to have to ask you to fuck off," the guy spat.

"Sir, obstructing an ambulance is an offense. Don't make me arrest you."

"You can't arrest me, you fucking failed doctor."

The EMT hauled off and punched the paparazzo in the mouth. The guy spun backward in a spray of spit and blood.

The EMT went to the Escalade, put it in neutral, and pushed it slowly backward off the road. It rolled slowly at first, the EMT grunting loudly. Then its wheels began the downhill slope away from the road, and the EMT moved away. The truck rolled down until it hit an old oak tree with a loud crash.

A cop car pulled up.

The commotion had caught the attention of the paparazzi waiting to get into Prairie Blossom. They were leaving their cars and grabbing their equipment from backseats. They began to race toward the ambulance, and the police met them halfway, yelling at them to stop.

The gurney wheeled down to the Tercel, and the EMTs pulled Seamus out.

When the crowd caught sight of him, their cries became deafening, and a barrage of flashbulbs burst over the scene like constant lightning.

"This is a police line," one of the cops yelled. "We need you to stand back."

The EMTs loaded Seamus onto the gurney. One of them shone a light into his eyes and took his pulse. He ripped an EpiPen out of his bag and plunged it into Seamus's chest. Seamus's eyes flew open.

"Turn the bus around," one EMT said to the other, who bolted to the front of the ambulance.

Nicola pushed to Seamus's side. She grabbed his hand.

"You're gonna be okay," she said. "We made it."

"No we didn't," he said, his eyes rolling into his head.

Nicola panicked. The EMT touched her arm. "He's going to be fine, miss," he said.

The driver backed the ambulance up to the front of the Tercel and got out. He opened the doors again toward them.

"Sir, we're going to move you to the ambulance now," the EMT said. Both men pushed the gurney along the uneven blacktop, with Nicola and Kara forming a human barricade against the camera lenses pointed at them.

Two paparazzi broke through the police line. They ran to the other side of the gurney, shooting off flashes at a blinding rate.

"Seamus, what's going on?" one of them yelled in his face.

"Seamus, who's this? Is this your secret girlfriend? What's her name?" yelled the other.

The movie star looked into Nicola's eyes and a tear spilled sideways down his face. He mouthed, "I'm sorry." Then he raised his hand at the cameras and yelled, "You fucking animals, leave her alone. She's not my girlfriend, she's my fucking publicist."

The gurney slid up into the ambulance. One EMT climbed in with Seamus, and the other pulled the doors closed, and seconds later the ambulance pulled away.

Nicola turned around, staring into shards of white light punctuated by tiny red bursts. She took a deep breath. "Okay, publicist, what fucking happened?" snarled an old guy at the front of their ranks.

Nicola took another deep breath, cleared her throat, and in the sudden silence that followed, she spoke.

"Seamus O'Riordan suffered an accident on the set of his movie tonight during sword training. He is suffering from a severe concussion and we are rushing him to the hospital to make sure it's nothing more serious. Thanks for your concern, but we really need to get to the hospital, and these lovely policemen are going to make sure you can't follow us."

The crowd started yelling angrily. The old man in front stepped toward Nicola, and one of the policemen raised his arm to hold him back.

"So tell us one more thing," the old guy barked. "Tell us the truth—you're the secret girlfriend, right? You're Seamus's secret girlfriend!"

She froze for a second, and Kara nudged her with an elbow.

"No, sir, you're wrong. I'm Nicola Wallace, his publicist."

CHAPTER 35

YOU'RE GLOOMY TODAY, NICOLA THOUGHT. She looked at herself quickly in the rearview mirror of her brand-new Audi A6 and saw that her mouth was set a little harsh. She took a deep breath. She was nervous. *The Tercel would never have made it up this hill.*

She missed the Tercel. She'd paid to have it freighted home for her brother to use, and the thought of that turquoise beast with its custom Hemi engine driving around Dayton never failed to make her smile.

The winding road led up and away from the Pacific Coast Highway, and the landscape turned immediately to low gray desert. *This is what the Hollywood Hills will look like after all the people are gone*, she thought. *After all the vines and earthquakes destroy the gaudy houses and the coyotes reclaim it all.*

She looked at her GPS and saw that the "hidden driveway" promised in the brochures for Malibu's most exclusive rehab facility was just a mile ahead. Gaynor had warned her that she'd probably overshoot it on her first visit, and if she did she'd have to drive all the way to the top of the canyon before she could turn around and make her way back to the driveway.

She had requested to visit Seamus earlier, but his sober coach had nixed all visitors for the first month. Even Bluey had been unable to gain access, and only Seamus's agent had seen him. Nicola heard that visit had been angry and brief, since it concerned Seamus being fired from the blockbuster in Ojai. Agents don't like losing money.

As she approached the driveway she deliberately accelerated. She drove by the heavy, nondescript wooden gate, and continued all the way to the top of the canyon. At the crest, she pulled her car into a turnout and got out.

She was standing on a cliff that dropped hundreds of feet below her to forestland, that low Malibu scrub that covered the jagged rolling hills along the coast. She could see the ocean stretching out below her all the way to Australia. The mist was light and crisp and she could see Catalina outlined against the horizon.

If she looked a little ways north, she saw the kelp forests, and thought back to her first date with Seamus, the exhilaration of jumping from the roof of the yacht into the emerald Pacific, with Seamus holding her hand. As fucked up as things had gotten with him, it was impossible to deny that moment and its perfect happiness.

She surveyed the canyon for the rehab facility, but its location was as inscrutable as promised. It was deep inside its own canyon, unable to be seen from anywhere nearby.

Out of habit, she pulled her phone out of her pocket and was relieved to see that she had no service. She watched a pair of hawks riding the thermals. She slid her phone back into her jeans and reached her arms up to the sun, taking a deep breath.

"Okay, chickenshit," she whispered to herself. "Let's go do this."

※　※　※

After clearing three security gates, Nicola was surprised to see that the facility had valets parking cars. As she slid her new Audi into the valet queue, she had another pang of missing the poor old Tercel. Now she was just another Hollywood publicist pulling into a valet line in an Audi.

The valet did not make eye contact as she got out of her car. He handed her the ticket and drove her car twenty feet into a parking spot.

"Because I could never have done that myself." Nicola turned and looked at the building, a sprawling California bungalow surrounded by forests of succulents. The fences around the property were shrouded in massive hot-pink bougainvillea, and Nicola realized that the preponderance of spiky plants was just a pretty way of enforcing prison walls.

Nicola opened the leadlight door and stepped inside a regular living room. No desks. No nurses. She was surprised.

A woman in her late fifties with long gray hair walked up to her. "Ms. Wallace?" she asked.

"Yes, but please call me Nic," Nicola said, and the woman hugged her.

"Welcome," she said softly. "I'm Nina. Do you have any questions before I take you out to see our boy?"

"Not really," Nicola said. "I read your e-mail; I know how he's doing and I know what we can and can't talk about. Is there anything else that I need to know?"

"There's been progress," Nina began quietly. "He hasn't been a fan of the process, but in the week since he heard you were going to visit, he has been improving rapidly. We're not sure if that's a part of his new sobriety, or if it's because he likes you."

"Hopefully the former, huh?" Nicola said with a weak smile.

"Yes, of course," Nina said. "If you're ready to go, he's waiting for you outside."

Adirondack chairs were strewn across an obscenely green lawn, and at the back of the yard an azure pool nestled into a small canyon. Behind that, another wall of blinding-pink bougainvillea made sure nobody got out. She saw Seamus sitting in a red chair, drinking a glass of water and fussing nervously with his T-shirt hem. She pushed the door open.

As he caught sight of her, his face broke into a smile and he stood rapidly, knocking the glass of water off the arm of the chair. He ignored it and started to walk toward her, his arms open.

She walked down the several steps to the soft grass and was

instantly enveloped in his strong arms. He squeezed her so hard she could barely get her arms around him to return the hug. She felt him press his nose into her hair and take a deep breath. "Oh, Nic, it's so fucking great to see you," he said, still squeezing.

Gradually she gently pushed him away, breaking the hug. He took her face in his hand and stared into her eyes. She could see tears welling along his bottom lashes and broke contact before one of them could make an escape.

"Thanks for coming," he said.

"Well, thanks for having me," she responded.

"Don't be silly," he said, taking her hand. "I've wanted to see you since I got here, but, you know, I had this whole junkie thing to take care of."

Nicola sighed. "Too soon," she said.

"Sorry." Seamus looked at the ground. "This isn't easy."

"I know," she said. "It's not easy for me, and I'm just here for an hour. I'm not doing the hard work you are."

"I was a jerk," he said. "This is the least I could do."

She looked into his eyes, and his chin started to tremble.

"Please don't cry," she said.

"I'm doing my best," he said with a half laugh. "I'm just pretty raw, and I've been doing my forgiveness work, and Nic, you're the only one whose forgiveness I really care about."

"So, do you wanna walk around or sit somewhere?" she asked.

"That was your least subtle deflection yet," he said.

"Yep. Clumsy as fuck." She laughed. "Wanna sit or walk?"

"Let's go sit over by the pool; nobody goes in the pool."

He led her by the hand to a bench beside the pool. He threw some pillows from nearby chaise longues on top of the cement bench. Nicola sat, and Seamus followed suit, sitting so close to her that their thighs touched. They sat in silence for a full minute.

"I've missed you," he said softly.

"I'm sorry," she said. "I really am. I wanted to come up and see you, but we had to agree to a one-month lockdown to make it look serious to the studio. And the insurers."

"I know," he said. "I'm just sorry that you had to go through all this, too."

Nicola flashed back to the days after the overdose, the hiding out at Gaynor's, having to change her cell number, hiring security for a week, finding a new apartment in a security building, her mom being besieged by reporters, even though her mom had loved it. It had been a nightmare.

"It was pretty bad," she said. "But look on the bright side. I got a new phone, a new apartment, and a new car."

"And a promotion," he added.

"Yes, I did get a promotion, but not the way I wanted to get one."

"You gonna stick with it?"

"Yeah; like you said, this whole town is about lucky breaks, and that's definitely the only way I can look at this. I mean, I'm currently working as publicist for a man I nearly loved, a friend who sold me out, an heiress who hates me, and a movie star who tried to bite my face off. My client roster is like Dante's ninth circle of hell. Or a John Waters movie."

Seamus chuckled, and Nicola's heart ached in her chest.

"So, before we talk anymore, I do have to ask one thing."

"Seamus, don't; not here, not now," she said softly.

"I know the answer, but I have to ask."

Nicola focused on a hummingbird that was skimming around the pool.

"Is there any chance for us as a couple when I get out of this place?"

"I've thought long and hard about that," she began hesitantly. "And I think that for now, for the sake of both of our sanity, we should keep it professional. I'm still processing everything, Seamus. That was too much of a zero to sixty for me. And once again, as soon as I think I can trust someone, I get run over by a truck."

"You're not Hollywood, Nic," Seamus said. "And I mean that as a compliment; that's probably why I fell in love with you. You're not a desperate vulture looking for a corpse to feed on. You're fucking cursed with integrity, and I love that about you, even if it's destroying me right now."

"I don't want to be Hollywood long term; I know that for sure now. But I can't go back to Dayton, so I'm going to stick around for a bit until I figure out what's next. I keep some big-ass walls around me, and they're up real high right now. I don't want to string you along and say I can forget what happened. I don't know if I can. But if you're happy with me as your publicist, and maybe some blurred lines later on, I'm down. I don't hate you. I nearly fell for you. You're in a pretty special place in my heart. But if you ever . . . ever . . . lie to me again . . ."

Seamus started to weep.

"Fuck, I love you," he said through his tears. "Nobody ever talks to me the way you do; nobody surprises me like you do. And thank you, for all of that."

"So do you want the business update?"

For once, Seamus was grateful for the deflection.

"Sure," he chuckled, wiping his nose with his wrist. "Lay it on me."

"The studio gave your role to Ethan Carpenter," she began.

"Oh, shit, that's hilarious. He's way too young."

"Well, not now that they've turned it into a CGI-laden generic tween flick. They had to scramble to save money after your incident, and that's how the bean counters decided to go."

"Hey, it's their two hundred million bucks. They can blow it however they want. Is he still dating Billy?"

"Oh God no. He's had to go back fake-straight to steal your job."

"Of course he did." Seamus scowled. "Is Billy okay?"

"Uh, well, he's been hanging out with Bluey. A lot."

Seamus rolled his eyes.

"Why doesn't that surprise me? Actually, it kind of does. What a dynamic duo. Anyway, what about you?"

"I have my own office at Gaynor's, and I have clients. Gaynor's so much happier now that she's not representing Zetta anymore, and that whole scandal pretty much blew over for her. Not so much for Zetta. He can't get hired for shit, but hey, he's the most popular meme on the Internet. The tagline goes 'It's okay to love Jesus, but . . .'"

Seamus laughed and took Nicola's hand, rubbing his thumb absently on her palm.

"Are you and Bluey on good terms?"

"Yes, we are," she said. "It was points in his favor that he'd been trying to get you to quit for years."

"Yeah, he's a good guy."

They sat in silence for a long time, looking at the pool. Nicola leaned her shoulder against his.

"We really almost became something, didn't we, lass?" he said, his voice mournful.

"Maybe, sure."

"I'd say it was more than maybe," he said.

"That's because you're an actor and you're used to getting your way," she said seriously.

"Ouch," he said, pulling back slightly.

"See?" she laughed. "That's why I can't date an actor. You guys take yourselves too seriously."

"Yes, Nico," Seamus said with a sly grin. "I'm exactly the same as everyone else in my profession. And no, generalizations and exaggerations never get old with me. Never."

"That's better," she smiled. "And yes, if it helps, I think we were on the verge of being something, but now we're on the verge of being something else."

"Well, at this point in my recovery, I'll settle for anything that keeps you around me. I'm happy that you know I love you, even if you aren't sure about little old ex-junkie me."

"Thanks, O'Riordan," she said. "It's been a hell of a ride."

"That it has, Wallace," he said, kissing the top of her head. "That it has."

✳ ✳ ✳

An hour later, Seamus returned to his room. He sat on the embroidered quilt on his bed and burst into tears. He let the sobs wash over him and he felt the pain in his heart grow and grow instead of wearing out. He punched his fist over and over into the quilt as the tears continued to flow. He had never been this much of a crier before Nicola.

His breathing started to calm, and he shook off the last wave of sadness and looked up at his dresser. He saw himself in the mirror, his face puffy and red, and streaked by salty tears.

"What the fuck are you crying about?"

He looked up. SaraBeth Shields was standing in his doorway in dirty white shorts and a plain black T-shirt.

"Hey, this isn't a good time."

"Tell me about it." SaraBeth walked in. "I just had a visit from fucking Amber Bank. I've been cast on her fucking reality show. My agents signed the deal already. I can't get out of it."

"Well, I guess that could make your day worse."

"I saw you with your girlfriend just now."

"Did you then?"

"She fucking assaulted me at Freddy's. You shouldn't date her. She's a boring, hungry tiger."

"You sound just like Amber."

"Yeah, she just visited me. I just told you that. They're shooting scenes where she's pretending to be my sober coach."

Seamus laughed bitterly. SaraBeth was more fucked than she knew.

"Anyway, movie star, she asked me to give you this."

SaraBeth tossed an envelope onto the bed.

"Have a nice day." She turned and slouched out.

Seamus eyed the blue envelope suspiciously. Amber had written his name in full, in childish writing with a heart over the *i*. He reached for it slowly and tore it open. The card was a generic photo of a bunch of blue flowers with *Thinking of you* in gold script across the top.

He opened the card and read the childish inscription.

"Hey, shithead—don't forget who your real friends are. Love you. Amber."

A small foil package fell from the card to the floor. He bent over and picked it up, pressing it between his fingers, feeling the contents. He tossed it onto the top of the trash in the can beside his bed, and stared at it intently as he sat back and started crying again.

CHAPTER 36

NICOLA LAY ON HER BED in the middle of her new bedroom. She looked to the right, and then to the left. She'd never had so much space around her bed. The walls were so far away. She gazed at the gray sky outside the huge three-panel window. She wondered if it would rain.

"Dear Santa," she said quietly. "I'd like it to rain for Christmas."

She felt a gust of warm air as the central heat kicked back in, and collapsed into her bedding. She looked at the pristine flat white ceiling of the apartment. She hadn't realized how much she hated the stale gray popcorn ceiling at the old place. Glancing at her phone, she realized she'd been lying there for nearly forty-five minutes. The Rolling Stones record she'd put on before she came into her bedroom had ended a while back, but she couldn't be bothered getting up to flip it over. Kara and Billy had decided at the last minute that they just couldn't be without a Christmas tree on Christmas Eve. They'd been gone since lunchtime, and it was about to start getting dark.

Forcing herself off the bed, Nicola let her feet sink into the soft dark-gray carpet. Every time she touched the carpet, she told herself that it alone justified the apartment's $3,200 monthly price tag—a price she hadn't been able to bring herself to tell her mother. She walked slowly into the kitchen and pulled a bunch of finger-food packages out of the freezer. She turned the oven on and pulled out her phone just as the door opened and Billy's ass entered the room first, followed by the rest of him, carrying the trunk of a rather long but spindly tree, the end of which was being carried by Kara in a floor-length red North Face puffer, a scarf, and a matching wool cap. It was sixty-five degrees out.

"Looks like it's gonna be a very Charlie Brown Christmas," Nicola quipped as Billy and Kara leaned the forlorn tree up against the bare wall near the television.

"It was the last tree in the lot; we felt sorry for it," Kara said, rubbing her shoulders for warmth.

"Ignore her, K," Billy said. "Let's go back and get the rest of the stuff from the car."

And they were gone again.

Nicola walked over to the record player and flipped the record. She dropped the needle to her favorite song, and Mick Jagger started singing to Angie, asking when the clouds would disappear. She gazed around the nearly empty, vast open-plan living space, their old couch and dining table occupying opposite corners and nothing in between, and she suddenly felt the same chill that Kara was apparently battling.

She checked her phone again. Nothing. Two days after her only visit with Seamus in rehab in late October, he had inexplicably checked out and moved to a high-security rehab facility outside Seattle. This time he did not have access to a phone, and his seventy days had started all over again. She hadn't heard from him in two months, but Bluey had kept her updated, and assured her that Seamus was taking it seriously "this time," which worried her. The other day he had let slip that Seamus had earned pay phone privileges, and she wondered why he hadn't called. She hated herself for feeling so needy, but dammit, it was Christmas Eve.

The door opened and Billy and Kara tumbled in, dumping armloads of shopping bags onto the carpet.

"Look, Nico," Billy exclaimed proudly. "Nothing says Christmas like Home Depot and the ninety-nine-cent store."

"Gurl, he basically forced me into the ninety-nine-cent store at gunpoint," Kara joked. "The last thing I need is to get papped having a ghetto Christmas."

Nicola shook her head. Maybe it had been a mistake to forgive Kara and continue to live with her. At least this time it was Nicola's name on the lease. The increasing obsession with fame was getting tiresome. *But hey,* she chided herself, *it's Christmas. Let bygones be bygones.*

"So what's in the bags?" she asked with as much enthusiasm as she could muster.

"Sit on the couch, babe! We have surprises." Billy was so excited that it was almost contagious. Almost. She took her seat as Billy played game show host and Kara vamped up the hostess role she'd no doubt play in the distant future. They'd bought a tree stand, lights, and a hundred yards of tinsel at Home Depot, and hundreds of colored glass balls "for just $22.99" at the ninety-nine-cent store.

"I thought we were going to have a gift-free games night," Nicola sniffed. "I was excited for vintage Trivial Pursuit and gossip."

"We discussed that," Kara said. "But none of us have any gossip. We've all been working so hard that none of us would win."

It was true. November and December had seen all three of them working long hours. Nicola and Kara barely crossed paths, which immediately after Ojai suited Nicola fine. They'd agreed to continue living together; Kara had found the apartment at the foot of Runyon Canyon, Nic looked at it on her lunch break, and they'd moved their stuff in separately. They'd only begun joking around with each other again in the last couple of weeks. Billy's new *Spyglass* gig kept him busy, and he'd been spending nights with Bluey, who suddenly had a lot of time on his hands now that Seamus was locked up.

"So we can just play Trivial Pursuit, then," Nicola whined. She'd bought an original 1983 version of it on eBay. "We can do shots every time none of us have any clue what the question is even about."

"I have an idea," Billy said, sensing that Kara was about to refuse altogether. "Let's save the trivia for New Year's Day. And we all have to have a story. Because I sure as hell don't have one now. But I do have a present for each of you. Let's decorate the tree, heat some food, watch Pee Wee's Christmas special, and do gifts."

"That works for me," Kara said quickly. "I'm gonna go sleep over at my folks' tonight anyways, since for some reason they want us all to wake up at home tomorrow. It's gonna be a Very Brady Kwanzaamas at the Jones house."

"A certain Aussie is on his way back from Seattle today, and he's gonna pick me up by eleven."

Nicola was suddenly alert and hated herself for it.

"How's Seamus doing?" she asked. "Did Bluey say?"

Billy shrugged.

"He always says the same thing. He says Seamus is either 'right as rain' or 'coming along nicely.'" Billy changed the subject. "But wait—Nic, I don't want you to be alone on Christmas morning."

"Thanks, B, but I'm fine. After the year I've had, it'll be perfect to sleep in, and hopefully it'll be a bit foggy and I can hike Runyon and call Mom and Biscuit, and then I'll see you at Gaynor's for Christmas dinner."

"That actually sounds perfect," Kara said. "But now, I'm starving. Let's get those snacks in the oven and decorate the world's saddest tree."

✳ ✳ ✳

The record had reached the end of side two, and the needle was clicking against the label, sounding like an offbeat clock in the silence. Nicola looked at her phone. It was nearly midnight. Billy, Bluey, and Kara had left just after ten thirty. Nic had poured herself a shot of bourbon neat and put the Rolling Stones back on. She considered calling her mom, but it was too late, and sitting by herself in silence felt much more attractive.

She got up and took the needle from the record and walked

toward the balcony. Dragging open the sliding glass door, Nicola stepped outside. The concrete was cold against her bare feet and the chilly night air slid inside the neckline of her flannel pajamas. She took a deep breath and surveyed the night sky over Hollywood Hills. No stars, no moon, just a uniform silver blank screen. She saw an owl circling around the silhouette of an oak tree. It landed and hooted twice, breaking a profound silence that Nicola only noticed when it was gone. Hollywood was preternaturally quiet tonight.

The cold started to get to her and she went back inside, the plush gray carpet warming her feet immediately. She walked over to the couch that was still strewn with wrapping paper and her gifts from her friends.

Billy had given her a beautifully wrapped and rather large box that he had filled with "free shit from work," including two phones and assorted beauty products, beneath which she found a framed photo of the two of them. In the photo, she was fourteen; Billy was fifteen. The quarry pond was behind them, and the wet hair and broad smiles on their faces told her that they'd just jumped off the cliff together for the first time.

"Oh, no fair," Kara had said. "I got her a photo, too."

And she had. Nicola opened the simply wrapped gift slowly, slightly nervous. A small five-by-seven frame contained a photo of Seamus and Nicola. Shot from behind, on the film set in Ojai, it showed Seamus leading Nic by the hand toward the spaceship as the sun set over the mountains in the distance.

"This is the only photo I shot that weekend," Kara began. "I promise."

"It's beautiful," Nicola said softly. "Thank you." Then she punched Kara lightly on the arm. "And thanks for not selling it."

Nicola stared at the photos sitting in their nests of wrapping paper. She got up and took them into her bedroom, placing them on her too-small bedside table. Turning in the near dark, she saw another gift sitting on top of her Pottery Barn covers. Her shoulders dropped.

It was small blue box with silver candy canes printed on it, tied with a silver bow.

Nicola lifted it tentatively. It felt light. She shook it, and was relieved to not hear anything rattle. No jewelry. She pulled the ribbon undone and dropped it to the bed. Lifting the lid, she saw a small gift tag. TO: OHIO, FROM: EDINBURGH.

Beneath the tag was a folded note. She lifted the note out, revealing the box's contents—a woven nylon bracelet, strands of pink, lavender, and silver braided together. She unfolded the note, handwritten. She'd never seen Seamus's handwriting before—like him, it was irregular and a bit childish. It made her smile.

> *Dear Nico. A very happy holidays to you, my sweet. I made this for you. No matter what happens, I hope you can wear it and let it remind you that you're not Hollywood. Miss you madly, love you more. —S*

She put the note and the box next to the photographs on the table and tied the bracelet around her left wrist. She walked around the apartment, turning off all the lights. Returning to her room, she pulled her curtains wide open, letting the silver moonlight flood the room. Nicola looked up at the night sky and felt the rasp of the nylon against her wrist. Then she climbed under the covers, shivering as she waited for them to warm up.

acknowledgments

First, we want to thank our patron saint Lindsey Kelk for her guidance and her generosity—a fine quality that exists all too rarely these days. Not only was she kind enough to read *Blind Item*, she championed it tirelessly. Without her love and support, our book wouldn't be in your hands. If you liked *Blind Item*, you should read her books. They're awesome.

We are so lucky to have Erin Stein on our side. Erin, we cannot thank you enough for gambling on us and being an incredibly kick-ass ally/editor/tiki drinks provider. We are also massively grateful to the entire *Blind Item* team at Imprint—Rhoda Belleza, Natalie Sousa, Mariel Dawson, Ashley Woodfolk, Alexei Esikoff, Raymond Colón, and Nicole Otto. Drinks, New York, soon.

Kevin would like to thank: Lindsey Kelk (again, but this time for being an amazing coconspirator, as well as a one-woman twin-dater support group and music obsessive), my parents Jim and Vonnie (for letting their weirdo kid be weird and having all the patience in the world, and so much more), Steve Gidlow (for a lifetime of love and support through all the unfinished books that led to this one), Jay Tag (for laughter, music, listening, and for understanding that we had to drive ten hours home at three a.m. because I'd figured out the end of this book), my dogs Jack and Tuna (for sleeping inside my shirt while every page of this book was typed), Jack Ketsoyan (for years of hilarious, unprintable friendship AND this book), and to the First Draft Club—Giselle Knight Trowbridge, Heather Taylor, Skye Pyman, Emily Thompson, Ken Taylor, and Eric Williams—who loved the earliest version of *Blind Item* enough to convince us it was worth the hard work to whip it into shape. Lastly, I want to thank George Castro for his love, his laughter, his faith uh faith uh faith in me, and for being my sounding board for the madness of Gaynor *en español. Te amo mucho.*

Jack would like to thank: My mom—sorry, Mom, I know you wanted me to be a pharmacist but in the end life had other plans. I love you. The Huvane Baum Halls team who gave me my first job in PR at the age of nineteen, from there on the rest has been history. This journey that I have been on for the past seventeen years has had its challenges, roadblocks, and heartache; I will never want to go back and change things or regret anything I have done. Jenny McCarthy, thank you for your support and all the advice you gave us on writing this book and not letting us give up. Mom and Sam, thanks for always believing in me and for your unconditional love and support no matter what. Dad, I know you're up there in heaven watching me and I hope I make you proud. My friends who I consider my second family—without you guys life wouldn't be the same. I love you all (and sorry that you had to hear me talk about this book for the past three years). My business partner, Ben—we have been through it all; thanks for not giving up. Chad, thank you for everything that you do; I could not have done it alone. Mariam and Zaven, you kids have changed my life—thanks for bringing joy to our family. My clients, I thank you for your loyalty—no need for names, you know who you are. Kevin, my writing partner, what can I say besides we did it . . . and that it's not the end.

DON'T MISS THE SEQUEL!

THE SEQUEL TO THE *LOS ANGELES TIMES*—BESTSELLER *blind item*

guilty pleasure

KEVIN DICKSON
& JACK KETSOYAN

[Imprint]

KEVIN DICKSON is an author, musician, and animal lover who resides with his husband and Chihuahuas on the fringes of Los Angeles. A former journalist, Kevin spent most of this century in the tabloid trenches, dealing with the darker, more desperate side of fame. After leaving that world he set to work capturing it in the novels *Blind Item* and *Guilty Pleasure*, while touring and recording with his band, the Chew Toys. He is currently working on several new books and plotting new music. Kevin is sporadically available for a chat on his website, kevinjamesdickson. com but is more often found hiking or watching the river otters at the Los Angeles Zoo. Those playful mammals are both entertaining and a reliable cure for writer's block. Their help on this novel was greatly appreciated.

JACK KETSOYAN is widely known as one of LA's most sought-after publicists, and has earned his place as an elite businessman in the entertainment industry. With over ten years of experience, he has worked with some of the largest agencies including Huvane Baum Halls and PMK-HBH, and molded the careers of many A-list celebrities such as Helen Mirren, Paris Hilton, Rachel Weitz, Pussycat Dolls, and Erika Jayne, among others. After gaining a long list of loyal clients, Jack opened his own boutique agency titled EMC BOWERY, where he focuses on building careers and crisis management. Jack co-wrote the *LA Times* Bestseller *Blind Item* with veteran journalist Kevin Dickson. *Guilty Pleasure* is its sequel. Currently, Jack continues to expand his firm EMC Bowery, spends time with clients, and creates content for his novels.